THE FALL
OF THE UNITED STATES?
THE RISE OF ISRAEL

THE FALL
OF THE UNITED STATES?
THE RISE OF ISRAEL

Will the United States survive

the Coming Apocalypse

RONDEL W OSBORN

PREFACE

FOR THE COUPLE—JIM AND NANCY Jenkins, a happy, young-aged couple who lived in a nice suburb in Phoenix, Arizona—it all started five years before the end. Both had good paying jobs in their fields, Jim, an engineer, owned his own business and was a part time woodworker while Nancy is a successful insurance adjuster. They are in their late twenties and were doing well financially. They also had inherited funds from each of their families. By secular standards they were a very successful, happy family. Jim and Nancy attended a local church most Sundays and so, by current religious standards, they were considered 'Good Christians'.

Everything was good, until it wasn't. The first sign was a lump in Nancy's annual breast exam. The biopsy came back with the bad news that it was cancer. The doctor was very encouraging, stating that the treatment of this form of cancer would be with radiation. The radiation treatments were uncomfortable but worked, and the cancer was eradicated. She had been tested every six months to verify that the cancer had not reoccurred, and she was clear for two years, then she was not.

Nancy knew no pain or discomfort anywhere, but she knew. She prepared as well as she could. Making a new commitment to Christ, she thanked Him for the notice of the upcoming end. She wrote letters to her family that told of her love for Christ and encouraged them to make deeper commitments to Him. She did this before the report came back from the doctors that indicated the cancer had metastasized and was attacking her lungs, liver, and bones.

Nancy's last six months of life were horrible. The treatments became just a way to slightly prolong her life. She finally requested that they be stopped, and her last days were at home where she was more content. Jim, in fact, renewed his hope she might recover. He sat holding her hand, day, and night as she rested quietly. On the morning of her last day, she opened her eyes and looked at him and said, "Jim, you have many more years to go; find someone to share them and find love."

He wanted to reassure her that she would get better, but he knew she was aware of what was coming soon.

Again, she spoke. "I see Jesus coming for me!" With these words she raised her right hand and took the hand Jim could not see but felt a tingle in the hand he was holding. She was gone.

Their families came and were there when she died in peace. Everyone was certain she went to Heaven. The funeral was very nice, as funerals go, with many people attending.

Eventually the well-wishers, family and friends were gone, and Jim was left alone. He had prayed Nancy would recover and then when it became apparent the prayer would not be answered, he prayed she would not be in pain. The final prayer had been answered. He tried to continue a relationship with the Lord, but he felt lost and very alone.

He had no debt as Nancy had insisted, they purchased enough insurance to cover cancer costs, as it seemed to run in her family. In addition, she insisted on carrying additional life insurance in case she did not recover. By most standards Jim was wealthy; his house was too large for two people and ridiculous for one. He sold his business as he had lost interest in it, a business he had previously loved. There was nothing holding him here and he now disliked the house that had been a joy. The furnishings he and Nancy had accumulated and enjoyed were now burdensome. Nancy had been a sewer of clothes and quilts and had a room full of expensive machines and fabric. Her sister wanted it all, even though she could not sew on a button, so one room of the house was soon emptied. He advertised items for sale and slowly things went, and the house sold at a good price due to a surge in local real estate. A high-end used furniture store bought the rest of the furnishings. All that was left was Jim's tools and a few boxes of pictures and books, which he put into storage. He had a wood-working shop and had made much of the furniture in the house. He purchased and moved into a rather nice motor home and purchased a like-new Jeep which he towed. A not-so-new small motorbike was carried on the back of the motor home. As he drove away from his beautiful home, with no idea where he was going, he was aware that his life as he knew it was ending.

For a year Jim toured the country. He spent a few days with his brother and then some of Nancy's family, but he didn't seem comfortable being so close to them, so he moved on. Everyone encouraged him to reopen his business, make new friends, or find some way to be happy. Probably good advice, not a solution.

The motor home was very comfortable, and he liked to drive it, but he soon tired of seeing things alone, so he began to look for a place to settle. He was in Colorado and on a back road in the foothills of the Rocky Mountains when he came to a small town named Pagosa Springs. It was a delightful town with several quaint stores like many small towns. It had restaurants, an ice cream shop and an array of small stores and most importantly very friendly people. He attended a small friendly church the next Sunday and the pastor, a young man with a big smile and an open personality and preached the gospel. The message encouraged the people to seek the Lord's directions and follow His will. The people he met were friendly and accepted him, even without a wife, it felt like this could be home. On Monday he visited a real-estate agent, who showed him several cabins which could be rented or purchased. Nothing seemed right, either too big, or too small or too crowded in the town. Leaving the motor home in an RV park, he drove the Jeep around the area where he came across a small community. It was a sub-division with about a dozen houses. The structures were small, but larger than the weekend cabins he had seen in the town. At the end of the road, he practically ran into the 'for sale' sign for a very nice log cabin on several acres. The cabin, two story with no garage on a wooded lot. The water was provided by a well and a small water tower. With all the trees, it was difficult to see the surrounding mountains. It had nice, covered porches on the front and rear of the cabin. Nancy would not have liked it as there were no flower beds and no garden, but for Jim it looked promising.

CHAPTER 1

New roots
Three years before the end.

THE REAL ESTATE AGENT WHO had listed the cabin was a young woman named Julie and she was anxious to sell the property. She was a tall brunette, dressed in tight jeans and good looking. She apparently was new to the business and not comfortable being alone with Jim, so when they met at the cabin her husband was with her. He waited by their car. Jim did not understand her concern but thought perhaps it was because he did not have a wife with him. She did not explain why and perhaps not unusual for women in the business.

"The cabin is owned by the heirs of the man who lived here most of the time. He rented rooms to hunters during the season. There are several small bedrooms upstairs. His family did not want the furniture, so it comes furnished," Julie said as she opened the door, trying to be very upbeat and relaxed.

They went inside. Julie left the front door open. The house was fully furnished with old but nice leather furniture in the living room and oak furniture throughout. Everything was well worn and would not have pleased Jim's wife, but he liked it. It felt homey. The house had an office with a desk and table and several chairs. The walls were covered with built-in bookcases. Most of the books had been removed. There had been numerous pictures and animal mounts in the house which had also been removed. Other than some paint and repair of nail holes, Jim saw nothing seriously wrong with the house.

Julie talked continuously as she walked through the house showing and describing everything. He did not really need to be told there were eight chairs when he could see them. "The house is very comfortable, and the fireplaces should keep everything warm in the winter and the fans are nice in the summer," she said, without mentioning there was no air conditioning. Going to a bookcase, Julie pushed a hidden release, and the bookcase swung out, revealing a safe. It was a mid-sized gun safe that would probably hold fifteen to twenty guns. Jim had seen safes like this and knew it was worth a couple thousand dollars.

"We think the safe is empty, at least the family says it is, but no-one seems to know the combination and the local locksmith says the door would be damaged to open it. It may be just an unusable oddity," Julie quipped with a smile.

Jim just nodded and walked out onto the back porch which was covered with screens and sliding windows. "Tell me about the property," he inquired.

Julie, disappointed that he had not gone upstairs or asked about a lower price, thinking he was not interested, replied, "There are five acres, all wooded, except what you see here, and the back of the lot connects to the National Forest so no-one will ever build there. There is a fence around the property."

"I would like to have a good inspector go over the house and check everything. If nothing serious is found, I believe we can come to an agreement," Jim said, surprising Julie.

"I can have a contract this afternoon; I believe the sellers will agree to pay for any repairs the inspector finds," she said giddily.

With one visit Jim had purchased a cabin in the woods. Even though he had not closed on the contract, he moved the motor home to the side of the lot and lived in it; no one seemed to mind. He did not go into the house but spent his time going over the property, planning where to put a garage and shop. On Sunday he went back to the church he had previously attended where he had met the friendly people who accepted him, even without a wife. It seemed this would be a very good place to live.

The inspector found many things needing improvement or repair. The seller was a law firm handling the estate and just wanted the deal closed, so they were agreeable to anything remotely reasonable. It took a week to get all the paperwork done and the property closed. It was up to Jim to direct the workers on the repairs who then billed the law firm. It was a workable arrangement. The repairs took three months, but Jim took possession after the paperwork was signed.

Jim wondered about the old safe behind the bookcase. Everyone would write the combination down somewhere as forgetting would be a disaster. He looked around the safe and the compartment where it was housed but found nothing. The next logical place would be the little office. There was an old desk and some chairs and a table, along with a file cabinet. Some of the papers had obviously been removed, but several remained. It was not in the papers; he found it written in pencil on the side of a drawer in the desk. He opened the safe and it was mostly empty but did contain a .338 caliber rifle, a true long-range rifle with a very nice scope. There were also records of the hunters who had stayed in the cabin over the years. Jim put his rifles, a tactical vest and all his ammunition in the safe, not filling it.

With a rented truck, everything in storage in Phoenix was recovered. In the cabin, he moved the big table out of the way and put his workshop in the dining room, something his wife would have never allowed. Using his equipment, he built additional tables and bookcases to fill the spaces in the house. He also replaced the handrail on the staircase as several of the spindles were broken. This made a real mess of the cabin as sawdust covered everything.

A problem in living far from a large city was the lack of a good hardware store to buy lumber and supplies. It was necessary to go 40 miles to the nearest large town where Lowes and Home Depot stores were right across the street from each other. To carry the lumber, he purchased a rather pathetic-looking used trailer. After replacing the wheel bearings and tires it was usable, but not much to look at!

The next project was building a garage and workshop. Picking a space back under some large trees, he framed the concrete base and hired a local contractor to pour the cement. It was a local crew that did all kinds of construction, they started by taking out some trees with a small dozer. Then framed the slab and did a good job of pouring and smoothing the cement. The building itself was all metal from a commercial company. It came on a large truck that had trouble reaching Jim's cabin. He had another local man bring a big forklift to unload the truck and stack the material near the building site.

All this work got the attention of the neighbors in the sub-division, and they came by to meet Jim and comment on his construction. They were all surprised that he was single and would take on this task alone. He learned that the largest cabin in the area was owned by a family named Ashcroft who seemed to have homes in several states and several foreign countries. They were not there often so Jim did not meet them. A local man named Duncan managed the Ashcroft property and soon became a friend to Jim. In fact, Duncan spent so much time at Jim's cabin Jim wondered how he made a living.

Duncan was not there when Julie, the real-estate agent, stopped by. The man Jim had assumed was her husband was not with her.

"Hello, Mr. Jenkins, I brought you a housewarming gift," she said as she walked to the construction site carrying a large potted plant. "You have done so much work on this place, I just had to stop and see it."

Julie was dressed in some rather close-fitting clothing. She looked better than he remembered from their prior meetings. She was also not wearing a wedding ring. The previous attitude of being uncomfortable around Jim was gone.

"I am just taking a break for lunch. Would you like to join me for a sandwich?" Jim asked, then immediately regretted it. Julie's reaction was a big smile and a very slight motion of her hips. This was not a business call about houses, but maybe a call about monkey business!

Going into the cabin, Julie brushed her finger across a chair back and said, "I know a group of women that clean houses. I use them when I list a house that needs a deep cleaning," she said, laughing while looking at the tools in the dining room.

They ate sandwiches in the kitchen and Julie seemed unable to stop talking. "I want to thank you for buying this house. It is the first full commission in a long time, and I really needed the sale. I was beginning to wonder if I was in the wrong business."

"You did your job well, very professional," Jim replied, not knowing what else to say.

Julie continued talking, confusing Jim as to the point of her visit. He even began to wonder if she was on something, like drugs.

Duncan rescued him. He showed up, knocked, and walked in without being asked. Julie seemed frustrated, excused herself and left with the comment, "If I can help with anything, feel free to call." She said this while doing something with her eyes. Women seem to have a way of using their eyes to communicate, something men are unable to do.

"I hope I am not interrupting anything," Duncan said, chuckling.

"I am not sure. She seems friendlier now than when she was showing me the cabin!" Jim replied, with a roll of his eyes.

"There are many lonely people looking for someone. It is natural to be with someone." Duncan commented, one of the few times he discussed feelings.

The garage and workshop went up quickly with the aid of the same crew that poured the slab. The front of the building had two high garage doors built for the motor home. The second door was for the Jeep. Jim built a partition in the back half of the building and moved his woodworking tools into it. He finished that room with insulation and sheetrock and added a small potbellied stove for heat. Air conditioning was not required.

With the new building weathered in, Jim spent most of his time exploring with the Jeep and the small motorcycle. Having been warned by Duncan that the winters could be severe and even limit travel, Jim ordered some freeze-dried survival food and purchased a storage container for water. When both arrived, he was surprised that the food was a pallet load, brought on a truck. He had the pallet unloaded and placed in the shop, thinking he would move it into the house later. He set the water tank by the food and filled it up. He had made another purchase that also cluttered up his new building. In driving around the village there was a family who was selling a motorcycle trailer that their son had used with his big Harley Davidson motorcycle. The boy had an accident, and the family was practically giving the trailer away, so Jim bought it and made a hitch so he could tow it with his small cycle. With no immediate need for it, he set it behind the Jeep in the garage. His shop was getting crowded.

When fall came and the trees changed into beautiful color, he took a break. When the end came, Jim was on a camping trip in the mountains on his cycle.

CHAPTER 2

The Beginning of the End

W ITH A DESIRE TO SEE the fall color and enjoy the crisp air, Jim took his motorcycle and backpack and left for a three-day outing. He had put a bar, called a sissy bar, on the cycle that stuck up behind the rear seat which would allow a passenger a backrest. With no passenger, he attached his backpack to the bar and took off. He did not bring the trailer, which he had never used. Traveling off-road trails about 20 miles into the forest he found a nice place on a hillside and set up camp in an open area. By any measure the view was breathtaking; the trees lining the valley below were arrayed in their full splendor. He enjoyed the view and wished he had someone to share it with. The feeling of loneness was nearly overwhelming.

The weather was quite cold at night so he camped where the morning sun would provide some warmth. Gathering some firewood, he boiled water and rehydrated some of his freeze-dried beef stew from his pallet of emergency food. It was not bad and with some coffee, also instant, made a fair meal.

It was the third and last night on this trip. In the early morning hour, he was considering whether to get up or stay in the warm sleeping bag. His bladder voted to get up and go outside. As he stood there looking at the stars the flash occurred. It was not blinding, but bright enough that he was glad he had not been looking directly at it. He did, of course, look in its direction, a natural reaction, and saw a glowing ring in the high heavens that got bigger with time. In the east he saw another ring from a flash over the horizon. There was no sound. He glanced at a distant farmhouse just in time to see the lights go out.

He felt a chill, for he suspected this was an Electro Magnetic Pulse (EMP) attack which had been discussed by scientists and those in high governmental places for years. If the worst happened all electrical devices would be fried, resulting in no electrical power. Cars would not start, and phones or computers would not function. This would be a major disaster for the United States as everything worked on electrical power.

Going to his motorcycle he removed the space blanket he had placed there to dry. The thin blanket had an aluminum lining which had gotten damp from the dew during the night. He used the kick starter and the engine roared to life. Maybe it wasn't an EMP attack, or maybe the blanket protected the circuits or maybe the simple engine did not have much in the way of electronics. It was a relief when it started as his food supply and water were getting low.

As he took down the little tent and was packing everything, he saw smoke in the south. It came over the trees in large black billows; whatever was burning was very hot. "This is not good," he thought. He had the uneasy feeling the fire was near his home.

With great urgency he began the slow trip down the little trail and more than two hours had passed when he reached the turn off to his subdivision. A sick feeling arose in his stomach when he saw a car stopped in the road with two bodies beside the car. As he neared, he saw bullet holes in the car. This had not been the site of an accident, but double murder.

Shutting the cycle off he pushed it into the forest and went on foot. He had brought his old army 45 pistol which would take care of any small animals but would probably only make a big bear mad.

It would, however, accomplish the task for which it was designed, to take down a man.

Staying near to the houses and on the edge of the forest, he passed several cabins. The air was smoky and filled with ash to the point it was difficult to see. The dry wood in the log homes had burned quickly and several had already burned out. Two houses had visible bodies lying in the yard. His cabin was still burning. It had fallen in and was beginning to cool. It was completely consumed with the sheet metal roof covering most of the remains. The metal shop/garage was still burning on the front. The metal was melted and beginning to fall in. It must have been sprayed with something flammable to keep burning with no wood for fuel. He ran around the side and opened the door to the shop, which was not on fire and retrieved an extinguisher and put the fire out.

Had the person who had done this fled? Or was he still lurking about admiring his work? Running back, he got his cycle and drove around the little subdivision. Every house had been set afire. He found other victims lying in their front yards; there may have been others dead in the rear of the houses, but he didn't look. It was a disaster.

He went back to his cabin, or now pile of ashes and looked at the damage. The cabin was destroyed. He could see a pile of burned logs and books where the office had been and a raised area where the safe was now buried. The garage and shop, however, fared better. The front of the building was badly damaged. Going inside the shop in the back, he found it undamaged. Entering the garage from the shop he found that both the motor home and Jeep had front end damage and were probably undrivable. He just stood there looking at the vehicles, angry but sad.

"Jim, are you there?" The voice was shaky and strained and belonged to Duncan.

"Come in Duncan! I am all right," Jim called.

Duncan was dirty, his face covered in mud and his cheeks streaked with tears which were still dripping off his chin.

"Thank God, someone is alive!" he said in an almost panicked voice.

"Tell me what happened," Jim said.

"I recognized them. They were a bunch of thugs from the mosque in town, dressed in black and pretending to be ISIS. They came in three pickups that had a big black flag on each one. Most had machine guns. They shot everyone they saw. Maybe some ran into the woods. I tried to call 911 but my phone wouldn't work. My God, I didn't do anything! I just ran away! I am such a coward. Why would they pick this little area to attack?" The tears started up again in earnest and he started shaking.

Jim took Duncan into the garage and entered the motor home. He prepared meals from the survival food supply. After a while a neighbor came and joined them with her sister. Their husbands were away and missed the event. The two women had run into the woods when the shooting began. They hadn't known what to do as none of their cars would run. Jim and Duncan walked around each cabin in the subdivision and found eight more bodies. Most had been shot but some killed with a knife. Months would pass before the gruesome scenes would not disturb Jim's sleep.

When evening came the two women lay down on the bed in the motor home and Jim and Duncan went to the Jeep. With their feet sticking out of the doors, they lay down. No one slept.

The next morning Jim worked his way to the safe in the burned cabin. With an ax and a shovel. He got to the safe door, and it was surprisingly undamaged. He opened the door, and the inside was completely untouched. He removed all the guns and ammunition and put them all in the motorcycle trailer. He loaded the trailer with a five-gallon gas can, a five-gallon water jug and a box of freeze-dried food. With all the guns and ammunition, the trailer was well overloaded. Jim hoped the little motorcycle would pull it.

By midmorning the police and several people from the nearby town arrived. They were on a flatbed farm trailer, pulled by a tractor which had not been affected by the EMP. The two women's' husbands were among the arrivals. Brief tearful reunions were held. The Chief of Police and two other officers were there and took statements from Duncan and the two women. They gave good descriptions of the men that did this. The police chief and several others knew exactly who these men were. They had arrived and lived in the small nearby Muslim community for the last two months. Most of the people in this community were polite and nice, even though they did not mix with the town's people or participate in any civic activities.

With nowhere to stay in the subdivision, everyone went back to town. Jim followed the flatbed trailer on his cycle, towing his little trailer. When they arrived in the town a large crowd started toward the Muslim community; they were not happy.

The Imam, the head of the Mosque, came to meet with them. He was waving his left hand and speaking loudly. "We did not know what they would do! We just gave them a place to stay for a while! We did not know! We are sorry; we are peace loving and good neighbors!"

A group of about twenty people came with the Iman, men, and women, to give him moral support.

Jim discreetly said to the police chief, "We cannot see their hands."

Just then a young girl behind the Iman said in an audible, but low voice, "Kill the infidels wherever they are!" Not a good time to quote this scripture from the Koran.

An older man, carrying a shotgun used for fifty years to hunt birds, screamed at the Iman, "You bastard, you killed my family!!"

The old man raised his shotgun, and the Iman raised his right hand which contained an AK 47. The old man was faster and fired the shotgun at a range of ten feet. The shotgun was loaded with number four bird shot and at short range it came out as one mass. It hit the Iman in the chest and blew a hole completely through him severing his spine. He was dead before he hit the ground.

What happened next was indescribable. Many of the Muslims were armed as were most the town's people. Shots were flying everywhere. Jim did not see anyone with a gun pointed in his direction, so he did not shoot. When the smoke cleared, the Muslims were all down and most were dead. Of the town's people only one man was slightly wounded. It got quiet for a moment, and then a shot came from the mosque and hit one of the policemen in the chest. He was wearing a vest, but it knocked him down. Jim aimed at the mosque and fired his AR-15 through and around the window. No more shots came from within, but the crowd opened up on the mosque. It was quickly full of holes.

The town's people went through the Muslim community and there was a slaughter. An older lady and two or three children escaped and were never seen again. The rest died in their homes or in the street. The mosque was searched, and a large cache of weapons found. The militia became very heavily armed. All the houses and the mosque were burned to the ground. The bodies were disposed of by tossing them into the fire.

Most of the people gathered at the church in the center of town and the preacher addressed them with a prayer. "Lord God, we have been attacked and we defended ourselves. We thank you for the victory and if we acted rashly, we ask for your forgiveness and we praise You." There were lots of "Amens" after the prayer. Julie, the realtor, looked at Jim dressed in his vest with several clips and the rifle across his chest. A look of fear replaced the previous very friendly attitude.

The police report of the incident stated: "The Muslims fired on the town's people who returned fire. Sixty-three died, all of whom were Muslim. The entire incident was ruled self-defense."

Jim went up to the police chief and said, "Several months ago I signed up with a militia group. It is a casual group who publish an online newsletter. I have never met any of the members. Awhile back the newsletter gave a gathering point location, west of here, to meet if there's trouble. I don't know if anyone will be there, but I think I will drive over that way and check things out."

"If no one is there, come back. We could use you here. We will organize men to watch the town. If communications ever come back, maybe the Army can help us out. Thanks for your help today," the chief responded as he shook Jim's hand.

Jim was almost ill as he rode back to his burned home. A lot of blood was spilled today, and he felt it was not the last. He prayed and asked God to watch over the Nation and wondered what was going on everywhere else. He rode with his headlights on and after arriving at his burned home thought the bright headlight might have been a mistake; he had been an easy target. 'I will need to be more careful and watch what I am doing if I am to survive,' he thought.

Jim pulled the cycle close to the garage and slept in the motor home. Surprisingly, he slept better than he had in several nights.

CHAPTER 3

On the Road to the Militia

RISING BEFORE DAWN, JIM PREPARED breakfast from the freeze-dried food. It was not too bad, and he already regretted he would need to leave most of it in the shop. He gathered a few more items before leaving. There were three motion sensors around the property which would emit a signal on a remote speaker if movement was detected. All were battery powered and might be handy. Most of his spare batteries had been in the cabin, but he had a few in the shop. He topped off fuel in the motorcycle by siphoning the Jeep fuel tank.

Jim retrieved his old laptop from the back of the motorhome, and it surprisingly booted up. Perhaps the steel building had protected it from the EMP. He wanted to see the e-mail about the Militia meeting place but, of course, there was no internet service. He remembered the general location and would go there, hoping it was correct. He shut the computer down and put it back in the motor home cabinet. It would be of no use without internet service.

Ready to leave, Jim stood and looked at the ashes of the cabin. Everything but a few tools were gone. For the first time he kind of understood Nancy's death. She would not have been able to handle the loss of everything. The furniture would not have bothered her but all the pictures and handmade things they had accumulated over their years together would be very hard to handle. In addition, he did not think she could have survived living in a tent or sleeping on the ground and seeing all the death. Jim, on the other hand, looked at the ashes and strangely felt relief at no longer having the responsibility for all the clutter. He got on his knees and prayed for guidance and for forgiveness of his sins, which were many. Not knowing why, he had survived, he asked to be used to fulfill God's plan, whatever it was. He started the cycle and moved down the road without looking back.

As he rode, he saw a few cars moving; it seemed the attack had not destroyed every vehicle. Many people were walking, and several tried to flag him down, but he did not stop as he could not help them. He did stop at a stalled car along the road. Sitting in the shade was a young woman with a baby and two boys, the oldest around ten. They looked anxious and frustrated. "I was just driving along, and my car stopped. I don't know why if won't restart."

"My husband should have come looking for me," she said, clearly afraid of Jim.

Jim thought that he probably did look fearsome with a rifle across his chest and a vest with clips and a pistol. He said, smiling and attempting to be friendly, "Something bad has happened and most cars will not run right now. Maybe he is looking for transportation."

"My cell phone doesn't work either and the baby is hungry," she said almost crying.

"I have nothing for a baby, but here is water and some food bars," he said as he passed out two canteens and the bars. They ate like they were starving.

"Can you charge my i-pad the older boy asked?" holding up his now dead device.

"All he wants to do is play games," the woman said.

"I am sorry young man; those devices will not work. You will have to learn to live in the real world and help your mother. Where do you live?" Jim asked.

"Just a few miles down the road," she replied.

Jim put the two boys on the trailer and had them hang on. The woman holding the baby sat in front of him as he slowly pulled onto the road, hoping nothing would break, as he was greatly overloaded. As they gained speed, her skirt blew up. She didn't care as modesty was not nearly as important presently as it had been a day or two ago. A lot of things had changed in the last few days.

It was ten miles to a small village and a tearful reunion. Jim later wondered why the man had not attempted to locate and assist his family. He could have just walked to where his wife was and help them. Perhaps he just didn't know where they were.

Jim, continuing his trip to the militia camp left the pavement onto a gravel road, a shortcut to the meeting place. It was late afternoon when he saw a small car moving on the road ahead of him. In the distance he saw another vehicle, a truck on the side of the road. Around the truck were several figures that seemed to all be dressed in black, not a good sign. He sped up to try to catch the car, but it rounded a little bluff and disappeared from his sight.

As he approached the bluff, he heard two shots, followed by screaming and shouting. He parked the cycle and began running to the bluff. Sounds were a combination of small children crying and men laughing and screaming. He looked over the bluff and saw a few black-clad men standing, watching as one of their number ripped clothes off a woman. There were several children around crying or screaming. The men were laughing like this was a comedy.

Two of the men stood a distance behind the others. Jim aimed his AR-15 and fired at one. The silencer on the gun did not make if silent but the muzzle blast was reduced and with all the noise and commotion, the men did not notice the shot. The man in his crosshairs fell, and the one beside him laughed even more thinking he had just stumbled. The next shot took out the second man. A third man seemed to realize what was happening but was hit before he could react. One of the black-clad figures was a woman who began screaming as she realized they were being fired upon; no one paid any attention to her. Another man brought his rifle up to return fire but did not see a target. He went down with the fourth shot. The man attacking the woman was bent over her and unaware of what was taking place. Some of the children were behind him so a fatal shot was not possible, but his rear seemed to be in the clear. Jim shot him in the hip joint, breaking his pelvis and rupturing everything inside. It must have been very painful. The woman in black was the only perpetrator left. She screamed and fired her pistol in Jim's direction, missing him. He shot her in the chest. The firefight lasted ten seconds.

Jim walked up to the area where the man wounded in the hip lay. He was screaming in a language Jim did not understand. Jim said, "Say hello to Satan, you bastard." Jim shot him in the head as he was reaching for a pistol.

It got very quiet. There were six children and a woman, all with stunned looks on their faces. Jim was probably a scary figure with his rifle and military dress. He walked to each body to verify it was dead. All were. One of the youngsters, who Jim guessed to be a teenager, was an attractive blond girl. She was helping the woman cover herself. The woman had scrapes and bruises but didn't appear to be seriously hurt. The children were clearly not from the same family. Two were black and two seemed to be of Indian descent. The teenager, a very pretty girl, looked to be from a Scandinavian country or maybe from northern Germany. The sixth one seemed to be Chinese — a real United Nations group. The age of the youngest child was probably five or six, and the oldest was the teenage girl.

"I will get my cycle and come right back," Jim said as he walked away. No one answered. He looked at the truck which had obviously belonged to the thugs and saw a wheel had broken loose and was at an odd angle. They had broken down. The woman's car had been disabled by the gun fire. Why had they damaged the car if their truck was inoperable? They must have help coming, the only logical answer.

He drove the cycle with the trailer to the small, frightened group. He retrieved his sweater from a bag and gave it to the woman so she could cover herself. The sweater was large on Jim and looked like a tent on this small woman. She smiled a little and said, "Thank you."

"I think more of these people are their way. We need to leave here quickly," Jim stated.

"Do you happen to have any water?" the woman asked in quite a pleasant voice, considering the circumstances.

"I am so sorry," Jim said as passed around his canteens and the food bars.

"We left in a hurry and did not bring any food or water. They attacked our school and were shooting everyone. I just took my class and ran," the woman said very sadly.

"I will take two of the children to a campsite a few miles away and come back as soon as I can. I cannot take you all at once."

She looked very concerned and said, "I don't like the idea of separating the children."

The teenage girl said, "I will go and take care of Lee until the rest of you come."

Jim walked to the woman and took off his watch and handed it to her and said, "I will leave my watch for security."

The woman took the watch and with tears in her eyes and a little smile said, "Thank you for saving us. My name is Hannah White."

Jim stated his name and took out his pistol and handed it to her. She took it without another word.

Jim took the little Chinese boy and put him on the bike in front of him and the young girl sat behind. She gripped him very tightly.

He drove as fast as he dared on the gravel road, went about five miles, then turned off onto a path up a hill. On the top was a treed area that was fairly level, a site he had found in a previous exploration. The site was not openly visible from the surrounding country-side. He quickly unloaded the trailer and took off the top.

He looked at the girl and assured her that he would be back as soon as he could.

She looked at him very sweetly and said, "My name is Rhoda, and we will be fine."

Jim went back faster than he should with the empty trailer bouncing behind him. He returned to the site in less than fifteen minutes. He quickly went over the bodies and took weapons. There were four almost new AK47s along with belts of clips and pistols. There were two additional rifles that were worn out, so he threw them over the side of the hill. In addition, he found a leather pouch which contained some papers and a handheld radio. He also took those items.

Three children fit into the trailer, sitting on the ammunition and emptied pistols. They held the four rifles with the barrels sticking up. They looked like miniature warriors. Hannah sat behind Jim gripping him tightly; the closest a woman had been to him since his wife died. It was nice. The remaining child, a small black boy sat in front of Jim and laughed all the way back to the camp. He was a delightful, upbeat child.

The last rays of daylight were disappearing when they reached the camp. He had not used the headlight to be as inconspicuous as possible. In the distance he noticed headlights of vehicles coming down the road toward the dead. He ascended the final knoll when the radio came alive with chatter in a language he did not understand. He finally switched it off. Parking the cycle and trailer behind a bush, everyone unloaded.

Rhoda had already begun setting up camp by unrolling the little tent. She did not know how to set it up, but she had placed it in a level place. With a little instruction from Jim the tent was soon up and ready. The only equipment Hannah and the six children had was a thin blanket for each, no spare clothes, food, or water. They would have been in trouble even if the terrorists had not stopped them.

Jim refilled his canteens from the five-gallon water container and passed them around. Everyone was hungry but he did not start a fire because of the nearness of the trucks which had now reached the dead bodies. Jim lay on his stomach at the edge of the hill and watched the new arrivals through his rifle scope. They were using the truck headlight to light the area, clearly not afraid of being seen. The dead were searched, as well as the damaged truck and car, in an obvious search looking for something important.

"What are they looking for?" Hannah, who had crawled up beside him, asked.

"I don't know, maybe this leather pouch. It has papers that I cannot read." Jim paused, and then continued, "These men are more disciplined, and they have guards watching with night vision goggles. I don't understand all the lights, but they are not sloppy like the ones who stopped you."

"We can take them if we have to," Hannah said, surprising Jim who turned and looked at her. He noticed, again, that she was actually quite pretty.

"What are they doing?" she asked.

The men had dragged the bodies to the side of the road and laid them side-by-side. Two of the men were putting a little pile of dirt on the chest of each body.

"I have no idea. Maybe that is a ceremonial burial. Maybe Muslims must be buried by a certain time," Jim speculated.

"With all those men they could have buried them properly," she replied.

The trucks drove away in the direction they had come from. Then Jim took some of the scraps of wood the children had gathered and built a very small fire. While it burned down to hot coals, he took a small pot and went down the hill to a stream and filled it with water. From his pack he took a water filter device and hooked it to a tree. It had a container at the top and a hose which went into the collapsible five-gallon container. He poured the water in the top and it slowly trickled out into the larger container.

Rhoda, the oldest of the children, followed every step in the process. She asked questions about how the filter worked and if it could filter really dirty water. It was clear she enjoyed being with Jim.

Jim busied himself preparing the freeze-dried food by arranging hot coals around the same pot he had used for water. He filled it with water from one of the canteens. When it was hot, he added a packet of freeze-dried food, mostly pasta with some chicken. Each packet supposedly made four servings, but it took three packets for this crew. Jim had brought enough food for several weeks just for himself, but it would last just a few days with this big family. At the time he packed he had put in a packet of thin plastic bowls for no reason. He was glad to have them now. Hannah helped him with the preparation and clean up but spent some time just observing Jim. The children seemed to have lost all fear of Jim and enjoyed being near him, making him a little uncomfortable.

Not wanting to build a large fire which could be seen for miles, they sat around hot coals, adding a little dry branch now and then. The sunset was gorgeous adding to the pleasant experience, making it almost like a family outing.

Hannah smiled at Jim and said, "Let me introduce us. I am Hannah White, this is Rhoda, she is from Sweden, Lee's family is from China and Shelden and Handle are from India. Bobbie and Billy are from Mali in Africa. This is the class of English-as-a-second-language from the school in Bayfield." Each of the children smiled and nodded as they were introduced; they all seemed very relaxed.

Jim wondered where all these kids' parents were as Hannah was clearly not their mother. Out of courtesy he just said, "My name is Jim Jenkins, and I am from a little community just outside of Pagosa Springs."

The tent was made for three adults, but all six children crowded in. Jim donated his sleeping bag which he opened as a blanket for everyone. The six got settled in more or less comfortably. No one complained.

Jim refilled the water filter bottle so it would continue cleaning water through the night and made two cups of instant coffee for Hannah and himself. They sat by the coals and talked.

"These kids are not yours; where are their parents?" he asked.

"Shelden and Handle have two parents, or they did. The others seemed to have only a mother; at least I never met a father for them. Rhoda looks older but is only 12 and she had no parents at all. I don't know where they went. When the attack came the whole town just seemed to explode. The school was completely destroyed, and we were on a day trip to the park or we would have been killed. My car was nearby, and we just jumped in it and ran. I am sure if their parents are alive, they think their children are dead. I will get word back when I can."

Just then a deer and her fawn came out of woods. The fawn quietly came near, and Hannah with an outstretched hand touched its nose. Before they ran off.

"How about that!" Jim said.

"A good sign, maybe we will be all right," she replied, and then continued. "I have my blanket I will share with you."

With an uneasy feeling, Jim lay down with his head on a little rise in the soil. Awkwardly he held his arm out for her to lay her head on it. She slowly eased to the ground, snuggled closely and covered them with her thin blanket. It felt good.

After a few seconds, Hannah raised herself on an elbow and put her face near Jim's face and remarked, "We would certainly be dead or most of us dead by now if you had not come along. There is no way we can thank you but know that I realize what has happened, even if the children don't understand." She paused, then said, "I am Jewish."

She waited to see if he had a reaction to this revelation, he had none.

She lay her head back on his arm and almost immediately was asleep while Jim lay there, enjoying her presence, and trying to understand what had happened that day. He started this morning completely alone and now was with a group that depended on him for their very survival. It was almost like a really large family.

He finally dozed off and slept fitfully until the sky began to lighten. Rising, trying not to awaken the quite lovely young woman, Jim started gathering wood for a fire. The coals from the previous night were still warm and he took some dry pine needles and laid them on the coals and blew. They quickly burst into flame. Not worried too much about the light, he built a bigger fire.

"Are you sure you are not an angel?" Hannah asked, still under the blanket. "You started the fire by just blowing on it."

"The coals were still hot. I assure you I am not an angel!" he replied, chuckling.

The children drifted out of the tent, one at a time, and stood around the fire wrapped in their little blankets; no one had a coat.

Breakfast went easily and quickly. Everyone seemed to be hungry. Jim made instant coffee and a chocolate drink, also from the packets. Cleanup also went quickly, as everyone helped. In short order the tent was packed, and the food put away.

"I think we can get everyone on the cycle if we leave everything. However, leaving all the camping gear means we will be in difficulty if we do not meet someone before evening," Jim said to Hannah.

"We will do what you think is best," she replied.

Hannah went to the guns Jim had taken from the dead men and selected a pistol with a holster and strapped it on. Jim watched her and went over and put new holes in the belt so she could fasten the buckle around her narrow waist. He thought this was very strange as she did not look like a person who had ever fired a gun. He refrained from questioning her. Pulling her big sweater down over the pistol completely covered it.

Jim topped off the fuel tank from the five-gallon container, almost draining it, and filled his four canteens from the plastic container. After taking two boxes of food bars out of the food container he placed the box behind a rock further up the hill. All the pistols and rifles from the attackers were placed on the food box along with the camping supplies. The cover from the trailer hid everything reasonably well.

Five of the children crowded into the trailer, not very comfortably, but inside so they would not fall out. Hannah would ride behind Jim and Rhoda in front of him. Jim's rifle lay across the handlebars and his pistol in his vest. It was very tight. They crept down the hill, barely moving, then sped up a little when reaching the gravel road.

CHAPTER 4

The Militia Base Camp

THE SMALL GROUP HAD TRAVELED about thirty miles when they came to what looked like a hunting camp. It had a sizable lodge and several out-buildings. A very large American flag was flying from a flagpole; giving Jim confidence here they would be among friends. A hundred yards from the buildings was a gate with several heavily armed men. The men were tense and very alert, but relaxed when they saw the children on the cycle and in the trailer. Jim got off and, keeping his hands clearly in view, walked up to the men and handed them his membership in the militia organization. It was a simple card that only indicated he received their e-mail newsletter, but it was enough, and the men welcomed him into the camp, although one of the men held Jim's guns until meeting the man in charge.

The man in charge was named Captain Masters and was an officer in the Colorado National Guard, an actual US Army military man, the first Jim had seen since the EMP event. While pleasant, he was definitely a no-nonsense man and in charge. While Jim explained his unusual family, the captain was doing a thorough visual check of each member.

"I have left guns and supplies at our last camp and will need to retrieve them," Jim stated.

"We have no reports of problems in that area, but we had no knowledge about the men who stopped this family either. Be watchful," the captain replied.

"I will go with you and help," Rhoda the twelve years old, going-on-thirty, stated.

Jim looked at Hannah who just smiled and rolled her eyes at him.

The captain had a young man fill the cycle's fuel tank. The man, about twenty years of age, was obviously more interested in Rhoda than what he was doing. Jim watched and thought, 'Lord, this girl is going to need your close protection.'

Going much faster than when heavily loaded, Jim sped out of the gate, leaving Hannah and the other five children standing and waving. Jim watched for any movement ahead and to the sides but knew it was unlikely he would see a sniper in time. None had been there a little earlier in the day, so he felt fairly confident he would be safe if he could make the trip quickly.

He turned off the road two hours later and went up the path to the previous night's campsite. Rhoda jumped off, fresh as a daisy and quickly ran behind a bush, the children's' bathroom. Jim took his scope and looked at the site of the gun battle and observed that nothing had changed. The bodies all remained in a row and seemed undisturbed. No one had been there except a few vultures. Jim topped off the fuel tank, draining his fuel container. Rhoda helped load the trailer and seemed to be enjoying herself. Everything fit in the little trailer, even the guns taken from the dead. When they departed, they left no sign there had been a camp.

The trip back to the military encampment was a little slower but went well with no unwanted surprises. At the camp an old yellow school bus had arrived while they were away.

Captain Masters greeted them. "I am glad to see the guns. The reserves have government M-16's, but the militia is armed with such a variety of weapons and calibers the government does not stock ammunition for," he said, ignoring the fact that most of the militia members had a good supply for their weapons, at least for the present.

Suddenly Rhoda griped Jim's arm and said, "What is happening?"

Jim followed her gaze and saw a group of mostly women and children around the bus. Hannah and the other children were in the group.

Jim, with Rhoda hanging onto his arm, walked over to Hannah who was keeping the other five children close. For the first time since she was attacked, she looked frightened. All the children came to Jim as he approached and surrounded him. Most were crying except little Bobbie whose smile was greatly reduced. Captain Masters soon joined the group.

"We have been sending the dependents to a camp a hundred miles north of here. They will be safer if the enemy is coming. At that location there is a tracking system to unite families who have been separated during the attack," the captain explained.

Hannah was not crying, but close to it. She worked her way through the children to stand very close to Jim. She paused a moment then said, "They are sending us away. Jim, I, I." She stammered.

"You will be safer there and I will come as soon as I can," he replied.

As they stood nearly touching, she finally said, "This happened so quickly." With no warning she stood on her tiptoes and kissed Jim on the cheek, her first expression of affection.

As the bus drove away the six faces were looking out the back window. Even Bobbie was crying.

"I didn't understand you were married and those were your kids," the captain said as he walked up to Jim.

"No, we are not married. I met her and the children only two days ago. She is their English teacher. We seem to have bonded quickly," Jim said, not covering his emotions at all.

Having more important things to discuss, the captain said, "The leather packet you brought had plans in them. There were three sets in different languages. We could read the Spanish which is an attack plan to take over the South Western part of the country, basically New Mexico, Arizona and southern California which would become a part of Mexico. We cannot read the other two languages, one is Arabic we think, and is longer so it may say something different. The plan is to take control of the country well north of Arizona and New Mexico and then ask for peace with the condition of retaining those states. It seems crazy for Mexico to go along with this plan. The US can easily trounce Mexico even in the weaken state it is in."

"Maybe they are planning to get additional help from another source, or plan to use nuclear weapons to quickly win a victory," Jim replied.

"Our communications are limited. The old Ham systems, especially the old tube units, were not affected by the blast so we have some communications. It is not secure and we have no encryption so anyone who has a Ham unit can hear and understand us. Some officers from the active service are on the way and they may change our plans. Right now, I have lookouts on the mountain tops watching for activity and they have short range walky-talky radios for communication. I plan a probe south to see what we can find, and I want you to be a part of it," Captain Masters stated.

CHAPTER 5

Lookout 18

At Lookout 18, one station Captain Masters had established, four men were on duty— two watching and two resting. On watch currently was Private Amson, nineteen, an active Army Reservist, and Bill Davis, twenty-six, a militia member. God had provided a long-range target shooter in this group of patriots. Bill's rifle was his property and his prized possession, a fifty-caliber rifle with a top-of-the-line scope.

A problem with being on remote watch is boredom; nothing happens for long periods of time. The men knew not to play cards or anything else which would distract them. But it is difficult to stay alert when the only sound is coming from birds in surrounding trees. As they engaged in small talk, they had not noticed a group of men in dark clothing crossing a ridge nearly two miles south. Establishing an ambush site along a road at the base of the ridge.

After several hours on watch something caught their attention—a bus going north along the road, one of the few vehicles running these days. Why it was operational when most vehicles were not was a mystery to these men. They watched the bus through optical devices, Amson, a telescope, and Davis, his rifle scope. They discussed who might be on the bus, where they were going and, of course, wondered if any good-looking women were on board.

They both were watching when they saw a black clad man appear with an RPG, a small handheld missile launcher. Both men cursed as the small missile hit the front of the bus, destroying the engine. Bill Davis uttered a curse about his previous inattention and then a prayer to guide his shot. Five or six men rose from their cover and began running toward the bus, all armed with AK-47s. Bill aimed ahead of the leader and fired, knowing he could not hit a moving target at this range. He certainly could not, but the Lord God could. Four seconds later the lead man's head exploded. The terrorists stopped, not understanding what had happened. The only noise they had heard was the splat when the bullet hit. Two seconds later a bullet struck a rock right beside the, black-clad renegades, blowing it to pieces. They all turned and quickly disappeared over the ridge.

The rear door of the bus opened, and people streamed out. There seemed to be many children and four or five adults. Absent of serious injury, they began moving down the road in the direction from which they had come. Moving rather slowly, some of the adults seemed to be suffering from old age with stooped shoulders and shuffling of feet.

Private Amson grabbed the handheld radio and called, "This is lookout 18, and a bus going north has been attacked and is disabled! There are survivors!"

At the Base Camp a man ran to Captain Masters who was still talking to Jim, yelling, "The bus has been attacked about ten miles north of here across from Lookout 18!"

More words were spoken but Jim heard all he needed to hear. He ran to his cycle, quickly threw everything out of the trailer, and with only his rifle revved the engine.

The captain yelled at him, "Wait, we will send back up!"

Jim was already out the gate.

The little motorcycle's top speed was sixty-five on the speedometer and it was pegged out. The little trailer was airborne a good part of the time as he sped along.

It was less than fifteen minutes, but it seemed like forever when he saw a long line of people scattered along the road. He slid to a stop just short of them and got off, greatly relieved to see familiar faces, his new family.

The six children had been terrified by the attack but screamed in delight when they saw Jim. They ran and surrounded him, grabbing on and all talking at the same time. Rhoda leaned over the little ones and whispered in his ear. "I think God is telling you we are your family," she said, as she kissed him on the cheek.

Hannah stood back while the children greeted him and in turn, she slowly came to him. The children parted to let her in.

Jim said to her, "I was afraid I had lost you forever."

She looked him in the eyes and replied, "I beg you don't ever send me away again."

She then rose and kissed him on the mouth, hugging him for a moment.

One of the other passengers, an older woman, said to Jim, "It is a miracle, but your family is safe."

"Yes, yes they are," Jim replied to her, never taking his eyes off Hannah.

"Go ahead. Take your family to safety; we will just hold you up," the only adult man in the group commented.

"We will all stay together. Is anyone else in the bus?" Jim asked.

Jim was just ready to walk to the bus when two pickups came up the road. Each had a small American flag on the fender to inform any militia which side they were on. The men on board were all militia, and obviously trained. Several took up defense positions, while others moved toward the bus. They carried back a man, badly wounded and burned, but alive. They placed him in one of the pickups and loaded the rest of the adults. Jim repeated the loading of the small children and with Hannah behind and Rhoda in front of him, they started back to the Militia Camp, moving slowly.

CHAPTER 6

The Small Mansion

ARRIVING BACK AT THE MILITIA Camp they were greeted by Captain Masters.

"I am happy you are all allright and it looks like you will be here for a while. I can put you in bunk houses, but it will break up your group. They were designed for men or women, not family units. Another option is a small cabin, shack really, down by the creek. It will be crowded but you can be together and out of the weather," he added.

After a short walk to the little cabin, Jim saw that the captain hadn't misstated his assessment of the structure. It was small. The captain went along to observe the reaction of the rather big family unit. Lee, the Chinese boy, shouted, "It is a mansion!" when he saw it.

It was a pretty cabin, bigger than a shoe box, but not by much.

Hannah grabbed Jim's arm as they entered. She had a big smile and a twinkle in her eyes.

The cabin had three rooms. The biggest was the living, dining and kitchen, all in one. It had a worn couch, three small chairs, and little table along one wall. The far end was the kitchen which had a gas stove, a refrigerator, a sink, and little wood burning stove with a cast iron frying pan on it. The room also had a stone fireplace at the opposite end. It was quite nice for one or two people. The second room was a surprisingly large bathroom. It was tiled and had both a shower and a tub. The third room was the bedroom, which was large, compared to the rest of the cabin. It had a queen size bed with sheets and blankets. The room also had a good-sized closet, the only storage in the cabin. The little house was clean and had been well maintained. Oil-lanterns were in every room, indicating the electrical power had never been reliable. Currently there was no electrical power.

"This was the caretaker's cabin and he moved to the main house just days ago right after the 'event'. Do you think you can all fit in here?" the captain asked.

"This is just wonderful, it is perfect, and we love it!" Hannah replied, almost unable to contain herself. The children all yelled "Yeah! Yeah!"

"I will have someone round up additional bedding and send it over," the captain said as he left chuckling.

Hannah immediately began planning how things would be arranged to allow the children to sleep in the main room. It would involve moving chairs and the table to one side in order to open some floor space. "You will be comfortable in front of the fireplace," she said to them.

"Might I sleep on the floor in the bedroom with you and Mr. Jim?" Rhoda asked Hannah.

"No!" Hannah answered, and they both laughed.

Jim looked the living situation over and said, "Hannah, I don't know how this is going to work. These sleeping arrangements are going to be tight. Maybe I should sleep at the lodge."

"Jim, we will be fine, together. What will happen, will happen. You may be tired of me in a few weeks and want to get rid of me, for I cannot conceal all my bad habits forever," she coyly replied.

"What bad habits can you have, except you seem to collect children from all over the world?"

"Well, that is certainly one, and sometimes I get short tempered and I like to sleep naked," she stated, very seriously.

They both laughed and Jim replied, "Well, that last is certainly not a problem for me."

"Jim, I want to tell you. When the man on the road was attacking me, I prayed. I prayed someone would come and help me. I then heard a voice that said, "Do not be afraid a man will rescue you and will care for you all of your life." She paused then continued, "I won't obligate you, but I believe I am yours."

The discussion was interrupted when the young private arrived with the promised bedding. He had four small mattresses and several blankets. The mattresses were rolled up—good for storage, but thin on the floor.

The young man, looking around for Rhoda, stated, "We have received a message from the parents of two of your children, Shalon and Handel. They are grateful their children are all right and will come for them when it is safe. It is not clear when that will be as there are roaming groups of terrorists near them."

Hannah, moving between the private and Rhoda replied, "I will pass the message on to the children, and if you get any more word, we will appreciate it. Also, you should know that Rhoda looks older, but is twelve years old."

The young man looked surprised and stuttered a reply, "Sorry, I didn't mean any disrespect. I almost forgot! Captain Masters would like to see Mr. Jenkins early in the morning at the large building by the entrance." With that the young private left in a hurry.

That night Hannah demonstrated the last of her bad habits and they became a couple in their living arrangements.

The next morning Hannah was up very early and made breakfast with the help of Rhoda, who seemed very interested in Hannah's cheery attitude. Rhoda was not satisfied with the response to her inquiries. "I will discuss this when you are a little older!" was Hannah's standard reply.

Hannah thought about the young soldier and decided she needed to talk with Rhoda sooner rather than later.

CHAPTER 7

The Patrol

JIM HAD ASSUMED THE MEETING with Captain Masters was just between the two of them, but when he arrived there was a group of men and women, several hundred of them. The group consisted of a wide age range from very old to quite young, mostly people he had not seen earlier. The group drank coffee and visited, getting to know each other before the meeting began. Most of the men and women in the militia were hunters, shooting enthusiasts, or ex-military personnel. There were some Reserve members, not formally activated, but acting as such. Hannah had not been invited but she joined Jim just as Captain Masters was beginning the meeting.

"There is much I do not know but I will bring you up to date with the information I have. The EMP was devastating, but not everything has been damaged. We have some communication, using the old Ham radio network. I was not aware it was still functioning at all, but there are a few stations around the country the locations a closely guarded secret. Not all vehicles or aircraft are down. Most military vehicles seem to be functional and older trucks and cars are fine, those without computer control. The central government is functioning, and aid is on the way. The country is under attack on several fronts and the military is responding. We have been attacked on a broad front from Mexico. Since we have a strong civilian militia, it will be up to us to defend the southern border of the US until the military arrives. The attack is on a broad front all along the border with Mexico."

The captain paused to let this sink in before continuing.

"The invaders are a mixed group. A few are clearly ISIS types, and wear the distinctive black garb and are Arabic. Others seem to be foreign and local Muslims, some of whom dress in black. The involvement of the Mexican government is a question. I have been told they deny being a part of the attack; however, large forces could not have been in their country without their knowledge. In addition, we have in our possession documents indicating a plan to give Mexico the southern states as a reward for their aid."

A second pause as the captain gathered his thoughts.

"I am establishing two probes, patrols of a sort, to go south and investigate the situation. We do not know of any forces in strength near us, no tanks or artillery or a massed army. However, there are signs of small groups of the enemy ravaging the towns so it is likely you will encounter hostiles. Any information from captured prisoners will be helpful, and any documents found are very valuable. Be on the lookout for this type of pouch containing any papers." With that he held up the pouch Jim had retrieved from his first encounter.

The captain concluded his speech with the comment, "I know most of you are volunteers and this mission is no exception, however, it is vitally important we begin to resist. I will meet with the officers and they will contact each of their teams for final instructions. You are dismissed."

"We need to get our gear together and get ready," Hannah stated.

"What?" Jim replied.

"We are a team and I will go with you. Rhoda can watch the little ones and the next cabin has two older women who will help if needed," she paused then continued, "I can help, let me go with you."

"All right but this may be dangerous," Jim replied.

The 'troops' left the next morning well before dawn. In the lead was an army Humvee with Lieutenant Simons, the officer in charge of the mission. The lieutenant was a young reservist with no combat experience or leadership training, but he was a nice young man. Following the Humvee were three duce & a half army truck that were popular in WWII. Perhaps these could have participated in that conflict. The trucks flew small American flags. Jim and Hannah were in the back of the second vehicle along with fifteen other men and women. Some were dressed in military garb and others in civilian clothing. One man was dressed in a navy uniform. All were armed with some type of weapon; many, like Jim, had an AR-15 or an M-16 which looked similar. Jim was dressed in his tactical vest with a small backpack. He carried eight clips for his rifle. In addition, he had his old army forty-five pistol and several clips for it. That along with several canteens of water and food bars made his load heavy. He hoped he would not have to walk much. Hannah also had a small pack with water and food. Her weapon was the pistol in nine mm. The gun was well concealed under Jim's old sweater which she was wearing with her jeans.

The destination was a town in northern New Mexico, a town of about ten thousand people, mostly Navajo with some Hispanic and a sizable number of European Americans, a typical town for the area. The trucks spread out as they came into the town square where they quickly unloaded. Everyone was on high alert knowing there might be someone in the area that might shoot at them. The people of the town were disturbed at their presence and while they acknowledged them with a nod of the head, were obviously nervous.

The first thing Jim noticed was the old church that had been burned. It was made of blocks which were still standing, but the roof and interior lay in ashes. Jim had visited here years earlier and remembered a grand old building, probably Catholic.

If there was a plan on how to proceed, Jim and the other volunteers were unaware of it. The lieutenant, along with two young women, walked along the street and pleasantly inquired about a mayor or someone in charge. While he was smiling and pleasant, four men in army uniforms followed, scanning their surroundings for any problem. The biggest complaint of the residents was the lack of electricity and wondered when it would be back on. No one had an answer. The few who would engage in conversation mentioned there had been several strangers in town, but no terrorists. They would not discuss the burned church. The most noticeable thing was their fear, and no one seemed to know of the mayor's whereabouts.

Jim went a short distance down a side street to look things over. Arriving at a corner, an old man with a bad limp slowly came toward him and greeted him with a big smile, showing bad teeth. Then it happened. The old man, it seemed, was not so old. He grabbed Jim's left arm and another man appeared from a nearby doorway and grabbed his right arm. They pulled his arms away from his weapons. Dragging him through the doorway into a small room, Jim cursed himself for letting this happen. Inside the room a woman, laughing at how stupid he was, came to take his rifle.

Suddenly there were two deafening shots. The two men holding Jim's arms fell, both shot in the head by Hannah who had followed the trio inside. The woman still held the stock of Jim's rifle when he grabbed the rifle and slammed the butt of the gun in her face. He heard bones break. There were other men in the room, two on his left and one on his right. A fourth man sat at a desk dressed in some sort of uniform. The men went for their holstered pistols but were too slow. They should have been ready; Jim was not the only stupid one. He shot the two men standing on his left while Hannah shot the one on the right. Jim shot the man at the desk in the chest and Hannah shot him between the eyes at the same time. Seven people lay dead or dying on the floor.

Jim then heard a noise of someone moving in the next room, so he quickly fired six shots through the wall in the direction of the noise. He heard a moan and a body fall.

It suddenly was very quiet with Jim and Hannah standing side by side in the smoke-filled room. It had happened so fast they were stunned at what had just occurred.

The calm didn't last more than a few seconds. The lieutenant ran into the room with his four guards and yelled questions at Jim, questions which had no answers. Things finally settled down and Jim explained what had happened. It was suspected these men wanted a prisoner for some reason. Maybe they thought Jim knew something; he didn't. One of the guards with the lieutenant was a sergeant, and the smartest one present. He took charge and checked the bodies. The woman had died. The man in the adjoining room was alive, but his spine was broken. This man was a high-ranking officer in the Mexican army and would never walk again. The four men in the room also wore Mexican uniforms.

In a back room of the building they found the mayor and three other officials of the city. They had been tortured by thugs wanting information about the US defenses, information the city leaders didn't have. A few days previously a group of twenty or thirty men had come into town and declared the area was now part of Mexico. They damaged several buildings, raped a few women, shot some policemen and burned the church. It seemed the church, while Catholic, had other Christian groups meeting there during the week. Why they did this made no sense to anyone. All the invaders had left the town except the eight men, now dead or captured.

The wounded officer, a major in the Mexican Army, talked freely. He indicated a division of troops was on the way and the town was destined to be a fortified city on the new northern boundary of Mexico. He thought the division would arrive in two or three days. They had taken Jim hoping to gather information concerning US defenses. In addition to the mayor, they found boxes of documents, in Spanish and other languages, which would take interpreters and many days to review. They also found radios and additional arms; it had been a big haul.

Finally, Jim and Hannah had time to speak to each other. "You saved my life. I didn't know you were so capable with a pistol," Jim stated.

"I took a course some time ago to get a carry permit. I couldn't let them hurt you," she replied with a smile.

"You are amazing and continue to surprise me," he replied.

The two of them went across the square to the burned-out church and just inside the door got on their knees and prayed, asking God to forgive them for taking lives and then asked for guidance for the future. When they got up, they discovered ten other men and women outside the entrance on their knees, joining in their prayer.

CHAPTER 8

The Indian Camp

WITH THE INFORMATION FROM THE wounded Mexican Major, preparations for a major battle commenced. The prisoner was sent back to the Base Camp along with the recovered papers. Jim sent a note to Rhoda to get his sniper rifle, ammunition, camping gear, and send it with the new troops. He had assumed Captain Masters would, in fact, send additional men to defend this town. A few militia men would not be able to stop a full division if they were really coming. The Mexican Major might not have known the plans, or he may have just been lying. Captain Masters would have to make some hard decisions.

The first of the reinforcements arrived at dusk. It was quite a sight. The same truck which had taken the prisoner back lead the pack pulling a flatbed trailer loaded with gear and men. Captain Masters was in the cabin. The rest of the vehicles consisted of a variety of old vehicles. Anything that would run was brought along. Nearly all the troops from the Base Camp had arrived, hoping the information the captain had was correct.

One of the vehicles in the convoy was Jim's motorcycle with the trailer. Driving the cycle was the young private, whose name was Jones. Behind him and clinging tightly was twelve-year-old Rhoda.

"Rhoda, what are you doing here?" Jim and Hannah yelled at the same time, louder than they should.

"I am sorry, but she was very persuasive," young Private Jones said, looking at the ground.

"Hannah, please I want to help. I cannot stay behind," Rhoda said, pleadingly.

Jim and Hannah looked at each other in exasperation. Hannah finally said, "There is nothing we can do. There is no way to send her back. You will have to stay close to us young lady and who is taking care of the children." The last statement she directed at Rhoda with a very stern look.

Rhoda squealed with joy and hugged them both, "the ladies next door are watching them."

Private Jones interjected, "I will be glad to watch her."

"No, you will do your duty as your officers direct you!" Jim said, attempting to give him a stern look, not very successfully.

The discussion was interrupted by Captain Masters when he called a meeting of everyone.

The captain stood in the back of a Ford pickup and spoke as loudly as he could. It looked like everyone in the Militia Base Camp was there, about five hundred men and women, along with some children. Jim thought, 'If an air attack occurs now, we will be completely wiped out.' Thankfully, there was no attack.

The captain shouted, "We have received information that a full army division has crossed the southern border of New Mexico and Arizona. The army consists of heavy tanks, trucks and perhaps as many as five thousand men. This information is from prisoners and captured documents and is considered creditable. We will establish a defensive line in the mountains along the path where we believe they will come. Commanders have been established who will assign you a position. Our objective is to stop the advance of the enemy and hold them until regular army troops arrive. Be prepared as these troops may arrive at any time completely unannounced. Good luck and God Bless the United States!!"

Jim's individual commander was Lieutenant Simons who they had met earlier. He looked at Hannah and nodded then at Rhoda for a longer time but made no comment.

"You have your cycle so I will assign you the more distant location. It is on the state line between New Mexico and Arizona, overlooking the desert where we believe the enemy will come. The hills to the east will be occupied with group C. This is just south of the Navajo Reservation. They have agreed to fight with us, but not join ranks or take orders from us. I'm not sure how that will work but try not to shoot any Indians. Take supplies for two or three days. If you are there longer, we will send a truck with provisions."

Private Jones had come close to Jim and his family, obviously hoping to be assigned a spot close to them but his placement was about two miles northeast.

Jim put everything he could in the little trailer. Rhoda had packed well, and all the camping equipment was there as well as his sniper rifle, a good supply of ammunition and the last of the freeze-dried food. The trailer was packed tightly. Rhoda had added a pistol to her wardrobe, another nine mm, the gun a little smaller than the one Hannah continually wore. She gave no explanation as to where she got it. Being only twelve years old, Jim wondered whether she had any experience with firearms.

All three mounted the cycle with Rhoda in front and Hannah's out-stretched arms holding them together from behind. The threesome was a crowded, but happy family leading the convoy south. Captain Masters stood with Lieutenant Simons looking as if he didn't believe what he was seeing. A larger group of men cheered them on as they departed.

Going south they passed through Indian towns that seemed untouched by the conflict. The only thing unusual was there seemed to be few men present. If there were enemy patrols watching their activity, they were well hidden. It was a very peaceful and pleasant trip. Reaching their defensive area, the group stopped, and the lieutenant again went over the individual positions the men were to take. Private Jones looked longingly toward Rhoda who, of course, noticed and smiled slightly, playing hard to get. The trucks split up, going went east down a paved road. Jim, with a pickup following, continued south. The pickup turned onto a dirt road and a mile further, Jim found his assigned unpaved road. The road became a trail as it ascended. The little cycle struggled, making slow progress through dense forest. How anyone knew about this place was a mystery.

They approached the edge of the bluff which overlooked the vast plain to the south where they spotted their camp. Stopping, they were very near to riders on horseback standing quietly under the trees. Jim thought he had again made a mistake and entered an ambush. One of the men slid off his horse and approached them as the three of them got off the cycle. The man was clearly an Indian. He even had a cloth tied around his head with a feather stuck in it. He carried an ancient rifle which looked like it had belonged to Geronimo. He was a big man, well over six feet and looked to be about eighty or so.

He addressed Hannah saying, "You are a lovely lady and will give me many children to fill my tepee and your father may live nearby," 'father', apparently referring to Jim.

Hannah, taken aback by the statement, noticed the other Indians standing nearby were smiling broadly, so she replied in kind. "I am grateful for your generous offer, but I belong to someone already."

The big man sighed and then turned to Rhoda and went to one knee and said, "My dear, you are young and will have many children. Will you come with me?"

Rhoda, always the ham, moved her hip to one side, put a hand into the air and replied, "Alas, my heart belongs to another and I cannot love any but him!" When she said 'heart,' she moved both hands to the center of her chest. It was a performance any Shakespearian actor would be proud of.

With that everyone laughed. A female voice in the back said, "Do not be concerned ladies. He is bragging about capabilities he no longer has!"

The woman moved to the side of the big man still on one knee, helped him up with the comment, "Professor, you will scare these lovely ladies and you, old fool, should know better!"

The man got to his feet and smiled. Displaying a set of perfect white teeth, the tall Native American and said, "Welcome family Jenkins! We were notified you were coming and glad you are here. My name is Samuel Wolf and this elderly woman is my wife, Rose, and my grandson, Cecil. Young lady, Cecil is not as encumbered as I with a wife, so be on your guard." With that remark from his grandfather, young Cecil lowered his head with embarrassment.

Jim introduced his family and found these Indians dressed as wild men and savages were college professors and businessmen. Samuel Wolf was head of an engineering department in Flagstaff and his wife, also a doctor, was head of the Nations' school system. The group consisted of ten men and four women, all with college degrees. This rag-tag group was very impressive.

They were taken to the Indian's camp, well away from the edge of the bluff; it, like the people, was impressive. A large military tent contained cooking equipment, an array of radios, and stores of food and ammunition. Other smaller tents housed sleeping quarters for individuals or families. No children were visible. In a clearing were two sizeable solar panels used to charge phones or other batteries. The sophistication of this setup made the Militia Base Camp look amateurish and ill-equipped.

In the center of the camp was a small fire, producing little warmth. Rhoda said to a woman there, "I can build the fire up so you will be warm."

The woman smiled and replied, "White men build big fires which can be seen and sit far away, the Indian builds small fires which cannot be seen and sit close." She laughed a little and Rhoda joined her, learning something.

Samuel Wolf, actually Doctor Samuel Wolf, was a very serious man, a complete change from the jokester they first met. He took the three of them to a nearby level spot under tall trees.

"This is a good spot for your camp. We have food supplies which you are welcome to share. There is a shortage of blankets and tents, so I hope you came prepared. The water in the stream is bitter but will not harm you. We have containers with filters in the big tent for drinking water which remove most of the bad taste. If you have any needs, please let us know and we may be able to help. In the morning I will show you a good shooting position; I understand you have a long-range rifle."

This turned out to be a rather long speech for Samuel. When finished with instructions, he then left them alone to set up camp.

Too thickly forested for the cycle, some of the Indians disconnected the trailer and carried it to Jim's campsite, saving Jim a lot of walking. While Hannah and Rhoda set up the tent, Jim unpacked the trailer and checked his sniper rifle. The case had protected it. All the freeze-dried food was removed from the trailer and taken to the big tent in order to share what they had. It was not needed. Hanging in the back of the tent were two cleaned deer, and the table was covered with various leaves and roots. A big pot was cooking something on a small wood burning stove. The Indians were living off the land and living well.

An elderly woman came to them and looked at their freeze-dried food and said something in the native language to Rose Wolf. Rose turned to them and while laughing said, "Cactus Wren has refused your food. She is our guide on natural eating. I hope you will not be insulted, but please keep your food. We may need it later. It seems we more modern Indians have lost the skill of living off the land. We are lucky Cactus Wren is with us. She has knowledge of the old ways and we will flourish only because of her. I am trying to get our young ones to learn from her, but they show very little interest. It does not look good for our future generations."

Hannah and Jim gathered their packaged food and prepared to leave when Rhoda said, "I will be along in a while."

She walked over to Cactus Rose who was working on some of the roots and said, "I would like to go with you to gather the food. I want to learn your ways."

Cactus Wren looked at her for a very long time, as if waiting for her to leave, then replied, "I will leave at first light in the morning." She spoke in perfect English but did not smile.

Rhoda, however, smiled broadly and replied, "I will be here."

An unlikely budding friendship would develop between the aged Cactus Wren and the young Rhoda.

The little family ate a quite tasty meal with the Indians who talked in both English and Navajo. Everyone was very friendly, and they felt welcome in this group. Later they made bedding in the small tent and were comfortable, but of course the arrangement stopped an enjoyable activity with Hannah.

Before going to sleep, Hannah said to Rhoda, "I need to talk to you about men and boys. You are a lovely young woman and will attract attention from them. I don't want you to get hurt."

Rhoda smiled and patted Hannah on her hand and replied, "Mom, I know boys and men are hot-to-trot and look for girls. Years ago, I made a pledge to wait until marriage before making love and I intend to keep it."

Hannah thought for a moment then replied, "That is the best way; if you have any questions; you know you can ask me anything. Also, I want you to know, Jim and I have made a commitment to each other and when we find a preacher we will be married." The conversation between Hannah and Rhoda took place within earshot of Jim. There had been no serious dialog between the two adults concerning marriage. This was the first time Hannah had indicated she was willing to marry Jim, and he was surprised she had revealed it to Rhoda and not him.

CHAPTER 9

Preparations for Battle

SAMUEL WOLF ARRIVED WELL BEFORE dawn. He came and sat by the smoldering fire Jim had built, the night before rekindling it without making a sound, but somehow awaking Jim. Jim exited the tent to the smell of coffee boiling on the coals of the fire, using Jim's coffee pot. Hannah crawled out looking sleepy and provided four cups, only three needed as Rhoda was still soundly asleep. They talked quietly, but within minutes Rhoda scrambled out fully dressed, ready to join Cactus Wren for her first adventure of gathering food.

Hannah prepared breakfast for the four of them from the freeze-dried packets. Samuel ate and seemed pleased while downing it with an ample supply of coffee.

Taking a canteen of water, Rhoda scrambled off to find Cactus Wren. She was clearly excited to go with her new friend. Jim filled several canteens from his little filter system, and with his small pack and tactical vest was ready for the day. Hannah gathered her small pack with food and water. She carried the AR-15 and Jim the heaver .338 sniper rifle. Samuel carried a small pack but had no rifle or weapon of any kind.

The three of them walked about fifty yards through heavy timber to the edge of the bluff. There were two young men in army fatigues sitting there looking to the south. Samuel gave them a thermos of coffee, but no food. They drank the coffee and waited without any conversation at all.

As the sun came over the horizon and lit the summit to the south, several flashes came from the hill. Someone with a mirror was flashing a signal.

One of the young men in fatigues named Eagle Eye, perhaps a real name, uncovered a mechanical device with mirrors. He aimed the device at the light and flashed it three times. Jim had seen things like this in movies, signaling from ship to ship in WWII, but had never seen a real one.

"This is a Heliograph machine to communicate with our most distant observers. We just don't have enough radios. It is not secure as anyone can see the flashes," Samuel explained.

"What did they say?" Hannah asked.

"Nothing other than they are there and watching. Our signal says the same thing. If they see suspicious activity, they will send a message in Navajo, which likely outsiders will not understand. There is a big negative using this method of communication; it gives our position away. Anyone can see the light even if they cannot read the message."

The three walked on another hundred yards or so along the bluff and came to a rather extensive shooting station. A long trench, designed as an observation point, over the valley. Several feet apart were individual stations with wooden tables and chairs for the shooters. Somewhat weathered, this installation had been constructed with careful planning and appeared to have been there for a good while.

Samuel explained, "We constructed this place to hunt game. We can see deer and elk in the valley from this height, and with our long-range rifles can get meat almost any day. We have young men with radios which we direct to the animal. It works very well."

"What weapon do you use?" Jim asked. "It is a very long way to the valley floor."

Samuel smiled a little and went to the center table and removed a tarp exposing the weapon.

Jim was surprised. He had thought his .338 caliber rifle with the expensive scope would be the most impressive weapon around, but under the tarp was a .50 caliber rifle with a fancy electronic scope, one Jim had never seen. The big rifle was equipped with a long silencer and was the most sophisticated weapon he had ever laid eyes on. He was ashamed of his previous assumption that the Indians would be hunting with bows and arrows.

"Someone is coming!" Samuel said as he recovered the big rifle.

Jim looked but saw nothing. It seemed the aged Samuel had excellent vision. The other Indians said he could see a flea on the nose of a hog at a thousand yards—maybe an exaggeration, maybe not.

Samuel turned and went down a path, down the almost sheer—cliff. He moved like a mountain goat, nearly running. Jim thought to help Hannah, but she was following Samuel. Jim struggled behind, avoiding a fall to a sure death down the cliff. Just before reaching the valley floor he saw a truck in the distance; it was towing something large.

It had taken about twenty minutes to reach the road with the truck still a good distance off. There were four other Navajo men there in army fatigues, each armed with M-16s, fully automatic rifles. The truck was a heavy-duty Ford pickup, towing a school bus, which was towing a flatbed trailer. The pickup was loaded with suitcases and bags tied down with rope. The bus was overloaded with people as was the big flatbed trailer. There was a small community in the overloaded vehicles. The fact that the truck could pull all this weight was amazing.

When the driver saw the armed men ahead, he stopped and everyone in the cab raised their hands, so they were clearly visible through the windshield. It was a tense moment; the men guarding the road were very military in their behavior, and the people in the convoy looked startled. The truck, a crew cab, held seven adults who exited with their hands raised.

"Where are you from and are you armed?" Samuel asked in a rather gruff voice.

"We started in Phoenix and have been picking up people along the way. There are guns in the truck. The Mexican army is not far behind us. Where is the US Army? We are being invaded!" the words tumbling from the driver's lips. He was a white man about fifty years of age, well dressed, a successful looking man.

When requested, the seven produced drivers' licenses identifying them as US residents. With this information everyone relaxed, and a friendly atmosphere ensued. The bus, built for sixty children, contained one hundred and fifty riders, men women and children. As they unloaded the smell was unbearable; they hadn't made enough bathroom breaks. The people on the flatbed trailer were in worse shape. They had had a very rough ride and suffered from the dust of the leading vehicles. Surprisingly, everyone was smiling and grateful to be stopping. They had reached what assumed was safety.

A woman wearing expensive jewelry and clad in a now dirty, but expensive dress, came out of the bus and went to the side of the road, hiked her dress and squatted on the ground, relieving herself. Jim thought 'how terrible our people are reduced to animals.' The woman stood up and walked back to the group then spoke to Jim. "We didn't have any water to drink on the bus, so I was able to make it without soiling. We are safe from those wanting to kill us. Isn't God gracious to us?"

"God has a plan and with people like you and He will certainly accomplish it," he replied.

Jim walked up to the driver, who introduced himself as Sloan and asked, "How is it your truck still runs?"

"I don't know. My cars would not start but the truck was in my metal building and seemed to be fine."

While Jim and Hannah talked with driver Sloan, a couple walked up to them and the woman asked, "Are you Ms. White?" The inquisitive woman was clearly from India as she was wearing the customary dress and a red dot on her forehead. The dark-complexioned man with her was dressed like a businessman. They were in expensive, but now dusty clothing.

"I am Hannah White; you are Shalon and Handel's parents. I am very sorry to have run off with your children, but I did not know what else to do. They were shooting everyone," Hannah explained.

"Oh, thank you! We were all told our children were dead, but you have saved two. We are most grateful." With that statement the woman began to cry and hugged Hannah, who had to hold her up, she was so distraught.

Just then a black lady came from the crowd; crying and so excited she could hardly speak. "I am Sheila Parker and my children are Bobbie and Billy. Do you have them?"

"All your children are at the Militia Base Camp. I believe this road will go by there. They are with the other children from my class, in the cabin by the river. Feel free to stay there until we return," Jim stated to the man and two women. The man was attempting to be dignified but tears were freely flowing down his face through the heavy dust as he tried to comfort his wife.

About twenty-five of the newcomers presented themselves to Samuel and volunteered to join the resistance fighters. Many, but not all, were veterans. Some were couples and some women seemed to be alone, but all were armed with a variety of weapons. Most were hunting rifles, but many had AR-15s in addition to their bolt action rifles. They unloaded their gear from the pickup. After preliminary instructions, they left in the direction Samuel had given them. They would cover a high mountainside to the east and wait until Samuel shot a flare as a signal to fire, when necessary to do so. Jim thought these men, while disorganized, would be a significant fighting force.

The truck, bus and trailer continued its journey with a new woman driver and much lighter load. They would stop at the Base Camp and then most would proceed north to a refugee camp, the only thing the US Government had provided.

As they pulled away, Samuel's radio buzzed with a message the enemy was in sight of the southern—most observers. The group began the long hike up the hill to their shooting stations. As they climbed, Hannah seemed very tired. Jim took her pack and rifle, ignoring her objections. When reaching the top, she gulped a long drink of water and immediately threw up.

CHAPTER 10

The Battle

A LARGE PLUME OF DUST ALERTED the watchers of the advancing vehicles. The large army was spread across the entire width of the valley. Tanks were leading the masses of vehicles and troops on foot. There were thousands of people, some armed and some not. Many peace-loving families in Mexico had been forced to cross into the US on foot. It was possible these were human shields. Among this ragtag group were young US Hispanics who had joined the invaders, wanting to help occupy this part of the US for Mexico. Absent were older Hispanics who had come to the US because they preferred it over the corrupt Mexican Government. The young Hispanic citizens had no memory of living in Mexico and somehow thought it would be better under Mexican rule.

Some of the tanks and trucks carried large ISIS black flags and some had the Mexican flag, a few had both. The black clad ISIS troops were at the front of the group walking alongside the tanks. It was more like a very wide parade an advancing army.

Since crossing the border into the US, the mixed group had been troubled by snipers. An occasional shot would ring out and someone would fall. The truck-mounted machine guns would return fire and the sniper would either be killed or retreat. They were an annoyance rather than a problem. There were, however, a dozen wounded, now being carried by fellow Mexicans.

The tanks were American made, older models, surpluses by the US army years previously, old but functional and dangerous. The commander of the tanks was a Mexican general who proudly rode in the turret of the lead tank, standing tall, visible from the waist up. The man hated the United States and always felt Mexico had been taken advantage of by the 'Devils to the North'.

Suddenly the flair went up from Samuel's shooting position and hell broke out. One hundred and twenty rifles fired in a volley. The general in the lead tank would have certainly been targeted were it not for the black clad ISIS fighters. The third round of shots took them all out. The proud strutting was replaced by a pile of black, blood-soaked rags. The general lowered himself into the turret and slammed the hatch, just in time as bullets began hitting the tank. He screamed into the intercom to fire the main gun. He had no target but was eager to fire at something.

Hidden among the brush three hundred yards ahead of the tank was a sixteen-year-old boy with a bolt action 30.06 rifle, his deer rifle. When he left to join the militia, a neighbor, an old man, had given him a small box of ammunition. It was a mixture of brands, mostly surplus army rounds from a military range, long closed. They may have been older than fifty years old. The boy thought the red ones might penetrate the tank, so he loaded them into his rifle. The lead tank fired, and the shot went over the youth's his head and exploded near a gate in a fence. The boy shot at the tank and was surprised with the red streak that followed the bullet. It was a tracer round which exposed his position.

In the lead tank the gunner, after firing the first round, opened the breech and ejected the brass casing. Opening the safety door to the locker which stored the thirty rounds the tank carried, he took one round out and left the door open, a no-no in loading protocol.

The tracer round was destined to hit the tank and bounce harmlessly off, but the Lord God took control of it. The bullet went into the end of the barrel of the main gun on the tank and directly into the gunner's compartment. The gunner had the second round in his hands, preparing to slide it into the barrel when the tracer bullet sliced through the brass into the power charge, setting it off. The explosion set off the thirty rounds in the locker and fire and heat set off the explosive charges in the projectiles. There was a massive explosion; the tank turret flew a hundred feet into the air and came down on a following tank. The lead tank blew into thousands of pieces which went through enemy troops like a hot knife. Many of the troops within one hundred yards of the tank were wounded or killed. It was a massive blow.

The other tanks came to a halt. They had been told the US Army would not be here as their trucks and other equipment would not function due to the EMP attack. The only resistance would be a few farm boys, and most of the locals would welcome and join them.

Commanders of other tanks in the convey either ducked inside the turret or died in a hail of bullets. One of the tank drivers, one with a dead commander, saw the lead tank burning and the tank right beside him disabled so he decided it was enough fighting for him. He put his tank in reverse and very quickly backed over a dozen troops and fled. He was immediately blinded by the dust but proceeded south as fast as he could. He ran into a fuel tanker, nearly running over it. The tanker exploded in a huge ball of fire. The crew escaped the tank but burned to death in surrounding flames.

In the rear of the convoy, one of the few ISIS soldiers remaining was being carried on a litter. He had twisted his ankle and could not walk without pain. ambling along in the same area was a Catholic priest and his flock, carrying large crosses. The priest envisioned himself as carrying the message of Christ to an unbelieving land. He may have been correct, however, the ISIS fighter on the litter hated him and his message. With the shooting and explosions, the advancing army began falling apart; the men carrying the litter dropped it and ran. Bouncing off the litter the anger in the man in black boiled over. He picked up his AK-47 and began shooting the men carrying the crosses. The bullets cut through the tightly packed group of men and women, killing dozens. He was reloading his rifle when the first bullet struck him. It was a small .22 caliber but did not disable him. Looking around, he found the rifle was held by a small girl, a member of the group of Catholic marchers. She continued to shoot. The rifle held fifteen rounds and she emptied the gun. Only eight hit him but that was enough. His last thought was 'I have been killed by a woman, worse, by a child, a female child. How will Allah accept me?'

The men, women and children had scattered, running in every direction. Some had sought cover in adjacent trees and bushes but were cut down by the militia, men and boys, with shorter range weapons. The tanks and trucks turned south in the direction from which they had come, running over many of their own. The area was the site of a massacre.

The initial leader of the army had been a member of ISIS, but a Mexican general was the leader of their forces and the only one left alive. He was in an armored carrier, well back in the pack, and safe. He screamed into the radio, attempting to get control, but no one was listening. Eventually he joined the retreat.

After traveling about ten miles, the general in his armored carrier got to the head of the pack and managed to stop the exodus. Those on foot would arrive much later. He contacted Mexico City and reported to his superiors, who were very unhappy with him. His orders were to establish a base and hold it until reinforcements arrived. He again was promised air support, assured the US had no functional aircraft, and that the US Army was occupied elsewhere. In addition, he was assured that numerous people of Hispanic heritage would soon join them. The general did not believe one word of what he was told, but as a dedicated soldier would follow orders. In an hour the men on foot began arriving. The general climbed atop of his armored vehicle to address them shouting as loudly as he could.

On the side of the mountain, just a little less than a mile away was a lone man. He was a member of the long-range target club and had a rifle very similar to the one Samuel had been shooting. Even at the long range the general was an easy stationary target. With the steady pull of the trigger, the bullet passed through the general's chest with little decrease in speed. He was dead before he hit the ground.

The attack from Mexico to the Colorado border had failed. Many of the attackers threw their guns down, thinking no one would shoot them if they were unarmed. They were wrong. The men in the mountains followed the masses trying to flee and shot them without mercy. Additional men and women had come from the surrounding towns and lay in wait and attack the hoards as they passed. In a short time, the fleeing men ran out of water and food and the danger of medical collapse was just as prevalent as being shot. Groups of men, militia and others, followed the remnants of the invaders. When they came across communities of Hispanics, the communities were wiped out even if not involved in the invasion. The genocide also included any person who looked like a Muslim or Arab. The southern part of New Mexico and Arizona was strewn with dead bodies. By any measure, the carnage was horrible.

The invading army had come north with nearly ten thousand people including tanks and trucks. Less than three hundred made it back to Mexico.

The punishment of Mexico was not over.

Within days two US aircraft carrier task forces arrived off the west coast of Mexico, leaving their patrol area in the Sea of Japan These carriers were well outside the effects of the EMP attack and their weapons were functioning. The aircraft swept over Mexico and in one day destroyed the airfields and aircraft in Mexico. The Mexican Army had no reliable defense to the more modern aircraft.

Mexico tried to contact Washington for terms of surrender but got no response. Their appeal to the US Embassy in Mexico City brought sympathy, but no solution.

CHAPTER 11

After the Battle
(What is going on?)

FROM THEIR SHOOTING POSITION JIM and Samuel watched the invasion crumble. Between the two of them they had fired over one thousand rounds. Hannah and Rhoda had been with them and loaded the empty clips from containers of loose shells. The battle had not lasted long, but they were all exhausted, particularly Hannah. She was seated in the bottom of the dugout and when all the clips were reloaded lay her head on the ground and did not move. Rhoda noticed her first and moved to her side, yelling at Jim, who was intent on observing the fleeing troops. He forgot everything when he looked at Hannah. He tried giving her water, which she threw up. He, then, picked her up and carried her to the tent, where he lay her out of the sun. She was protesting that she was allright, but she clearly was not.

Samuel gave orders to young men nearby to pack the guns and then put them in Jim's trailer.

"We need to get her back to camp! There are doctors there," he said solemnly after looking at her.

The camp was quickly broken down and the equipment loaded into the trailer. Jim carried Hannah, under protest, to a truck where he got into the cab and held Hannah on his lap. Rhoda led the procession on the cycle, driving it for the first time, traveling too fast. They reached the Indian encampment in record time. Hannah slept the entire way.

There were a few wounded men from the battle, mostly broken legs or sprained ankles—very few with bullet wounds. Because of Samuel, Hannah received immediate attention. The doctor was an older man who examined Hannah. He determined immediately she was dehydrated and instructed a nurse to insert a saline drip. When the needle was Inserted Hannah woke up and said, "Ouch!" and smiled. She was already feeling better.

The doctor said, "Young lady, you seem to be a little low on water and are probably very tired. This stress is hard on everyone. You've had a traumatic reaction which is not unusual. Is it possible you could be pregnant?"

"I may have been exposed," she replied.

In the back Rhoda was heard to snicker.

The doctor, trying unsuccessfully, not to smile replied, "I think we might assume you are. I don't have the equipment here to test you. I want you to stay in bed for two days and if you are completely recovered you may resume normal activity, but no more warfare for you. I suggest a doctor's visit for a pregnancy test when you can. I would keep you here, but we are expecting a lot of injuries."

The nurse returned when the drip was complete, and after assurances from Hannah that she felt fine, the nurse released her. They left the hospital with a supply of vitamins for expectant mothers.

Jim, like many men in this situation, became overprotective of Hannah, much to her chagrin. She insisted she was fine and could do anything as before, but just needed to drink more water. Whether or not the pregnancy was true, Jim had been terrified at the thought of losing her. He insisted she ride in a truck instead of the motorcycle back to the larger Militia Base Camp and their cabin by the river. On the cycle, Jim and Rhoda followed the truck, a trip which Rhoda seemed to enjoy.

During their absence, the Militia Base Camp had changed. The big open field was now full of green army-issue tents and rows of trucks. Apparently, the trucks had survived the attack or been repaired. The population had doubled or tripled with uniformed troops everywhere. A very interesting addition was a new-looking helicopter sitting in an open area. It was a large passenger carrying machine with perhaps a dozen seats. It obviously had not been affected by the EMP attack, or had been repaired, a good sign.

The truck stopped at the main camp and Hannah got out. She insisted on walking to their cabin instead of riding with them on the cycle. "I need to stretch my legs after bouncing in the truck," she explained. Jim drove the cycle beside her and noticed she was walking slower than usual.

The five children heard them coming and all five tried to climb into Hannah's arms at the same time. They nearly knocked her down. They were all yelling at the same time and Hannah enjoyed it all. Jim parked the cycle and helped her by picking up Bobbie and Billy. It was a heartfelt welcome. Shalon and Handel's parents, Jason and Asha, along with Sheila, the black boys' mother, stayed on the porch smiling broadly. Asha had on her customary Indian dress, while Jason was dressed in jeans and a plaid shirt.

"Welcome home! Come in and eat and rest!" Asha stated with a big smile. It didn't seem to bother her that her own two children were greeting Hannah and Jim as 'Mom and Pop', the same as the other three children.

The aroma inside the little cabin was inviting as Asha had prepared ethnic India food—a lot of food. Apparently, the food supply had improved with the arrival of the army. There were also additions to the cabin. Asha was cooking in large pots and the table was set with plates and glasses. The plates were plastic but had not been present before. The little table could not accommodate everyone, but the smaller children seemed happy sitting on the floor in a circle. The five adults and Rhoda ate at the table. Before eating, Jason stood, and they all bowed in prayer.

"Lord, we are overwhelmed with gratitude at your many blessings. We again thank you for the return to life of two of our children. We thank you for the safe return of Jim, Hannah and Rhoda from the conflict and pray for peace. And Lord, we thank you for Your protection during the persecution of our country and pray we will be a better country because of it. We also thank you for this bountiful feast you have provided and the wonderful friendship with your people. Amen."

As they began passing the food, Jim thought, 'This couple has lost three children and all their possessions except the clothes they are wearing, and they thank God for all their blessings. What a great testimony.'

They ate and were filled for the first time in days or weeks. It was wonderful.

Jason and Asha insisted Jim and Hannah take the bedroom with the only real bed in the cabin. Jim protested, but finally agreed. Hannah, looking so tired, convinced the group all she needed was rest. She did not object when Jim suggested she turn in early. Sleep came quickly. She did not stir when they quietly made beds for Rhoda and Lee on the floor at the foot of her bed.

Jim woke up alone in the bed and found Hannah and Asha in the kitchen. Hannah smiled at him and gave him a kiss and a cup of coffee. "Join Jason on the porch while we women do woman things." She seemed to have recovered and felt fine.

Jim took his coffee and joined Jason on the front porch. As he sat down, Jason said, "Good morning, I hope you slept well."

"I did and I think Hannah did also. She seems to be much better today," Jim answered.

Jason continued. "There are buses leaving today to take civilians to the refugee camp north of here. They have requested all civilians go and this camp will be soldiers, army personal and militia. I know you will probably stay as you are one of the fighters, but we will take everyone else and look after them if you desire."

Jim didn't answer right away as he thought about how things would change when everyone he knew had gone.

Before he could answer, Hannah came outside carrying a cup of coffee and stated, "I am not going to leave you and it is not open for discussion. It probably is better if the children go. They will be safer and better provided for there, especially if we need to leave for another fight."

"I am not going either. I can help, and I don't want to leave. You are my only family," Rhoda emphatically stated, as she came out carrying a cup of coffee.

Jim looked at the cup, then at her. Catching his examination, she continued with a little smile on her face. "Coffee is not an adult beverage," she knew it melted his heart.

Jim finally got a chance to speak. "It will be difficult to send the children away, but it is probably the best. There is no way to know what will happen here."

By this time the news had spread to the children. Everyone gathered on the front porch. The children begged Jim, Hannah and Rhoda to go with them promising everyone would have a good time. It was clear Jason and Asha had talked to the five children earlier and they understood they must go.

The discussion was interrupted by a young corporal in uniform who came jogging up. "Excuse me Mr. Jenkins. Your presence is requested in the main tent in the compound. The information meeting will be in twenty minutes and please bring your arms in a safe condition." The young man then saluted and turned and headed towards the other cabins.

Jim said his goodbyes to the five children, all who cried and made him promise to come and see them soon. They were sad and would miss their current caretakers but were anxious for more adventure.

Jim walked alone to the meeting and as requested, carried his AR-15 rifle without a clip and the bolt back. He had eight clips in his tactical vest so it could be used in a matter of seconds. He thought it strange to go to a meeting armed. A uniformed sergeant met him at the entrance to the big tent and looked at his rifle, turned to a private at a small table and said, AR-15, with silencer and a forty-five. Jim gave his name to the private and entered. The sergeant had checked to assure the AR was empty, but had ignored Jim's pistol, which was fully loaded and 'cocked and locked,' as they say. A man with one star on his collar stood up to speak; he apparently had been introduced just before Jim arrived. A one-star general is a big deal for such a small group; maybe they were planning to expand their number.

"Men, as you know our nation is under attack from foreigners. Our valiant Militia has broken the attack of a greatly superior force from the south. This force consisted of ISIS troops from the Middle East and the Mexican regular army. These forces included a dozen tanks and many trucks and as many as twenty thousand troops."

He paused to let the numbers sink in. Jim noticed the welcome did not mention women, of which there were many present, and the Navajo Indians who had been pivotal in the defeat of the invaders. He also thought the estimate of twenty thousand was greatly exaggerated.

The general continued. "We have several prisoners, both ISIS personnel and Mexican officers and have received valuable information from them. Please treat the information I am going to give you as classified and keep it limited to friendly forces. First, the ISIS forces considered this mission to be a suicide mission; they did not believe their small force plus the Mexican Army could defeat the US Army forces, even with the electronic attack. To get the Mexicans to join them, ISIS lied to them. The Mexican government was told all electronics would be disabled; no communication existed in the entire US and no vehicles or aircraft would be operational. The US military would be completely disabled. They were further told that when they reach the northern borders of Arizona and New Mexico the US would agree to give this land to Mexico in exchange for peace. Because the population in this area is primarily Hispanic already, the Mexican government was led to believe their troops would be welcomed. Like I say, they were lied to and it seems the Mexican government bought into it."

The general paused again and took a drink of water. Watching the crowd to access their reaction. Jim was growing suspicious the information being given was not the complete truth.

"Our plan is to move our troops from here to the west and confront invaders in California. These attackers are like those we faced here. It is possible the enemy in California will rethink their attack when the reports from this area reach them. The army will transport the regular active troops in the trucks outside. The Militia is encouraged to move with us but must provide your own transportation. Once active troops are in position, the trucks will return here and take those willing to go. The Militia arms have been recorded and ammunition will be provided as soon as possible, but it may take a few days. We will begin our move west tomorrow."

When the general's speech concluded, another man stood and requested everyone conserve water and food as supplies were limited.

Jim stood for a few moments after the meeting and thought, 'Where are the US forces? Where are the aircraft, the tanks and artillery? We have the strongest military in the world. Why are these few troops and the Militia defending our borders? Something is not right; maybe the EMP attack was more crippling than the general indicated'.

Outside the meeting Hannah and Rhoda were saying goodbye to Sheila, Jason, Asha and the five children as they loaded onto one of the five school buses. It was heart breaking for all. The children requested Jim and Hannah to come and get them soon. Jason and Asha noted again their children, Shelon and Handel, calling

Hannah "mom," which they thought was endearing. The buses left with an army Humvee leading them. Hannah remembered her trip in a similar bus with the children, which resulted in a disaster. She was worried and hoped the convoy would arrive safely and the camp would be secure and comfortable.

As the two women, actually one woman and a girl, were walking back to the cabin, they caught up to two men each walking a bicycle, one with a flat tire. The men looked like they were exhausted. They resembled hoboes with dirty clothes too large for them, held up by belts with the ends well out of the buckle. As they passed, one of the men said, "Mam, do you know where we can get some water?"

"I have water," Rhoda said as she removed her pack, which she now always carried.

The men nearly collapsed as they lowered their bodies to one of the few benches along the walkway.

Hannah and Rhoda waited while they drank the contents of the little bottles. "You must be sisters," one of them said.

Hannah, at thirty-eight, could easily pass for thirty and Rhoda at twelve could be eighteen or nineteen, so being sisters was not out of the question.

Hannah responded, "I thank you, but Rhoda is twelve and I am much older!"

Rhoda, who wanted to be treated as an adult, said, "I am actually thirteen, and mom here is a little bit married and a little bit pregnant."

Hannah turned to her, surprised, and said, "Rhoda, when did you have a birthday? Why didn't you say something?"

"We were a little busy shooting people and the timing didn't seem right!" she replied.

The comment confused the men even more. Why a mother would not know the birthday of her daughter, and how could these two women, or girls, shoot people?

"Let us introduce ourselves. I am Harold Taylor, and this is my brother Ralph; we are from Phoenix."

Ralph continued, addressing Hannah. "A little pregnant is not a condition. Are you pregnant?"

"I think I am, very early, but I am not sure," she replied.

Ralph reached out his hand toward Hannah's breasts and said. "I am a doctor. Do you have any discomfort in this area?"

Harold stated a little fearfully, "Brother, if you don't want to be shot, get your hand off that woman!"

Both men turned and looked at Jim who stood there with a stern look on his face. At six foot two inches, dressed in his black tactical vest with a pistol, and his AR across his chest, he did look imposing, like someone ready for action.

Hannah looked at him and exclaimed, "Darling, these men are from Phoenix. They rode all the way on bicycles!"

Rhoda looked at the men and chuckled at their reaction and exclaimed, "Pop, your wife was in no danger," as she opened her jacket exposing her pistol, which she had also added to her daily attire.

Jim broke into a laugh and said, "I never worry about my women. Hannah is a better shot than I and Rhoda is a true vixen if she needs to be."

Ralph, who had pulled his hand back, noticing both women were armed, said, "I feel like we have walked into a den of wolves."

Jim introduced himself and stated, "Let's get you something to eat and maybe you will tell us how it is in Phoenix.

The five of them went to the Chow Tent. The food provided by the military, was very basic, but wholesome and filling. It would not last forever.

Harold and Ralph filled their plates twice. Hannah and Rhoda shared one. Jim drank water and coffee and ate a piece of pie.

After stuffing his face, Ralph stated, "My brother and I are failures; we decided this on the way here."

"Perhaps you could elaborate on this statement," Jim requested.

"It is by the evidence. I am a doctor and have treated many patients, including myself and my brother. The medical profession treats problems by prescribing pills, and sometimes surgery. When the transportation and electricity went out, pills could not be shipped. We ran out very quickly. It is true some people suffered, and a few died a little sooner than they would have with treatment. However, both my brother and I are more atypical is correct. Without pills and transportation our health improved. We walked everywhere, we lost a great deal of weight, and now we feel much better. We are, or were, both diabetic and the disease has now disappeared without any medication. I would have been a more effective doctor if I had just taken away peoples' cars and food."

Harold continued when his brother paused. "My experience was no better. I am a pastor of a church, a fairly big church. I thought we were doing pretty well; our offerings were good, and we gave to missions and did a great deal in the community. When this attack happened, our parishioners fell apart. Some of the people had stockpiled food, and even water, but would not share with the ones who had nothing. I think some of our congregation died from lack of water. A few of us tried to help. We carried water around the neighborhoods, but it was extremely taxing. People even put big signs on their houses stating, 'NEED FOOD AND WATER!!' But they were not willing to walk a few miles to carry the water back. A group of young people even put a sign saying, 'NEED HELP TO CHARGE I-PADS'. The people would not leave even when the dead were piling up. Without air-conditioning it is almost impossible to survive in Phoenix in the summer. My brother and I finally decided we must leave. I don't know if we did the right thing, but we were not helping anyone there. I feel as though God would not have let this happen if our churches were doing their jobs."

The five said nothing for a while. Jim knew, even in September the heat could be severe in Phoenix. It was very cool in Colorado and they were wearing Jackets, but Phoenix was in the desert and almost impossible to survive without air-conditioning.

"Perhaps God has a mission for you here. Do not be discouraged. God has a plan. In fact, we should all rejoice, that God considers us worthy for discipline. He could have easily destroyed us all," Jim stated.

Harold the pastor then asked, "We are a Christian Nation. Why would God not protect us?"

Jim replied, "It is only my opinion, of course, but while the US claims to be a Christian Nation, we have, in general, forgotten about God. The church attendance has plummeted and while many have a Bible, few read it. In addition, children born to single mothers is at an all-time high and growing. God has made it clear that sex between same sex people is wrong, but society has accepted it as another lifestyle. In the Bible, in Sodom and Gomorra, homosexuality was practiced but the great sin was they, as a society, accepted it and even stated the practice was desirable and good. Sounds like us. I think the biggest thing, however, may be the murder of children. In ancient times some worshiped a god called Molech who demanded child sacrifice. In the US we abort more children every year or two than were sacrificed to Molech in the many years the religion existed. Even worse, in the ancient times, the children were killed to satisfy a presumptive god, but we just kill our kids for convenience. We are much worse than they were, and God wiped them out."

"You are right, of course. The US has fallen far from God's will and we deserve His wrath, but He has a plan."

The voice came from behind Jim, and when he turned to see who had spoken, there sat the general who had presented the plan going forward for the military.

"General, I arrived too late for the meeting this morning and did not hear your name," Jim stated.

"I am Mike Christy and I apologize for listening to your conversation, but I think you are spot on."

"Join up please, we are just relaxing and having this very strong coffee," Hannah requested.

The general moved to their table joining them and introductions were made all around.

Involving the general into their conversation, Jim asked, "How bad is it General?"

"To be very honest, I don't know. Much of the military equipment was unaffected by the EMP attack, but our equipment was already in pathetic condition. Proper maintenance had not been done for years due to a shortage of spare parts. The big problem is communication. We have become too dependent on the internet and computers which were damaged, perhaps severely. The nation will not fall but will be changed. Your militia has successfully repelled the attack from the south in this area, but that is not the case in California. ISIS personnel are as far north as San Francisco. It seems the Californian's are not as well armed and do not have the where-with-all to fight for their land."

The general paused and Ralph, the doctor, asked, "If ISIS know they cannot win, why are they doing this?"

"I think this is a worldwide plan. I believe they want to establish enclaves of terrorists' groups in the country, but the immediate effort is to cause the US to withdraw from the Middle East. I think the goal is to divert attention away from the Middle East in order for Islam to try to wipe out Israel. Russia and China are involved in some way to encourage them. With the US occupied here, Russia can move into Eastern Europe, and China into the South China Sea and take over Taiwan. Their plan is actually working; we have moved our carrier task force from the East China Sea to our west coast and have attacked Mexico with our aircraft."

"How long will it be before our military recovers?" Hannah asked.

"Our immediate needs are to get the vehicles running and communications online. Both of these require parts now made in China.

What a stupid thing we have allowed to happen. The parts we need for fighting are made in a country we may have to fight. We have been going down a wrong path for years. The fox has been guarding the henhouse too long."

"I have a motor home and a jeep in a metal building at my cabin. I assumed they would not run, but maybe I was wrong. The metal building may have protected them," Jim stated.

"Any running vehicle is needed right now. Moving our forces west will take all the vehicles we have. You have a couple of days before we are to move," the general replied.

CHAPTER 12

At the Cabin

A S THE THREE WALKED BACK to their little cabin by the stream, Jim stated, "I think I will go back to my house and check the motor home and Jeep. If it will run, the motor home will be a good place to live, and we can certainly use the vehicles if we move west."

"We will all go," Hannah stated, as if it had been decided.

"I think it would be unwise for you to ride on the cycle for such a distance. You need the rest, and the two of you can care for each other."

Hannah started to protest but then thought better of it, being concerned she might lose the baby on a rough trip, if, in fact, she had a baby to lose. Rhoda was about to request she accompany Jim, but he gave her a look indicating she should care for Hannah. She just nodded in agreement. Maybe she had matured since turning thirteen.

Jim took the cycle with the empty trailer and left the camp. If the vehicles would not run, he could load more supplies in the trailer. He was armed even though this part of the country was supposed to be safe. The roads were mostly deserted; the few cars moving were full of people moving to the refugee camp where there was food and water. How they knew to go there was a mystery to Jim.

The trip was about seventy-five miles and took a little over an hour. Reaching the subdivision, he slowed to a crawl, not knowing what to expect. The cycle at idle did not make much noise. He slowly drove through the neighborhood. Hearing voices, he shut the cycle off and went on foot with the rifle ready.

The sound was coming from the big Ashcroft cabin, or its burned remains. In the side yard of what had been a beautiful cabin were several tents and about twenty people. It looked like a very large family with men, women and several children. They were Hispanic. No one appeared to be armed.

Jim stepped into the road in front of the property and slowly walked toward them with his hand on his rifle across his chest. When they saw him, the adults stopped their activities and stood, obviously afraid, and the little children raised their hands above their heads. What a pathetic scene!

"Jim, don't shoot!!" Jim's friend, Duncan, shouted as he ran to get between Jim and the group. "They are citizens and needed a place of safety."

"I'm not going to shoot anyone," Jim stated as he took his hands off the rifle and spread them out so they could see they were empty.

The tension eased a bit as Jim took his rifle and leaned it against a tree. Duncan explained, "These people are from the town and attend the church there. They have been in this country for many years but are afraid. The rumor is the Militia is shooting anyone who looks Hispanic."

The leader of the extended family, a man named Hernando, greeted Jim and explained they were simply afraid to stay in the town. He spoke without a trace of an accent so Jim believed he had lived his life in the US, not that it mattered to him.

"You may be wise to take precautions. There is a lot of craziness going on. I pray it will not last long, but be careful," Jim stated to Hernando. Turning to Duncan he continued, "I am going to check the vehicles in my garage and see if they will run. It seems some vehicles avoided damage by being in metal buildings."

Jim retrieved his cycle and drove to his burned cabin and garage. It looked like no one had disturbed anything. He unlocked the side door and went into the dimly lit garage. Reaching to a shelf he turned on a battery powered light which worked. The only difference in the garage was a thicker layer of dust; no one had been there. He took the light to the front of the motor home to check out the damage. The front of the garage had been burned and the doors damaged but remained standing. The insulation on the garage doors had fallen out and covered the fronts of the motor home and the jeep. Removing the debris, he was pleasantly surprised. The paint was blistered, and the plastic trim pieces melted and warped, but the vehicle looked basically intact. The windshield was not even damaged.

Duncan and Hernando arrived and helped Jim get the door to roll up. It had to be forced as the panels were warped. When in raised position, it had to be tied up with a rope. Outside, the children and other adults were clearing the burned trees and other debris from in front of his garage. Jim checked the fluid levels in the vehicle. Everything was allright, just as he had left it a few months ago.

It would all be for naught if the motor home would not run. He started the motorhome generator to put an additional charge on the batteries, then waited a few minutes. Everyone stood back when he got in the driver's seat and pushed on the starter. The engine turned over a few seconds then started with a roar. Smoke filled the garage. A big cheer went up from the group. Moving the RV down the driveway a few feet allowed the smoke to clear from the garage. Leaving it running, he checked out the Jeep. It was in similar condition and he soon had it running. Instead of trying to open the other garage door, he just backed it up and drove out the door already open. He was surprised to see the crowd of people washing the motor home, using buckets and ladders from the garage. He checked all the tires, ducking the water. The mood was festive and the children, especially, were having a good time.

Jim went through his shop and took a few tools. With the generator he could run the electric drills and saws so he loaded up a plastic container with all the tools it would hold. He then took two more containers from the pallet of freeze-dried food and loaded them in the motor home. Duncan helped him lower the garage door and lock it.

Taking Hernando back into the shop, Jim told him, "The garage is unheated, but the shop has a pot-bellied stove which will warm the room very nicely. The temperature is going to drop as winter comes on. There is propane in the tanks and a little camp stove in one of these boxes. The food on the pallet is available if it lasts. Most of it is prepared by just adding boiling water. Here is a key to the side door; feel free to use this building as you see fit."

"You are very kind. I assure you nothing will be missing, except some food, when you return. I confess I have been praying for help because we are running out of supplies," Hernando stated. Jim noticed Hernando's eyes tearing up.

Jim spent a few minutes hooking up the Jeep behind the RV and putting the cycle on the rack attached to the rear of the motor home. After the trailer was tied on the top of the Jeep, he was ready to go.

Duncan came to Jim and asked, "If the weather gets too bad, may we move them into the garage? It will be warmer than the tents."

"I gave Hernando a key to the door; use anything here you need. I hope this madness will not last much longer, but you were right to hide your friends and family. There are some crazy people out there," Jim replied.

Jim got into the RV and noticed the women had cleaned the inside as well as the outside. He pulled out in what seemed like a giant rig while the people lined the road and waved goodbye. New friends.

CHAPTER 13

Back to Militia Camp

Jim drove the RV out of the subdivision and onto the state road. It was almost deserted. He came to a small town and noticed a church sign ahead. It was an electric sign, now off, of course. The sign read, "Church will meet this Sunday, everyone come!" Jim wondered how many churches in the country would still be meeting. A man stepped into the road in front of him and pointed to the entrance to the church parking lot and waved for Jim to enter. Jim had to either stop or turn in. The other option would be to run over the man. It somehow seemed right to turn in. It was mid-afternoon on a Saturday and a service the next day would be nice. As he turned, the man smiled and waved at Jim. He looked familiar, but Jim could not place him. The parking lot was not large, and he parked the RV along the far end, hopefully out of the way. He got out to speak to the young man, but it seemed he had disappeared.

It was then that Jim noticed the church, which sat on the back of the property, had been burned. The brick walls were standing but the roof had fallen in and the stained-glass windows were smoked, those which had not broken. It had been a nice building. Since the young man was gone, Jim decided to go on as there still was some daylight left. Before he could get inside the RV a man in a police uniform came into the parking lot, riding on a horse.

"I see you are a bit early for the service tomorrow," the policeman said with a smile, as he dismounted.

"It seems the building is not usable. Will the church meet?" Jim asked.

"Oh yes, we will meet, we never missed a Sunday. They came on a Wednesday and burned several buildings and shot several people. I lost three deputies and the church lost its pastor. I was out of town or I probably would be dead. It was a horrible blow."

"I just made some coffee. Would you join me?" Jim asked.

"Yes, I would enjoy a good cup. Maggie, in our office, brews something but it doesn't taste much like coffee. My name is Teddy," he said, as he held out his hand to shake Jim's hand.

Jim introduced himself and retrieved two chairs and a small fold-up table from the storage bin under the RV and stepped inside and poured the coffee. As he stepped back outside, he pushed a button and the awing extended providing shade.

"How is it your motorhome still runs?" Teddy asked, taking a sip of the coffee.

"It was in an all metal garage, which seemed to protect it and the Jeep as well."

"That was fortunate; nothing here seems to work. I need to get going, I am glad you stopped, maybe a good omen," Teddy said as he mounted his steed.

"Do you have another preacher to lead the service?" Jim asked.

"No, the pastor's wife has been a real trooper. She has kept the church functioning even though it has been a real burden. I never realized how strong and talented she is," he replied as he rode off.

Jim waved at the cop and thought, 'Christian people will survive, even in hard times.'

Jim turned in early and for the first time in a long time felt completely relaxed and safe, although he still kept his pistol by his bed. With the windows open and a cool breeze, he slept better than he had in weeks.

Jim got up early, made a full pot of coffee and put two pans of muffins in the oven. They would provide snacks for several days, and Hannah's kids would like them.

With a cup of coffee and one of the muffin pans, he stepped outside to sit in one of his chairs. He opened his Bible for his regular reading as was his custom. It was a great relaxing time.

Jim looked up as he turned a page and was surprised to see three young girls standing right next to his table. They were very quiet, two of them were looking at him and the youngest was looking at the pan of muffins. The oldest was about seven or eight, the middle one maybe six and the youngest four or five. All were dressed up for church with nice, clean, fancy dresses.

"Would you like a muffin I made them this morning?" Jim asked.

They all smiled, and the oldest girl replied, "Yes, please."

Jim went back into the RV and returned with paper plates, some cups and a pitcher of water, the only drink he had.

When he stepped out, a young woman stood there, also dressed nicely for church. "I hope they haven't bothered you," she said. Her smile disappeared and she began shaking and slurring her speech.

Jim, thinking she might fall, helped her to a chair. "They have been no problem at all. I hope you will join us in a little snack," he said.

She looked up at Jim with tears running down her face. "I have come to the point of losing my faith. Last night the girls prayed that God would send someone today to give us some bread. I did not believe that God would do that. I guess I did not believe God could do that. And here you are."

"May, I have another one?" the youngest girl asked.

"No, we don't want to eat all your food," the mother said.

"I have plenty. I stocked up because this is the only thing I know how to prepare," Jim said chuckling.

"We prayed someone would come and help us," the older girl said. "Did an angel tell you?"

"Perhaps an angel did tell me. I was driving by last evening and a young man directed me into this lot. By the time I got parked, he was gone. He was young, maybe twenty, a good-looking young man. Any idea who he might be?" Jim inquired.

"I don't know, most all of our men are gone," the mother replied, sadly.

"Our father went to heaven with a lot of other people," the younger girl said.

"I am sorry, we are being rude. My name is Alice, and these are my daughters. Their father was the pastor here."

"I am Jim Jenkins and right now live at a militia camp north of here," Jim said, thankful at the change in the conversation.

Jim noticed Teddy on his horse stop at the edge of the lot and tie his horse to a tree. He started in their direction. Jim got up, went inside and returned with a full pot of coffee and the other pan of muffins.

Teddy arrived and greeted each of the young girls by name and then their mother. He gave each a smile as he called their names. Alice returned his smile and Jim thought he noticed a mutual interest between the two.

With only two muffins left in the second pan, Jim said, "I will make some more in case they are needed."

"Let me help you, but we don't want to eat all your food," Alice repeated as she got up from her chair. Her attitude of despair seemed to have passed.

Jim followed her inside the motorhome.

"This is very nice! Is it your full-time house?" she asked.

"It is now. I just retrieved it. It was in a garage when my house was burned down, maybe by the same people who came here."

Jim prepared the mix and put the freeze-dried apples in water while Alice washed the two muffin pans.

"Our town is out of everything. There have been no supplies since the electricity went off. We are mainly living on small gardens around town. I don't know how much longer we can survive, especially with winter coming," she stated sadly.

"Teddy seems interested in you and your girls. Maybe he could be a help and an emotional support for you," Jim said as he hoped he wasn't speaking out of turn.

"I am a very recent widow. It would not be proper for me to be close to Teddy, he is just a friend," she replied, without a smile.

"Alice, I don't mean to interfere, but we are in a war and likely will be for some time. The normal rules of etiquette do not apply. Consider allowing him to come close without feeling any guilt. It may be necessary to survive," Jim said, hoping he had not overstepped. He also considered taking his own advice as far as Hannah was concerned.

She stood and looked at him for a long time before answering. "Jim are you sure you are not an angel. My daughters seem to think so and you have certainly been an answer to our prayers." She then came and gave him a little hug and added, "Thank you!"

She went outside and moved her chair to sit next to Teddy. He looked at her with a smile and a nod of his head. Non-verbal communication.

After a few minutes, the crowd had increased to about thirty people, mostly women and children. Jim scanned the group looking for the young man who had ushered him into the parking lot the day before. He wasn't among the worshipers. They sang a few songs without books accompanied by a woman with a guitar. An older man then stood and read a few scriptures from an old Bible and led a prayer. Alice then went to the front of the congregation and stood on a step to the burned church and spoke.

"My friends, I want to share with you a blessing which my family has experienced this morning. Last evening, my daughter prayed to God that he would send us some cake or sweet rolls today. I did not believe that would happen and, furthermore, I did not believe God could make it happen. I am sorry for my unbelief. Today we have a visitor in the giant vehicle who fed my daughters and myself some very good sweet muffins. My girls believe this man, named Jim Jenkins, is an angel, something he denies. However, I am not so sure. Be sure to stop by and greet him and welcome him to our church, which we will rebuild. I want to thank God right now for a renewal of my faith."

She ended her talk with a big smile, something they had not seen in a long time.

The crowd responded with applause and shouts apparently ending the service.

While Alice was talking with congregants, Jim said to Teddy, "I would like to leave a few things for Alice. Would you deliver them after I leave?"

"Of course, it would be a pleasure. I want to thank you for helping her. She has been in a deep depression since her husband was murdered. I have been concerned that she might harm herself," he said with a sad look on his face.

Jim replied, "I think you could be a big help to her and who knows what the future holds?"

Jim opened a bin in the back of the RV and filled a bag with a couple of boxes of the muffin mix and some packets of dried milk. In a second bag he placed some packets of freeze-dried food, hoping it was something the young girls would like. In a third bag he placed a four-roll packet of toilet paper, which someone had mentioned was in short supply. He handed the bags to Teddy who responded with a big smile and the comment, "I will see she gets these, and I will check on them often. I cannot thank you enough for stopping here."

Jim place the remaining six muffins on a paper plate and covered them with plastic wrap and handed them to the oldest girl. "This may be good for a snack or breakfast," he said.

The smallest girl came to Jim and said, "Would you thank God for me?" With that she followed her two sisters toward home.

Jim was getting ready to put his table away when he noticed it was covered with fruit and vegetables from gardens all over town. The people had been generous. He put them in a bin under the RV and stowed the table and chairs.

Alice finely freed herself from the last of the people and came to him. "Jim, I cannot express my feelings for what you have given me. I was in a bad place and you rescued me. I want to thank you, but it seems insufficient. Come back and see us if you can and bring your family." With that she gave him a very tight hug and kissed him on the cheek and turned and walked quickly away.

Jim started the motorhome and slowly drove out on the previously deserted street, but now full of people waving to him as he continued his journey.

What a wonderful stop. He wished he could thank the young man who waved him into the parking lot, making all this possible. But he was not to be found.

He continued his journey, hoping to get back to camp before dark. After a few miles, he took a detour, a short cut on a forest road. No traffic at all. He was cruising along at a moderate speed when, rounding a curve, he saw a young girl sitting in the middle of the road. He slammed on the brakes and steered for the shoulder of the road, barely missing the girl. He finally stopped the rig and jumped out.

A woman appearing out of nowhere had picked up the small girl and was hugging her. In addition, the road was now full of people, mostly children but several adults.

"My God! Is she allright?" he asked.

"Sally is fine; she should not have been in the road, although there has been no traffic for days," the woman holding the girl stated. She did not seem angry with either the girl or Jim.

Jim looked around and saw no buildings, just a small school bus and a large van parked among the trees. Several adults and more children came running from the woods.

"What are you doing here?" Jim asked, a foolish question as it was obvious the bus had stopped when the EMP attack occurred.

"I am Pastor Bill. We have been here almost two weeks. Our bus just quit running and we can't seem to get it started. A few trucks have gone by, but no one has stopped. We were expecting people to look for us when we didn't arrive at the retreat camp," said Bill, a pleasant looking, fit man, about thirty-five years of age stated as he held out his hand for Jim to shake.

Jim shook his hand and gave him the sad news. "No, and I am afraid there will be little traffic. It seems we have been attacked by some weapon which has disabled most all electricity and nearly all vehicles. I am afraid this is very serious as our country has been crippled."

"I see. Well it explains why no one has come looking for us. We are certain God is in control and His will be done."

The response surprised Jim, and he did not reply to Pastor Bill who seemed completely unconcerned.

The lady holding Sally came to Jim and said, "I am Angie, Pastor Bill's wife. I am so glad you stopped. The children have not had anything to eat for two days. We had some supplies, but they ran out."

"Come with me, I have some food," Jim replied, and she accompanied him as he went to the motor home.

Jim stood aside to let Angie enter first, and then several children followed her. The RV was suddenly crowded.

"This is very nice," Angie said as she stopped in front of the sink. "Do you have any water to spare? The only water we have had is from a stream and it has a bad taste."

"Of course," Jim replied taking little sleeves of plastic cups from the cabinet.

The eight children, all very well behaved, and looked to be six to ten years old, sat around the table and on the couch. They each took a cup and drank several refills from the RV water tank. After they had finished with the water, Angie accepted a coffee cup full of water, and for the first time really smiled at Jim.

"We all thank you!"

"I made a few of my secret recipe muffins this morning. There are five left, maybe you can divide them among the children while I make some more," Jim said as he got out a bowl and a box labeled 'Muffin Mix'. In a second bowl, he put some freeze-dried apples and added some water. When the apples had rehydrated, he added the muffin mix and some dried milk powder. Stirring, he moistened the mix with water. Jim then took two muffin tins; each holding six muffins and added the batter. The two tins filled the small oven.

"It will take fifteen or so minutes," he stated to all.

"Why is the recipe a secret?" Angie asked.

"Well, I made some of these, years ago for our church class. Several women asked for the recipe and I told them it was a family secret. I always told my wife she married me to find out my recipe. It was kind of a joke, since this is the only thing I know how to cook."

This got Jim another smile from her. "Where is your wife?"

"She passed away several years ago," Jim replied while thinking 'Am I married or should be married to the woman I am living with?'

A small girl, maybe six, came to Jim and touched his arm. When he looked at her she said, "When you get to heaven will you tell my mom I love her and miss her?" She then went back and sat down.

Jim knew he should say something to her instead he just glanced at Angie with a questioning look on his face.

Angie watched Jim for a moment then explained. "Last night when Pastor Bill prayed, he asked God to send a messenger with help. He asked earnestly to send some food. The young ones may think you are an angel or something."

Angie turned away from him and looked down into the sink. "I didn't believe Pastor Bill's prayer would be answered. When you talk to God would you ask for forgiveness for me for my doubt?"

"Of course, I will, but I am sure God hears you as plainly as He hears me," Jim replied very quietly. It was obvious this woman was very troubled. He also wondered why a wife would refer to her husband as Pastor Bill, instead of just Bill.

"I pray often but never hear an answer and I pray for a child of my own, but it doesn't happen. I even doubt if anyone is there to hear me."

She looked at Jim and he saw she was crying. She quickly looked away, ashamed to let him see her grief.

The tension in the camper was broken by a voice from outside. "Something smells very good in there."

A second woman in the group stepped into the RV and smiled at Jim, extending her hand. She introduced herself. "Hi, I am Donna, and my husband's name is Troy. We are the parents of Tommy and Mary, motioning toward two children on the couch. The other children are from the class at our church."

When Donna introduced her children, Jim noticed Angie turned her head away.

Jim removed the muffins from the oven and refilled the pans with the rest of the muffin batter and placed them back in the oven.

"Am I allowed in?" a female voice from outside the RV asked.

"Of course," Jim replied. When she stepped in, he was not sure he had done the right thing.

The woman was a younger version of Angie, with the same facial features, but her clothing and shoes was covered with black mud of some kind.

Angie introduced her, "Jim, this is Bernice, my sister. She fell in a pit of something yesterday and we have no extra clothes."

Bernice correctly stated, "I am afraid I am not socially acceptable," as the smell of whatever the "mud" consisted of filled the camper.

"In the back there is a shower. I am afraid I have no clothes that will fit you; take whatever you need from the closet," Jim said, pointing to the rear of the RV.

"Oh, thank you!" she replied while advancing to give him a hug. Thankfully, she changed her mind and gave him a big smile instead. She went to the back, picking up a muffin on the way.

Angie called after her, "Don't use too much water and dress in *something* before you come out!"

Jim glanced at Angie with another questioning look, thinking this was beginning to look like a rather strange group.

She explained, "Bernice sometimes is a bit wild and rambunctious!"

From the back of the RV came Bernice's voice, "I heard that!" followed by laughter.

Jim stepped outside the vehicle to get more packets of dried food and found the two men standing there talking. "Come in if you like," he said.

"It seems a bit crowded, and it is more important the children get something to eat," Pastor Bill stated.

Jim opened a second compartment and removed two folding chairs for the men.

"I cook very little, but I have a packet of oatmeal, which is quick and will give some nourishment."

"That sound very good and will set well on an empty stomach," Troy, a man of very few words, stated.

Jim retrieved his largest pan and put the oatmeal on the stove. Angie and her friend Donna were busy washing the plastic dishes from the Children's' breakfast and wiping off messy fingers. The children, unbelievably well behaved, remained seated and quiet.

Bernice emerged from the back of the RV, dressed in one of Jim's dress shirts and obviously, clothed only in the shirt. If she was embarrassed about her dress it didn't show.

Angie gave her sister a stern look, which was returned with a smile. "I washed my undies and they'll dry in a few minutes," she stated. She carried her muddy outer garments in her hands.

"There's a small washing machine next to the shower; just toss and add a little soap," Jim said while intentionally not looking at Bernice, but suddenly missing Hannah and wishing she were here. He started the generator so the coffee pot and washing machine would function.

While the oatmeal cooked, Jim opened some dried strawberries and rehydrated them. Jim fumbled in the cabinets and found a packet of thin plastic bowls. Angie filled the bowls with oatmeal, Donna added a layer of strawberries and Jim topped each off with a spoon full of honey and a little powdered sugar. The children finished eating and were escorted to the bedroom in the back. It was the adults' turn and the two men and the three women crowded around the small table.

Before eating, Pastor Bill bowed his head for prayer. All at the table lowered their heads, except for Angie, who stared at Jim.

"Lord we thank you for sending your messenger with this food which we so badly needed. We know you always hear our prayer and we praise you and thank you again for loving us and providing for us."

The five adults ate quickly as if they were starving. Jim served water, coffee and the rest of the muffins.

"Jim, sit down; I'll serve the table," said Bernice, as she got up, showing more leg than she should.

Jim held up a hand and said, "No please, you need to eat, and we need to discuss what you want to do."

Pastor Bill paused for a moment before speaking, "If you could take one of us to a town, we could call someone to come with another bus to take us on."

"Pastor, I'm afraid you do not understand the seriousness of the situation. There are no phones working and very few vehicles. We have had an invasion from the south which has occupied some of the United States. I don't have any way of knowing how much territory is lost but many cities are under siege. The situation is dire," Jim replied, speaking slowly.

No one spoke for a moment as the position they were in began to sink in.

It was Angie who finally spoke, "Jim what do you recommend we do?"

"You must all go with me, even if we must leave some of your gear. We'll crowd everyone in, and I can take you to the Militia Camp north of here. From there transportation will be provided to a refugee camp near Denver where you should be safe. There's some communication there and perhaps you'll be able to contact your families," Jim said to a now silent group.

Just then the dryer sounded. Bernice got up and said, "I'll dress now," the flirtatious or silly attitude she had before, completely gone.

After only twenty minutes everything was loaded, and the RV made ready to move. It seemed the luggage and many of the supplies for the church group had been transported in a pickup a day earlier and was probably at the retreat site. The van traveling with the campers had contained several cases of fresh fruit and snacks which was a God send. This had sustained the group.

With Jim driving and the children in the back bedroom there seemed to be plenty of room. Pastor Bill rode 'shotgun' in the right front seat.

Continuing north on the back road for twenty miles, they reached the turn-off for the church retreat site.

Jim, concerned about the narrow road and the lack of a place to turn around, stopped the RV without turning down the road. "How far is the camp?" he asked.

"There are supplies at the retreat for two or three weeks, but no more. Our men driving the pickup should be there and may be isolated," the pastor remarked.

"It's about a half a mile and has a good place to turn around," Pastor Bill stated not understanding Jim's hesitation.

"I'll walk down and check it out. If I am not back in thirty minutes, or if you hear shooting, drive on," Jim cautioned as he stood and put on his tactical vest which was stored by the driver's seat. He took his AR rifle from a hidden rack above the windshield, causing a shock among his passengers. He stepped out of the motor home and had taken just a few steps when Angie appeared at his side, followed by her husband, Pastor Bill.

"You should stay; it's probably allright but no reason to take a chance," Jim commented to the pastor's wife.

"I'm going with Jim. You should go back, Angie," Pastor Bill stated.

She looked back at him. "No, we'll both go; we know the camp, and Jim doesn't."

Going further, they noticed clothing and empty suitcases strewn along the road. Jim motioned for the couple to get behind him as he put the rifle to his shoulder, ready to fire. Coming to the edge of the clearing they stopped in the trees. In the clearing were several buildings and people moving about, some children playing, others leisurely going about daily tasks. Armed men were spotted at random positions engaging in what appeared to be friendly exchanges.

"There are Bryan and Barry," Angie whispered, pointing to two men on the porch of a small cabin at the side of the clearing.

"I don't think we should approach those men," Jim stated.

Angie waved but the two men did not notice her.

Jim took a signal mirror out of a pocket of the vest and flashed one time in the direction of the cabin. Instantly the men raised their heads and looked in their direction. Pastor Bill stepped out a little and waved for them to come. One of the men nodded and glanced at the armed men, casually they moved around the cabin into the woods, more out of the view of the guards. In just a few minutes they arrived where Jim and their friends awaited on the road.

"Thank God, Pastor! We had about given up hope," one of the men stated quietly.

Both men hugged the pastor and Angie, one with tears running down his face.

"What is the situation with this group?" Jim asked, without being introduced.

"They are a displaced community. They came several days ago and just moved in, took over the whole camp. They could be really dangerous if challenged," the one crying lamented.

"We should leave it to them and go on," Jim said.

The five moved quietly back down the road and broke into a jog as soon as they got away from the clearing. They loaded up and got underway quickly. The people at the camp were unaware of the visitors.

Jim drove and the four men sat at the table while Bernice and Donna prepared food for Bryan and Barry, using the microwave. They also brewed a pot of coffee.

With the right seat open, Angie joined Jim up front. She was quiet for a moment then said, "Jim could you've killed the men with guns?

Jim paused, thinking, 'What kind of a question is this for the wife of a minister'. "Yes, I probably could've shot the four-armed men. They seemed to be armed with pistols and shotguns and we were pretty much out of range for those weapons. There's no way to know what others inside the building were armed with, so the end of a conflict would be just a guess." He paused, and then continued. "I didn't think there was anything there worth killing over."

"No, of course not, and we couldn't have stayed there very long. It just seems wrong, what they did, just coming in and taking our things and our food."

"You're right but, this is a different time. People who are hungry will do things they have never done before. They will rob, steal and even kill to survive. I am sure most will feel guilt later, but the deed will be done. We must be prepared to protect ourselves and our families," Jim replied.

"Shouldn't God protect us, so we don't have to fight? Pastor Bill has said as much in his sermons." she said very slowly.

"That is a question I cannot answer. In the Old Testament, sometimes God protected Israel by fighting a battle for them, other times God protected them by helping them fight. The answer is to listen to what God's instructions are for each occasion. Sometimes he simply places soldiers where they are needed. Miraculous thing can happen when God is in full control."

"*If* He talks to you," was her only reply.

Just then Pastor Bill walked to the front and Angie jumped up giving him her seat. She went to the back without another word.

Pastor Bill sat and said to Jim, "You handled the situation perfectly. Those people taking over our camp were just looking for food and anything else they needed or wanted. They did not mistreat Bryan or Barry and they were not held captive. There is no doubt they would have fought to maintain control of the place and you avoided bloodshed by simply leaving."

"It is good they didn't see us; they may have shot at us thinking we might have something worth taking. It turned out allright. They'll have to do something when the food runs out."

They came to the end of the short cut and to the main four lane road. He stopped to look both ways, and of course there was no traffic. Turning onto the main road, he felt more comfortable driving a little faster. Just as he got up to speed, he saw a group of maybe ten people walking along, two carrying a stretcher with a person on it. Some of the adults were carrying small children, all looking exhausted. He stopped and checked his pistol as he got out. A large, older man said, "Thank you for stopping; we could use water if you can spare any."

The group had no packs or supplies of any kind. "Where are you going?" Jim asked.

"We understand there is a refuge just down the road with shelter and food," the man stated.

Jim wondered how this rumor had gotten started, the refuge was many miles to the north, and these people had no hope of making it. "Get in and I'll take you to a camp where you can get transportation to the refuge," Jim informed him.

The motor home, already full, became uncomfortably crowded. The newcomers immediately collapsed on the furniture and floor. An older woman asked if she could have some water for the children. Angie, Bernice and Donna retrieved leftovers to give the newcomers.

"Take all the water you want, and in the upper cabinet are some food bars. Pass them out. They will provide some nourishment," Jim remarked as he got underway.

The old man said they were from Show Low in Arizona and the town had been attacked. Several in the community were killed and the churches burned. They had paid a man to take them to the refuge in an old truck. The man let them out and told them it was only a couple of miles. He had lied. After drinking water and eating the food bars, everyone settled down, and some slept, until Jim arrived at the Militia Camp.

At the Militia Camp, the old man insisted that Jim accept all the money the group had. He refused; they would need it much more than Jim would. The surprising fact was that money had lost most of its value since the attack, although people still used it in an exchange. Bartering had become much more common.

The guard at the Militia Camp did not seem surprised at the large number of people in the motor home. Recognizing Jim, he waved him through. Another soldier in uniform directed them to a parking area, now full of army trucks. Everyone slowly got out of the motor home, some with help at the steps. Most shook Jim's hand, some hugged him and all thanked him for saving them.

Bernice, the flirt, came and hugged Jim even giving him a little kiss on the cheek. "Jim, I know you have a woman now, but if something happens….." She said this with a spark in her eyes.

Angie then came and hugged Jim for an embarrassingly long time. She whispered in his ear. "Jim, I cannot express how much meeting you has affected me. Thank you, and when you talk to God, please ask Him to remember me." With that she walked off.

Next, the little girl, Sally, came to Jim. "Mr. Jim, thank you for coming from heaven to answer our prayers. I was in the road to watch for you and wasn't afraid you would hit me with your truck. I was afraid you might not see us and we were so very hungry."

Jim bent down on one knee to talk to the little girl. "Sally, sometimes God does send someone from heaven to help us, but usually He gets someone nearby to come. I was nearby and came and am glad I could help. When you pray, ask God to send a message to your mom about how you feel. I am sure He will do it. Your mom is still with you as long as you remember her and you can talk to her and I think she will hear, even if she can't talk back."

The little girl gave Jim a hug and then ran off to be with the others.

Last Pastor Bill came and took Jim's hand. "Jim, I am forever indebted to you for rescuing us. I don't know how to say it, but my wife has been troubled for some time and I seem unable to meet her needs. You are everything I'm not and I think if you would have asked her to stay with you, she would have."

Jim, with no idea how to respond, said, "Pastor, your job requires a lot of time and with the situation we have, there will be more demands on you. Your wife has needs and desires and she is important. Perhaps what she needs is to know that she is, in fact, a priority to you. In any case, I am sure she loves you and would never leave."

"I hope you're right," he replied. "Thanks again, and I hope to see you again."

The pastor joined his wife and took her hand as the entire group went into a building with food and showers. Jim watched and was glad Angie did not look back at him. Bernice however did look back at Jim. She pointed to the pastor and Angie and raised her hand and signaled an OK sign. She then waved and smiled for the first time as a friend, not a flirt. He watched them go, sadly realizing knowing he would never see them again.

Jim drove the motor home to the little cabin and was glad to see Hannah and Rhoda rushing out to meet him. Hannah ran to Jim while Rhoda looked at the motor home.

"It's so big and beautiful," she said in awe as she walked around it. "Oh, you poor thing," she continued when reaching the front with the blistered paint and melted rubber.

"I'm surprised it would start. Did you have any trouble?" Hannah asked.

"Not really; everything seems to work fine. I guess the metal building protected it from the EMP attack. There may be a lot of undamaged vehicles in garages all over the country," Jim replied.

Going inside, Hannah and Rhoda inspected the facility in some detail. "This is certainly a man's house. There are hardly any cooking utensils, pictures or pillows," Hannah said laughing.

"It is wonderful!" Rhoda added.

There had been a picture of Jim's wife, Nancy, on the wall, but he had removed it before leaving the cabin. Perhaps they could obtain a picture of his new family to hang in its place.

The little family vacated the cabin by the river and moved into the motor home. There was a shortage of living spaces as new people were arriving every day, many from as far away as California.

As they prepared to go into the motor home for the first night, Jim took Hannah's hands in his, and said. "Hannah, I think we should formalize our relationship and get married."

"Why, Mr. Jenkins, are you asking me to marry you? Don't you remember, we made a commitment after our first night and I have considered us married since then? Besides, where would we find a judge?" she questioned.

"I don't know any judges, but I do know a preacher and I believe he can do the job," Jim answered.

"Of course, I will marry you any time you wish!!" she replied, with dancing eyes and a broad smile.

CHAPTER 14

Going West

THE MARRIAGE WAS NOT TO be, at least not yet. A uniformed, active duty soldier came running to the cabin. "Sir, Mr. Jenkins, Captain Masters has requested you meet with him about a convoy which is presently getting underway. Your motor home is greatly needed," he stated, out of breath. The young man then ran to the next cabin, the best replacement for the lost phone service.

The Militia Camp was a beehive of activity. Jim parked the motor home in a closed gasoline station adjacent to the camp. He had noticed a sewer clean-out before and thought he could empty the holding tank into it. If he had need for the motorhome during this mission. He didn't regard this as luck but as God providing.

Captain Masters spotted Jim and waved to get his attention. "I hope you are planning to go with us toward California. We have received several vehicles from the army but are still short of transportation. I think you know these men two who have volunteered. Perhaps they could ride with you."

The two men were Harold and Ralph Taylor, the pastor and doctor who Jim had met on the road. They would be good company.

"Of course, they are welcome, and they can help drive if we have long days," he replied.

The men stepped aboard with practically no luggage. The doctor had located a few medical supplies and carried them in an old canvas bag—not a very sterile arrangement.

"I understand you are a preacher. May I ask what denomination?" Hannah questioned, with a knowing look at Jim.

"I am a Baptist; we try very hard to follow the teaching of the Bible in our beliefs. Our doctrine can briefly be summed up like this: There is One God in three persons, the Father, the Son and the Holy Spirit. Three persons but one. I think this concept is difficult to completely understand. We believe Jesus, the son of God and somehow a part of God, died on the cross and rose from the dead. His sacrifice paid the price for our sins, and our belief in Him will save us, and we will join Him in Heaven when we die," Harold stated in a serious tone.

"What do you think of Messianic Jews?" Hannah continued.

"Ah, the Jewish question. The way of salvation is the same for Jew and Gentile. Paul in his writings made this very clear. He also described the advantages of being Jewish, which are many. God's plan for Jews has certainly not been completed and in the final days they will be a central part of what happens. I believe, in the end, all or most all of the Jews will be saved and be a great missionary force to the entire world," he stated with a big smile, and then continued. "But I believe you already know this."

"Well, yes I have read the Bible several times and have made a commitment to Christ and am a Messianic Jew. I have, however, not been faithful to attend worship services as I should. I do not feel like I am doing the right thing much of the time," she answered.

The conversation was interrupted by Captain Masters when he arrived with a dozen men and women, all adults and all armed. "We need to transport these troops with you. I know it will be crowded but it is necessary. I think it would be better to disconnect the Jeep and let the sergeant drive it. I hope this is all right with you."

The captain was not asking permission, but simply trying to be polite while informing Jim the vehicles were under control of the military. This was not a surprise to Jim as he expected it and, in fact, thought the Jeep might be confiscated. But keeping the motor home for his family was a priority for him.

Five of the men crowded into the Jeep and went ahead of the motor home. The captain also had boxes of equipment loaded into the storage compartments of the RV. When ready to leave, both vehicles were crowded and probably overloaded.

The convoy was led by four armored Humvees with heavy machine guns. Following them was a truck with a tank on a flatbed trailer, also pulling a small artillery gun. Following the truck was a mixture of military and civilian vehicles with Jim's motor home almost at the end of the line. The last vehicle was another armed Humvee.

Jim drove the crowded motor home with Hannah in the front seat and Rhoda sat in the floor between them. The entire vehicle was packed with men, women and guns. An effort was made to keep a path to the bathroom open. The convoy stopped every four hours or so for the troops to get out, stretch and relieve themselves. Both men and women did their job without seeming to be embarrassed. Ralph took over the driving after the second break and Jim and the two ladies sat on the crowded couch and tried, unsuccessfully, to snooze. A small tanker truck refueled all the vehicles and they continued for thirty hours with only rest stops, arriving in California in the middle of the second day. The towns they passed seemed undisturbed and people came out to watch them go by. Two hours into California this changed. A small town by the highway had burning buildings and additional destruction. The soldiers in the front of the convoy went through the town and found the attackers had left two days before. They had come into the town without any warning and simply shot people for no reason and then burned all churches and government buildings.

A young soldier came running by the vehicles and told them the convoy would be taking a longer break, and the additional men in Jim's RV were needed to assist in searching the town.

To the side of the road was a building with a Star of David with a cross overlaid. It was a Messianic Jewish Church. The front was damaged, but the building was standing. Several people were gathering outside the building getting ready for some kind of service.

Hannah watched them for a few minutes and then said, "I have to go to this church meeting." The tone of her voice indicated the statement was not open for discussion.

Harold Taylor, the pastor, then commented. "My brother and I are Jewish by birth but have never been involved in the Jewish religion, but right now I feel like I must go to this religious service. I don't understand it, but we must go."

Hannah and the Taylor brothers got out of the motor home and started down the bank to the building which was now beginning to be crowded as people were arriving from all directions. This left Jim and Rhoda alone in the vehicle.

Jim watched Hannah and said to Rhoda, "We must find out what is going on; this is not normal."

Jim and Rhoda caught up with Hannah and the brothers just as they reached the church. The building was already full but with the front wall partially open from some type of explosion they could see and hear what was happening inside.

A man in dirty street clothes stood at the front of the assembly, perhaps the Rabbi (or preacher) of the church and was already speaking. "My friends, the rumors we have heard are true. Israel is under attack! The enemy is gathering a large number of troops on the borders to attack. The danger is real and imminent."

Jim wondered how the speaker knew this as communication was almost nonexistent.

The man continued. "We have been granted a great honor in being invited to go and fight to defend our homeland. The United

States and the Israeli governments have agreed to provide air transport to Tel Aviv and will be leaving soon. We will be taking any person who is Jewish and any non-Jewish family members. I feel like God Himself has called us, and most of our surviving congregation has already volunteered to go. If you are called, you may sign up at the table here in the front. Some of the aircraft have already arrived and we will be leaving late tonight or early in the morning."

Jim was surprised the US would use the few flying aircraft to transport people around the world when the need was so great here. He had come up behind Hannah and placed his hands on her shoulders. She did not move and was as rigid as stone. After what seemed like a long time, she turned to face Jim. She had the strangest look as she was smiling and crying at the same time. "Jim, I hope you know I love you with all my heart, but I cannot marry you. I must go to Israel! I don't know why, but I must go! I do know I will miss you every day."

With this statement she rose on her toes and kissed him lightly on the lips. She turned to go but he held her and said, "Wife, we are one and will stay together, wherever we go, we will go together." Rhoda piped in, "What about me?"

They waited in line to register. Jim noticed several of those in line were militia members from the convoy, quite a few of them. Reaching the head of the line, Hannah spoke to the man taking names, and introduced herself as Jewish. He accepted this at face value. Hannah nodding in Jim's direction, said, "This is Jim Jenkins, my partner; we plan to marry, and this is our ward which we plan to adopt."

At this statement, Rhoda grabbed Jim's arm so tightly it hurt a little.

The man at the desk looked at Jim, who was still dressed in his tactical vest with a pistol and several rifle clips, Rhoda and Hannah with their pistols. He thought these three look like they could actually fight if need be. He started typing on the form, on an actual typewriter, as he stated, "This trip is for Jews and family members. That is the agreement with the US government."

He handed the paper to Hannah and said, "The aircraft are at the base north of town, go one mile west and then follow the signs. Next please."

Hannah, not understanding if Jim and Rhoda could go, looked at the paper.

1. Hannah White Jenkins Jewish
2. Jim Jenkins Husband of Hannah
3. Rhoda Jenkins Daughter of Hannah

Hannah turned to Jim and Rhoda and while crying and laughing at the same time said, "We can go!"

They walked back to the RV, with them the two brothers, Harold and Ralph, who had also been accepted as Jewish on their word only. Jim thought there might be a problem. They had committed to Captain Masters their service and they had some of his equipment and were transporting several of his troops. Arriving back at the vehicle, there was the captain himself, supervising the unloading of the boxes of supplies from the storage bins in the RV into a school bus which had not been in the convoy. With the captain were six men and four women, all armed and dressed in fatigues. Jim thought they looked Jewish, with their olive skin and facial features.

The captain smiled and said to Jim and his now official family. "I was expecting you would want to make the airplane trip, so I have taken my supplies and exchanged your passengers for these who also will be going with you."

"I feel bad. We had committed to you to assist in freeing the West Coast," Jim remarked.

"Do not feel that way; you are on God's payroll, not mine. He will provide for us here while you do His work in the Holy Land. I wish I could go with you. May God be with you my friends." With this statement, Captain Masters uncharacteristically hugged Jim, then Hannah, and then Rhoda.

"I will leave the RV at the airport with the keys. Consider it yours," Jim replied. The Captain smiled at him and responded, "I will send someone to check." He then got in the bus and drove off. Jim thought 'What will he check? He knows something I don't'.

One of the young men called to Jim from the rear of the RV, "Your Jeep is hooked up and the transfer case in neutral. It should be ready to tow." Jim had not noticed the Jeep was there. The ten soldiers, the brothers and Jim's family all crowded into the motor home, standing room only, and drove west to the airport.

CHAPTER 15

The trip To Israel, the Holy Land

ON THE WAY TO THE airport the ten soldiers began singing a song, and Hannah joined in. They sang in Hebrew and Jim didn't understand a word of it. Neither did the Taylor brothers or Rhoda. Hannah came and whispered in Jim's ear. "The song is about going to Jerusalem next year. We sing it at the New Year's dinner. This year it will be true." The tears had finally stopped and she was smiling and giddy. Jim also felt at peace, as if he was doing exactly what he was born to do.

The trip was so enjoyable Jim was actually a little sad it was ending.

Arriving at the airport, a guard stopped them and allowed them to enter after presenting the papers from the man at the church. The guard was stoic but finally directed them to bypass the terminal and go directly to the runway. The scene upon rounding the building was surprising. Sitting on the runway were two Boeing 707 four-engine aircraft, planes not in service in the US for at least forty years. They looked in good shape except that some symbols on the tail had been crudely spray painted over. Another big surprise was a huge black C-5 aircraft, the Air Force's largest cargo craft. The tail ramp was open.

A man on the runway with a flag directed Jim to drive the RV toward the C-5. As they got near; another man directed them where to park. Rhoda, looking through the windshield, wide eyed, said, "My gosh it is so big! Can it really fly?"

As they began unloading, Jim began gathering his clothes and guns. Everything else would be left in the motorhome. A man who looked like he could bench press a truck appeared, and without introducing himself, asked. "You own these vehicles?"

"Yes," Jim replied.

"You won't need to transfer you personal items," The big man replied without any explanation.

When they stepped out of the motor home, they saw the Jeep had been disconnected and was being driven up the ramp into the C-5. A camouflaged-clad young man soon arrived, slid into the RV driver's seat, and followed the Jeep into the aircraft. They were taking their vehicles, something Jim had not even imagined was possible.

"You may fly in the cargo plane, but the passenger jets will be more comfortable," a young woman in uniform stated to them as they watched the loading.

"Let's fly in this big one!" Rhoda exclaimed excitedly.

It took two hours to load and secure the vehicles. The bay was less than half the capacity of the large aircraft. The seats along the side walls were small with no armrests and were designed to be folded down when needed. The five sat together side-by-side near the front of the huge cargo compartment as the aircraft took off. The sound was deafening but quieted a little when they reached cruising altitude. Several Air Force personnel took seats opposite them, also strapped in. The two old 707's left just before them and were not seen until they arrived at their destination in Maryland.

As the aircraft leveled off, one of the airmen approached. He had been eyeing Rhoda since sitting down. "Would you like a tour of the upper level? It's quite different." He asked Rhoda but indicated with his hand the invitation was for all five of them.

They climbed a small circular staircase to the flight deck area of the aircraft. The young man was correct; the upper level was much nicer than the cargo area. The cockpit had the door, propped open, unlike commercial aircraft. Behind the cockpit was a passenger area with about twenty seats and a small area for the off-duty crew to sleep. The noise level here was much reduced. Jim wished there were seats available, but all were taken. Some were military but most were families, even a few children. There were arms stored in bins near the ceiling. Jim walked to the front where he could see the cockpit and noticed lights on the ground, electric lights.

"They have power down there!" he stated to no one in particular.

A man at a big instrument panel, the Flight Engineer, looked up at him and replied. "A few cities and some small towns have gotten their power plants operating and some farms seem to have large generators. I don't think any of the interstate electrical grid is up yet, but it will be soon. We are recovering slowly."

The two brothers, Harold and Ralph, found someone to talk to, and two empty seats on the upper floor so Jim, Hannah and Rhoda returned to the cargo bay. Rhoda suggested they sit in the RV, which was a disappointment for the young man who had guided them, as he wanted to spend more time with her. It appeared many men would be disappointed until she got older.

The RV door could be opened as there was a space between it and the vehicles beside it. Upon entering the three noticed the engine sounds were greatly diminished, in fact, it was quite comfortable in the vehicle. They were surprised to discover they had electrical power from the extensive aircraft power supply. The propane was shut off due to fire danger, so the electricity was needed to operate the refrigerator, and of more immediate need, they could make fresh coffee. Rhoda lay down on her bunk and Jim sat in the front passenger chair which could swivel to face the rear. He was looking at a map when Hannah brought two cups of fresh coffee. She put the coffee down and sat in Jim's lap, snuggling up.

"I know you don't understand my sudden need to go to Israel and I can't explain it myself, but it's real. I would've missed you every day and every night if you hadn't come with me. There are no adequate words to express how much I love you," she said, whispering in his ear.

"Where we are or where we're going doesn't matter as long as we're together. I think your desire came from God Himself. Jesus said 'in the last days all Israel would be called back to the Holy Land. I think that is what is happening," Jim replied.

Hannah snuggled even closer and watched Rhoda as she drank her coffee. Rhoda quickly went to sleep, and Hannah said, "Come with me."

They went to the back bedroom, closed the door, and joined the 'Mile-High-Club'.

The C-5 landed at Andrews Air Force Base in Maryland. The huge base was brightly lit and very busy. A 'follow me' truck directed the big aircraft to a side parking area near one of the smaller hangers on the base. The aircraft turned around so the tail and loading ramp faced the hanger.

Jim, Hannah, and his "daughter," stayed in the RV using its seatbelts during the landing. It was more comfortable and probably just as safe as the little bucket seats along the cargo hold.

When Jim opened the side door of the RV, he almost hit a large man in an unfamiliar uniform. The rather handsome, rugged looking man, probably around fifty, seemed surprised someone was getting out of a vehicle, part of the cargo.

"Your door will probably be blocked with the additional cargo," he said, matter of factly, without smiling or being overly friendly.

"I will lock the door open; perhaps we will be able to get in and out after loading the cargo," Jim stated. The man just looked at him and observed the two ladies following him out.

Jim latched the side door open and he and his little family got out of the way.

The uniformed man directed the loading of cargo, a lot of it. Pallets were brought in using fork lift trucks along with vehicles being driven in. The aircraft would be fully loaded with all this additional gear. The loaders, some in uniform, others not, were yelling to each other to be heard over the noise, some in Hebrew and some in English.

Hannah, not fluent in Hebrew but understanding a little, leaned over close to Jim and said, "They are calling him General Steinhoff. I think he is a general in the Israeli Army."

It was unbelievable that a general would be directing the loading of an airplane in the United States, but here he was, and very competent in doing so. The loading went very quickly and the weight was evenly distributed fore and aft of the aircraft. Jim was impressed. After the pallets and vehicles were loaded and tied down, the men came, lots of men, and a few women. The aircraft which had looked cavernous and empty on the first leg of the trip now was crowded and looked overloaded. The loading was completed in an amazingly short period of time and the ramp closed. They hadn't had the opportunity to get off to stretch their legs.

The general came to Jim with a smile, the first they had seen, extended a hand to Jim and said, "I apologize for being so short with you; I was not informed of your vehicle. My name is Benjamin Steinhoff."

"I am Jim Jenkins. This is my wife, Hannah, and daughter, Rhoda," Jim replied.

"I am glad you are aboard, especially you, Sister Hannah," the general said, somehow recognizing Hannah as Jewish. He continued. "Perhaps your vehicle will come in handy. We have more people than seats in this aircraft, perhaps some of us could ride in your truck, especially if there are seat belts."

As the engines were fired up Jim went into his RV which had open access, even with the crowded load. He retrieved the seat belts from under cushions and with Hannah's and Rhoda's help, picked up everything to make room for additional people. The RV was quickly packed—all the seats were occupied and then more. Jim sat in the driver's seat, which only faced forward, and Hannah sat in the right seat. Rhoda sat on the floor between them, no seat belt. Most of those on board were young and there were a few children sitting in laps. It was noisy as everyone was joyful and all talking in several languages. Jim understood none of it. Hannah and Rhoda joined in and chatted with those closest to them. Women seem to have an ability to understand several people talking at the same time, a talent men do not have. It was a great start of a very long trip.

The big aircraft reached cruising altitude and word was passed along that seatbelts were no longer required. People began moving about. Several came into the motor home out of curiosity and asked if it was some kind of command vehicle. They were disappointed to find it was not, and left questioning why it was being brought along, a question Jim also was asking himself.

After several hours into the flight, boredom set in, and the general stepped into the motor home. All the other occupants exited out of respect, fear, or awe of the really big boss. "Mind if I come in and relax a bit? The noise is deafening out there," he said.

"Please sit down. Would you like a cup of coffee?" Hannah asked very pleasantly.

The general sat on the short couch along one wall with Rhoda on the other end. His size dwarfed Rhoda.

"My! This is comfortable isn't it? Is this your fulltime home?" he asked, taking the cup from Hannah.

"I lived in it for a few years after my first wife died then when my home was destroyed, this vehicle survived. We just got it running again," Jim explained, incompletely.

"So you haven't been married long?" he pried.

"We committed to each other and to God several months ago," Hannah answered, trying unsuccessfully to explain and excuse their relationship.

The general smiled and ended the discussion with the comment, "There is nothing quite like a Jewish wedding for a Jewish girl, especially in Jerusalem."

Jim, changing the subject, asked, "General, we were invited on this trip and Hannah felt the need to respond. What can you tell us about the trip's mission and why we seem to be involved?"

"Call me Benjamin please. You are not in the army. We believe, and Washington agrees, the attack on the US is a diversion. ISIS has no hope of defeating your country, not at the present time. Their plan is to draw the US forces away from the Middle East and leave Israel defenseless. This, of course, is nonsense. The Lord God will defend us as He sees fit. I believe the Jews have finally been fully called back to Israel as told in the scripture in the Book of Revelation. I may be mistaken, of course, but I believe the end times are upon us. I am not mistaken to state 'God is in control of events'. To answer your question, this trip has two purposes. The first and most important is to give a way for Jews to return. The second is for the US to provide needed military supplies. Entire opposition armies are amassing in yet another attempt to push us into the sea. Many on this and other aircraft are trained soldiers, most, but not all, Jewish. We will stand against this massive onslaught as before and will be in God's hands as always. Perhaps we will see the second coming of the Messiah or perhaps we will be coming back with Him if He takes us out of the world before then."

"You are a fellow believer in Jesus," Hannah said quietly.

"Absolutely, the scriptures are clear and our people, the Jewish people will soon be open to the truth," he replied.

"Tell us about yourself, General," Jim added to the conversation.

He thought for a moment then stated, "I am a military representative of my government at the Pentagon. When the attack happened, the Pentagon emergency generators were protected and unaffected. I was able to maintain communication with Israel. The thinking is the attack on the US is a diversion to draw the US forces back home. This appears to be correct because as vicious as the attacks are, the magnitude is not close to being sufficient to cause the US to surrender. Mexico has been duped into thinking the US will surrender southern states and part of California to achieve peace. This will not happen, of course, and Mexico will suffer a disastrous defeat."

The trip, many hours long, seemed to pass quickly. The general visited for a few hours and drank many cups of coffee, joined in snacks, and finished his visit with a bowl of soup from the store of freeze died food.

They landed in Paris and refueled. No one got on or off the aircraft, apparently due to a clearance problem. The takeoff signaled the last stop before their arrival in Israel, and perhaps a serious war with overwhelming numbers of the enemy.

Other came and went during the remainder of the trip. It was the quietest place and had the best seats on the aircraft. It also had a clean and adequate bathroom. Within an hour or two of final arrival the group in the motor home consisted of young adults, some dressed in fatigues and others in jeans and civilian clothes.

A young man, who looked less than eighteen and frightened stated, "I have heard they are using sarin gas and maybe even nuclear weapons."

Jim who seemed to be the oldest, and therefore should be the wisest, respond. "We don't know what they have, but I bet Israel does. As far as we know there has been no attack yet."

In truth, neither Jim nor the young man knew what was going on in Israel as the communication to them had been nonexistent.

The young man, looking far off in the distance, quietly said, "I wonder what it is like to die."

The little room got very quiet. Many of these kids were going into the unknown, having never fired a shot at anyone or even heard a shot fired at someone. Just like any green troops going into combat for the first time, they were scared.

Jim, who did not feel wise but felt he needed to reassure them, spoke up.

"I want to tell you a little story. The last time my mother visited me at my house in Tennessee she was quite old and would not live long. She could not see well and got confused easily. She could not climb the stairs, so she slept on a foldout bed in my office. She used that room and the little eat in kitchen and the bathroom around the corner. Only three rooms in the house. I was at my desk one afternoon and realized she was not there and went to look for her. She was in the family room past the bath, just standing there. I asked her if she was all right and she said, 'I don't know how to get back to my bed. This looks like a nice room, but I can't see it very well.' I helped her back to her bed in the next room. She was just confused in an unfamiliar place."

He paused and the young people looked at him, wondering what this story had to do with them. Jim continued.

"I think we are like my mother. In this life we see a little bit of God's creation, but we are partially blind. When we go to be with Christ, we will see him clearly and He will show us the heaven He has prepared. The few rooms we see now will not compare to the wonderful house He has made; a house with many rooms and many floors. It will be a wonderful place."

"Are you saying we should try to die?" the frightened young man asked.

"Not at all! We should always fight to live and look for a way to please God. We should always fight death, but not because of fear. The Lord put us here to do His will and, in His time, He will call us home. While here, seek to do His will and when He calls you home, go without fear. Right now, we have a job to do and it may or may not involve dying. In either case, we should not fear, that is if you are a believer in Jesus as your savior. If not, your priority is to get to know and trust in Him."

The group in the motor home was silent and in thought, but through the window, opened for ventilation, Jim heard comments, "Amen" and "That's right!"

Outside in the cargo bay stood several people who had been listening. The group included the Taylor brothers, Harold and Ralph, and General Steinhoff.

The group in the motor home began leaving quietly. The young man who had started the conversation came to Jim and shook his hand. "Thank you! I feel all right now. I may still be a little afraid, but I am better."

"I'm here if you want to talk and there's a pastor on board, Harold Taylor. I am sure he will be happy to discuss anything with you," Jim replied.

Finally, the only one left was a young woman. She came to Jim and said, "My name is Laura. I was raised in a strict Jewish house and we were never allowed to say the name, Jesus. We just said, 'That Man'. I would like to feel like others who accept Him, but I cannot."

"You are fortunate to be a Jew, God's chosen. When Jesus was on earth, He was a Jew, also. Let me give you a Bible to read. Read it and one day Jesus Himself will speak to you, and if you are receptive, He will save you. I am here and my wife Hannah, like you a Jew, are available to talk any time."

Jim took a Bible from the cabinet and handed it to the girl who gripped it close to her chest and left the camper.

"That was your favorite Bible in both Hebrew and English you gave her," Hannah stated.

"I know, and I can get another in Jerusalem. She needed it now," he replied.

Rhoda came to Jim and for the first time sat on his lap and laid her head on his shoulder. "Papa, I think you may be a preacher in the making. You made us all feel better."

For the first time Jim thought Rhoda looked younger than her actual age and for the first time she called him Papa. It was great.

Hannah looked at them and just raised her eyebrow a little and smiled. She began washing up the glasses and cups in order to stow them before landing.

CHAPTER 16

Arrival in The Holy Land

THE PEOPLE IN THE AIRCRAFT were mostly silent as they approached Tel Aviv, each deep in their own thoughts. Harold and Ralph Taylor joined Jim and his little family in the RV as seats with seatbelts were in short supply. They were all buckled in during the smooth landing. Jim had never met the flight crew but knew they were very capable.

The airport in Tel Aviv was busy with aircraft landing and taking off continuously. The big C-5 followed a pickup with a sign on the back stating, 'FOLLOW ME' in several languages. It led them to a remote hanger, obviously for the military.

The unloading of the C-5 could best be described as slightly organized confusion. The troops deplaned first and stood in loose ranks while Israeli soldiers tried, somewhat successfully, to organize them. More people arrived, apparently from passenger aircraft from the US and other countries. It turned into quite a large group of volunteers. Information about them had been sent ahead and names were called, and the new troops slowly separated into groups, presumably dependent on their skill or training. Jim and his family were assigned to a group of others with an unknown or no-skill category. Weapons were inspected to verify they were unloaded to minimize the risk of an accident.

The vehicles were unloaded, and regular troops quickly surveyed them and put them in a line, ready to move out. The RV with Jeep in tow was put to one side, as no-one seemed to know what to do with it. General Steinhoff seemed to be one of several in charge of the confusion. He took Jim and his family along with a dozen in their group of 'unknown' category.

The general addressed Jim with an apparent infield promotion or joke. "Captain Jenkins, your vehicle will be useful for transporting personnel and equipment." He stared at the RV and continued, "It is certainly a beautiful vehicle; I just wish it was painted a more subtle color."

It was true; the RV was painted in bright colors and was very reflective. It would visible for miles in the desert sands of Israel.

"How much weight can the vehicle tow?" the general asked Jim, now apparently a captain.

"It is rated to tow a trailer of ten thousand pounds, or forty-five hundred kilograms. I will need to change the hitch to a ball hitch," Jim replied.

The general did not speak but nodded his head in agreement.

Jim began disconnecting the Jeep while someone got into it and started the engine. He was surprised to see it was Rhoda behind the wheel. She, of course, had no license, but seemed to understand the transmission and quickly backed it up and parked it beside the RV. Jim just stood there for a moment watching her as Hannah came to him and said, "Our daughter is certainly growing up fast." Jim just smiled at the thought, and then removed the tow bar and placed it in a storage bin. He swapped it for a receiver hitch with a two- and one-half inch ball, the largest he had.

An Israeli officer of unknown rank requested Jim drive the RV to a side lot to pick up a trailer. The officer accompanied him to a row of trailers in the back of the hanger. Jim, using the camera on the rear of the motor home, backed up to the trailer without help, impressing the officer. They quickly hooked up the trailer and towed it back to the front of the hanger where a forklift had a large box ready to load. The box was set on the trailer over the wheels. It did not seem to be heavy as the trailer did not sag very much.

Over the next two hours, equipment was issued. Everyone without a uniform was issued one were told to change while standing in ranks. They all stripped off their clothes, down to underwear and put on the uniforms. Hannah was embarrassed but Rhoda seemed to enjoy providing a show which all the men seemed to appreciate. All in all it was time of good humor and something to remember and joke about in the future. Duffle bags were issued with spare clothing and a few toiletries. They put their civilian clothes in the bags and tied them up. A simple tag identified the owner. The bags were then stacked on the trailer in front and behind the box and a couple of men secured them with a net, tied to the trailer.

The group was directed to a mess hall for lunch or dinner. Since it was mid-afternoon it could be considered either. The food was some kind of meat on very hard bread with a cup of something cold, which was quite good. While there, an officer without any display of rank addressed them in English.

"Attention please! You have volunteered to serve in the Israeli army, and you are now soldiers. We understand you are not trained but it is necessary to put you in the field immediately. You are being assigned to an area north of Jericho, along the border with Jordan. We are not expecting a serious invasion in this area, but it is possible. Most likely, small groups may attempt to cross there and get behind our lines. We believe our major attacks will come from the north, from Syria and from the south from Egypt, who seems intent on violating the agreement with us. Your presence will free up some battle-hardened troops to defend our northern and southern borders. Do not believe, however, your positions are without risk. There will certainly be small groups trying to infiltrate and a remote possibility exists of a major invasion from Jordan. If that happens, it will be your job to hold the line until reinforcements arrive to back you up. This afternoon weapons will be issued to those unarmed. We will leave at four hundred—that's in the morning. Rest this afternoon; it will be the last free time for a while."

Leaving the mess hall, Jim, Hannah and Rhoda were joined by Harold and Ralph. The brothers were not to be issued weapons as one was a chaplain and the other a doctor. Jim looked for someone in charge to offer available space in the motor home. A quick look at the activity around the RV indicated no permission was required as all the storage compartments were open and being loaded with boxes. It seemed the motor home was now the property of the Israeli army, which was allright with Jim as he had not initially planned to bring it.

Near the hanger where they had left the C-5, now gone, was a building with the Star of David and a symbol indicating it was a synagogue.

"Let's go in; we may not see one of these for a long time," Hannah said.

A sign hanging on the wall of the building stated in four languages, "All are Welcome Here!"

Going inside, a Jewish service was underway with a Rabbi speaking in Yiddish at the front of the sanctuary. Hannah was looking at a sign in four languages on a door to the side. The English part stated, 'Weddings Performed Here!'

"Will you marry me now?" she asked.

"You know I have always been anxious to marry you," he replied, matter-of-factly.

Rhoda said nothing but jumped for joy and giggled like the little girl she was.

Going into the room they found it was set up for a typical Jewish wedding with a canopy at the front and seating for perhaps twenty people. A woman at a small writing desk looked up smiling and said, "The Rabbi is not available until tomorrow morning. I am very sorry."

"I am trained as a Rabbi and am now a Messianic Pastor; I would be honored to conduct a wedding for these two friends of mine," Harold Taylor said to the woman.

She started to ask if he was licensed in Israel to conduct weddings but thought 'what difference does it make.' "That will be fine," she said.

The wedding was simple, with Ralph Taylor standing by Jim, and Rhoda by Hannah. Hannah was given a large silk scarf to cover her hair and drape down her back, the only formal addition to her fatigues. Pastor Harold took a small Bible from his pocket, and opened it, but never read from it. He had the words memorized.

He ended the brief ceremony with, "Now my dear new friends, it is my pleasure to pronounce you man and wife. Jim, you may kiss your bride."

Cheers went up all around them. When they turned, they found the room filled with people from their flight who happily congratulated them.

Rhoda was saying, "Mom and Pop got married!" causing a lot of confused looks in the group.

The woman at the desk was filling out a marriage document and asked Harold to sign as Rabbi.

Hannah asked her, "Would you put the date September 7, this year, when we actually made the commitment to each other and to God?"

The woman just glanced at her and complied, thinking, 'this union is probably not legal in Israel anyway'.

For Hannah, not having a Rabbi or a minister perform the ceremony didn't bother her. They had committed to God, which was all she needed. However, she knew their arrangement had bothered Jim, so she did this for him. It was nice.

Wandering around the big air base they came across a store, kind of a PX where they picked up a few things to add to the stores in the motor home. Coffee and snacks had been depleted on the flight from the US. Returning to the RV, a military sewage truck had finished emptying the tanks on the motor home and a small fuel truck had topped off the fuel. The motor home was ready to go.

Jim, Hannah and Rhoda spent the night in the RV alone. The Taylor brothers went to the barracks. Going to bed early, they expected the next day to start very early. Hannah and Jim enjoyed their first night as a married couple, with their teenage daughter in the bunk at the other end of the RV, not a typical arrangement for newlyweds.

CHAPTER 17

Ongoing Conflict in the USA

WHILE JIM AND HIS FAMILY, with the others called by God to go to Israel, were in the air, the US was invaded again, this time in southern California. A large number, perhaps a thousand terrorists, most from Africa, had come into northern Mexico. They had, with the government's help, rounded up Mexican civilians to occupy the state of California and claim it for Mexico. The group led by six Mexican army tanks, had crossed the border and proceeded north. Following the tanks were the foreign terrorists and members of the Mexican Army. Staying east of the heavily populated coastal cities, they went through many smaller towns and cities with heavy Hispanic populations. Meeting no resistance, many in these towns joined the march. The border patrol was no match for the invaders and vacated their posts. With the lack of effective communications, a defense could not be mounted.

Captain Masters with his force, mostly militia from Colorado, Arizona and New Mexico, were also no match, but formed a defensive line to meet the slowly moving invaders. He regretted losing the two hundred men and women, including Jim and his family, who went to Israel. Clearly, they had been called by God, and in any case, he had no control over the decisions made by volunteers. Masters had added more people and vehicles along the way, most of them hunters and target shooters.

Ahead of the invaders were refugees fleeing from towns and farms. Some were in older vehicles and farm equipment unaffected by the EMP attack. The majority of the people, however, were walking. Many pushed wheelbarrows or pulled toy wagons with a few possessions. It looked like pictures he had seen of civilians during World War II; it was heartbreaking.

The captain established checkpoints for the refugees fleeing north in an attempt to check for weapons or explosives and identify terrorists among them. It was impossible. The evacuees were of all races and although they had few possessions, searching them was impossible. Many Hispanics were in the group, people who did not want to live under Mexican rule and believed the US would drive the invaders back.

A young man requested to see the commander and was brought to Captain Masters.

"Captain, I am Hernando Garza, mayor of El Centro. I am pleased to finally meet the US Army who will defend us," the man stated with a big smile.

"Well, Mr. Mayor, we are not the US Army but are primarily a militia group from the southern states east of here. I see in all these people coming north many able bodied men and women. Why are they not defending themselves and their country?" Captain Masters asked, in an unfriendly tone.

Hernando, who was shocked that anyone would suggest the people could actually do something to defend themselves, replied, "This army coming has weapons and tanks, we have nothing. None of our people have guns. We are defenseless. It is the army's job to defend us." The man paused and sensing Captain Masters was getting agitated at him, continued. "Sir, the State of California decided long ago to not allow weapons of war into the state. This is for safety to prevent disruptions to society."

The captain, indicating with his hand the long line of refugees, questioned, "How is that working for you?"

The discussion with the two men was interrupted by one of the militia who interjected, "Captain we have found a trailer filled with marijuana and what we think is cocaine."

Hernando with raised voice, countered, "Captain, the medical supplies are from our legal dispensary! We have many people with medical issues requiring these medications!"

"You supply cocaine? Are you a drug smuggler?" The captain yelled back, now angry.

Hernando lowered his head and almost whispered, "We do have an arrangement. It brings in funding."

"Dump it and burn it!" Captain Masters commanded his soldier.

"No, please!"

"Get him out of here! If he interferes, shoot him! My God are these people really part of the United States?" the captain queried, ending the meeting.

By the time Captain Masters was in position to intercept the Mexican invasion, two US aircraft carriers were off the coast of California. Their aircraft had attacked the Mexican airbases, destroying the civilian and military aircraft there. They had been unopposed as Mexico had not anticipated the attack. The aircraft carriers were now in a position to defend their homeland. The pilots, unused to defending the homeland since the United States had not been invaded in their lifetime, were anxious.

From the air the invaders looked like a flood, like a river of people moving north. Leading the mass was the six tanks and additional support trucks. Most of the people were on foot, so the progress was slow. There was a group of black clad men, well-armed, leading a portion of the group. They were shouting words of encouragement to those following, mostly who were unarmed. When they came to a city or village, the churches were burned and anyone in the structures killed. The rest of the city would be left unharmed.

Occasionally residents asked to join the troops with the promise that when they took the state everyone would be given a mansion in Beverly Hills. It would be a life of luxury and plenty. Most of those who joined were young men looking for adventure.

The first aircraft came from the south. A helicopter hovering out of sight with just its antenna over a hill sent targeting information to the aircraft which locked its missiles on the six tanks. The aircraft screamed over the hordes of people and launched six missiles destroying the six tanks in the first pass. The explosions filled the sky with smoke and fire. For the first time the people thought they might not have been told the complete truth. Two more aircraft followed, dropping fragmentary bombs. These bombs, developed in Vietnam, exploded one hundred feet in the air and sprayed the ground with sharp fragments. The bombs were not effective against armored vehicles but deadly to troops, or in this case, civilians. The bombs were dropped along the length of the mass of people moving behind the tanks and armed men. The result was utter devastation. The dead and dying numbered in the thousands. Most survivors had been wounded.

Captain Masters saw the explosions from a distance. His vehicles, flying huge American flags, approached the site. The dead lay everywhere and the few alive were trying to help the more seriously injured. Many sat crying, holding dead loved ones. The captain had seen atrocities in foreign lands, never on this scale and never in America. The carnage was so horrific that McMasters and his men became sick with many throwing up. This was a major disaster. The pilots of the aircraft would later testify they had seen weapons throughout the mass of people and concluded they were attacking an invading army. In some ways they were right, in some, not so right. They were not charged with any crime and, in fact, given medals.

So, the invasion of California from Mexico was crushed with a very heavy loss of life.

Navy personnel, now soldiers, from San Diego, arrived in a variety of vehicles. They reported the military, Navy and Marines, had protected the city from invasion but were still rooting out snipers. The city itself and the harbor were secure and would be completely cleared in a few days.

On his own, Captain Masters took his men south without resistance and entered Mexico. He went to the Gulf of California and set up a defensive parameter giving the US a harbor on the Gulf. Mexico could lose territory instead of gaining the southern states as promised.

The captain left a detachment of men to guard the new southern border and went north with the majority of the men. Word had come that Sacramento was in flames. He confiscated all the vehicles which were operational and raced north. Sacramento lay in ruins. Many of the leaders of the state had been publicly hanged as the state capital building burned. Bands of people, many illegal aliens, roamed the streets shooting at everyone who didn't look like them. The weapons, most of them AK-47 fully automatic rifles, had been smuggled into the country over several months. The men firing them were untrained, so they rarely hit their targets. The populous, being unarmed, could do nothing but flee. Captain Masters arrived in a fully armed Humvee. A large group of men charged him in an open street, with most of the shots fired in the air. The heavy machine gun on the Humvee very quickly cleared the street, leaving it littered with dead terrorists. It would take weeks to clear the city, one building at a time.

The war was not over. Armed terrorists were entrenched in the surrounding cities. They had infiltrated unchecked during previous months and had taken over neighborhoods of several cities, roaming the streets causing havoc. In San Francisco a huge atrocity occurred. A group of gay men and women in their outlandish outfits gathered to welcome the black clad terrorists, crazily thinking any anti-establishment group would befriend them. Word had spread about a celebration in one of the big open arenas. They came by the thousands, a very colorful group. After a massive group had assembled, the exits were blocked, and the entire throng massacred. The state was in chaos and unable to restore local services and reestablish food supplies.

The effect of the terrorism was regional. In Oklahoma City, a city full of independent thinkers, a church was attacked. One of the terrorists, a six-foot four-inch man clad in black, came through a back door and nearly knocked down a seventy-year-old woman who was tending the nursery. He screamed 'Allah Akbar!' and went on toward the sanctuary carrying an AK-47. The woman pulled a small thirty-two caliber pistol from her purse and shot the man in the back six times. The small caliber bullets hit nearly every vital organ in the big man. When he fell, she went over to him and kicked the rifle away, as she had seen Joe Friday do on TV, and bent down to the man. She quickly told him about Jesus and how He would save him if he would only accept Him. It was to no avail as the man died cursing the woman and her God. He would immediately regret it when he stood before the same God, she told him about. Three other terrorists came into the church through the front door also shouting 'Allah Akbar'. The congregation, now alerted by the shots from the older woman, was ready. Twenty-three men and women in the church shot them down before they could fire their machine guns. Two people were wounded by friendly fire. The Imam of the local mosque was identified as the driver of the van who delivered the men and had waited to pick them up. His previous claims of Islam as a peaceful religion fell on deaf ears. He was locked up for life.

Finally, the Federal Government in Washington woke up and revoked the visas of anyone involved, or related to those involved in terrorism, and they were deported. The mosque in Oklahoma City burned to the ground and the Muslim garb, commonly seen disappeared.

Captain Masters' group continued to grow as more and more volunteered. Splinter groups also formed with some of them no better than criminal gangs who had no reservations about shooting people to steal whatever they wanted. The situation was volatile and would be for some time.

The plan to disable the United States was going exactly as planned. The invaders who died on the field were part of the plan.

CHAPTER 18

The Eastern Front in Israel

IN SPITE OF THE FRIGID temperature, Jim awoke early as usual and got his family up and off to the dining hall well before daylight. The entire airfield was brightly lit with spotlights. There was apparently no fear by the Israelis of air attack. Jim hoped they were right. The dining hall was overcrowded; another group of volunteers had arrived and were eating, still dressed in civilian clothes. Those who had arrived in the C-5 in Jim's group had sand colored fatigues and were armed. With their duffle bags packed on the trailer, he guessed the new comers must have slept in their clothes or underwear. They found the Taylor brothers and joined them at their table, crowding in. The food was hot and good.

Over the din of noise in the dining hall an announcement could just barely be understood. "The troops in Group 70, assigned to General Dementri, will assemble near the trucks, at the hanger where you arrived. Prepare to leave immediately. Do not delay."

Being in group 70 was news to Jim, if it had been announced previously, he had missed it. In any case, it was a good number. It was still very dark when the group got together. Standing with hands in their pockets and shoulders hunched over due to the cold, conversations were in subdued voices. Anticipation ran high. The company assignments were made according to aircraft of arrival. The C-5 passengers were assigned to Group 70, subgroup BB. This didn't seem to be normal military procedure, but it was easy to remember. The officer in charge of their subgroup was introduced as Captain Glaser. The captain was a man about fifty, a quite pleasant military man. In spite of his mild mannerisms it became clear he was a no-nonsense man in charge. Jim liked this guy!

Captain Glaser took his troops, numbering around one hundred, off to the side and addressed them. "Gentlemen and ladies, soldiers of Israel, we will defend the east border of Israel. Group 70 is to defend the section from the north end of the West Bank, south to Qumran at the Dead Sea. Our assigned location as subgroup BB is the mid-section of this line. All of this territory is in the West Bank. Our information is that most of the residents have moved from the West Bank into Jordan, but we cannot assume there are no enemies in our territory. There may be pockets of agitators to our west, behind us. Our subgroup will follow Subgroup AA, assigned to the northern most section. Our group will be proceeded by two Merkava Tanks; following them will be the armored Humvees. The open trucks will come next, along with the bright motor home. Our subgroup will end with additional Humvees. Group CC will follow us. Each vehicle has been assigned a number displayed on the dash and another attached to the rear of the vehicle. Please check those numbers and fall into numerical order. If a vehicle breaks down, try to get if off the road and you will be picked up by the last vehicles. We are not expecting an attack but be on guard. We will leave in ten minutes."

The captain repeated the message in Hebrew, which seemed to take very little time.

Jim went to the motor home and checked the hitch for a third time. He walked around looking at each tire, opened the door and got in the driver's seat. Hannah was already in the passenger seat and Rhoda sat on the floor between them. Jim glanced back and saw that most of their passengers were young attractive women.

"They are nurses assigned to our subgroup," Hannah remarked as she observed him while he looked over the group. "Several of them were at our wedding," she continued, smiling, reminding him he was a married man.

The floor was covered with boxes with red crosses on them. Jim thought the RV was most certainly overloaded, but on smooth roads it should be allright. In the rear of the motor home were the Taylor brothers, sitting on boxes. They were chatting up the young nurses and all were having a great time. Jim, laughing to himself, hoped the Reverend Harold Taylor remembered his profession.

Jim put on his tactical vest and got his AR-15 and laid it nearby. He put in a clip but didn't put a bullet in the chamber. Hannah and Rhoda strapped on their pistols. None of the nurses were armed.

The truck Jim was assigned to follow was a cargo truck loaded with boxes of equipment. It pulled out and he followed. The convoy drove from the airfield and onto city streets. The local policemen cleared the roads and were stationed at intersections, so they proceeded without stopping. The streets were lined with cars. If there was a war these people didn't seem to be aware of it. Leaving the city of Tel Aviv, the speed increased to one hundred kilometers, or about sixty miles per hour.

The distance to the West Bank was only twenty-five kilometers and took less than one half hour. There was a large wall Israel had erected to stop terror attacks. The gate was open and guarded by Israeli soldiers. The convey was waved through. At that point the two tanks joined the and led the convoy, slowing them to the speed of the tanks. The machine guns on the tanks and Humvee's were manned in case of attack. The situation changed immediately after entering the West Bank. All appeared quiet. The villages were completely deserted. When passing through the ancient city of Ramallah, they saw not a single person. The stores were boarded up and not even a dog was in sight. This big city was deserted.

"Israel will be insane to let all these people back in if we win this war. It was a big mistake in 1968 to give this territory back as well as Temple Mount," Ralph Taylor whispered in Jim's ear after working his way to the front of the RV.

"I think things will be different this time. The world will again make demands from Israel in order to achieve peace. In '68 Israel gave up a lot and did not get peace; I doubt they will make the same mistake again," Jim answered.

Those in the motor home got very quiet as the convoy slowed when approaching the Jordan River. Across the river, east side, the lovely farms could be seen covering the gentle sloping hills. It was peaceful and beautiful, a view the younger Jewish generation had not seen. The Palestinians in the West Bank had not farmed the west side of the river, even though the land was rich.

Jim was very uncomfortable. The entire line of vehicles was in open view and in range of snipers, who could be anywhere in those hills. No shots were fired as the convoy split with some going north and some south. Along the shoreline Israeli soldiers were dug in. These were the troops they would replace. Jim was directed to park behind a bank a short distance from the river. The RV was fairly well out of view from Jordanians. He felt safer here, but if they were overrun there wasn't an escape route for the vehicle to take. Everyone unloaded and Jim set the jacks to level the unit.

Captain Glaser came by and nodded his approval of the location of the RV and directed the medical personnel to set up a tent in front of the RV for a field hospital. All hoped it would not be needed. Apparently, the motor home would be a support vehicle for the hospital.

Jim and his little family were assigned to a small bunker remaining from one of the many previous wars. It had a long open station for several shooters and a small cave like structure. Concrete had been used to construct the bunker which was still fairly well intact. It seemed several of these bunkers existed along the borders of Israel.

Most of the other shooting stations were open pits. Most of them were full of sand and other debris. It seemed Captain Glaser had a motive for assigning Jim and his two female companions to the nicer bunker. They immediately began cleaning it out. Using brooms, a shovel, and other supplies from the motor home, the women cleaned out buckets of sand, along with remains of animals and plants. Jim carried the buckets and dumped them over the front of the shooting station adding to the protection from hostile fire. It took most of the day to clear the bunker, which turned out to be roomy, for a bunker, that is. In the back of the covered portion was an exit which led to a shallow ravine. If they kept low, a person could go from the bunker to the hospital tents without being seen from Jordan. A lot of thought had gone into the construction of this unit.

"If we had beds, running water and a bathroom, we could live here," Rhoda quipped.

Jim looked at the four stone and concrete walls and thought, 'The requirements for living conditions for her have certainly deteriorated in the last weeks.'

Several days went by with no activity from the east. The IDF (Israel Defense Force) had a drone capable of flying several miles into Jordan to detect activity over the mountains. It was quiet for the present. In fact, even the expected attack in the north had not occurred. Jim had noticed several old tanks on the hill behind them. He questioned Captain Glaser and was told they had been abandoned in the war in 1968, and were useless. Jim suggested if Israeli flags were flown on them if might confuse the Jordanian army as to their location. The captain did not think it would work, but saw no harm in doing so, so the flags were placed on two of the old tanks.

Laura, the young nurse to whom Jim had given his Bible came and confessed a belief in Jesus. She was saved amid joy from some of the group, but distain in the practicing Jewish members. Harold Taylor, the nearest Christian minister, took her and four others down to the Jordan River and baptized them. It was somewhat of a risk as they were completely open to sniper fire from Jordan. The next day he repeated the process with twenty-three others. Captain Glaser then intervened due to the risk. He directed them to another location upriver which had a little better protection from sniper fire. Pastor Harold, along with two other ministers, baptized people every day.

The whole exercise of them being there was turning into a vacation. If it were not so cold, Jim was sure the young people would be striping down and lying in the sun. Rhoda and Laura became close friends, even with the difference in age. They and Hannah spent time discussing a variety of things in the sun in the bunker. Laura was interested in what it was like to live in the US, and told of conditions in Israel. Both of the young women questioned Hannah about what it was like being married. Even whispering as they were, Jim on watch nearby could hear some of the conversations. He wisely pretended he didn't hear anything.

There was peace, until there wasn't. The drone gave a warning. Trucks pulling artillery and several tanks were climbing the far side of the mountain, coming toward them. The Israeli front went on complete alert and a request for air support was sent up the chain.

It was the fifth day of their assignment when the barrage began. All the fire was over their heads on the ridge where the old tanks were located, a natural defensive position. The hospital staff, having no patients yet, came crowding into the more secure bunker. It was the first time any of them had been in such an attack. The concussion of the explosions, even though not very close, was painful and almost deafening. A few of the inexperienced warriors began to cry, with a fear they had never before experienced.

Looking through binoculars, Jim saw the enemy tanks headed toward the Jordan River, shooting as they came. Troops on foot were following. This looked like a real attack, not the diversionary one for which they had planned.

The two Israeli tanks, latest design from the US, were far superior to the Jordanian tanks. Being dug in they were practically invisible. They took out six of the enemy tanks in rapid succession with just six shots. The assault slowed but did not stop.

Jim began firing his .338 rifle when the attackers were about a mile away, the extreme of his effective range. Hannah watched through the spotting scope and tried unsuccessfully, to help him correct his fire. A retired IDF soldier manning a big Browning fifty caliber machine gun opened up. It could easily hit targets at the one-mile range. A lot of ammo was fired for a few hits, but enough to slow the enemy.

The front was very wide, at least four or five miles. The few tanks the Israeli's had been too far apart to cover the whole battlefield. To cover the gap there were teams of troops with handheld missiles, very effective at short ranges. As the tanks approached the river, the missiles took them out. Seeing the majority of their tanks in flames and the heavy fire from rifles and machine guns, the forward motion of the attack was broken. Many of the enemy troops dug in near the river and the rest fled. The remainder of the day was spent sniping at each other. The Jordanian artillery fire had stopped when it looked like they were ready to cross the river into Israel. The firing resumed when the attack stalled. Fortunately, the Jordanian artillery was not very accurate, thanks to the mercies of the Lord God. The requested aircraft were slow in coming and when it arrived it was a single aircraft, but quite effective. Flying over the front, it took out the artillery on the east side of the mountains, halting the bombardment.

The attack on the eastern front was, as Israel predicted, designed to draw some of the Israeli troops away from the main attacks coming from the north and south. Jim and the other green troops from the US had, to some extent, nullified their plans as the front line Israeli troops were free to fight the major battles.

A diversion or not, the casualties in the attacking Jordanian forces were heavy compared to the green troops wounded and killed, but the little hospital quickly became filled to overflowing. The bedroom in the RV became an operating room for the most seriously injured. It was cleaner and had better lighting. Even though they tried to keep it clean, the mattress became blood stained and the interior of the unit was contaminated and damaged. It was a small price to pay.

Just as quickly as it started, the conflict was over. The badly damaged Jordanian troops pulled out. At the command of someone with little or no battleground experience, the move to retreat during daylight hours made the Jordanians sitting ducks. Many more were injured by the accurate sniper fire that rained down on them as they pulled back.

After one day of quiet on the front, General Steinhoff called a meeting. It took place in Subgroup BB as they were centrally located. Captain Glaser invited Jim to attend, just because he was there and convenient.

When everyone had gathered and quieted down, the general addressed them.

"Gentlemen, we have done well. As far as we can tell, the Jordanians did not intend to cross the Jordan River as they had no equipment to do so. This was a diversion, a costly one for them, but a diversion. They apparently thought our forces would be badly damaged and ineffective. They were wrong. With their withdrawal we have an unforeseen opportunity. Our drones have found no forces east of us. The enemy has apparently have moved all their troops to the south where they are waging a strong offensive against Jerusalem. I have requested permission from Headquarters to move into Jordan and then south to flank their army. I have received permission and a portable bridge is on the way. We will cross into Jordan tonight and hopefully surprise them. This is a great opportunity given to us. Get ready to move and rest as much as possible for we will be very busy for the next few days."

The general then gave a shout in Hebrew, which most understood, and many shouted back joyfully. Apparently, some type of war cry.

The bridge arrived but Jim doubted it could support the tanks, or even the trucks. It consisted of small floats which supported steel rails tied together, and to the shore with cables. It went up quickly with IDF engineers. When completed, men walked back and forth on it, demonstrating great courage. A group of men were sent across it to provide security to the east side of the river.

The crossing commenced at dusk. The first big tank rolled to the bridge and with great courage drove onto it. The pontoons sank until only the very tops were visible. The tank rolled off the other side to a great cheer. After this first test things moved more quickly. Only one vehicle at a time was on the bridge but there was no delay, when one rolled off the far end another rolled on the west end. In two hours, all the vehicles were across.

Jim, plus his two companions, were assigned to drive a Humvee. Apparently, he had been promoted to a real soldier. One of the nurses drove the motor home. This was a real military convoy with men and women who had actually been in combat. It helped that Israeli aircraft were providing cover. The group had also grown in size. There were now perhaps four or five hundred soldiers and a couple of small artillery pieces. In addition, they were supported with ten additional armored transports and Humvee's. As armies go it was a very small but substantial force, and with God's presence, they could take on anyone.

A small force remained on the Israeli side of the border in case a second attack came. If so, the general could return quickly. Going up the slope in Jordan, unopposed across fields, they came to the north-south highway number 65. It was a nicely paved road and the convoy turned south on it, moving as fast as the tanks could maneuver. They went through a small farm community and the residents ran out to wave and cheer them on, thinking it was a Jordanian force. When they saw the Star of David on the vehicles, their demeanor changed instantly. These people would certainly notify the Jordanian military of Israeli presence.

The landscape turned from fields of crops to desert as the altitude quickly dropped further below sea level. As they approached the large city of Alwestah the tanks left the road, as did the Humvee's armed with the heavy machine guns. They spread in a line across the desert. In the city was a major traffic jam with trucks, cars and donkeys stalled on the main road west to one of the few bridges over the Jordan River. The traffic consisted of Jordanian military vehicles and trucks carrying troops all congested to a point they could hardly move. In another situation it would have been humorous. Men were running everywhere shouting to get someone to move. The Israelis practically drove into the town before anyone seemed to even notice them.

General Steinhoff, over the radio, ordered everyone to concentrate fire on the military vehicles. The tank guns roared, and it seemed the entire town burst into flames as fuel tankers and trucks with ammunition exploded. Then the fifty caliber machine guns on the Humvees opened up. Bullets went through houses and trucks, neither of which provided much cover. People fell like flies, as the pathetic saying goes. Several Jordanian soldiers jumped from their trucks and valiantly formed a defensive line, but they were no match for the tanks and armored Humvees. As if to stomp on someone who is already down, the fighter jets strafed the town and the road, all the way to the bridge. The devastation was complete. The firing stopped when white flags began waving all along the line. Men arose from the carnage with their hands up, hundreds of them. In addition, there was a huge number of wounded in the city and all along the road.

General Steinhoff proved his leadership capabilities as he quickly assigned about fifty men to guard the prisoners and another dozen or so to help the medical staff. The Jordanian medical personnel were identified and aided the Jews as they worked together to set up a quick field hospital. The wounded were moved by prisoners and cared for as well possible under such conditions. Historically, the Jordanians had not been hostile to the Jews thus the prisoners cooperated and some even apologized for attacking Israel. It had been a total victory with not a single Israeli causality, praise be to the Lord God. Rhoda, greatly disturbed by the huge number of injured people, stayed with the nurses, the first time she had been separated from Hannah.

The general didn't spend more than an hour setting up the prison camp when he commanded the group move west to another conflict on the Israeli side of the border. They reached the bridge in less than an hour. It was unguarded, another oversight on the part of the Jordanian Command.

The army roared into the ancient city of Jericho. The Jordanian troops there did not oppose them and seemed to think they were friendly reserve troops. For some reason they were unaware that their troops had been destroyed or captured in Alwestah. Didn't these men have radios? None of them seemed to know what was going on behind their lines. The main facility in Jericho was a large modern field hospital caring for wounded soldiers, Jordanian and Israeli, both being cared for equally well. In addition, the Jews captured the main Jordanian command post housing the highest-ranking officers in the Jordanian army, all without firing a shot. This conflict was beginning to look like a minor disagreement between brothers, except, of course, for the hundreds of dead and wounded.

Again, leaving a few men to guard the prisoners, the army moved toward the front lines, now in Jerusalem. To Jim this seemed very strange. The enemy seemed completely oblivious to the fact, that Israel was fighting back. Did they really think Israel would just run away and jump into the ocean?

Jim was driving the Humvee with a retired Israeli soldier in the right seat, a gunner on the roof and several men in the back. Hannah was sitting just behind him. One of the young women, a medic, was with them and Jim heard her say, "Hannah, are you all right?"

"What's wrong?" Jim asked, louder than he intended.

"Hannah? Hannah, are you allright?" The young woman asked again.

"I, I am fine, I think," Hannah stated in a very shaky voice.

Jim pulled to side of the road, a violation of his orders.

"Take over!" He told the man in the right seat. The man complied and the vehicle soon joined the convoy a few vehicles further back.

Jim moved back to Hannah and squeezed into the seat beside her. Holding her tightly he asked, "Hannah, what is wrong?" She felt warm, too warm and soaking with sweat.

Hannah replied very weakly, "Jim there was a woman back in that town with a little baby in her arms, both dead. What are we doing, why are we even here?"

With that statement, Hannah passed out.

The young medic asked Jim, "Could she be pregnant?"

"I am not sure, but we think so!" he answered.

Hannah rallied and with fear in her voice said, "Jim, am I going to lose your baby, our baby?"

"I don't know what is wrong but we need to get her out of the war zone. It may be just the pregnancy; it makes some women extra sensitive to trauma, and we certainly have seen a lot of it. She may just need rest," the young medic stated, not convincing Jim.

General Steinhoff's voice came over the radio in the vehicle, "We are approaching the rear of the Jordanian forces, the artillery. We will spread out and attack them and attempt to save some of the artillery."

The convoy stopped and Jim stated, "I'll get out here. Good luck!"

Without waiting for a response, he opened the door and stepped out of the Humvee with his rifle over his arm and carrying Hannah.

He walked a few feet, and in the dust obstructing the drivers view, nearly got run over by his own motor home. The RV was covered with dirt, the windshield was cracked and there were at least two bullet holes in the side near the roof. It was worse for wear.

The door swung open with a bang and the young nurse, Laura, jumped out.

"Jim, what is wrong?" she nearly shouted.

"I don't know but something is not right," Jim replied.

"We're stopping just down the road; get her inside and we'll check her out."

Jim got her inside with difficulty, the RV being full of people and medical equipment.

Hannah, beloved by all, was treated like a queen. She was placed on the rear bed, the one used for surgery. Two doctors, one being Ralph Taylor, began an examination of her. He first checked to see if she was bleeding, a sign of miscarriage. She was not. A nurse began taking her vitals.

Jim was sent to the front of the RV to get him out of the way. When they reached the location for the next field hospital, he helped unload the supplies.

After what seemed like a long time, Ralph came to him and stated, "Jim I think Hannah will be fine. She is exhausted and dehydrated. We will give her fluids and let her rest. Understand, she is tough, but also a pregnant woman and not a hardened soldier. She shows no sign of losing the baby now, but of course there are no guarantees. You should do your duty and leave her in our hands and in the hands of God who is in control."

So, Jim slipped in, kissed Hannah on the forehead as she slept, gathered his gear and left for the front, wherever it was.

Jim caught a ride to his assigned Humvee in a pickup, which was trailing the convoy. The armored vehicles spread out and approached the Jordanian artillery units from their rear. They drove to within a hundred yards of the big guns before the Jordanians seemed to notice them. It was amazing how a military unit could have no guard at their rear. The artillery unit had a command tent which directed the fire of the big guns. The commanders looked up and seeing they were under the guns of the Jews, simply got up and raised their arms in surrender. The rest of the gunners did the same. The Jordanian artillery company was captured without firing a shot.

The prisoners were taken to aside with a few men to guard them. The command tent had detailed maps of the battlefield ahead. The Israelis, using their own radios, contacted their counterparts defending Jerusalem and received the location of the enemy them. With that information and the captured maps, they redirected the big guns and fired a single burst of six shots. The Jordanian radio in the tent came alive with an excited voice, "Cease fire you are hitting our own troops!!!"

General Steinhoff replied on the radio, "This is General Steinhoff of the Israeli Army, we are in control of your artillery and you are surrounded. There is no further need for loss of life. Surrender now and let us stop this foolishness."

There was a pause on the other end as the commander of the Jordanian forces was brought to the radio. "This is Mohammad Hurtol, Commander. We have met, General. It seems you Jews have an unbelievable ability to survive. We, of course, surrender without terms as I know we will be well treated. I would like to personally apologize for this action. I never agreed with it."

The front-line Jordanian soldiers, now prisoners, came marching out carrying their wounded. It was a strange surrender; some of the stretchers had a Jordanian on one end and a Jewish soldier on the other. In other cases, groups of men from both sides were walking together, chatting like best of friends.

Thus ended the war in the east with Jordan.

The prisoner of war camp for the Jordanians was unusual. Instead of a ten-foot barbed wire fence around it, the boundary was marked with plastic ribbon tied between trucks and sometimes just posts. Anyone could easily step over it or raise it up and walk under it. There were guards, of course, but they were fairly relaxed. Trucks came from Jordan bringing supplies and sometimes even family members of the prisoners. The prisoners were supported by both Israeli and Jordanian supplies. It was strange indeed.

Jim caught a ride back to the hospital tent and looked for his two ladies. Hannah wasn't in a bed but helping a doctor perform some type of surgery on a wounded man. She had on sterile gloves and was handing him instruments, like a nurse. The doctor spoke to her in excellent English. She looked like she felt fine. The doctor was a Jordanian from the hospital in Amman and the patient an Israeli soldier.

Rhoda was on the other side of the tent holding the hand of a young Jordanian soldier. She was speaking to him, words he probably did not understand but seemed content to listen and look at her. Another doctor, working near Rhoda, was changing the dressing of the young man's stump of his left leg. When asked, Rhoda would hand him something but always held the young man's hand. It was a touching scene.

Both of his women were still in their fatigues and both were blood splattered, as were the doctors. For the first time Jim noticed Hannah had a small baby bump. Jim just stood there for a moment and basked in his love for both of these women.

Hannah finished her duties with the patient and saw Jim standing at the entrance to the tent. She came to him taking off her gloves with a big smile.

"I've heard the plan for our group is move north this evening. You should stay with the medical people. I'm afraid your episodes could be a sign of something serious and to be around doctors might be a good idea," Jim said as softy as he could.

Without touching him with her hands Hannah rose up on her toes and kissed him. "This medical unit is going with you. All these patients are going to hospitals in Amman or Jerusalem. So you can't get rid of me yet, and I am fine," she said with a smile.

"You are not fine and I am afraid for you and our son. Maybe you should go the hospital in Jerusalem."

"No, both of us will go with you and stay with the medical units. I think we can be of some help here, and we may be having a girl," she stated.

Rhoda had joined them by this time and added, "Dad, we really do seem to be helping here and they are really shorthanded."

Jim kissed Hannah on the lips and Rhoda on the forehead. Directing his comment to Hannah, he said, "All right but please take care of yourself. What you are carrying is important, but not as important as you are."

CHAPTER 19

War in the North

Gᴇɴᴇʀᴀʟ Sᴛᴇɪɴʜᴏғғ ᴄᴀʟʟᴇᴅ ʜɪs ᴏғғɪᴄᴇʀs together to give new directions. They were joined by regular Israeli soldiers from Jerusalem, now without a battle to fight. The general, even though retired from active duty was the ranking officer and took charge of the meeting.

"Gentlemen, Jordan has surrendered, and we have accepted. The conflict with them is over, but be on guard, not all of their units may have received the message, and some may choose to disregard it. Do not fire unless fired upon.

Group 70 will move north along Highway 65 and engage the Syrians now attacking the Golan Heights. The prisoners will be guarded by units from Jerusalem. Our injured will be transported back to the hospitals in Jerusalem which, at this point, are still untouched. Additional supplies are available. We will pull out at dusk; everyone should eat and relax. It will be a long night and an active day tomorrow."

Jim met Hannah and Rhoda at the tent where rations were distributed. It was military something and they ate, thankful for it. The RV was loaded for the trip with medical supplies and nurses, so they relaxed in the shade of a truck. Jim actually dozed.

Hannah got a seat in the RV, something Jim wanted her to have. She would be near the best doctors in the group, and the RV would be more comfortable. Rhoda stayed with Jim who rode in a Humvee. She now had an M-16 rifle and several clips in a vest. She had copied the men and wore the rifle across her chest, held by a sling. These, along with her pistol, made her look more like a seriously dangerous person, not at all like a person her age should be. Jim wondered what these events were doing to the young people in both Israel and the United States.

The army now had six of the latest model tanks from the US leading the convoy along highway 65. Moving at sixty miles an hour on the smooth highway, they reached the eastern shore of the Sea of Galilee in an hour and a half. This is the area were Jesus drove the demons from the man living in the wild into the pigs. They didn't see any pigs but there did seem to be several crazy people along the road. They lined the road and threw rocks at the vehicles, cracking a few windshields. The soldiers ignored them.

They slowed as they climbed the Golan Heights and saw bombed vehicles and other signs battle. The lead vehicles made radio contact with the Israeli defenders on the heights and began to spread out in battle formation. The enemy ahead was a mixture of Syrian, Iranian and Iraqi forces, along with many other groups including the remnants of ISIS. Many of these groups were ancestral enemies of each other but had joined to fight Israel. Unlike the Jordanians, these fighters were vicious and had no affection or mercy for anyone.

Group 70 moved further east along the border of Jordan and Syria. They were in the open but didn't attract any unwanted attention. Perhaps they were mistaken for a Jordanian group. The convoy drove past an enormous UN refugee camp consisting of hundreds of white tents. There were a few visible UN troops who stood and watched the convoy pass.

The plan was simple; Jim's unit would move northeast and then turn northwest to move behind the Syrian forces attacking the Golan

Heights. If the plan worked, the Syrian's would have Israeli troops in front and behind them. If the Syrians had troops in reserve, Group 70 could be in the same trap. It was a risk; even with air surveillance they could not be sure. The medical personnel quickly set up a field hospital as the combat units moved on.

Group 70 moved northwest behind the enemy troops and attacked them from the rear. General Steinhoff hedged his bet a little by having two tanks and six Humvees, along with fifty soldiers, to protect his rear. The remaining forces attacked the Syrians from their rear. Rhoda fought right alongside of Jim. She shot her M-16 with surprising accuracy while Jim, using his sniper rifle, took out the snipers and more distant targets on the Syrian side.

The battle was furious. The Syrians, unlike the Jordanians, fought to the death. The attack was less than stellar because the Israelis on the Golan Heights were so badly hurt they could not mount an offensive. In fact, they were very close to being overrun. Raging throughout the day, causalities mounted on both sides. The Syrians surrendered only when their ammunition was exhausted as Group 70 was blocking the resupply and reinforcements.

Just as the fighting was winding down and Jim was unable to find additional targets, a strange feeling came over him. It was as though a soft hug enveloped him and a quiet voice in his head said, "We love you and will wait for you."

As mysteriously as the first emotional sensation had come, as second wave, one of dread and fear, came over him. Rhoda exchanged looks with him; she had felt something, also. "What just happened?" she said as she came near.

"I'm not sure, but something has occurred. I'm afraid of what this may mean," he answered.

Even though they were both exhausted, Rhoda and Jim began running back to the hospital tents. A truck picked them up, carrying them the last few miles. As they rode, Jim tried to convince himself everything would be allright, but the feeling was something else.

As they got off the truck at the tent, Harold Taylor, the pastor, came to meet them. The look on his face said it all. "Jim, I am so sorry. They think it was a stroke; she died peacefully."

It was like Jim had been hit with a hammer. Harold held him so he would not fall and helped him into the tent. Hannah was lying adjacent to an area where the deceased had been placed. She was on a stretcher all alone. She was beautiful and at peace. Jim sat next to her taking her hand, with Rhoda beside him. Neither felt shame as their tears flowed freely. Both would struggle with the loss of this lady.

Time passed and as the arrivals of the injured slowed, the medical staff got a much-needed rest. Laura, Rhoda's friend, came and sat by Rhoda to lend support. Then one by one, others came. They were not alone for long; other soldiers came to mourn the loss of their friends.

Jim prayed silently, "Lord, I just don't understand! You have taken two women that I loved and You have chosen to leave me here. I know You have a plan and are in control of everything. Help me understand."

Jim finally stood, as did Rhoda. "She is with the Lord now," he said.

"I am thankful God allowed me to know her and share a little of her life," Rhoda stated.

Jim replied, "Amen." Out of the mouths of babes comes wisdom, he thought.

CHAPTER 20

The Iran Affair

IN IRAN THE SUN WAS just setting over the desert and the moon would not rise in the east for another 3 hours. It was dark on the ground but not at 38,000 feet where the Turkish airliner was flying over the water of the Caspian Sea, north of Iran. Unknown to the pilots of the airliner, they were being shadowed by another aircraft, flying just behind and below their aircraft. The two aircraft appeared as a single return on the radars tracking them from Iraq and Iran. The airlines had been careful to file flight plans with several countries in this volatile and war prone area. The shadowing aircraft, a four engine jet cargo plane, had filed no flight plan and displayed no insignia or nationality on its flat black paint, and it broadcast no identifying radio signals. Two of the three pilots in the cargo aircraft were tasked to monitor the airliner for a change in speed or direction as the aircraft were very close.

The cargo compartment contained a single item, a six-foot diameter sphere about 35 feet long. The aft end had four control surfaces, vertical and horizontal. It looked more like a big torpedo than a flying machine. On the top were folded wings and a rocket motor. The vehicle not only looked strange but was unique in that no part included in its manufacture had numbers or writing on it.

The outer hull, coated with the latest stealth paint, was constructed of tightly wrapped paper, held together by a flammable resin making a heavy, but strong, frame. The nose of the missile contained a titanium disk capable of penetrating barriers, the only metal in the hull. Inside the vehicle were 60,000 pounds of high explosives. This type of explosive was developed in the United States. The formula, stolen by Chinese from the US and stolen by the Russians from the Chinese, was now commonly manufactured in many countries. The missile was designed for concussion and contained no metal fragments other than the nose piece. It was designed to leave no identifiable component after the explosion.

When the two aircraft reached a point directly north of Tehran, the cargo door of the trailing aircraft opened. A drag parachute pulled the missile from the cargo bay. The wings opened and the drag parachute detached. The little rocket engine engaged and the missile gained altitude.

At this time a meeting in Tehran was just getting underway. The meeting was in the uniquely designed main government building. It was nearly round with a very high ceiling with small desks for the delegates. The front of the meeting room was raised and there sat the ruling Muslim Clerics in their robes and beards, along with the civic leaders, the president and his cabinet. No one at the meeting was there to make decisions; those were made by the clerics before the meeting was called. Essentially everyone in the Iranian government was present. The subject to be discussed was the ongoing battle to drive the Israelis into the sea. The elected official's responsibility was to implement the decisions of the ruling clerics. These representatives of the people had little power of their own.

Meanwhile, 200 miles to the north, the stealth missile reached 80,000 feet and the rocket burned out and dropped off. It would fall in the sea and be lost. The missile, now a glider, flew on.

Tehran was defended by a ring of radar sites consisting of the latest Russian equipment and was manned by Russians. The radars were very powerful and included the latest technology. All believed this system could detect any stealth aircraft. It couldn't, however, detect a stealth glider at high altitude. The Russian technicians were alert and monitored aircraft out to the borders of Iran. Airline schedules were included in the verification system. The goal was to detect everything in the airspace. Monitoring technicians knew there was always a risk of an Israeli attack on the nuclear facilities where Iran was developing an atomic bomb. On this particular evening the aircraft over Iran consisted of two commercial passenger aircraft. In addition, there were the routine six military flights monitoring the airspace near the nuclear sites. It was a very quiet evening.

Most of the ranking generals of the Iranian Army and Air Force were present in the meeting. In addition, to show their support for the regime, Russian civilian and military representatives were present, but off to the side. Another reason for their presence was to keep track of what Iran was doing. Apart from the Russians, there were Chinese and North Korean delegations. All three of these countries, not necessarily allies, had a single objective. They agreed it was in their interest to weaken the power of the United States. By assisting the Islamic states in destroying Israel, these countries believed Iran would be indebted to them.

The Russian military advisor, General Ivan, was bored and daydreaming. He thought he was dreaming for sure when he noticed the point of something coming through the ceiling. It seemed to him; everything was in very slow motion. At first, he thought a small aircraft had crashed into the roof of the building, but as it continued into the large room, he saw a missile and he knew he was finished. His last thought was, 'what an attack, everyone in the government will die.' It then exploded and vaporized everyone.

The thousands of pounds of explosive raised the pressure and temperature in the room hundreds of times the normal and everything was incinerated. The roof of the building rose several feet before crumbling into rubble. In addition to the large main meeting room, the building consisted of several wings of offices. The explosion extended throughout the halls and blew out the windows and collapsed the wings of the building. After the dust cloud settled, the place where the large and beautiful building had stood was a depression in the ground filled with broken concrete and dust. The loss of life would never be accurately known but was around twenty-eight hundred. There were no survivors within the building.

Dawn finally came to Tehran and the extent of the damage became more obvious. The fact that it was an explosion was clear, but the cause was not. The concern that it was nuclear was quickly put to rest by inspectors from one of the nuclear facilities. The damage went well beyond the main building. Other buildings as far away as a mile suffered damage. Through the night the main effort had been to search for survivors. None were found in the main structure, although there were many injured outside the facility, primarily from flying glass.

Overnight an aircraft arrived bringing Inspectors from Moscow. These Russians were not invited by Iran. Speculation that it was a natural gas explosion was quickly dismissed due to the extent of the damage. A natural gas explosion might be used in a public announcement if it became politically expedient. Chemical analysis determined the carnage to be the results of standard explosive material used in bombs—materials manufactured by several countries, including Russia, the United States, China and Israel. Russia was eliminated from consideration by a directive from Moscow, although their integrity was questionable, as everyone understood. The actual perpetrator could be one of many countries, like Saudi Arabia, Israel or the United States. Many nations had concerns about Iran's nuclear program and their ties to terrorism. Iran sponsoring the current attacks in Israel was not a secret to anyone.

The next question for the investigators was 'How was an explosive delivered?' No parts of a missile or any evidence of one was found. An examination of the radar records turned up nothing.

The possibility of a bomb brought into the building was suggested, however, with the type of explosive it would need to be the size of a tractor trailer truck load. With few records remaining from the explosion, there were few clues regarding recent shipments into the building. One of the engineers from Russia surmised that this was a very large missile attack, based on his evaluation of the damage. It was his opinion, but without any physical evidence to back it up. His opinion was never released to the public.

As some of the US satellites had survived the EMP attack, Washington was aware of the explosion. The few remaining talking heads in the US news media reported the event as an explosion of unknown origin. Israel did essentially the same, neither taking credit for the attack. If it was a missile attack the weapon was clearly a new, previously unknown device. The Russians didn't think that Israel had such a missile and it was unlike the Israelis to attack the heads of state. It would be characteristic of Israel to target the nuclear facilities themselves. The Americans would normally be capable of doing something like this, although, in the current state of the country, it was considered unlikely. In addition, none of the many Russian spies in the US had reported activity concerning the development of a secret stealth missile, and it was unlike the US to attack without warning. Other mid-eastern countries, like Saudi Arabia, would attack the leaders of a country without warning, but no one believed they had the capability to do this.

As the day after the attack progressed and no announcement came from the government, Iranian people began to realize that they, in fact, had no government. All their top civilian and military leaders were in the destroyed building. In the middle of the afternoon that day an older woman, in her head-to-toe black burka, walked over to where a guard was partially buried. She removed her burka and stated, "It is enough!" in a rather loud voice. There were men and women, curiosity seekers, in the area observing the devastation. One of the men decided the woman needed to be taught a lesson and came toward her screaming obscenities. He stopped when she picked up the AK 47 that the now deceased guard had been carrying. She didn't point it at the man and she didn't know how to fire it, but the man immediately stopped with a look of anger and fear. A young man stepped forward and stood by the woman in support. Following a momentary pause, nearby women began removing their burkas and throwing them on the ground. An Imam came running to intervene, but the now-gathering crowd ignored him. Surprisingly, most men didn't object, but rather supported the women. At first there were only a few voices, then rupturing into a rallying cry, "It is enough!" arose from the restless onlookers.

By evening of the second day, as news of the event spread around the world, leaders of nations began to understand what had happened. The entire government leadership of a country had been removed by an unknown entity. If that could happen to a heavily guarded place, like that in Tehran, with the most sophisticated defenses, it could happen in their country. This was not an uprising that overthrew the government. This event simply removed the government. A wakeup call had just been issued throughout the region, especially in dictatorial regimes like North Korea and most Middle Eastern countries. Even in the United States some congressmen had the sobering thought, 'If that can happen there, it could happen here.'

A military commander, Mohammad Atta, arriving from one of the larger bases, saw opportunity and took control. He activated all military units and recalled units from Syria and Iraq. His objective was to maintain control of Iran as the unrest over social and economic conditions had been spreading for months.

Atta feared the Russians would take over the country and issued an order for them to stand down. He stated, "No foreign rulers here."

Whoever was responsible for the attack on Tehran created a big impact on the Syrian attack in northern Israel. It would take several days for Iranian troops to return and assist their interim government in maintaining control, but the effect on the battlefield north of Israel was immediate.

CHAPTER 21

Victory in Israel

GROUP 70, NOW VERY LARGE in size, swept over the Golan Heights and attacked the main forces invading Israel. The invaders had attacked along the northern border from the Mediterranean Sea to the Sea of Galilee. The most hardened fighters on both sides were fighting on this front. Israel had been pushed back with heavy losses on both sides. When Group 70 attacked the flank of the enemy at the same time the Iranian forces were ordered to withdraw, the attack fell apart. The members of ISIS would not accept that the Iranians would disengage, so fighting between the two groups occurred. Many of the invaders saw confusion and simply retreated.

The Turkish forces were in contact with their country's leaders and advised them the invasion had failed. Turkey seized the opportunity to take advantage of the situation and attack the Kurds, their perpetual enemy. All along the border of Turkey and Syria, fighting broke out between the two groups. The Kurds, well-armed by the US and Iran were looking for a way to obtain a country of their own, fought back valiantly.

Israel, taking advantage of the withdrawal, charged north into Lebanon taking territory all the way to the outskirts of Beirut and into Syria, as well, taking Damascus. The Arab armies fled but many thousands surrendered. The Iranian forces escaped across Syria heading for home, not knowing what to expect there. Many of these soldiers were tired of the rule of the Mullahs and wanted to find a way to live in peace.

The UN, no friend of Israel, demanded a cease fire, trying to stop Israel from enlarging their territory, a demand Israel ignored.

Israel, not making the mistakes of the past, evacuated the populations of the captured cities along the coasts and the countryside of their captured territory. This was area Israel decided would be kept as a part of Israel. The mass exodus was made using trucks and buses while many walked. This was unique in modern warfare and Israel would be criticized for it by world governments.

Fighting finally ceased. Jim, with Group 70, was near Damascus when the fighting ended. The Arab armies were surrendering everywhere, throwing their weapons down and abandoning their tanks and other equipment. Rhoda had stayed right beside Jim through the weeks which had passed since Hannah's death. She was the only reason he had a desire to live and, in fact, he hoped many times he would be killed to stop the pain. Rhoda, also saddened nearly to death, had tried to help Jim in his depression. She saw things no one should see, especially a young girl—things which would haunt her the rest of her life.

Then it was over. The volunteers from the US were directed or allowed to return to Tel Aviv. The regular IDF personnel would take over the occupation of the captured territory. It would be months before the final borders of the countries involved would be defined. Israel would never again trade territory for the promise of peace—a lie which would not be believed a second time.

Jim and Rhoda found Hannah's grave in a new garden, just north of Nazareth where Jesus grew up. It was a beautiful spot and now would be occupied by Jews. She was home. The two stood for a while and wept, but thankful they had known this wonderful woman.

Driving the Jeep, he had brought with him from the US, Jim and Rhoda returned to Tel Aviv. It was practically a miracle it had survived, and they had been able to recover it. Riding with them was Harold and Ralph Taylor, the pastor and doctor who had been on the original flight from the US. Good company.

All along the busy roads were prison camps holding thousands of men and a few women. The task of feeding them must have been enormous.

The entire city of Tel Aviv was in celebration of the victory. There were parties in the streets; it reminded Jim of New Orleans during *Mardi-Gra*. Many thousands of native soldiers had been killed but Israel was the victor, so they celebrated. The soldiers, including Jim with his Jeep, ended up in a parade through the streets of the city with people along the way waving throwing kisses and shouting at them. Jim smiled and waved back, displaying a happiness he didn't feel. When the parade ended, they continued to the airport and were directed to the same hanger where they had first arrived. All the men and women formed into ranks, loosely organized in the groups with whom they had fought. Jim and his group were with Captain Glaser and General Steinhoff. The Israeli Prime Minister, Joshua Salon, spoke to the group and thanked them for their help and thanked the United States for their support, support which Jim thought was lacking. Everyone was given a small medal, and a military campaign ribbon was given to non-Jews. Registered Jews were given a slightly different medal. Records were kept and Captain Glaser distributed medals, giving Jim one for himself and a different one for Hannah. Rhoda received one of the non-Jewish medals. The gesture was appreciated.

As the group was dispersing, Prime Minister Salon came directly to Jim.

"I want to express my sadness at the loss of Hannah. I have received reports of her dedication to Israel and know she will be remembered as a valiant daughter of Israel; she will rest with her people. Both of you have shown great courage in coming with her and fighting with us. It would be an honor if you chose to stay here and live with us," he said to Jim and Rhoda.

"I thank you, Mr. Prime Minister; it has been an honor to do a small part for Israel. I may, in the future, accept your offer to relocate here, but now I believe we need to return to the US to help with their many problems," Jim replied.

"I understand and thank you again," he stated with a smile, as he shook their hands and moved on to talk with others.

CHAPTER 22

Home to America

A C-5 AIRCRAFT SAT ON THE tarmac near the hanger. An announcement was made indicating it would be leaving for the United States in four hours. Documented soldiers wishing to return could board after the vehicles, and cargo were loaded. Jim parked the Jeep near the aircraft, hopping it would be taken aboard.

"I hope the Lord leads us back here someday," Rhoda said to Jim as they walked to the small base store.

Jim did not answer but thought, 'How did this young girl become such a believer in God to say such a thing? There is more to her than I had thought.'

The thoughts he was having were disrupted when a group of young Jewish men walked by and she checked them out, rather closely, and they, in return, looked her over.

Jim chuckled to himself and said, "Rhoda, there are young men everywhere in the world."

Showing no embarrassment, she replied, "Oh I know, but God has a place for me and He will provide a man if He wants me to have one."

"What!?" he asked.

"Oh Pop, you worry too much! I know more than you think I know. I am sure God has a plan for me for the rest of my time. Besides, I know you'll never let me go astray!"

That statement told Jim Rhoda intended to stay with him. It had been a question going over in his mind since Hannah had died. He and Rhoda didn't know each other prior to Hannah and he, in fact, didn't know if she had relatives in her native country or in the US.

His thoughts were interrupted when a motor home drove by. It looked similar to the one he had brought from the US, only this one looked new. It was painted in desert camouflage common on Israeli army vehicles. It sped by, driven by a soldier with a big grin on his face.

The two of them went into the base store to get some supplies for the trip. Using some of Jim's money he had been carrying since leaving the US, they picked up snacks and a few souvenirs to help commemorate the time spent in Israel. Rhoda also got a small survival blanket in a small pouch, stating, "That cargo plane is cold, and we won't have your camper to snuggle in for the long trip back." They were taking home something money couldn't buy—the gratitude to God for the opportunity, and safekeeping He had provided, while helping defend Israel.

Putting their purchases into the packs they now always wore, and carrying the rifles and pistols they had, they walked to the dining area in a hanger. No one seemed to notice or care about all the weapons present. The Taylor brothers joined them for the late lunch before boarding the aircraft.

"I thought you might be staying here," Jim commented.

"We'll be coming back, but we have people we need to help in the US now. I think when we return, we'll be bringing most of my congregation," Pastor Harold remarked.

"What about you two, have you considered staying?" his brother, Ralph, asked.

"Yes, we have, but it seems right to go back for now. The US is in such a mess and it will take some time to set things right, if that's possible," Jim replied.

"And I have a marriage proposal to consider!" Rhoda added.

"What? You are thirteen!" Jim said, surprised.

"Well, Samuel Wolf directly asked me to have his children! I assumed he planned to marry me," she said very seriously.

"Samuel Wolf is at least eighty-five and has a wife!"

"Well, there are those things to consider!" she replied. They all burst out laughing.

By this time several people around them were laughing and the discussion was repeated to those further away in the room who also joined in. By the time they left, the entire room was in an uproar. It seemed that after the conflict everyone needed a release and it felt wonderful to experience genuine laughter again.

As they left the lunch area three soldiers stood in a row and one of them stated to Rhoda, "We would love for you to stay and have our children, and you may choose any of us to marry!"

"I am so sorry, but before I can consider other offers, I must answer my Indian chief," she said, causing an increase in the hilarity in the room.

A dozen other Americans from the dining area joined them for the walk to the aircraft. The vehicle loading had been completed and the passengers were being checked in before being allowed to board. Apparently, in order to return, your name had to be on the list of those who had come on the cargo aircraft originally.

The man checking the list addressed Jim. "Your wife, will she be coming?"

"Hannah will be staying here," Jim replied with downcast eyes.

"I am very sorry sir," the man stated, seeing the grief on Jim and Rhoda's faces.

The only mention of the weapons they carried was a request that the rifles be unloaded to avoid any accidents. Many of the men and women on the aircraft were armed. Jim still had the rifles and pistol he brought with him, and Rhoda had her pistol and an M-16 rifle, not legal in the US for private ownership. At this point no one seemed to object.

Walking up the ramp, the huge cargo area seemed to be nearly empty. A few vehicles were tied down in the center of the bay, and additional chairs were bolted to the floor in rows. Backed into the aircraft was the motor home they had seen speeding by earlier.

Rhoda said, "They have painted our house!"

Jim looked more closely at the unit. It was his motor home. It had been repaired; the windshield replaced, and it was painted the desert sand color. The door was unlocked so they went in. The inside had also been redone. The cabinets were refinished, and the mattress replaced. The unit completely cleaned, it truly looked new. Tied to the table was a very pretty plant with a packet of papers and an envelope. Opening the envelope, there was a letter from General Steinhoff.

Jim and Rhoda,

I want to thank you again for your service and to express my grief at the loss of your wife and friend. Know she will rest with her people. I hope we have restored your vehicles adequately. Sorry for the paint. We did not have any of the flashy original colors it came with. I, along with the Prime Minister, will welcome you any time in the future should you choose to return.

Benjamin Steinhoff,
General IDF

"Well, this was unexpected!" Jim said as he picked up the packet of papers. Opening the packet and seeing the papers nearly took his breath away. They contained what would be his most prized possessions. There were pictures of him, Hannah and Rhoda. The first was a picture of the entire group when they arrived at this very airport six months ago. He located his family way in the back. The next picture was of his wedding to Hannah. He had not seen a photographer that day. There were pictures of them in several locations in the various battles and one of Hannah standing by a tree wearing her pistol and a big smile. The last picture was of the burial of several soldiers, including Hannah, all in wooden coffins.

By the time he got to the last picture, he had tears pouring down his face, as did Rhoda, as she took the pictures from Jim. To them it was a treasure of great value, the only pictures of Hannah either of them had.

The aircraft had such a small load Jim wondered why they were using it. Maybe it needed to be returned to the US. The seats along the wall were not all filled, and his vehicles and two pallets made up the cargo. The upper floor seats were nearly full, but still the aircraft was lightly loaded. One of the airmen told him these were all the troops wishing to return who had come on the three fully loaded aircraft from the US. The rest had chosen to stay or were now buried in Israel. If they chose to stay it was something to celebrate; if they had died, it was for a worthy cause.

The big ramp closed, and the aircraft took off. It reached cruising altitude quickly and leveled off. There was a little snack bar with coffee and other drinks and a bin full of sandwiches, which didn't look fresh. Rhoda, now acting as the lady of the house, prepared soup from cans from the RV storage for the three men, Jim and the Taylor brothers. They were chatty and Jim appreciated the distraction from missing Hannah.

"Pop, there is frozen meat and fish in the freezer and the cabinets are full of canned food. Someone stocked the camper," Rhoda said as she opened doors and drawers. "Do you know how to cook?" she continued.

"I haven't a clue; I guess the general wanted to restock the unit to the condition it was when we arrived," Jim responded.

"Did mom have a cookbook? Maybe we could learn!" she responded.

"I doubt it, she seemed to know how to fix anything," he replied sadly.

"We'll learn," Rhoda said, regretting the conversation.

"Maybe the general thought food would be in short supply in the US and right now it's plentiful in Israel," Ralph Taylor stated, wanting to change the conversation.

With the light load and extra fuel stored somewhere, the C-5 flew from Israel to Andrews Air force base in Maryland without stopping. It was a very long trip, but they all got some badly needed rest.

As they neared the US an airman came to the motor home and knocked on the door. Rhoda jumped up and opened it and a young man stepped in. "Mr. Jenkins, greetings from the flight crew. We will be landing at Andrews soon. It seems you have a choice—to leave us there or continue to California. I am afraid those are the only choices. The layover in Andrews will be about six hours."

"I think we should continue. Being in California will put us closer to where we started, and I do have property in Colorado. In addition, we abandoned Captain Masters near there; maybe he still needs our help," Jim stated to Rhoda and the Taylor brothers.

They all seemed to agree as all were from the west and being closer to home seemed logical.

The landing at Andrews was smooth and the aircraft taxied to the hanger area. The loading ramp lowered, and men immediately began coming aboard. An officer walked to the motor home and stood there for a moment, as if he couldn't believe what he was seeing. The man was probably in his fifties, and even with no rank visible, carried himself like a high-ranking officer.

He walked to the open door of the RV and asked in a pleasant voice, "May I enter?"

"Of course," Jim called.

"I am Colonel Slone of the Twelfth Battalion. We have just arrived from Germany and have been reassigned to California. This aircraft is for our transport. I was informed there were a few militias on board. No one mentioned this vehicle."

He spoke in an authoritative manner, not unfriendly but leaving no doubt he was in charge.

"I am Jim Jenkins, my daughter Rhoda and this is Doctor Ralph Taylor and his brother Pastor Harold Taylor. These ladies are nurses with the militia," Jim stated, indicating each person in turn. "We have returned from Israel and plan to go on to California. We had previously been with a Captain Masters there."

The colonel looked at Rhoda for a moment, seeing her as very young, asked, "You took your daughter to a combat zone?"

It was Harold who spoke up. "Sir, this young lady has fought the invaders in New Mexico and in several battles in Israel. She has fired hundreds of rounds at the enemy."

The colonel looked shocked and at Rhoda with a new respect. "Young lady, you have more combat experience than any of my men!"

He turned to the door where two of his aids stood and said, "This vehicle will remain. See to the loading, and work around it, and quickly get the men aboard."

Three Humvees were quickly loaded, each with a trailer containing duffle bags and boxes of ammunition. Two separate pallets contained boxes of food and water. Then the men came, marching in file, all well equipped with vests and weapons. They sat along the sides of the bay and in seats provided across the aircraft. There were, perhaps, two hundred men. The aircraft was packed. Rhoda and the nurses, looking out the windows of the RV, got the attention of many of the men. As they say, men will be men.

The now heavy aircraft took longer to reach altitude but the air was smooth. Colonel Slone returned and joined them in the RV. Rhoda served fresh coffee and a pastry, warmed up from the refrigerator, a gift from Israel. The colonel smiled at the luxury these people had, and in the middle of the cargo bay of a flying aircraft. He also hoped his men could not see him as they had nothing but cold food from their packs.

"Tell me about the fight in New Mexico," The colonel asked.

"It was a substantial force, consisting of Mexican military and some ISIS members. At least they were dressed as ISIS. In addition, there were hundreds of civilians from Mexico and from US towns in the southern parts of the state. They had a few older tanks and most were armed with AK-47's. It seemed the Mexicans had been told the population of the southern states would welcome them and join in the march north. They were right to some extent. What the invaders did not count on was the civilian population that was armed, some well-armed. From the first crossing of the border, snipers hindered the progress. The tanks and armored vehicles were unaffected of course, but the troops in the open were vulnerable. The organized militia gathered in southern Colorado and moved south to northern New Mexico and met them in the mountains. We had the addition of men and women from the Navajo and Apache tribes in the area, hardy warriors. With all the snipers in the hills, and most of the invaders on foot, it was a slaughter. The Mexican Army didn't seem aggressive in the conflict. After the first tanks were knocked out the rest fled, actually running over their own people. I don't know how many tanks or troops made it back to Mexico, but I am sure it was a small number."

The colonel thought for a moment and asked, "So, the US Army was not a part of the conflict?"

"There were a few of the local Army Reserve but the main contingency was the militia. We had perhaps four hundred men and almost the same number of Indians," Jim answered.

"What weapons does the militia have?" he asked.

"I have an AR-15, the most common gun I saw. The rest are a variety of mostly hunting rifles and even shotguns. In addition, I saw a variety of handguns. Some of us have sniper rifles and are quite good with them. As the fighting went on, many picked up the automatic AK-47's and even some light machine guns. The militia is now armed as well as most military units anywhere," Jim replied, smiling.

"It seems the invasion in California did not go that way. The invaders came north without any significant opposition. I don't understand the different responses between the states," Colonel Slone said.

"It is not complicated. California has strict, restrictive gun laws. The population is simply unarmed, even with basic weapons."

"I think you're right. I'm from California and the emphasis has been to restrict gun ownership for years, even for military personnel like myself. It seems this has been a mistake made by the government," the colonel stated thoughtfully.

Jim did not respond, but thought 'The people elect the government, so it's been a mistake made by the people themselves!'

"My brother is a representative in the state legislature; I will talk to him about this. I am interested in your opinion on the subject," he requested.

"In my opinion, gun control is not about crime control or accident prevention as we know the most stringently controlled states also have the highest crime rates. Gun accidents are truly a small number. I think governments that restrict gun ownership do so because they believe they need to maintain control of the people. If the population is armed, a dictatorial power can be overthrown. Gun control is really about the government wanting control, nothing else," Jim answered.

"I believe you are right and perhaps these events will change the way people think," the colonel stated as he got up to leave the RV.

As the long flight seemed to go on forever, the soldiers in the cargo bay began moving around, tired of uncomfortable seats. A few at a time came to the RV to look in, pretending to be interested in the vehicle, although probably more to look over the nurses inside, or perhaps to request a good cup of coffee. They met several nice young men and a few women in the group.

The aircraft landed at the same military base in eastern California and quickly unloaded. The active duty soldiers deplaned and stood in ranks while their commanders gave them information about their assignments. This group was proceeding to San Francisco where the fighting was continuing against entrenched terrorists. The fighting there would be building by building, difficult and dangerous.

Jim and the rest of the militia would join Captain Masters, now located north of Los Angeles. Jim would be driving his RV, towing the Jeep, and the remainder of the militia would travel by two Greyhound buses, arranged by Captain Masters.

Jim noticed one of the large hangers was full of people—Muslims—as the women were wearing head scarves. There were armed guards at the open doors of the hanger to prevent people from wandering off. These people were captives for some reason, guarded, but not closely, unlike prisoners of war.

An Air Force medic came by and Rhoda asked him, "What is going on with all these people?" indicating the hanger.

The young man smiled at her and stated, "They are being deported, to Syria, I think. They have overstayed their visas or are relatives of known terrorists. Most were given deportation orders weeks ago, orders they disregarded. They're people the government now considers undesirable. I'm afraid, in some cases, it's just a purge. Their names and fingerprints are being recorded, and they probably will never be allowed back into the country."

As the medic walked away the obviously disgruntled people in the hanger began moving to three 747 aircraft to be flown out of the country. Jim and Rhoda, along with the Taylor brothers, watched them leaving, having mixed feelings. By their dress it was obvious these people had not integrated into American life but living in a free society had rights. Probably none assembled there were terrorists, but many sympathized with them. This was a troubling situation and Jim was glad he was not part of the decision-making process.

The Taylor brothers joined Jim, Rhoda and the militia nurses in the RV for the trip west. The brothers seemed to enjoy keeping the nurses entertained. Jim drove, quietly missing Hannah. Rhoda rode in the passenger seat, probably doing the same. Jim followed the two buses carrying the militia. They drove 85 or 90 miles an hour, faster than Jim liked to drive, but he pushed it and kept up.

It was a short trip to the militia camp in the south end of the Joshua Tree National Park. The camp occupied a small tourist area with a few stores and cabins used by park rangers. Most of the militia lived in tents, set up in an open area. Jim and Rhoda, of course, lived in the motor home, the best facility in the camp. Captain Masters lived in a tent and came by to see them as soon as the RV arrived. The park had electrical power; things had improved since they left the country seven months previously.

Captain Masters gladly accepted a cup of coffee offered by Rhoda. "We are really in a holding situation here. We monitor the north south traffic from this point to the Arizona border. There are troops along the border of Mexico, so we are a second line here. It has been very quiet, a good rest. The army troops finally arrived three months ago and are carrying out inspections from LA to San Francisco, apparently one building at a time. Very bad duty. Most of what we see here and further south are people from Mexico south leaving the country. We don't hinder them if they are unarmed. Anyone who looks like they're from the Middle East we hold until we can determine who they are and whether they are wanted any-where. If not, we release them. Like I say, it has been quiet and several of our men have gone home. In fact, I may give it up also. I am ashamed to say some members of the militia forces have formed corrupt gangs, robbing everyone they come across. It's more like the old west and will take a long time for the government to establish control."

"What about us? Can we be of service, or do we need to just get out of the way?" Jim asked.

"You could stay if you wish, but it's not necessary. If you go back to Colorado, you could do me a favor and take some our people with you. They need to return to their home areas. Some have been wounded and would do better in a real hospital near their homes. If you could be on call if the need arises, it would be helpful. The cell system is working in most places now, so I could reach you."

"We certainly will transport any we can, and it will be good to get back home. I have a daughter that needs to be in school; she has played hooky for far too long." Jim smiled and Rhoda made a face at him.

So, it was decided. For them the war was over. They loaded two men with leg wounds and three others who just wanted to go home. The wounded men were to be cared for by a young nurse who had somehow gotten very pregnant in the past months. The wounded men were placed in the bed in the back of the RV. Sleeping arrangements would be uncomfortably crowded for the two nights spent on the road. The other three men would follow in the Jeep. Other than that, it would be an easy trip to the militia camp in Colorado where all of this had started. The camp, now controlled by the US Army, accepted their passengers.

The RV seemed large and empty with Jim and Rhoda the only ones on board. It would be good to get back to his cabin and start rebuilding. As they were passing through a small-town, named 'Homestead', Rhoda spoke up.

"Dad there is a church, let's stop in their parking lot for the night and attend the services tomorrow."

"Sounds like a good idea, I am tired, and it is Saturday, isn't it?" He replied.

He pulled into the parking lot, well away from the building, glad to stop. They walked around the motor home, Jim checking the tires and oil. Rhoda went along, just stretching her legs. A city policeman, on a bicycle came by on the street, and Jim called, "We are early for Sunday service. Is it all right if we spend the night?"

The policeman, an older man, did not answer but just waved, smiled, and nodded his head in an affirmative answer.

Being tired they both turned in early and Jim slept well for the first time in days. The generator starting woke him. Rhoda was up in the kitchen and needed the power for the coffee and micro-wave. The smell of fresh baked muffins filled the motor home. The muffins, one of the few things Jim could make, came out of a box, which he added chopped up apples or nuts, they were very good. Before the event he had purchased two cases of the mix, which he had put in the rear storage compartment of the motor home.

It was a beautiful morning, crisp but pleasant outside, so Jim rolled out the awning and set up a table with two chairs for breakfast in the morning sun. When he came back out helping Rhoda carry the food and drink, they were greeted by two young girls, in pigtails, dressed for church. They were about seven and were obviously twins looking and dressed exactly alike.

"What is that smell, it smells good." One of the girls said, while the other mouthed the words.

"These are muffins from a secret recipe, would you like some?" Rhoda stated. "Dad get a chair for our guests." she continued.

"Girls, girls don't bother the people. I am sorry, I hope they have not been bothering you." A woman stated as she came up walking quickly. She was probably mid-twenties and dressed for church in clothes too big for her. She had probably lost weight in the last few months.

"They are not bothering us, but we have plenty, would you join us also." Rhoda stated as she went to greet the lady.

"I don't want to impose, but for some reason we cannot seem to get flour, or sugar anymore," she said sadly. "My name is Donna Right, and these are my daughters. My husband was the pastor of this church before he passed away."

Jim introduced himself and Rhoda as his daughter. Donna did not ask about his wife, a blessing.

Rhoda excused herself and went back into the motorhome and put on two more pans of muffins in the oven. She had run out of apples but added some nuts from a jar on a back shelf.

The five set around the little table and ate the six original muffins and six from the second pan. Jim had butter and honey, both from Israel.

"These are delicious." Donna stated and the two girls nodded in agreement.

By the time they finished the breakfast, people began arriving for the service. They came, mostly walking and a group on a horse drawn carriage. All seemed to be carrying bags and many had chairs.

"The church has been burned and we just meet in the parking lot for a service. Since the pastor has been killed someone just reads a scripture and we pray. We then have a community lunch with everyone bringing whatever they have. You and your daughter are certainly welcome to join us." Donna said, with a forced smile, while trying to be upbeat.

The church was a block building, and the walls were standing but the roof gone. Jim had not even noticed it had been burned and assumed it had a flat roof. The site had been cleaned up including the smoke damage on the outside, so the building from the outside did not look too bad.

A man in a suit came to Jim and introduced himself as George Bennett, a deacon in the church.

"Welcome to our church. As you can see, we are still recovering from the attack. About a dozen men, mostly dressed in black came into our city and burned all the churches and several other building.

They shot anyone who objected, about thirty in all. Our pastor, Donna's husband included. We are surviving and will rebuild but at this point supplies are very difficult to get. Our town will survive and maybe even stronger as we are turning to God more than ever before." He said with a smile, not forced.

Men carried tables and chairs from a storeroom in the back of the church and set them up in the middle of the parking lot. The people gathered around and the some set in the chairs and when all were full the rest sat on the ground.

The service was started with a man who led the people in several song with no music or song books. Then George read scripture from the Gospels of Jesus's sermon on the mount. A sermon Jesus had given on the north shore of the Sea of Galilee, very close to the last battle Jim and Rhoda had been in. Hanna was buried not far from this site. The message was not long but any church in the world would have been proud of it, a wonderful service.

After the service, everyone broke out the food they had brought. Several brought eggs and apples seemed to be in season, as well as corn. While the service was going on Rhoda had baked two more servings of muffins which she added to tables, along with butter and honey. Meat and bread were in short supply, but the fresh food was plentiful and the people friendly and happy. Rhoda spent her time with a group of high school aged youngsters and had a great time.

George joined Jim and Donna still at the little table under the awning of the motorhome.

"I understand you have just returned from Israel and the fighting there. What can you tell us, we receive no news all?" He asked.

Jim paused a moment before answering then said, "I went to Israel with my wife, Hanna and Rhoda. Hanna is Jewish and she very suddenly felt she needed to go to Israel, along with several other people in our militia unit. We flew to Israel and fought in several battles in Israel, Jorden, and Syria. They were hard fought, but God gave us the victories. Rhoda is young but fought right alongside of us. Hanna died, not of the battle and is buried there, near the sea of Galilee, where Christ preached the message, you just read from."

"What are you going to do now?" Donna asked.

"I have a place south of here. Well the house was burned, like your church, and I need to work on it. I also need to get Rhoda into school, she has missed almost a whole year." He replied.

"If you decide to resettle, Homestead will welcome you and your daughter. As you can see, we are a Christian community and should do well if we are not attacked again. If we are, God will protect us, perhaps using people like yourself and your daughter." George stated, very seriously.

"I thank you for the invitation, but I don't know what God's plans are for us. Right now, I feel no guidance and feel somewhat lost."

Jim and Rhoda spent two days in Homestead and discussed staying but somehow neither felt it was the right thing to do.

They left the morning of the third day with Donna and her two little girls, waving goodbye. It was good to have been with Christian friends.

Jim and Rhoda arrived at the remains of Jim's cabin. It was untouched. The family who had used the garage for a few months, just after the EMP attack, had left it clean and in the same condition as before. Most of the freeze-dried food had been used, but other than that nothing was missing. The tools were all there, dusty, but there. The electricity was on about half the time. The subdivision had a water tank, fed by a well with an electric pump. With only two houses occupied, the tank provided enough water for them, even when the electricity was off most of the time.

Rhoda, having never been there, looked around the property and decided it would be a good place to live if they could get the cabin rebuilt. She then started dusting the shop and the garage, something women seem destined to do.

Jim spent the first days getting the motor home into the garage. The doors were not functional, so he removed them, and after pulling the RV in, replaced enough of the door to provide some protection. The Jeep was left outside, as was the motorcycle.

The next morning, Jim and Rhoda went to the nearby town where there was a well-respected, religious, private school. In normal times it would take a year or two's wait to get a new pupil admitted, but society had been so disrupted and the school had lost several students, so they were open for new enrollees.

The admissions person who introduced herself as Caro, was a pleasant woman who took their information. Rhoda had no documents, which it turned out was not unusual since the EMP attack. Unsettled families in transition had been common during recent months. Information about Rhoda's whereabouts were shared. As Carol rapidly took notes. From time-to-time Carol would pause, her mouth would drop open, and she would look at Jim and Rhoda in disbelief and shock. Rhoda had a background like no other enrollee Carol had ever met.

Naming all the courses she had taken at her former school, Carol was very effectively going over Rhoda's education, as Rhoda remembered it. She decided Rhoda would be a sophomore, tenth grade, in high school. Rhoda would need a little extra tutoring on a couple of courses, but she would graduate as she normally would.

Jim paid the fee, not cheap, but the school provided lunch and transportation from door to door. Rhoda stood on her toes and lovingly kissed Jim on the cheek as she left for class. So Rhoda became a school girl again, a role she enjoyed as she was definitely a people person. Wherever they went, both were armed. Jim carried his pistol on his side, sometimes covered by a shirt or jacket. Rhoda wore loose fitting blouses and carried hers just under her breasts in a holster she had made. She let her teachers know about it and was instructed to not divulge this information to the other students. Most of the teachers were also armed. This was still a dangerous place.

Jim went by a hardware store to buy garage doors and other supplies. They ordered the doors, with no promise of when they would come in. The owner explained the supplies could not be obtained. Most manufacturing businesses had not reopened after the attack. In addition, the ability to ship products was limited as so many trucks had not been repaired. The store did have some lumber in stock, which Jim bought and loaded on his old flatbed trailer. He could repair some of the garage door frames. Before returning, he drove around the town. The once bustling town was now mostly dead. Few of the stores were open, and several working age-men were just standing around. At one end of town a line had formed to get food at an aid center. It reminded Jim of pictures he had seen of the soup lines in the great depression of the 1930's.

A few of the cabins in the neighborhood had been partially rebuilt. Everyone was probably waiting for parts and materials. Most of the cabins, however, were still ash heaps like his. He spent the morning working on the left side door, removing the old fire-damaged door and frame. He replaced the side members with new wood, about all he could do until the parts arrived.

Jim and Rhoda's life continued. Neither felt a sense of fulfillment. They both were restless. She went to school which occupied her time, a blessing. She didn't date boys, indicating they were too immature and only wanted to play around. Well, yes, they are boys. She had five, or six girlfriends she spent time with and enjoyed.

Jim fought depression and loneliness. He went hunting with Duncan, and sometimes Rhoda, and kept a good supply of meat on hand. He traded meat with a farmer for grain and vegetables, so they ate well. The two of them attended a small local church and had contact with a few people. Everyone seemed to be in need. There were very few jobs and no money. Merchandise was scarce even if one did have money. The country was sinking further into a depression. The government with an enormous debt due to many years of spending more than they took in, could not pay its bills.

Even welfare checks so many had depended on stopped, causing enormous problems.

Rhoda had her sixteenth birthday and they invited her friends, most of them girls, and a few boys. Also attending was Mary who was around forty. She was a neighbor living in one of the partially rebuilt cabins. Mary had taken a liking to Jim and Rhoda. Her husband had died, she never explained how. Jim helped her with things around her house, so she helped Jim with Rhoda's party. She was just a friend; maybe she wanted more but Jim was not interested in a relationship.

Jim turned thirty-eight and he felt like his life was adrift. He thought he had made a mistake leaving Israel. In addition, his prayers to God seemed to go unanswered. He thought he would get over missing Hannah, but he did not.

When not hunting, Jim took long hikes in the mountains. If Rhoda went along, they would sometimes stay overnight in his tent. It was enjoyable to be out. They seldom used the motor home to travel as fuel was in short supply.

CHAPTER 23

New Directions

JIM FINISHED SETTING UP HIS camp, with the little three-person dome tent facing east. He liked to see the sunrise each day. His camp was protected from the west by large boulders. Here was on top of this mountain, the air was clean and cold. Walking around the large rocks, carrying a cup of coffee, he went up a little rise to see the sun set. It was beautiful. He noticed a flash of red out of the corner of his eye. There sat a woman with flaming red hair, blowing in the breeze. He had thought he was alone in this remote place. He walked over, and without turning to look at him she said, "It's a beautiful sunset the Lord has given us."

"Yes, it is. I thought I was alone here. My name is Jim Jenkins."

She turned and looked at him smiling, a very pretty woman with smooth skin, too pretty to be real. She had to be an angel.

"I am called Hadassah," she said as she stood. She not only had a pretty face, but a nice figure.

Jim thought, 'I suppose all angels are perfect.'

Just then there was a loud boom to the west. They looked and black clouds were rolling in the sky toward them. It looked like something out of a horror movie. The lightning flashed and the wind picked up. The woman turned and Jim followed her gaze. They saw a blue fabric flying through the air.

"My tent!" she said, as she ran the short distance to her camp. The tent was a small one-man tent with a pole at each end. It had been staked but they had pulled loose in the strong gust of wind. "I will need to go down the mountain. Without a tent or sleeping bag I cannot stay here."

Jim thought, 'Well you could just spread your wings and go back to heaven.' He picked up her pack, still laying on the ground, and said, "It is not safe to go down at night, and besides, a storm may be coming. Come with me."

They walked back to his camp, protected by the big boulders, and he indicated she should enter his tent. She hesitated but entered after looking at him for a moment.

He added some water to his little pot and made a cup of hot tea and gave it to Hadassah.

"Thank you, you have rescued me from a very bad situation. But it is not proper for me to stay here and you only have one sleeping bag," she said.

"I don't think we have a choice. I can make the bedding work and we will be proper!" Jim remarked as he began unzipping his sleeping bag to make a wider bed. "We will stay dressed to keep warm and we'll be fine."

"Well, I guess we really don't have a choice," she said as she removed her shoes.

He noticed a birth mark on her right ankle, the only imperfection he had seen.

The storm raged and raged for days. They were cooped up in the tent, never more than a foot apart and they fell in love and eventually made love.

Days later Hadassah said, "I must go down the mountain, even if it is dangerous. I need to get medication as I don't want to be a single parent."

"Then we should get married, right away, you know I love you."

She looked at him with a big smile. Her hair was all a mess and looked like a big ring around her face.

Just then he heard a voice, Rhoda's voice. "Pop, Pop, you are talking in your sleep again! Wake up, wake up!"

Jim sat up with a start. He was in the RV, parked in the garage next to his burned-out cabin.

He looked around confused and sad he had not heard her answer. It had been so real. The dream was so real he at first thought being in the RV with Rhoda was not real.

"I think you were dreaming dad. It seemed like a good dream. I am sorry I woke you up," Rhoda said, smiling. "Was there a woman in this dream?"

"I think so," he said, remembering everything in the dream clearly.

"We need to find you a girlfriend! I'll look the teachers over at school tomorrow and check them out!" she said laughing. "I'm sorry I awoke you."

"It's all right; get some sleep. You have school tomorrow, and I don't need a girlfriend."

Still laughing, Rhoda went back to bed. Jim did manage to sleep, not dreaming any more.

The next morning, Jim and Rhoda went to Rhoda's religious, private school. It was customary for parents to come once a year to meet with the counselor.

The counselor was a pleasant fifty-something year old woman who went over Rhoda's records. They were, of course, excellent and certainly Rhoda was college material.

The woman's name was Hannah, the same as Jim's late wife. She was wearing a Star of David pendent around her neck, identifying her as Jewish. "My mother's name was Hannah. She died in Israel," Rhoda stated to the woman.

Hannah immediately got more interested in them and asked, "Were you in Israel during the war?"

"We were actually a small part of it," Jim answered.

"Would you mind if my rabbi came to talk to you? Our group is considering a move to Israel and we are looking for any information about living conditions, the political stability and anything you could share. Your experiences would be a help."

"Of course, I'll talk with him, although we didn't get involved in the private lives of many people," Jim answered.

Rhoda went on to class and Jim, towing his larger trailer, went by a hardware store which had finally received, after an exceptionally long wait, the two large doors to fit his garage. The doors were not exactly alike but would be much better than the fire damaged ones there now. With help he loaded the doors and some additional lumber to repair the front of the garage and drove back to the cabin.

He spent the morning working on the left side door, removing the temporary door and frame. He had just installed the tracks for the door when a car drove up. A man stepped out and walked to him smiling, a pleasant looking man. He was dressed in casual work clothes. He had on a black hat, a hat which would go with a suit, not a work hat. This man was a Jew and probably the rabbi.

"Hello, I am Jonah Steinberg. My wife indicated you would not mind my visiting you," he stated, continuing to smile.

Jim liked this man immediately. "I am always happy to see visitors. Come inside. I am ready for a break," he replied.

Going into the motor home, Jim poured two cups of coffee and warmed a couple of his favorite pastries.

"Your wife, Hannah, did not mention she was the rabbi's wife!" Jim stated as he took a bite.

Laughing a little, he replied, "Hannah speaks of me in the third person, even when I am present. A quirk, I think." Continuing with a little more serious look, "I understand you and your family were involved in the war in Israel and you lost your wife there. I am very interested to know about it as my plan is to move there and take as many of my synagogue members who wish to go."

"I'll be happy to share our experiences, but our involvement in the war was minimal; we just followed orders. My daughter, Rhoda, who will be home from school in a couple of hours, was a valiant soldier even though she is a young girl. My wife, Hannah, didn't die in combat but of a medical problem. The doctors thought it was a stroke, but they weren't sure. She is buried on the Golan Heights in an area with other soldiers. She is a believer in the Lord Jesus, so she is with Him now. I'll see her and perhaps our child again." Jim stated sadly, remembering it all again.

"I'm sorry for your loss. I cannot imagine living without my wife, but I know the Lord God would provide me with strength as I am sure He has provided for you." Pausing for the moment, he then continued. "I would like you to come and speak to our congregations and tell them about your experiences. Many are concerned about living conditions and safety, but I believe the Lord is leading us to go."

"Of course, I will gladly come any time you wish. Rhoda has school on weekdays, but I am available any time," Jim stated, glad for something to do involving people.

"We have two services. On Saturday we have a standard Jewish service for what I call the hardcore Jews, and one on Sunday for Messianic believing Jews such as myself. Actually, most people attend both services and those professing faith in Jesus increases every week. After the Sunday morning service, around 10:00, would be a good time. We provide a lunch and then have a Hebrew language lesson taught by Doctor Fitzgerald in the afternoon. You are welcome to attend if you are interested, although you may already know Hebrew."

"I do not, and we would be interested in learning Hebrew, although we found nearly everyone in Israel could speak English and several other languages as well. I felt really ignorant among the people there," Jim replied.

"Well then, we will see you Sunday. Now that I have delayed your work, let us put up the garage doors."

Rabbi Jonah worked like a hardened construction laborer for several hours and when Rhoda arrived, both doors were installed and looking good. The springs would need to be adjusted and the door openers hooked up. Another day's job and Jim was exhausted. Arriving home, Rhoda came and kissed Jim on the cheek, as was her custom, and asked, laughing, "Did you see Hadassah today?" Jim did not answer her question and the Rabbi looked a little confused.

Rabbi Jonah declined the invitation for dinner as he indicated his wife would have his supper waiting.

After the Rabbi left, Rhoda unbuttoned her loose-fitting blouse and removed her nine mm pistol which she carried in a handmade holster. "Everyone is still afraid of another attack, so most of the teachers are now armed, and maybe some other students. You should carry a gun everywhere," she instructed Jim.

The next Sunday Jim and Rhoda went to the synagogue for the service, the Messianic Jewish service. The chapel probably held one hundred and fifty people and was full. The service was very interesting. The Jewish influence was evident as most of the songs were clearly Jewish, one sung in Hebrew, most from memory. He and Rhoda knew none of them. Rabbi Jonah Steinberg gave the message. It could have been given in any evangelical church. He emphasized the Jewish basis for Christianity and went into detail of the Old Testament prophesies and how they pointed to Jesus Christ. It was a great service and Jim and his daughter felt right at home. There was no altar call at the end of the service but Jonah indicated he would be available for counseling after the service, or at any time. With a final song, again in Hebrew, the service concluded. Before Jonah dismissed them, he introduced Jim and indicated he would be speaking about his involvement in the war in Israel, if anyone cared to stay. No one left.

As Jim walked to the front, the worshippers chatted. The religious service was over and everyone there were friends. As he went to the front, he noticed a woman with red hair in the second row with her head turned speaking to the lady beside her. He couldn't see her face, but she looked familiar.

"Good morning," Jim said, and everyone became quiet and gave him their attention. It was Hadassah in the second row. She looked at him and dropped her books. He was also shocked; this was a woman from the dream, not a real event. They stared at each other for so long the audience was getting uncomfortable. The woman beside Hadassah picked up the books, but she ignored the gesture and just kept staring at Jim.

Finally, Jim snapped out of it and spoke.

"Hello, my name is Jim Jenkins and I am not a Jew but recently I was married to one. Her name also was Hannah," he said as he nodded at the Hannah sitting by Rabbi Steinberg.

We were part of a militia group, formed not far from here. We and our daughter, Rhoda, fought in northern New Mexico when the invaders came. We then went west to California, as they had requested help. On the way my wife noticed a synagogue and felt led to attend the service. There was a call to go to Israel and help with the impending war. She felt she had to answer this call and, of course, my daughter and I went with her, along with quite a few other volunteers."

Jim continued speaking for about thirty minutes and described, not in great detail, about the battles he was involved in on the eastern side of Israel. He concluded with a statement.

"It has been two years since we left Israel, and I miss it. The people I met in Israel are wonderful people. They are dedicated and love their country. If you decide to go you will be welcomed. The danger has been greatly reduced, but there are still occasional terrorist attacks. My daughter and I have considered returning, although not being a Jew is a bit of a problem. I would like to introduce my daughter, Rhoda."

At the introduction, Rhoda stood and smiled. She, of course, was not embarrassed.

There was applause and people stood, thanking him. The red headed woman remained seated as the congregants left, including Rhoda who had found several young friends. While people were still leaving at the back, Jim and the red head were nearly almost alone at the front.

"Hadassah, I don't know what to say," Jim stuttered.

"Jim, how can this be? How can this be?" She repeated herself.

Jim walked to her and she reached out her hand, which he took. She stood, very close to him, their bodies nearly touching as she looked into his eyes. Hers eyes were a radiant green, just like the dream. It was like they peered into each other's soul. He also smelled her perfume, the same as in the dream. This was really spooky.

"Join me; I am meeting my parents for lunch here at church," she requested, not taking her eyes off him, then continued, "I almost ran up to you and jumped into your arms when I first saw you! What would the Rabbi have thought?"

He reluctantly let go of her hand and followed her into a side room where the lunch was to be served. It seemed everyone was staying for the meal.

Jim followed Hadassah to a table occupied by an older couple. The woman, definitely Jewish, looked just like the entertainer, Barbara something. The gentleman looked Irish with ruddy red face and very red hair, now thinning and with a little gray.

The man's name was Andy Fitzgerald, and his wife, Ruth. They were perhaps midfifties, friendly, and in great shape.

"We really enjoyed your speech. I am sorry about your wife; it must have been difficult," Andy said with a very noticeable Irish accent.

"It was and is, but somehow it seems right that she should pass in Israel. I cannot explain it," Jim answered.

They visited for a few minutes and then Ruth asked, "Are you planning to stay for the Hebrew class the doctor teaches?" As she said 'doctor' she nodded toward her daughter.

"You're a doctor?" Jim asked turning to Hadassah, again lost in her eyes.

"I'm a surgeon," she replied still staring.

"You must be Hadassah; I am Jim's daughter, Rhoda," Rhoda interrupted as she approached with a group of young people.

"Call me Aliza; I don't use my first name very much," the red headed lady, now Aliza said, smiling at Rhoda. She put her hand on Jim's arm, a gesture of familiarity. All at the table noticed.

"Pop, we're going to stay for the Hebrew lesson, aren't we?" Rhoda asked as she was leaving with her friends.

"We are, I would not miss it," Jim said.

"Aliza, she called you Hadassah. You have not used that name for years. How did she even know it?" Ruth asked. Then looking at her daughter's hand on Jim's arm, she asked Jim, "How long have you known my daughter?"

"Well, Mrs. Fitzgerald that is a difficult question, difficult indeed," Jim responded with a non-answer.

"Mom, I will explain later, if I ever figure it out," Aliza quipped to her mother.

"Dear, I think we need to visit with these other people," Andy said as he stood along with his wife, clearly to leave Aliza and Jim alone.

"Jim, we have a few minutes. Can you tell me what is happening?" Aliza asked.

"I don't have a clue! I had a dream a few nights ago, a very vivid dream and you were in it. We were on a mountain top and your tent blew away and you stayed in my tent while a severe storm raged. I saw you had a birth mark on your right ankle. Everything was so real," Jim stated.

She moved her chair back and slipped her right shoe off and put her foot in Jim's lap. A move, more than a little forward.

"You may push my pant leg up. Check out my ankle," she said.

Jim pushed her pant leg up a little, noticing the nice feel of her leg. Just above the ankle was not a birthmark but a tattoo of a small Star of David.

"My grandfather requested I get this tattoo so I would never forget who I am. He was in Germany during the war and was very insistent," she explained.

Leaving her foot in his lap, with him holding it, she asked, "Jim, in your dream, how much of me did you see?" Her voice was almost like a plea.

"It was a dream, not reality," he replied.

"I think we know it was much more than a dream! Please tell me."

"I saw this tattoo and then Rhoda woke me up."

Aliza sighed loudly and said, "Thank You Lord Jesus and thank you Rhoda!"

"I must ask, what did I miss by waking up?" Jim asked with a smile.

"I'll not tell, but in my dream, we were there for many, many days as the storm raged," she stated, with lowered head so he would not see her very big smile while thinking, 'The happiest days of my life.' She then continued, "Do you know what mountain it was?"

"From the view, it looked like Mount Hermon, north of the Golan."

"Isn't Mount Hermon in Syria? Aliza asked. I have never been near there."

Jim and Rhoda attended the Hebrew class taught by Doctor Aliza Fitzgerald. They learned about the Hebrew alphabet and learned a few simple phrases. Jim was distracted by watching the teacher, a truly beautiful woman, and Rhoda was distracted by watching Jim watching Aliza. She would have questions later.

After the class, Aliza came to Jim and after a moment of just looking at him said, "Jim, I don't understand what has happened between us. I know two people having a joint dream is not possible, but it is the only explanation. Something happened between us and I cannot ignore it."

"I can't explain it either; perhaps it was just a strange dream and a onetime thing," he replied, not believing it.

"We should be aware, the Lord kept us there until ……" Aliza stated.

"Until we fell in love!" Jim said, completing her sentence.

She lowered her head and replied, "Yes until we fell in love."

Jim and Rhoda went back to their motor home and Aliza left with her parents. "I think you should see her again. She likes you and she's gorgeous," Rhoda said, smiling.

"All these people are going to Israel soon; there is not time for a relationship. I don't want to say goodbye to someone again."

Rhoda rode along quietly for a minute then stated, "Maybe we should return to Israel with them."

"Well, it is something to think about," he replied deep in thought. They, at least he, was not satisfied with the way life was going here.

That night it happened again. Jim went to sleep and dreamed. This time they were on Temple Mount in the old city of Jerusalem. They walked among the ruins of the Dome of the Rock building, destroyed during the war. He had heard it was damaged, each side claiming the other caused it. It was more than damaged; it was destroyed as was the mosque at the south end of the Mount. He and Aliza walked hand in hand and sometimes with his arm around her, causing hard stares from the Israelis working there. They didn't care. It was a little strange; Jim was dressed in his work clothes, jeans and boots, while Aliza was dressed in the same dress, she had worn in the morning service with high heel shoes. It was an enjoyable dream and nothing erotic happened like the previous dream. He woke up at the normal time for him and got up refreshed.

Rhoda was dressing and fixing herself as women do when the doorbell in the garage rang. Since the RV was inside the garage and the outside door locked, he had installed the bell which only worked if the electricity was on. He went out to unlock the door and there stood Aliza with a box. She smiled, leaned over and kissed him on the cheek and said, "Good morning, I hope you slept well."

Without being invited, she came through the garage and entered the motor home, to Rhoda's delight. She sat the box down and opened it. Turning to Jim she stated, "If we are going to continue to meet like this, I need to have some different clothes. My feet were so sore from walking in high heels all over Temple Mount. If I leave some clothes here maybe I could change before we go somewhere again." The questioning look on Rhoda's face indicated she knew she had missed something.

Aliza then began removing clothing from the box. She had casual slacks and walking shoes. In addition, she had a robe, a night gown and some socks and underwear. "I don't know what to expect, so I hope you don't mind if I leave these here."

Rhoda, almost giddy with delight, took the clothes and carried them to the bedroom in the back, "I know exactly where these go."

Aliza came close to Jim and said, "I don't know what's happening Jim, but I think we have a matchmaker and his name is God Almighty. I cannot ignore Him."

Rhoda returned and kissed each of them on the cheek and said with a little giggle, "I have to go to school; I hope you'll be here when I get home."

"I can't stay, I have hospital duty and I need to give notice to them. We're planning to leave in a few weeks," Aliza stated, with a questioning look at Jim.

Rhoda left, singing 'Oh Happy Day.'

Jim took both of Aliza's hands in his and they sat on the edge of the couch, Rhoda's unmade bed.

"Aliza, you need to think. We have only been together in our dreams and I have lost two wives. You would be getting someone very used. You are a beautiful woman and could have anyone. Why would you want to be with me?" he asked as seriously as he could. He actually wanted to grab her and kiss her.

"Jim, I think what is happening is bigger than both of us. I don't know what it is. If you stay here, I will not go with my family to Israel. I think I have fallen in love with you."

"You know I love you in our dreams, but I don't know what to do in real life," he answered.

"When we were in the tent, you said Rhoda woke you up. I remember you left for a little while but you came back. You were aware of everything we did there, weren't you?" she asked with a little smile.

"Well, we were there within a foot of each other for a week or more. We talked for a long time then what were we supposed to do?" he asked.

"I wish I could stay but I have to go to the hospital. Let me know what you decide about traveling." She looked around at the vehicle and continued, "This is a really nice vehicle, and if you go to Israel maybe you could find a way to take it."

With that statement she leaned over and kissed him passionately on the mouth and whispered, "Miss me!"

Jim did miss her before she had even gotten out the door.

Her car had just left the driveway when another pulled in. It was Rabbi Jonah Steinberg. He stood for a moment looking at the departing car and then came to Jim standing outside his door.

"Wasn't that Aliza Fitzgerald? I wasn't aware you knew her," he commented.

"Better than you or I know, it seems," Jim remarked as they both continued to look at the retreating car.

"She is a lovely girl, but I have come to discuss something else. I received information this morning from one of my perishers that several families from my flock have engaged a ship to take them home to Israel. They will be leaving in a month from Houston. It's a large cargo ship and it has been commissioned to serve as a moving van for those going back to our homeland. Most of our people are loading household about everything they own. It seems we will be able to take much more than we planned. What we are lacking is transportation to Houston and there is a concern that fuel may not be available along the way. My question to you is, have you considered going back to Israel?" the Rabbi asked, and then looked down the road where Aliza's car had now disappeared.

"We have discussed it. In fact, Rhoda brought it up again last evening. I'll ask her again, but I believe we'll go. When do we need to leave and who needs a ride?" Jim asked.

"If we left in two weeks, then allowed a week to travel, we would arrive a week before the ship is scheduled to leave. It should be a fairly relaxing trip. How many could you carry in your motor home?" the rabbi asked. He had obviously thought hard about using Jim's RV.

"We could take six or eight along with Rhoda and me, one or two more if people are willing to be crowded and less comfortable. I could tow the Jeep. Or someone could drive it, and five or six could ride in it. It's not legal to ride in it while it's being towed, but if I did tow it, then it could be loaded with goods. In addition, I have a flatbed trailer I could tow. It's open but can carry a substantial weight," Jim answered.

"I had a feeling I could count on you. You may make this trip possible. Come into town tomorrow and we will discuss the plans in more detail," the rabbi stated as he left with a list of things to do.

Jim had a lot to do, also. First, he called the realtor, Julie, who had sold him the house and property several years before. She came out in the afternoon to look at the property with the ruins of the burned cabin. Now she had a different last name and was pregnant and had two children in the car. Things change. She took the measurements of the garage and shop and some pictures. She left, indicating she would arrive at the listing price the next day. Jim had received an insurance payment for the cabin, so while he would definitely lose money on the property, he would recover some of his investment. He spent the rest of the day servicing the Jeep and motor home. He loaded some of the hand tools in a bin in the RV, not knowing if he could use the electrical tools in Israel as their standard voltage was higher than the US standard. He would have to leave all the big saws and larger equipment, a real shame.

Rhoda came home excited. Jim thought she had heard about the move, but she had good news of her own.

"Pop, the school has a good internet connection so yesterday I sent an email to my great aunt in Sweden. She answered me today. She was sorry she had lost touch with me and hoped I was well. I told her we had been to Israel but did not tell her we were in the fight. She replied, with my family history. When my grandfather fled from Germany, he changed his name from Haymes to Hayes because he thought no one wanted any more Jews. My family was never religious and we never went to church, but I am Jewish!!" By the time she got to the end of her story, she was nearly shouting. She jumped up and grabbed his neck and squeezed so hard it hurt.

Jim had been afraid Rhoda's news would be she was going back to Sweden, and he would have hated that beyond words. She was so happy! His news would make her more extatic.

"It seems your new identity will make you an automatic citizen in our new land," Jim said with a smile.

She squealed like the young girl she was and screamed over and over, "We are going to Israel!!"

The next day, Rhoda went to school as usual with plans to spend time with the counselor. She needed to obtain her records and notes from teachers about her current classes and how she was doing in them. She was so excited she couldn't concentrate on much of anything.

Jim took the Jeep and pulled the big ugly trailer to the synagogue, where Rabbi Jonah would give updates on the move. Several people were there, including Andy and Ruth Fitzgerald. They seemed to be just as excited as Rhoda, and instead of planning the trip, everyone talked about what they wanted to do when they got to Israel.

Ruth came to Jim and stated, "Aliza called me this morning and said she wanted to ride with you in the motor home. I don't know what is going on with you two but I think we approve. But please don't hurt my daughter. She has spent her life getting a doctor's degree and working. She has not taken time for men and doesn't have much experience. I had always planned for her to marry a Jewish man, but maybe that is not to be."

"Our relationship is complicated and we owe you an explanation, but it must be from both of us. It seems God is planning something with us, something we don't understand. But know this, I will never hurt Aliza," Jim responded.

The situation during the day could be described as slightly organized chaos. About fifty people would be traveling to Houston. Others would be going to Israel by air and leaving nearly everything. There seemed to be more vehicles than needed, although some of them looked in poor shape for a long trip.

"Jim, is it you?" The question came from two men in very casual clothing.

"Harold and Ralph Taylor, it is good to see you again! Have you been with Captain Masters all this time?" Jim asked as the three shook hands.

"We have acted as Medic and Chaplin for him until recently. His mission has changed to being a policeman—not very satisfying considering his former mission. The militia group has disbanded, since the government has finally stepped up. It's still an awful mess in California," Ralph stated.

"We heard about this group returning to Israel and we jumped at the chance. Rabbi Steinberg has welcomed us and given us jobs. We are helping organize the move, and by the way, we have contacted Prime Minister Salon. He is anxious to see you again," Harold said with a big smile.

"I am surprised he even remembered me. It will be great to get back there; I have just not felt like the US is home since being back," Jim replied.

"Oh my!" Ralph exclaimed as he looked over Jim's shoulder.

Jim turned and there was Aliza coming toward them at a quick pace. "Down boys, she is spoken for!" he said.

She came to Jim and put her arms around his neck and kissed him then said, "Jim, we are really going! We are going to Israel to live!"

Introductions were made and then everyone got down to business of loading the supplies. Everything Jim and Rhoda needed to take was already in the motor home. He would have a big problem if RV could not be loaded on the ship.

The rabbi had already loaded articles from the synagogue into cardboard boxes and sealed them. The building would apparently be sold or abandoned as all but one or two members were leaving. Jim unhooked the trailer and left it alongside the building for loading. Its load had yet to be determined.

Aliza came to Jim and asked, "Darling, would it be possible for me to put a few things on your trailer?"

He looked at her, picked her up and kissed her and said, "You, lovely thing, can load anything you like, as long as you come along!"

When he put her down, there stood Rhoda right beside them. She was smiling and hugged Aliza, then Jim. Then she hugged Harold and Ralph. "I had hoped to see you two. Isn't this exciting, and why aren't you two married?"

"We would love to be married but we've found no women who will put up with us!" Harold answered with a smile.

The two men helped Aliza and Rhoda load boxes from the pickup onto the trailer. It wasn't nearly full. Other people brought boxes with their names on them and placed them on the trailer. Someone, probably Jim, would need to repack and distribute the weight, but for now the boxes were stacked.

In addition, someone had brought a small moving van and people were loading furniture, special pieces they wanted to save. Jim hoped there wouldn't be too big a problem if all these possessions couldn't be taken on the ship.

Julie, the realtor, came by and gave Jim the going price for his lot. She apologized for the low price, but the market was almost non-existent. Even though Jim would lose money, he was not unhappy, and agreed to the price she gave him. Julie left happy with a new listing, one of her few. Jim's only regret was the loss of his woodworking tools.

The day was over and Jim and Rhoda left in the Jeep, with Aliza following in her car. Rabbi Jonah had three men stay the night to guard the trailer and the goods stacked on the ground.

Arriving at his property, Jim opened the garage doors to allow access to the RV.

Aliza had clothes, lots of clothes, in her car, and they carried them into the motor home.

"Aliza there are plastic boxes in the side bins if there isn't enough room in the closet," Jim said to her as she scurried around happily.

Aliza's car was a SUV and Jim hoped the motor home could hold anything she had in it. He was right, but only by a little. This girl had shoes, lots of them, and clothes enough to open a store. It was wonderful to have womens' things in the RV again.

Taking her in his arms, he asked, "Will you stay the night with me?"

"You know I want to but I have a surgery late this evening and my mom has asked me to stay with them tonight. I think she is concerned for my virtue," she said, laughing as she kissed him. Rubbing him a little with her body to insure he would miss her, she continued. "Perhaps I will meet you in our dreams."

Jim and Rhoda walked around the neighborhood and took some pictures to help them remember. They went through the shop again and took a few more tools. He opened the safe and removed his personal things, leaving the plans he had drawn for the new cabin. He wrote the safes combination on a paper to give to the new owner, or Julie.

They went to bed early but Jim did not dream.

In the morning Jim took Rhoda to school in the motor home, her last day there. She would pick up her transcript and reports from teacher and say goodbye to all. She was happy to be going but sad to leave friends.

The chaos at the synagogue was slightly more organized. Aliza's parents were there before Jim arrived, as were several other people bringing all sorts of goods. Jim's big trailer was not completely full but getting close. Aliza arrived, dressed in scrubs. She went into the motor home to change into casual work clothes, something her parents noticed. Had their daughter moved in with this man she had just met?

Aliza, with Ralph Taylor's help, loaded four boxes with Red Cross markings on them onto Jim's trailer. "These are medical supplies the hospital wanted to donate for our trip. We all hope none of them will be needed, but if there's an accident, it's better to be prepared," Aliza stated to anyone in earshot.

Even though people were scurrying around, everyone was joyful. They were starting on a trip most of their ancestors had wanted to make.

The caravan would consist of ten vehicles. Jim's motor home would lead, towing his old trailer, now fully loaded. His Jeep, driven by Harold Taylor with an older couple, towing another fully loaded flatbed trailer. The third and fourth vehicles were Mercedes Benz cars, one Aliza's, and the other, her parent's vehicle. The first would be driven by Ralph Taylor and would contain a man and his three daughters, much to Ralph's pleasure. The Fitzgerald's would drive their own vehicle which was fully loaded with things they were taking. The rest of the vehicles would follow. One man had a large pickup with a big fuel tank in the back, in case gasoline could not be obtained along the way. It had been reported fuel was available on the main highways, but in short supply elsewhere.

Rabbi Jonah and Jim walked down the line of vehicles to check them out. There was an old mini-pickup, driven by an older couple. The tires were worn, cracked and low on air. Jim could air up the tires, but this vehicle would never make it. In the back of the little pickup were two suitcases.

"Samuel, are these two suitcases all you are taking?" Jonah asked the driver.

"Rabbi, when my father left Germany, he was limited to one suitcase each so we limited ourselves to one. I know this vehicle is old and we may not make it but our only desire is to reach Israel and die there," the old man stated.

"I have room for the suitcases, if we can find seats for them," Jim offered.

Rabbi indicated he agreed and Jim took the two suitcases to his motor home. There was still a little room in one of the storage bins. Just as he was closing it, Duncan arrived.

"Jim, I understand you are leaving and I wanted to say good-bye," he remarked.

"Yes, tomorrow, is the plan. By the way, my property is for sale, if you want any of the tools or saws, feel free to get them. I was planning to come by your place this evening," Jim replied, shaking his hand.

"No need to move them; I just bought your place. Julie will be by for your signature on some papers any minute."

"Duncan, I am sorry. I did not know you were interested. I could have saved you some money by selling to you directly," Jim replied.

"Not a problem. Julie looked like she needed the sale and I have the cash. I hope you will come back some day and see what I've done with the place."

With that comment, Duncan left and shortly Julie arrived with a dozen papers to sign. He signed them and gave her a deposit slip for his bank account so she could deposit the money when it became available on final closing. She thanked him for the business and wished him well. Jim knew he was trusting that these people were honest and would carry through with their promises.

Jim backed the motor home and hooked up the loaded trailer. He checked all the tires and fluid levels for the third time. He repeated the effort with the Jeep, hooking up the other trailer, checking its tires and fluid levels. The two vehicles were ready to go.

Jim and Rhoda took showers and prepared to turn in early as they planned on rising at three AM to get under way by four.

There was a quiet knock on the door and when Jim opened it, there stood Aliza.

"Sir, I am homeless and have no place to lay my head. I seem to have lost all my clothes! Can you help?"

Jim stepped out, picked her up and carried her in, a little difficult to do through the narrow door.

Rhoda giggled as she watched.

After the three had a bowl of soup, Rhoda made her bed and climbed in stating, "I want both of you to know, I sleep very soundly and tonight I will wear ear plugs!"

Aliza went to her and said quietly, "Rhoda, you know your father and I are very much in love and we will marry when the time is right."

Rhoda said nothing but sat up and hugged Aliza and kissed her on the cheek. "Welcome to our little family."

Jim and Aliza went to the bedroom in the back and spent their first night together, not counting the days in the tent in the common dream.

The alarm went off at three AM. They both wished they could have spent the entire day in bed, but they got up. The vehicle was filled with the smell of sausage, eggs and hot muffins. Rhoda had gotten up early, set the small table and even had a small flower in the center. It was a wonderful gesture. Aliza had put on one of Jim's shirts, which barely covered her, while eating breakfast.

"The sausage is all beef, as I am now a Jew, I will need to read labels more closely. Maybe you can teach me the proper way to prepare food," Rhoda said to Aliza.

Jim gave thanks, a special thanks for the meal and for the addition to their family.

As they were finishing breakfast there was a knock on the door. Jim automatically said, "Come In!"

The door opened and Andy and Ruth, Aliza's parents, stepped in.

Ruth looked at her daughter, dressed in a man's shirt and said, "When you didn't show up at our house, I was hoping you would be here."

Jim stood up and Ruth tiptoes and kissed him on the cheek. "Take very good care of her, she is precious. I brought you some pastries, but I see you have already eaten."

Rhoda took them and said, "Thank you, they will make wonderful snacks."

Aliza slipped into the bedroom and quickly returned, fully dressed and hair combed, ready for the day. She hugged her father and whispered something in his ear, and he seemed to relax. It had been a shock to find his daughter shacked up with a man, even one he liked. The tension eased and they planned for the day.

There was a significant change. Someone had contracted with a local church to hire their small bus to take passengers, rather than drive so many cars. A local used-car dealer showed up and bought four cars on the spot. He probably cheated the owners, but the other option was just to abandon them. The caravan now consisted of

Jim's motor home with a trailer, his Jeep with a trailer, two Mercedes cars, two nearly new pickups, a moving van and the bus. The group was followed by the rabbi and his wife in their car. They pulled out at four thirty, almost on schedule.

The distance to Houston from their location was about 1100 miles, too far for one day's drive. Driving time in a normal situation should be around seventeen hours, but they would be slower as more rest stops would be required. Even with changing drivers often, they would need to spend the night somewhere. Due to fuel shortages on the lesser roads, they planned to take the major freeways where possible. They proceeded east and picked up highway 25 just after dawn and went south to highway 40. Jim drove the speed limit of seventy which seemed fine for everyone, at least no one complained. They communicated with CB radios. Jim had one mounted in the RV and the rest had hand held units. CB radios, popular years ago, were now used primarily by truckers. They worked just fine if they didn't get too far apart. Everyone, of course, had cell phones but the service had not been fully restored and there were broad areas with no service at all.

After several hours they pulled into a rest area on the highway, It was swamped with homeless people who sometimes posed a danger to travelers. Jim and Rhoda, with their pistols in open holsters, provided some security, as well as several of the other men in the group. The restrooms in the buildings were unusable as people were living in them, and they had not been cleaned in months. There was an RV dump station, so Jim hooked up the motor home hoses and people lined up to use his restroom. The men, and a few women, just went behind a vehicle and tinkled on the ground. The stop took thirty minutes, during which time a good part of their food was given to the less fortunate living there. It was a sad thing to see the situation these people were in, especially in the United States.

After the noon break, Andy, Aliza's father, took over driving the RV. People moved between vehicles at each stop. Jim sat on the couch to rest with Aliza beside him. She snuggled under his arm and both went to sleep, under the watchful eye of her mother.

It was late when they pulled into a large inn in Oklahoma City. It had rooms available and a nice restaurant which they all enjoyed. The Inn had an unarmed security guard outside, but Rabbi Jonah did not consider it sufficient. Rhoda insisted on joining several men in guarding the vehicles. Armed with her visible pistol, vest and M-16, she looked very serious. Jim took his turn as guard, with his newly acquired shotgun—one of the new, two tube guns which held twenty shells, a very scary looking gun. The night was uneventful and after a hardy breakfast they were off to Houston. It was late when they arrived. The group spent a second night in a motel near the port. The trip had gone very smoothly without any mechanical problems, and fuel had been available when needed. Thank be to God who watches over His own.

Jim, again, led the caravan to the ship port. It was crowded with many vehicles waiting to enter. The line was moving very slowly as each vehicle was checked and the travelers identified. Jim was beginning to wonder if they would even be processed before the day was over. Just then, a young man in an Israeli army uniform walked up to the RV. Jim stepped out to greet him and was surprised when the man came to attention and saluted, "Captain Jenkins, it is good to see you again. Both Prime Minister Salon and General Steinhoff send their greetings. I am Lieutenant Yaffe. I am sure you don't remember, but we met in Jericho. Your daughter was very kind to me when I was wounded."

Seeing the young man talking to Jim, Rhoda slid out of the vehicle and came to them smiling. "Yosef how is your leg? It is good to see you again, and standing," she said.

Yosef looked like he wanted to grab Rhoda but restrained himself and replied, "I am completely healed. Your father solemnly warned me you were only fourteen. You look much older now."

Rhoda replied, "Well three years have passed, and I have good news! It seems my family is Jewish, a fact I just recently became aware of," she said, smiling quite broadly.

The lieutenant, realizing he was gawking and forgetting his job, stood again at attention. "Captain, sir, if you will follow me, we will get you and your other vehicles on the ship."

Yosef, speaking rapidly in Hebrew, directed another soldier on a small cycle to guide Jim around the line, through a gate directly to the dock where a very large ship was tied up. It was not a pretty passenger liner but a rusty looking freighter. On the side next to the dock was a large door with a ramp into the cargo bay of the ship. They bypassed a long line of people who were not pleased with them.

Everyone left their vehicles and went to a desk on the dock to be identified. Rabbi Steinberg had sent all the passengers' names, indicating whether they were Jewish or not. Jim and Rhoda were not listed as Jewish but were accepted because of their previous service. The others in their party were Jewish or married to a Jewish person. The vehicles were looked over causally, checking for explosives. They were not interested in the firearms.

While they were talking, someone drove the RV and the other vehicles on board the ship. They looked puny in the vast hold of the cargo bay. The man who had driven the RV came to Jim, and speaking in broken English stated, "Sir, we locate your vehicle near the stairs to upper decks and there is electricity available to plug in. The propane will need to shut off. If there is anything you need, please ask."

Ruth, Aliza's mother, observing how Jim had been treated, said to Aliza, "It seems you have chosen a man well respected in Israel."

Aliza smiled at her mother and replied, "I didn't realize that, but I knew when I met him he was a good and honorable man, a man I am very much in love with."

From that day on Aliza's mother considered Jim a son.

People continued to load the ship. Most came carrying their personal possessions in suitcases. Others had sent ahead containers to be loaded on this ship. The cargo compartment was not completely full, but the number of passenger cabins weren't nearly sufficient. Rabbi Jonah with his wife, Hannah, and Aliza's parents each had a cabin, because they had reserved and paid extra for one. They had also paid a fee to bring their car. Jim's vehicles were considered a part of the Israeli Reserve Force and he was not charged and was not aware that others paid. Jim, Aliza and Rhoda would sleep in the motor home. Many of the people would sleep on mats on the floor of the cargo compartment and the open deck of the ship, not comfortable but they were happy to do it. They were going to Israel; no inconvenience could discourage them.

CHAPTER 24

Aliyah
(Immigration to Israel)

THE SHIP LEFT THE DOCK just as the sun was low in the western sky on Friday. The big loading door was closed, and the stairs and ramps removed. Tugs moved the big ship away from the dock and slowly turned the bow toward the channel to the sea. Passengers crowded the rail along the deck watching the shore move away, savoring, for most, their last look at the only home they had ever known. The main engine started producing a rumble throughout the hull which would continue until they reached port in Israel. Under its own power, the big ship moved slowly through the channel, past docked ships, lighted buoys and other channel marking. The lights of Galveston passed on the port side of the ship and another mile to the Number 1 buoy marking the port of Houston. They then picked up speed and moved south into the Gulf of Mexico.

It was a beautiful sunset at sea and the start of the Jewish Sabbath.

The Sabbath evening meal consisted of family gatherings throughout the ship, small gathering around the cargo on the deck, in cabins and all around the cargo area. Aliza invited her parents to the motor home, and along with Jim and Rhoda, conducted the brief prayer before eating. Aliza, as mistress of the house, conducted the prayer using the candles brought by Ruth. In addition to their family, Harold and Ralph Taylor were invited. It was a bit crowded, but very nice, especially for Rhoda, the first for her since knowing she was Jewish. The part about 'Next time in Jerusalem' certainly had special meaning.

The next morning there were five services conducted on various parts of the ship, five being the number of Rabbis on board. Rabbi Jonah Steinberg conducted a Jewish service, using the scriptures of prophesies of a savior, and that Jesus fulfills that prophesy. The next day, Sunday, he would continue the message that Jesus is the savior of the world, as prophesied. It was a wonderful two days.

The weather was kind and the sea smooth. The ship passed the southern end of Florida and the passengers saw the last lights of the United States, for most of them, for the rest of their lives. As they passed south of the Bahamian Islands the sea was completely void of sea traffic. The weather was sticky, hot, and humid, and the passengers spent most of the day and night on the open deck. Other than a lack of comfortable deck chairs, it looked like it would be a pleasant voyage.

The third day out a crew member, one of the few on board, came running about looking for the red headed doctor, Aliza Fitzgerald. He found her and Rhoda on deck leaning against a shipping container in the shade.

"Doctor, mum, Doctor Taylor has requested your assistance. One of the crew has gotten very ill."

The two women followed him to the ship's medical office, just a cabin with a bed and some nearly empty shelves. It was not clean. A very large man lay on the bed in pain. He, even though in pain, smiled at Aliza and said, "What a beautiful doctor; I should have gotten ill sooner!"

Aliza, used to such statements from patients, ignored his comment and looked at Ralph Taylor, another doctor. "I believe this man has appendicitis, and I'm concerned it has ruptured."

"If it's ruptured, he must be taken to a hospital. The danger of operating here is that of infection." Aliza stated as she pushed on the man's abdomen.

"Oh, that is painful but keep doing it; just having you touch me is a pleasure," the man stated. (Revealing the nature of horny ole men!)

Standing in the corner was the captain, an older man and also a Greek. He said, "We will not see land for a week; there is no possibility of a hospital."

"I agree with you doctor. His appendix needs to come out. If it's ruptured, I doubt we could stop an infection. The motor home is cleaner than this room and I do have some supplies from the hospital. Someone carry him there as easily as possible. We don't want to rupture it by dropping him." She, for the first time, looked at the man's face and smiled. "My name is Dr. Fitzgerald, I am taking you to my bedroom, so behave yourself. What is your name?"

"I am Atticus and I am from Greece and you can do with me as you will." He replied, trying to smile.

Two equally large men arrived and put Atticus the sick man on a stretcher and carried him out of the room. These men did not seem to speak English but understood the captain.

Aliza and Rhoda hurried ahead while Ralph Taylor stayed with the patient. They quickly reached the motor home and Aliza took command. She directed Rhoda to put a plastic sheet over the bed and told Jim to get the boxes with the red crosses on them from the trailer. She was like a different woman, completely in command of the situation.

Rhoda removed everything which might be in the way from the bedroom. Jim opened the boxes in front of the motor home while

Aliza scrubbed her hands in the sink, using liquid dish soap. Jim located sterile gloves and following her instructions, helped her put them on.

The crew carrying Atticus, who now was in more pain, was placed in the aft bedroom of the RV. Seeing Aliza, he grimaced and smiled, "A beautiful woman is taking me to her bed, do with me what you wish, Red," he said.

"What have you given him?" she asked Ralph.

"There was some morphine in the cabinet, and I gave him an injection," he replied.

"Good, all I have is a bottle of ether. Scrub up and prepare to apply it." It was not a question.

Rhoda also washed her hands and put on gloves, to assist by handing Aliza instruments, a job she had performed in Israel.

Until Atticus was sedated, Jim had to hold his arms down as he continually tried to reach up and touch Aliza. His actions didn't seem to bother her at all, probably a normal situation for her.

Aliza directed Rhoda to coat the area with a sterilizing liquid and she expertly made an incision. He moved a little and she glanced at Ralph, who added a little ether to the cloth over the man's face.

"Good. It is not ruptured! I need a bowl."

The appendix came out and looked very red and very thin and inflated, like a balloon. She carefully put it in the pan so as not to puncture it. It was now a matter of sewing up the incision and applying a bandage. The whole thing took less than ten minutes.

Jim had watched Doctor Aliza as she exhibited a completely different personality than he had seen. This was a skilled woman who exhibited a calmness, even handling the sick man's advances with style.

Atticus awoke in two hours in pain, but still making passes at Aliza. It seemed to be his normal way. He would spend the rest of the day and night in the RV and then return to his room, wherever it was. Also, he was to be relieved of duty for the remainder of the trip.

Aliza gave him some antibiotic pills with instruction, and she impressed on him the importance of not missing a one. He, of course, asked her to stay with him to remind him.

In the evening, with Atticus in the motor home and Ralph looking after him, Jim and his family found a place on deck to sleep. It was warm and humid so it was not too uncomfortable. They had blankets, not to use for covering with but for padding on the steel deck. Jim lay on his back with Aliza on one side and Rhoda on the other each laying on one of his arms. It was like being tied to a board. It was also great—two people who loved him—what could be better?

The next day Ralph examined the incision and found no sign of infection. He redressed it and got the big man up. He helped him walk a little. The man was in pain but complained more about why the red head was not helping him. He was getting back to normal! After ten or twelve days the stitches would come out, but he was still not permitted to do any physical labor.

It was a bit over 5000 miles to Gibraltar and another 2500 miles for the length of the Mediterranean. The ship traveled around 20 knots, not fast by modern shipping speeds. On the evening of the tenth day the cliffs on each side of the entrance into the Mediterranean came into view. They passed through at night, a disappointment as everyone wanted to see the land. The port of Gibraltar was on the port side of the ship, north of the entrance and brightly lit. Even at night it was beautiful. The ship traffic was heavy and ships from all over the world passed close by. Everyone was on deck most of the night.

Jim and Aliza, of course, spent the nights in the RV, alone at last, except for Rhoda in the other end of the motor home. She was occupied much of the time being escorted by Lieutenant Yaffe, the young Israeli officer. Aliza had a talk with her and was convinced Rhoda was not going to do anything unwise with this handsome young man. She was steadfast in her conviction of no love making before marriage, hopefully years away.

Atticus, now much improved from his surgery, seemed to have all types of illnesses needing medical attention. Ralph Taylor usually had success keeping him away from Aliza but he occasionally found her. If he couldn't think of an illness or pain, he wanted to discuss some medical procedure he had heard about. Aliza finally ran out of patience with him and mentioned it to Jim who was no help.

"Aliza, Atticus is a lonely man who has met a gorgeous red headed woman who took enough interest in him to show him compassion when he needed it. The fact that he is madly in love with you should surprise no one. I suppose I could shoot him or rip open his stitches, but beyond that, I am unsure how to discourage him," Jim said as seriously as he could, all the while chuckling.

"Pop, you must defend your woman!" stated Rhoda very indignantly.

Just then Atticus came wandering up, and spying Aliza, came straight over.

Before he could speak Jim, addressed him. "Atticus you seem to be healthy to me. I was talking to the captain and he suggested the forward anchor locker needed to be serviced. The winches need to be taken apart and lubricated and he asked me if you were well enough to do work like that. I suggested he talk to Doctor Taylor for an opinion as you seem to be getting along very well moving about the ship."

Atticus, not a stupid man, could figure this out. "Well, yes, but I think I have overdone it today. I think I will spend the rest of the day resting in my cabin. Good day to you all."

"Pop, you were masterful; I am glad you did not have to beat him up!" his daughter said with a smile.

"Rhoda, Atticus is four or five inches taller and sixty or seventy pounds heavier than I. I think I would be the one beaten up," Jim stated chuckling.

Atticus did not bother Aliza again.

As the ship neared Israel, everyone on the ship went to the bow and up in the superstructure, each trying to be the first to see land. Shouts went up when the tops of Israeli buildings could be seen. Everyone broke into song, a Hebrew song. Jim had never heard it and could not understand the words. Rhoda on the other hand had spent a lot of time with Aliza and knew Hebrew much better than Jim did. She even had taught Rhoda this song. The quality of the singing was not great but the enthusiasm was, with everyone singing with gusto.

A small boat came along side and a pilot boarded the ship. He took over the helm and guided the ship to a dock where inspections and customs were located. This seemed to be a usual procedure. The ship came along side the dock and lines were passed. For the first time in two weeks the engines were shut off and the ship became quiet and the vibration stopped.

From the dock, the stairs were rolled up to the ship and passengers were asked to wait until they were called. Military personnel were present at each exit of the ship. It would take a couple hours for all the people to disembark into a waiting area in a large building. The large door on the side of the ship opened and a crew began unloading vehicles. It seemed there would be an import duty on some of the vehicles. Jim's motor home and Jeep seemed to be exempt due to his previous military service. There would, however, be a charge for new license plates for the two vehicles and the two trailers. The plates were to be purchased from a civilian agency located nearby. Everything went smoothly as this appeared to happen on a regular basis. Jim and his family were special in another way. No one seemed concerned about his weapons, when others were closely questioned about weapons or knives. His RV and Jeep were closely inspected, as were the two trailers which were completely unloaded. Each box was opened and searched, but not very closely. The inspectors were careful with the cargo and very friendly to the new arrivals.

While the passengers were waiting on the dock, the crew of the ship stood at the rail and watched. Atticus was there. Aliza saw him and walked away from the crowd and shouted, "Atticus, take care of yourself and keep taking those pills!" She then waved and gave him a big smile, creating a jealous reaction among the rest of the crew.

Atticus waved back and called, "If you tire of that boy, I am available! And thank you again for saving my life!"

As she walked back to Jim, he said, "That was nice. He was a pain but I think a good man, and I'm glad I did not need to beat him up, as if I could."

"All men seem to feel it is their obligation to flirt with their female medical staff. I don't understand it, but have learned to ignore it," She quipped.

Jim didn't try to defend the male species, as he was as guilty as any of them. Well, men will be men.

The group from the ship gathered in a large room and several men proceeded to a platform with a podium. A man introduced himself and began giving directions in English.

"We welcome all of you to Israel and thank you for coming. We have much land to occupy, land gained in the war. Those of you who have a prearranged destination are now free to leave. You will need to provide transportation for yourselves and your goods. The guards at the gates will take your name and destination in case we need to contact you. We have established a new town in the northern providence, north of Golan Heights, a good town and a good area for you to settle. Infrastructure is in but the town is not complete. For now, accommodations have been made, and we will provide transportation for you and your goods. You, of course, are not obligated to stay there, but we do request you go and check it out. The area is good for farming and ranching. Again, the government of Israel welcomes you."

Jim didn't know what to expect when arriving here. It wasn't surprising that this group would be asked to occupy a new city. This was a group of people who had lived in close proximity and had worshiped together through the years. Probably very few were farmers or ranchers, but there was a good mix of businessmen and skilled tradesmen among them. It wouldn't be a difficult task to succeed in creating a new town organization.

"I think we will be going by Hannah's grave site I want to stop and see it," Aliza announced to Jim and Rhoda as they got in the motor home.

"I agree. We just made a brief stop before returning to the US. When the war was over, we were quickly routed out of the country. It would be good to visit, but I think we need to go to the new city and drop off everyone first and unload this trailer," Jim replied.

The 'everyone' Jim was referring to was the eight additional passengers who needed a ride to the new location. The convoy got underway, with Jim following an army vehicle with several soldiers, all armed. Apparently, peace was not completely assured. The rest of the cars and trucks followed the RV. The roads were in excellent condition and the trip north proceeded quickly. They passed the beautiful Sea of Galilee on their right; it was really a freshwater lake which had many names. After passing the lake, they turned northeast and went up to the Golan Heights area, the previous border of Israel and the area Jim, Rhoda and Hannah had fought their last battles. Much of the damage to the structures hadn't been repaired, but the road was in good condition. The road went past Mount Hermon on their left, the presumed location of Jim and Aliza's dream. They continued toward the city of Damascus, a once major city in Syria, now in complete ruins after years of civil war in the country and additional destruction in the recent war. Damascus was deserted.

The new city, unnamed, was located on a plateau with a clear view of beautiful Mount Hermon to the west and the not so pretty view of the ruin of Damascus to the east. At this point Damascus was a part of Israel, although the peace agreement had not been completely finalized. In the past, Israel had agreed to return land in exchange for a promise of peace, a mistake they said they would not make again. Israel had stated that all the land captured would become an integral part of their country.

Jim had expected the 'new city' to be a vacant town with a few temporary buildings, but they found a bustling community with many young Jewish families who looked like they could take care of themselves. Also, there were soldiers and walls protecting the city. They were near the now undefined border with Syria and past knowledge told them terrorist attacks were possible.

Their convoy of vehicles was directed by an official to the northern part of the town to some small empty houses. The official introduced himself in English. "Welcome to our city. My name is Sol Haymes and I'm mayor of this town."

Jim introduced everyone in the RV and then Sol continued. "We were told about this vehicle. I've never seen one like it. I understand it even has a bathroom. This area is not complete, but there is an extension of the sewage line by the pile of stones. You may park near there and drain your tanks if you like." As he spoke, he indicated a stack of construction materials nearby.

Jim moved the motor home to the stack of materials and near the sewer pipe which he would use to dump the holding tanks. It was a good place and he would leave the vehicle there for the time being.

"I may be related to the mayor," Rhoda said. "We have the same last name."

"It may be true; the Israeli government has an extensive ancestry data base. They may be able to help," Aliza responded and then continued. "I'd like to go find Hannah's grave and I'd like to go soon."

Jim didn't understand why Aliza wanted to do this, but he didn't question her. Some of the families with small children were being assigned to the small houses recently constructed, others to tents for temporary shelters as there were not enough houses. No money transactions were taking place. The properties were owned by the government and had been built for this purpose. Resettling Jews moving to Israel was big business.

The Jeep was pulled up beside the RV and the trailer unhooked, making his Jeep usable for traveling.

Jim and his family went to Mayor Haymes, who seemed to be in charge of getting everyone settled. "Mayor Haymes, we'd like to make a quick trip to visit some graves on Golan Heights. We'll be back before nightfall."

"If you and your family will be sleeping in the camper then you won't need a house," he replied. "You're certainly fee to travel as you wish. Today our goal is to get everyone into a shelter, however, tomorrow will be a busy day getting supplies unloaded and everyone settled."

"We'll be available first thing in the morning and when you have time, I'd like to talk to you about buying some land for a house and a woodworking shop," Jim responded.

"The northern part of the city will be private homes and busi-nesses. We'll discuss your needs later in the week. Just a word of caution, we believe the area is safe, but it would be wise to be armed, just in case," The mayor replied, obviously wanting to get back to his duties.

Jim and Rhoda, already armed with their pistols, picked up their rifles and put them in the Jeep. The three of them left the city headed southwest to the Golan Heights. With a map it was easy to find the cemetery. It was a large, fenced area, where there were hundreds of graves. The loss of life in the latest war was significant. There was an unlocked gate and a small, unmanned building. In the building was a book with a list of the dead and where each grave was located. It took about fifteen minutes to find Hannah's grave. It was marked with a concrete marker with a Star of David overlaid with a Christian cross, indicating she was a Messianic Jew. Her name and the date of her death were on a small brass plate attached to the marker. It had taken a significant effort to mark all these graves.

Rhoda got on her knees and placed a small bouquet of flowers and said very quietly, "I miss you Mom."

Jim stood there quietly weeping, and then said, "Hannah darling, I'll come by from time to time, and I'll see you again one day."

After a few minutes as they prepared to leave, Aliza said, "You two go on; I'd like to visit with Hannah for a moment."

Jim thought this strange as Aliza had never met Hannah, but he and Rhoda walked back to the Jeep.

Aliza knelt down and rearranged the flowers and said, "Hannah, I hope you can hear me from up above or at least know my thoughts. I wish I had known you in this life. I'm sure we'd have been good friends; we, after all, love the same man. I believe you arranged for the strange dreams your husband and I had, dreams where you introduced us. They were more than dreams and I thank you for them. Because of these dreams and our lives since, we have fallen in love and want to marry. I would like to have your approval, and if you can arrange it, would you meet me in a dream, just the two of us? If not, we will both be with you one day where you are now. I know we will all love each other. Thank you again for directing me to Jim."

CHAPTER 25

The New City

ALIZA WAS WALKING ALONG THE side of a beautiful river. Well, to be more precise, she was walking on the top of the water in the middle of the river, and she was not alone. Alongside her also walking on the water, was another woman and a child. Somehow this all seemed very natural. The banks of the river were full of flowers and trees; it was beautiful.

"What's your little girl's name?" Aliza asked Hannah.

"She doesn't have a name. We were here when she was born and names are given on the other side," she responded.

"What would you name her?"

"I think Blessing would be a good name. She has certainly been a blessing to me," Hannah replied.

"Thank you for allowing me to love Jim. He has made my life complete, and it seems so right to be in Israel, and Rhoda is a wonderful girl and wonderful company," Aliza commented.

"One day we will all be together here and it will be wonderful, and the Savior will be with us continually. Do not be concerned about me sharing Jim; we both love him and thoughts of jealousy are not present here," Hannah stated with a smile, which somehow filled Aliza's mind.

Suddenly Jim moved, waking her. Aliza was lying on his arm with her back pressed against his torso, their normal sleeping position. She was in the RV in the new city. It had been a dream.

"You were dreaming," Jim said quietly.

"Your daughter's name is Blessing. We should put marker on Hannah's grave. She's a wonderful child," Aliza said.

Jim, not surprised at the information from another strange dream, replied, "I will see if there is a way to put an additional name on the gravestone. Is Hannah happy and at peace?"

"Of course. She is with the Lord."

Jim thought for a moment then turned very close to Aliza's face said, "I think I've exposed you more than once, and you seem to not be with child, and I wonder why."

"Darling Jim, I'm a doctor and I know things. I did not want to be a single mother, so I took precautions until we marry. I warn you; I want to stop the medication; it is time to start our family. You have probably needed to marry me," she said, trying to be serious.

"I have asked you to marry me a million times," he replied, exaggerating but not by much.

"Well then, the answer is yes!" she replied as she kissed him passionately.

They were delayed in rising that morning—not an unusual event.

Jim got out the ring he had purchased for her some time earlier and put it on her finger. She wondered if it was the same ring, he had given Hannah but said nothing. It was not.

As it turned out, adding a small brass plaque to the marker on a grave required only a simple request. Jim offered to pay but no money was required. Again, it seemed he, as an honored veteran, had some privileges. The small plaque would read, 'Unborn Daughter of Hannah and Jim Jenkins named Blessing.'

The child would now have a name in Heaven.

The new city was being built on the Tel of a much older city. The previous city had also been Jewish, at some time, as artifacts consisting of small stones with a menorah etched on them were found in several places. The city, or maybe an outpost, was located on the ancient 'Kings Highway' the road from the powers to the north to Egypt. The name had been lost to history. This land was Israeli territory around the time of Solomon's reign. It had been a walled city and never excavated, which was a problem for new construction. Archeologists wanted to examine the old ruins before new construction began. With their fancy ground radar, they found evidence of early habitation everywhere except at the top of a little rise north of the new houses.

Jim took some sketches of a house, garage and a shop, similar to his Colorado cabin and went to the mayor, Shalom Haymes. His office was in the largest building in the new city. Jim was surprised when he entered and found General Benjamin Steinhoff present, along with several other military personnel.

Jim was further surprised when the general came to him, called him by name and shook his hand. "It is good to see you again, Captain Jenkins, and I am sorry I never expressed sympathy for the loss of your wife, Hannah."

"General, it is good to see you again. I am surprised you remember me; I was a minor player in the conflict," Jim replied, shaking his hand.

The general, chuckling a little stated, "I confess I was given a refresher about your family. It seems you have returned with your mobile house and have big plans for this community—a community that needs a name." The comment was directed to Mayor Haymes, one of the several townspeople standing by.

"I've come by to see Mayor Haymes about purchasing a plot of land for a home and a woodworking shop. I don't know the procedure for buying land. I did talk to the archeologists I met, and they indicated their test did not show any ancient structures on the hill one click north of here. If you're busy, I certainly could come back later," Jim stated.

"I would like to see your plans," the general remarked. It was clear he was in charge of the meeting, whatever the original subject had been.

Jim unrolled his plans, just an outline sketch he had made showing the garage and woodworking shop with a modest, by US standards, house. It would, however, be the largest house in the existing settlement. He was planning for an expansion of his family.

"How tall is this building?" The general asked, pointing at the garage and shop.

"The garage doors are twelve feet, so the building will be about sixteen feet tall, about five meters, and I had planned a flat roof to blend in with the other structures," Jim stated, pointing to the plans.

The general smiled about Jim's statement implying he would not know the conversion from feet to meters. He replied, "You have chosen a particularly good location, but one we are considering for a watch tower. As you know, many invasions of Israel have entered through this area. This city is on the front line of any future conflict."

Jim thought for a moment and then took a pencil and sketched a second story on the garage and added windows on all sides, with raised dome on the roof.

The general stared at the drawing for a long time; no one in the room spoke, so as not to interrupt his thoughts. "What is this dome object?" he finally asked.

"With this height, sensors could be installed which would have a 'line-of-sight for many miles and could be monitored by a crew in this room. In addition, we might both save money if we worked together." Jim's attempt at humor was met with thoughtful silence.

General Steinhoff asked the others in the room their opinions about this sudden proposal. Pouring over the drawing there were fingers pointing, nodding heads and hushed discussions. One officer said quietly, "If this could be made to look like a residence and not a military facility, it would reduce the risk of attack."

The general said, "Give us a few days for us to consider this, and I need to run this plan by a few other people.

Within days Jim had his answer when he received a phone call from the general. "We'll build this building, and you may use the first level as you show it here. The military will equip the second level and man the equipment. You'll be responsible for any construction within the outer walls for the first level. We'll want an outside access for the second level. Every attempt will be made to make it look like a carpenter shop and not a military installation." The general made the statement while pointing at the garage and shop building.

Jim thought for a moment before commenting. This would mean the military would own and occupy half of his building. The military is powerful, and he could be thrown out at any time, without recourse. On the other hand, he would, get his garage and shop for little expense. "With this arrangement, what you are offering is acceptable, and I, of course, will be glad to work out the legal logistics of the shared project. I hope you will not take offense if I move my house away from the garage a bit, just in case it becomes a target," he remarked.

The general laughed and Jim could hear him speaking to someone in the background. "Samuel, you will work with Captain Jenkins and develop a building plan." Then with remarks to Jim, "This is very important and is to be completed quickly. I will have our technicians coordinate with you to insure everything they need is included."

After numerous phone calls and inquiries, Jim's questions about buying land and construction approvals were still unanswered. It didn't matter. Samuel, the aide, was efficient and seemed to have endless energy. He took Jim's sketches and within days turned them into construction drawings. The building he drew was larger by fifty percent. It was longer and had three garage doors and a service door on one side, leading to an office, which would become an entry check point. There were two stairs to the upper level, one from the entry office and one on the backside to the much larger shop area. There wasn't much detail on the upper level, but the electrical plans exposed a lot. The floor and walls had many electrical outlets indicating an abundance of equipment. On Samuel's invitation, Jim added electrical outlets to the floor and the walls of the shop where he envisioned the woodworking tools would be placed. Apparently, Samuel's budget was not limited, so he added any amenities Jim suggested. Two weeks later bulldozers arrived, and construction began.

Aliza and Rhoda were not idle during this time. They located a dress shop in Dan, the nearest city, and purchased dresses, a wedding gown for Aliza and a very fetching dress for Rhoda, who would be her attendant. On a second trip into town, Jim was a member of the shopping party. A men's store was located where they purchased a suit for Jim. It wasn't his custom to have to stand while the tailor fitted it. This would be more formal wedding than his previous ones.

The synagogue/church in the still unnamed new city was under construction. Like the one in the US, the strictly Jewish service would be on Saturday and the Messianic Service on the next day. The Jenkins wedding would be the first service held there. It was a grand affair; everyone in the city came as well as many military personnel, including General Steinhoff. Also, Lieutenant Yosef Yaffe, one of the suitors for Rhoda, attended. He either was stationed there by some chance, or he knew someone important. The small worship center was packed. It was a beautiful ceremony, over which Harold Taylor presided, with a canopy and all the trimmings. Aliza was, of course, gorgeous as was Rhoda, looking older than her age; in fact, they looked more like sisters than mother/daughter. After the wedding there was a party in the Jewish tradition with dancing, eating and drinking. Jim noticed Aliza didn't drink any wine, but brought her own juice. He also noticed Rhoda was dancing with the lieutenant nearly every dance.

As Jim went through this event for the third time, he thanked God for giving him three lovely women to love in his life. He still didn't understand why God had taken the first two, but believed God had a plan. Maybe he was given a doctor because he would need one later.

In lieu of a honeymoon, Jim's family of three went to Tel Aviv.

"I'll be glad to stay home and let you two lovebirds have some privacy, and Yosef can look after me," Rhoda stated with a big smile. She was now eighteen and a beautiful young woman.

"I think perhaps we need to talk about boys again," Aliza said, and they both laughed.

In Tel Aviv they went to an international bank to transfer most of Jim's and Aliza's funds from the US to Israel. It seemed this was not a simple transaction due to US law and would take a few days. Next, they went to an industrial supplier where Jim ordered equipment for his woodworking shop. They had some of the saws in stock but since the building was not complete, he would wait and have everything delivered when it was finished. He also ordered a generator, as the electrical power in the new city was not reliable. The people were very helpful and spoke English which helped Jim as he was still not fluent in Hebrew.

They spent a week in Israel's biggest and very modern city, Tel Aviv, staying in a luxury hotel in a two-bedroom suite.

In a quiet moment Aliza stated to Jim, "Husband, as I mentioned, I stopped taking birth pills a few weeks ago, so you have an immediate responsibility to provide our future children life as we are not getting any younger." She said this as she slipped out of her gown and climbed into bed.

Jim did his best. It was a wonderful vacation.

CHAPTER 26

The Town of Jenkins

THE CONSTRUCTION OF THE HOUSE and garage/woodshop/military installation did not proceed according to the plans Jim had seen. The first construction was basements, not on the plans. The basements were the full size of both buildings and built without any partitions, just single, large rooms. They were heavily constructed with ten-inch reinforced concrete roofs, which were the floors of the ground level. Another thing not on the plan was a concrete tunnel connecting the basements of the two buildings. Apparently, the existence of the basements, more like bomb shelters, was a secret because until they were constructed and covered; everyone except Jim and his family were kept away. It was becoming apparent to Jim that he and his family were simply a front for the military installation. Hopefully it would not be a problem.

After the ground level floors were poured, and the entrances to the basements concealed, visitors could drive by and observe from a distance, but due to safety concerns, they could not come into the construction area. Amazingly, the construction went quickly. After the concrete floors and walls were poured, the windows and doors were placed according to the plans. From the outside, the buildings would look like the plans. The upper floor of the multi-use building was completed with special bullet proof windows. They, of course, were not bullet proof for anything larger than AK-47 rounds. Larger weapons, guns, and field pieces would penetrate, but the building was as fortified as well as it could be without being a bunker. The roofs of both buildings were flat and other than their large size, looked very much like the buildings in the new city. The dome on the garage was low and looked more like decoration than an observation center.

Jim and his family stayed in the RV in the still unnamed city. Rhoda, returning from her classes, came in and announced, "The people in town are calling our house and garage the Town of Jenkins."

"That's not a good name. I'm not Jewish and 'Jenkins' is not a Jewish word. It's also not a separate city from this one we are living in. The residences need to choose a name for both this city and our home to the north," Jim remarked, surprised at the thought of a town named after him.

Aliza, sitting beside Jim, said, "Look out the window. Between the town and our house is an ancient city. Archeologists will be working there for years. I'm told it was an amazing city and they are finding many artifacts. Apparently, this was a major Jewish city in the time of the kings of the united country—a city which is not documented anywhere. Our house will be separated from the city for a long time, perhaps forever, and the Jenkins family *is* very important." She paused and both she and Rhoda smiled at Jim's uneasiness about the name, then she continued. "I was told today a hospital will be built just a short distance from your garage and shop. It is to be a large hospital which will serve the entire area and will be a major surgery and trauma center. So, you see, your city is growing already!" she said laughing.

"Well, if it is going to be a city, we should name it something Jewish, not after some poor American," he replied.

Ralph Taylor, the doctor who had walked with Rhoda to the RV and was still standing outside the open door, added, "You are not a poor American. The people have not only named the town for you but are accusing you of stealing the hearts of two of the most beautiful Jewish women!"

"Come in doctor, you exaggerate!" Aliza said with a smile.

"I didn't misstate the truth! The people love you and what you did in the war. It's clear to most that the construction north of here is being done by the military, and they understand the need for secrecy. And I didn't misspeak about you stealing the hearts of two beautiful Jewish women," he stated as he stepped into the RV.

Doctor Ralph took a seat at the little table. He accepted a day old muffin and cup of coffee like it was his home. He and his brother were always welcomed.

"We received notification from Tel Aviv that your credentials have been approved and you may now practice as a doctor in Israel," he commented to Aliza as he handed her a certificate with the name Doctor Aliza Jenkins. Her specialty was as a surgeon.

"Thank you, Doctor," Aliza said with a smile, as she took the document. She had been helping at the small clinic in the new city for weeks, probably not quite legally. "What have you heard about a new hospital?"

"It's already under construction. I've seen the plans; it is huge but has only two stories and is being built in Jenkins, not far from your mansion."

As he spoke the name of the city, all laughed except Jim, who winced and muttered something under his breath.

Jim passed the days at the construction site, helping where he could. His presence wasn't necessary. The building crews were experts and followed the plan, except where they seemed to have a secret plans. Part of the secret plan was a freight elevator going from the basement to the upper level of the multi-purpose building. In addition, a separate small structure was built to look like a chicken coop which housed a very large generator, already running to provide electrical power. The chicken coop camouflage was not very convincing as it had two large exhausts for the engines stick-ing through the roof. He had wasted his money buying a generator which would be delivered with the shop tools. Perhaps it would be useful somewhere.

The two buildings went up quickly with nearly no lumber used. The walls and roof were all constructed of concrete. On site was a large concrete mixer, much larger than a truck and the cement was moved with a big bucket and a crane. He had seen things like this in the US, but for large projects like dams and large buildings. These buildings would last for a very long time if not destroyed by bombs or earthquakes. A similar setup was in use at the hospital site. That structure was going up in an amazingly short time. The interiors would, of course, take much more time, but the structures them-selves seemed to almost overnight. An exaggeration, of course, but not by much.

Between the hospital and the garage, a well was drilled. They hit a water supply at a little over a hundred feet, either very good luck or with some knowledge of where to drill. It was exceptionally good water and seemed to be of unlimited supply. More buildings were going up, taking advantage of the big concrete mixers. Some were businesses but many were dwellings. It seemed the city with no name was moving up the mountain nearer the Jenkins' home.

Jim moved the RV to a spot alongside his new but as yet, unoffi-cial house. A deed would be coming soon. Also, he had not paid for either the house or the garage. He needed to resolve this for peace of mind. The generators providing electrical power to the multi-purpose building also provided it to the house. The generators were more reliable than the power to the unnamed city to the south. A septic system was already in operation to support the hospital. With the utilities in and reliable, it made sense to move, and many did.

For the three of them the long days were filled with work. Aliza had an unpaid position coordinating orders for equipment and for the trauma hospital. Rhoda was busy in school but found time to help plant hundreds of apple and other fruit trees. Surrounding fields were plowed and planted with a variety of crops. Jim worked on the buildings. The garage was adequate with concrete walls and floor, but the woodworking shop needed to be insulated and have cabinets and shelving for tools. The larger woodworking equipment had arrived and needed to be assembled and set up. Workers on the upper 'secret' floor helped install the tools with the understanding they could use them for whatever they were building upstairs. In addition, the exterior of the house was completed, and the roof was on. No interior walls were finished and much was still to be done in order to make it a home.

Jim hired a contractor to work on the home, his first financial investment in the house. The workers looked like a group from the UN. Most were Jews with olive skin but there were Arabs and African blacks. Many were Christians, although some may have been Muslims. They worked as a team, like a family. The contractor indicated this group had been together for many years and had not been affected by the recent wars. Jim noticed at least four languages spoken by the group, one of them English. They all seemed to understand Hebrew, better than Jim did. The work went quickly with teasing and genuine camaraderie. Each morning Aliza inspected the previous day's work and made suggestions, becoming as much a manager of the team as was the contractor himself. Jim worked with the electrician running the wiring. The result was a well-insulated home with sheetrock ceiling and walls and a tile floor throughout. Aliza was happy, so Jim was happy, with the house.

On several occasions Jim accompanied Jewish soldiers, by their invitation, to the ruins of Damascus, now occupied by Israel. He took the Jeep and the large flatbed trailer. They had found slightly damaged furniture and other supplies of wood, which they thought would be of interest to him. They showed him a beautiful table with chairs in a bombed out building.

"I feel like I would be stealing if I took this furniture," he stated to the officer in charge of the group.

"This area of the city will be leveled very soon to reduce the chance of disease spreading. The dead are everywhere, and the risk will be reduced if everything is buried. What you do not take will become part of the rubble," the officer explained.

Jim took the furniture which he could repair in his now functioning woodworking shop. In addition to furniture, he found what had been a lumber yard of sorts, a section contained stacks of hardwood planks. It took three trips to transport the very nice undamaged wood back to his garage. This, of course, was spoils of war, but he still felt guilty taking things he did not pay for. He was not alone as others came on a regular basis and carried off items. The only inhabits of Damascus were located in a Red Cross tent camp. As victims regained their health, they were being dispersed among Arab countries, a part of the peace agreement made at the end of the war. Israel was not inclined to accept a large number of non-Jewish citizens in the captured territory.

Back in his woodworking shop, Jim began restoring a large desk salvaged from the ruined city. It had drawers on each side and broken legs. It could be repaired but it would not be the same as the decorative trim would be impossible to replace. The desk was unusually heavy for a piece of furniture this size, but maybe it was made from a very dense wood. He removed the broken legs and began fabricating new ones from the reclaimed wood. Removing the drawers, he noticed that above the drawers there seemed to be a boxed area. Searching around, he found a trip button and two additional hidden drawers popped open—secret compartments. Inside, the first thing he noticed was a German Luger pistol with a swastika emblem on the side. It was a German World War II pistol. In addition to the pistol were stacks of old German money and six small bars of gold. It was a treasure which had likely been stored for years. The money, of course, was pre-war German marks, and perhaps no longer worth anything. He didn't know. He did know this was not his money, so he sent a message to General Benjamin Steinhoff to come when convenient, without describing the purpose.

The general arrived the next morning, more quickly than Jim had anticipated. The general looked over what Jim had found. He wasn't interested in the pistol and handed it to Jim, indicating it was his to keep. Surprisingly, Steinhoff didn't know if the money had any value; of course, the gold bars did. They were worth many thousands of dollars, and a huge number in shekels.

"Can you take me back to where you found this desk?" the general asked.

"I believe so. It has been several days and the streets in the city all look the same, full of rubble," Jim answered, not sure if he could actually find the building.

A trip was arranged quickly and, this time, Jim traveled with the general in a Humvee, accompanied by two trucks with troops and some equipment. Jim found the building on the first street he directed them down, pleasing all, especially himself. The room where the desk had been found was on the third floor of what had once been a very nice apartment building. The third floor had been a single residence, indicating wealth, but the furnishings were worn and damaged to the point that no one had taken them, except the desk. They climbed across the rubble and entered the reasonably undamaged third floor; only the front wall was missing. The general walked throughout the rooms and by just pointing at a wall, one of the men with them, opened it up with a sledgehammer. It didn't take very long to find a large safe inside the wall. It was an ancient thing, undoubtedly pre-World War II. It was impossible to tell how long it had been since the safe was opened, but the wall it was behind had no door, just a solid wall. It was likely the current owner had not known of its existence.

The general surprised Jim again when one of the men accompanying them was a locksmith or a safe cracker, depending on how he operated. The man retrieved a small satchel and attached some tools to the safe and with a headset on, turned the dial. It took five minutes to open the safe.

Inside was a true treasure. On the top shelf were two small German machine guns, fully loaded. No one cared about them. Under the guns were more stacks of German money, and in addition, stacks of English bills, all very old. Under the money were six very heavy, wooden boxes, full of small gold bars, like the ones in the desk. Each bar was stamped with a Nazi swastika. This was a sizable treasure. There were also paper files in leather pouches, all in German. No one took the time to read anything; they just took everything in the safe, including the machine guns, and loaded them in the truck. They spent a few minutes going over the rest of the apartment and found nothing else.

The men were happy to finally leave as the smell in the area was overwhelming. Apparently, there were bodies underneath the rubble in the street.

On the way back to the City of Jenkins the general turned to Jim and stated, "As the finder of this treasure, you have some claim to a reward, but the state will keep everything from the safe. Most likely something will be done for you. It is doubtful the rightful owner can be found as it appears this money was stored during the war and then forgotten, not an unusual occurrence. I think it appropriate for Israel to forget about what you found in the desk."

"Im not looking for anything for myself, but if some funds to help the new city were available, it would be helpful. The hospital will need more equipment than has been ordered. It would be better if you took the cash, in case it is worth something, and if you don't object, I will keep the small bars for souvenirs," Jim replied smiling.

The general took all the cash from the desk, except a few bills for Jim to keep as souvenirs. In place of the cash he left a small bag in exchange. Later Jim discovered an additional ten gold bars in the bag. Each bar probably weighed a couple of pounds, so he had about thirty-two pounds of gold, a sizable amount of money.

There was no mention of finding the treasure in the media, probably to reduce the chances of a legal claim for ownership from the Syrian's, who had abandoned Damascus.

A few days later an army truck arrived at Jim's house, now occupied by his family. The truck was driven by Lieutenant Yosef Yaffe, much to Rhoda's delight. In the back of the truck was the large safe from Damascus. It must have been a monstrous job to get it into the truck from the third floor of the building.

"Sir, General Steinhoff thought you might like to have this safe to keep souvenirs in. In addition, he has sent you this letter," Yosef stated, as he watches Rhoda come to greet him.

"Well, yes, I suppose it would be handy! Would it be possible to put it in the basement of the house. We don't really have a place in the living area," Jim replied, as Rhoda stood beside him with a 'Cheshire Cat Smile'. She needed some lessons on playing hard-to-get!

A second truck rolled up with a big fork lift on it. It quickly unloaded the safe and placed it in the basement of the house. There was an offset along one wall that it fit in rather nicely. Jim had planned to build shelves there, but the safe fit fine. The man who had opened it had written the combination on the door in pencil. The pre-war safe was in remarkable shape as it had been protected in an enclosed area.

As the men were preparing to leave, Yosef turned to Jim and said, "Sir, my enlistment is up in a few weeks and I wonder if I could work with you in your shop? I have some experience in woodworking."

Rhoda, who had been ignored up to this point, added, "Dad, you'll need help. A lot of people have ordered furniture for their new homes."

"Come by when your enlistment is up. I'm sure we can make some kind of arrangement," Jim answered. Rhoda uttered a little sound of joy.

As Yosef was getting in the truck, he, for the first time, spoke to Rhoda. "It's very good to see you, Miss Rhoda. There is a play in town; perhaps you would like to go?"

"Perhaps. Let me know the time and date, and if I'm available, I'll be happy to go with you," she replied, trying, unsuccessfully, to act like she would think about it if nothing else came up.

Yosef smiled, saluted Jim, and left, driving one of the trucks. Jim turned to Rhoda, who said nothing, but smiled and giggled.

Jim opened the package he had been given. It was a letter from General Steinhoff thanking him for finding the gold. In addition to the letter was a government document, a deed, for the tract of land his house and shop were built on. It was about five acres of land, a huge size for a single family where most people lived in apartments or in row houses. On the deed was a note indicating the military would have access to a 'surveillance station' on the property. Jim's family had ownership of his house and garage with very little cost. It was quite a gift. Of course, the military had access to the garage's upper level and the basements of both the house and garage/shop. What the government gives they could always take away in an emergency, so his ownership was contingent on future events. But for now, he owned a very nice piece of property.

CHAPTER 27

New Discoveries and a Time of Peace

Yosef came to work for Jim as soon as his enlistment in the army was completed. He was a good, capable worker in wood. He also was an artist in creating figures from metal plate using the cutting torch. Best of all, he made Rhoda happy. She was so obviously in love with the young man it was a bit embarrassing to be around them. On Rhoda's nineteenth birthday they announced their engagement to no one's surprise.

The woodworking shop was closed on Saturday and Sunday out of respect for the Jews and Christians, and for Jim's family to relax. It was Saturday and Yosef and Rhoda had packed brunch and gone to a more-or-less secluded spot on the south side of the property. It was an eroded area in the hill forming a notch in the terrain. The site was invisible from the house but open to the south, overlooking the ancient city. Archeologists and teams of volunteers from all over the world were still sifting through the ruins. They had found thousands of artifacts which would take years to catalogue. It was a major find as the city had been occupied during the time of the monarchy. Since it's collapse, it had never been occupied again. Because of this, the findings would provide a clear picture of the life of Israelites living there at a particular point in history.

As the young couple, sat on a flat rock eating, they watched the diggers and enjoyed each other's company. They were interrupted by a woman coming to them on an old motor-powered bicycle. It was difficult to judge the woman's age as she looked trim and fit, but her face was deeply winkled and looked baked from many years in the sun and wind.

Smiling, she said, "Hello, I thought you might be some of our volunteers, and I was going to point out you are outside our search area and on private land. My name is Yenta Neumann and I am an archeologist in the dig."

Yenta Neumann, a famous archeologist in Israel, and in charge of the exploration of this site.

Yosef stood to greet her, "Please join us we have some sandwiches and cool drinks. I am Yosef Yaffe and this is Rhoda Jenkins."

She got off her small cycle and came to them. "Are you the daughter of Jim Jenkins, the famous soldier this city is named for?"

Rhoda stood and took her outstretched hand and replied, "I'm Jim Jenkins daughter, but if you meet him please don't refer to him in such a way. He's very embarrassed when people refer to this place as 'Jenkins.' He feels there are more appropriate names for the city."

They visited for some time and finished the food Rhoda had prepared. Yenta was very friendly and suggested the two of them could come and help dig out the site any time they wished. Then she stated, "This is an interesting rock you're sitting on."

The couple had not really noticed but the stone was very flat and straight and had smooth edges. It looked like a long bench made just for this purpose.

Without waiting for them to answer, she continued, "This is a cut stone. See the edges and tool marks? Someone placed this here for a reason."

Yenta took a brush from her belt and began brushing the stone where it extended into the bank. She had not cleaned the stone more than a few inches when she uncovered figures etched into the surface. She first saw a bird then with more brushing, other figures, mostly animals and plants appeared. There were some symbols that looked like words written in another language, not Hebrew.

"This looks like some form of Egyptian hieroglyphs. I believe the images covered the stone completely, but the exposed part has eroded away in the wind and weather. We must excavate this area. I know this is your father's property and I need to ask permission. This is very different and could be a major find. When we surveyed the area with the ground penetrating radar, we didn't cover this side of the hill because it's steep. Maybe we need to bring it back."

"My father is home today. He and mom are at the house. Come on up, I'm sure he'll agree." Rhoda stated.

The three of them walked up the hill to the house with Yosef pushing the motorized bicycle.

Jim and Aliza were home enjoying a day of rest. Aliza, now four months pregnant, was still working in the hospital when needed, but took off this Sabbath. She had felt very well with the pregnancy but needed rest more often than usual. They greeted the new arrivals and Rhoda served tea and coffee.

"We have found something unusual on your property and would like your permission to evaluate it," Yenta stated to Jim and Aliza.

Jim knew archeologists had sizable power in Israel and could get permission from the government to do anything she wanted. He responded, "Of course you can dig anywhere if you believe something important is there. I do hope you don't need to dig under the house. If you need to damage the roads, we can always work around it."

Yenta wasted no time in beginning the exploration. Within an hour she had red plastic ribbon markers moved to include the new site. Two teams of ten young people there clearing the debris from the stones. They removed the surface dirt quickly to expose the buried end of the rock. At that point the progress slowed as they searched for any artifacts. There were none and the entire bench which Rhoda and Yosef had been sitting on was uncovered. It extended fifteen feet into the side of the hill and was covered in symbols. The writing in the part exposed had been erased by the weather over many years, but the part under soil was preserved and very clear. What was not clear was what the writing meant.

A day later, Jim and his family went to the site where Yenta was studying the stone. She had taken many pictures and sent them to experts all over the world seeking answers.

"We can possibly recover some of the worn writing on the exposed part with chemicals, but only in the lab in Tel Aviv. It is possible this is a history of the Israeli people. The first part seems to describe the life in Egypt and then progress to the forty years in the desert and then the time of the prophets then the monarchy at the end." Yenta stated as she pointed out on the writing at each stage along the stone. She continued, "You notice at the very end the sunburst image and the single figure of a man. I think this is the Messiah they expected in the future. An image of the expected Jesus perhaps! I cannot be sure about this, as some of the symbols are unfamiliar to me."

They all stood quietly for a moment thinking about what she said, then Rhoda asked, "How in the world will you move this without breaking it?"

"We'll build a support and then cut the stone near the level we are standing on and take it all. It's almost a meter thick so it will be very heavy, but strong. We will need a sizeable vehicle and equipment, but it can be done."

One of the volunteers, a young man from Norway, working on the opposite side from Yenta and the others, spoke up. "Ms. Neumann, sorry to interrupt but I have found something. The stone seems to be cut already. All along the base at the ground level there is a straight line. This stone is not attached it is just sitting here. There are marks on the rock over here."

This news excited everyone, even Jim. They all scurried to the other side of the stone, the side which had not been completely dug out. The team of volunteers began digging with shovels, forgetting to work slowly in case artifacts were in the soil. Even Yenta encouraged them to hurry. In quick order the flat rock on which the stone sat was cleared. The flat rock was had deep grooves in a curved arch around the top of the engraved stone. It looked like the end of the stone, deepest in the hill was a pivot and the entire stone could rotate and swing along on the top the grooves.

"There must be something under this stone!" Yenta stated, trying very hard to control her excitement.

"It would take a bulldozer to slide this thing," Jim noted as he got down and looked at the grooves. The tops of the notches were scratched and the color of the base stone, but the bottoms or troughs were a different color, as if stained. "I think oil was once poured into these grooves which would have lubricated the stone and made it easier to move. I have motor oil in the shop we could try."

"No, they would have used olive oil, which is what we will use," Yenta stated.

The olive oil came quickly in response to Yenta's cell phone call, four five-liter cans of oil. Jim thought this must surely be expensive, but no one questioned the cost.

The cans were opened and poured into the grooves on the flat area where the engraved stone would slide. It took three of the cans to fill all the grooves.

Six of the husky young male volunteers put their shoulders to the stone and pushed. The stone didn't budge.

"Again," Rhoda shouted as she and the others joined in the effort, crowding in along the side of the stone.

With a grinding noise the heavy stone moved slightly, and once broken free it slid with surprising ease. As it moved it revealed a passage, a hole under the stone. Some pushing nearly fell into the hole. With the engraved stone out of the way, a rectangular opening was revealed and steps leading down into darkness exposed for the first time in thousands of years.

"Miss Yenta should go first!" someone said.

"No one can go in yet!" Yenta stated firmly.

She took a little box of matches from her backpack, got down on her knees and struck the match. She lowered it into the opening. It went out when the match was lowed just a few inches into the opening. Yenta repeated the test with the same results.

"There is no oxygen in there; we must wait unit the blowers are in operation. It will take a few hours. When an area is closed for a long time, the oxygen is depleted. This is true of caves like this and tombs. We must be patient," Yenta explained.

No one was patient but they waited and speculated on what might be inside.

Yenta did go down a few steps but kept her head above the opening while closely examining the sides of the passageway. "There is writing here!" she said. Taking her camera, she began snapping pictures of clear inscriptions all around the edge of the opening. "This is writing is an ancient version of Hebrew, and will take some work to decipher, but this looks like a reference to Solomon. My God this is amazing!!" she said almost shouting. Her normal calm reserved attitude was completely missing.

It took nearly four hours for a truck from the Archeological building in Tel Aviv to arrive. The truck was driven by a small man, introduced as Issa. He spoke to Yenta in a language no one other than the two of them seemed to understand. He unloaded a blower and large spool of wide flimsy looking tubing. The tubing was made of a strong plastic like the material used to make trash bags. Issa took a rigid ring and attached it to the end of the tubing which held it open. The tube expanded to about a foot in diameter. He moved very cautiously, and it seemed to everyone very slowly. He was being very careful. Meticulously he unpacked what looked like and probably was a scuba diving tank and mask. Issa extended the gear toward

Yenta as if asking if she wanted to wear it. Of course, she jumped at the offer. She put on the tanks and mask with the mouthpiece and turned to go down the steps. "Do not tarry; there is not a lot of air in the tank!" he said in a serious warning tone in Hebrew. With much anticipation, Yenta descended the steps carrying the end of the plastic tube and a large flashlight.

The plastic unrolled as she went down the steps. At the bottom of the steps she entered a tunnel and the light from her flashlight disappeared. The tunnel seemed to be quite long. As she progressed, Yenta carefully placed the tubing on the floor along one wall of the tunnel. It was only about five minutes when the plastic stopped feeding into the hole. Issa had watched it very closely to insure it did not hang up or become tangled. Yenta reached the end of the tunnel and placed the ring holding the plastic tubing. She did tarry a little as it took longer for her to reemerge from the tunnel.

Issa cut the plastic and attached the end to the blower and started it using a small generator in the truck. Yenta began telling what she saw. She was smiling broadly and talking so fast she was difficult to understand. Waving her hands as she chattered, no one there had ever seen her this excited.

"There are jars that may contain scrolls and stacks of bone boxes. One area has a wall of inscriptions engraved on it. If this tunnel was dug in the days of Solomon, it proves without doubt that Israel controlled this area."

The blower roared to a start and a musty smell permeated the air as the cavern was ventilated.

Yenta turned to Jim and said, "There seems to be a vent tunnel up to your property, near the house. It's closed as there is no light from above, but it was for ventilation. Perhaps we can find it."

"We will look, I hope it's not under the house," Jim replied.

It took about two hours for the little blower to clear the cavern. Yenta, now with a candle in a glass lantern, went down the steps until the candle went out. She repeated this until the candle burned brightly at the bottom of the steps.

Finally, the group began to go in with instruction that if anyone felt the least bit dizzy, they should say something and get out. Of course, no one would. Jim, helping Aliza, went down following Yenta and many of the volunteers. The steps were very steep and had no handrail. Apparently, the ancient Jews were more nimble than modern middle-aged people. Reaching the bottom, the passage opened up a little, wide enough so two people could pass each other. The entire cavern was cut from solid rock, a big undertaking without power tools. As they moved along the passage, Jim noticed clay jars everywhere. They lined the walls and were stacked in notches in the wall. If all of these contained scrolls, this was an enormous find and would take years for experts to evaluate. Among the round jars were many square boxes, probably containing bones of the dead, a method of burial used today. The site was a massive graveyard.

As most of the 'explorers' went further into the tunnel, Yenta stopped and was examining a notch off to the side of the tunnel. It was a very small room with a low ceiling. In the center was a pile of rubble, similar to sand, with several oil lamps sitting on top. Along the side was a decomposed body. Even the skull was nearly gone. Inconspicuous to most passersby, Yenta was glad she had let her curiosity lead her to this find.

Very quietly Yenta speculated, "This was a table with several oil lamps. This man was writing here. He is probably a scribe, writing records on scrolls and preserving them in the jars."

"Could it be that he was alive when the tunnel was sealed?" Jim asked.

"It is possible; he was likely responsible for all these records and insisted on staying when the tunnel was sealed. He would want to finish his work and store everything in the jars. Perhaps someone had hoped to come back and let him out," Yenta stated very reverently.

"My God, he suffocated or starved to death!" Aliza said, looking at the skeleton.

"It was a sacrifice he was willing to make," Yenta replied.

She then raised her voice, "Let's get everyone out of here before we damage something. It will take numerous hours of work to evaluate this find. Everyone, this may be the biggest most important find in any of our lives. We should rejoice!"

The young volunteers responded and soon Jim, his wife and Yenta were the only ones left. "I want to show you something," Yenta said as she motioned.

She went to the end of the tunnel and looked up. There was a shaft cut in the rock straight up, over their heads. It was about two feet in diameter and Jim wondered how they did this without a drill. It must have been a tight fit for a man working with only a chisel and hammer.

"If this is a vent it would have provided air flow for the tunnel, if the entrance was open. This is on your property, near your house. It would be good if we could open it," Yenta stated, still looking up.

"I may know where this is. There's a pile of rocks in my garden. I thought it might have been an old statue or marker for something. We moved the house a little so as not to destroy it. I'll check it over. If that's not it, we'll have to measure and try to find where this vent is on the outside," Jim replied.

Jim walked back to his house and around the back to the garden where he and Rhoda had planted vegetables. In the center was a man-made stone structure. It consisted of cut stone, a round tower about eight feet tall. It was about five feet in diameter at the bottom and tapered to two feet at the top. He had thought it was an old trail marker and had not disturbed it. He thought it was interesting and added something to the garden. Several ivy vines had been planted around it which someday would grow to the top. Now with the aid of a ladder, he went to the top, where he found a round cap stone. There had been an inscription on the top but was now too worn to make it out. With some effort, he pushed the stone off and it fell to the ground, exposing a hole through the center of the tower and down into the underground cavern. He could clearly hear the blower fan and felt the air flow.

He shouted down the hole, "Yenta! Yenta!"

"You don't have to yell, I can hear you," She said as she stood right behind him. "I had paced off the distance from inside the tunnel and then up to here. I think the vent is right here," she said laughing.

Rhoda and Yosef came up the hill, holding hands and joined them. "Let's go inside and get something to drink, and maybe a snack," Jim suggested.

Going inside, Yenta looked around and said, "I've heard about this house and what a grand thing it is. The stories I heard were not an exaggeration!"

"I thank you; my husband provides for me very well," Aliza said, as she came into the room. She went to Jim and kissed him and continued, "It wasn't busy at the hospital, so I came home; I am a little tired, but I have some food prepared."

As she always did, Aliza had prepared enough food for ten people. They always had leftovers for snacks and to give to any workers which might be there.

They gathered around the table and, as usual, Jim prayed, thanking God for all the blessings He had provided and for showing them the ancient treasure in the cave. As always, he closed the prayer, "In Jesus Name."

He didn't know if Yenta was a practicing Jew or a Messianic Jew. She didn't seem to uncomfortable with the prayer.

As they ate, Jim asked Yenta, "What do you think is in all those jars?"

"Well, at least one of them contains scrolls. They should not be opened until they are in the controlled environment in the museum. But I could not stand it and opened one of them and looked inside.

It contained three small scrolls. I'll claim the cap was loose," She answered, smiling.

"Maybe somewhere in the writings the name of this city will be found, and we can adopt it instead of Jenkins," Jim stated, still hoping the growing city would not be named after him.

Yenta, still smiling, replied, "Perhaps you should consider it an honor! In any case names of communities are chosen for many reasons. Your house was the first here so that may be reason enough."

Jim wisely stopped talking, but did not conceal his dissatisfaction about the name. The three women looked at him and just chuckled, no support at all.

Rhoda, wanting to help her dad, said, "Yenta when will we know what the scrolls in the jars say?"

"It will be awhile. The jars will be transported to the archeological museum in Jerusalem where they will be opened in the proper environment. It's likely the cave was closed shortly after Solomon, and if so, these will be the earliest documents ever found. The magnitude of this find cannot be overstated. Each scrap of parchment will be gone over by experts. It will be years before everything is reviewed."

Yenta left with the documents in two trucks equipped with special racks for the Jars. They also took the bone boxes for evaluation. These would be returned to the tunnel when the examination was complete.

Aliza looked at Jim and said, "Jim I want to go to the mountain were we first met. You thought it was Mount Herman and it is just west of here."

The request surprised Jim, as going there had never been mentioned. "Aliza, we can certainly go but I don't think this is the right time, you are, in fact, very pregnant."

"I am not that far along, and I feel fine. I just have a feeling that if we don't go now, we will never go, and I want to check it out. It is, after all, where we met!" She stated it in such a way that Jim understood the decision had been made. In addition, he recalled that the 'feelings' Hannah and Aliza had been very often true like a message from a higher being, and not to be ignored.

"You have responsibilities at the hospital. Could you get away?" he replied, thinking to delay the trip until after the baby was born, a losing proposition.

"I have nothing scheduled for several days, and we can take the Jeep most of the way to the top. If I think I'm getting in trouble, we can come back," she said, and gave him a smile that always worked.

Rhoda had walked up during the conversation and spoke up. "Yosef and I can go with you and help if we need to!" She was always looking for a reason to spend time with Yosef.

"Thank you, but no. This is a trip Jim and I need to take alone, and our cell phones work if we need help," Aliza answered sweetly.

Jim loaded the Jeep with his backpack, tent and everything he thought they might possibly need. They planned to spend at least one night on top of the mountain but he took food for a week. If there wasn't a spring or a water supply, there would be a problem staying more than a couple of nights.

They left before dawn the next morning. Jim was happy to be going with Aliza, even though he was concerned about her ability to climb. He was absolutely giddy and laughed and talked almost continually on the trip. The Syrian's had an observation station near the top of the mountain, used to observe the Israelis on the Golan Heights. The facility had been bombed early in the conflict and abandoned since, but the road, such as it was, still existed.

They arrived before noon and Jim put on the heavy pack. His only weapon was a pistol, as he was expecting no one would be there. Aliza would carry a small day pack with very little in it. Not wanting her to be disappointed, he said, "Aliza, you know our meeting was a dream; we were not really on this mountain, even if it seemed real."

"Perhaps," she replied with another smile.

Following a well-marked trail, they climbed the mountain on a dozen switchbacks. Aliza did well by resting every few minutes. It was slow going but they reached a flat area near the top. It was where the dream had taken place. He saw the boulder where Aliza had been sitting the first time, he saw her. It was spooky.

"It is exactly as I remember!" she said, as she danced around a little. "We were really here!" She came up and kissed him. "That was a very happy time!"

She was right; it was exactly like he remembered in the dream. Even the place where she had set up her tent was there. Across the flat area was the rocks where he had his tent in a protected place. "We were certainly here in spirit; this exactly like I remember," he said.

"I think we were here physically. Look at this!" She said as she held up a strip of blue fabric attached to a tent stake, her tent stake.

It was impossible. In one night of their lives while they slept, before they even knew each other, they spent many days here in a tent, Jim's tent, on a mountain thousands of miles from where they lived. They were really here, physically here. Even time had been adjusted as all the days occurring in a dream passed during a single night. Of course, Jim believed the all-powerful God is capable of anything, but why would He do something like this? Jim was speechless.

He set up his tent in the same place his tent had been in the dream, and used the same rock to drive the stakes into the ground. He put the packs in the tent and opened the sleeping bag, large enough for two. He cooked the evening meal outside as the weather was cool and clear. This was not the same as the dream where they were kept inside by the weather. They walked over to the western side to see the very beautiful sunset. There were no ominous clouds to threaten them with another storm.

Jim was trying to figure out why God had done this, but Aliza was just enjoying the realization that their common dream was real, physically real. As they ate the warmed-up soup for their evening meal, Aliza said, "I think the reason God did this was so we immediately would recognize each other and when we met, quickly fall in love. He trapped us here in a tent right next to each other by the storm.

"You are right, of course, but what I don't understand was why God did something so unusual for us. He could have just let us meet in a normal way. I would have fallen in love with you anyway we met. It's as if God has something very special in store for us," Jim said, still deep in thought.

She came over, cuddled up, and said, "It may not be for us, but our child, that God has something special planned. I think it's time for you to take me to bed. Remember what it was like the first time we were here?"

They spent two nights on the mountain enjoying the view and each other. It was greatly satisfying.

Rhoda had called every few hours to check on them. She had really wanted to come. Next time she would.

CHAPTER 28

Peace – For the Most Part

AFTER THE CONFLICTS AND WARS around the world, peace seemed to exist everywhere. The general opinion was that the UN had a lot to do with it. The new head of the UN, a man named Arie, from Greece, was an effective peacemaker. He had an unusual alliance with the Roman Catholic Pope, who was a Greek, also. They had known each other for years and had sone some traveling together. It was rumored that Arie and the Pope were related. They strongly resembled each other, both good looking men. Unlike previous leaders of the UN, Arie traveled worldwide. He was an amazing man. Not only was he as handsome as a movie star, he had a wonderful personality. When he entered a room, all attention was focused on him, and every word he spoke was valued as a nugget of gold. He had gone to most world leaders and convinced them that peace was the best path. Even vicious, hateful dictators agreed or were swayed by his messages. His successes are nothing short of amazing. Arie often traveled with Pope Constantine, as well as the ever present-present gorgeous lady named Ingrid. No one Questioned whether their relationship was professional or personal. Perhaps it was both. The Pope spoke of peace on earth and seemed to accept and approve every religion, a strange position for the leader of the

Catholic Church. Acceptance of all religious views were effective in molding the world in unity, respect and tolerance for all nations. All conflicts on earth seemed to disappear. After decades of division and upheaval, it was a time of hope, prosperity and calm.

While everyone seemed to love and respect Arie, Jim had an uneasy feeling about the man. His casual familiarity, his constant smile, his words of promise and his magnetic personality were not normal. Jim was confused by his own uneasiness, as the man was clearly brilliant and very charismatic. Was he too good to be true? Could he be trusted? The Bible in Revelation spoke of a man, the Anti-Christ who would have these same characteristics. Was Arie that man?

Jim and his family continued their life with Jim working with Yosef in the woodshop making or repairing furniture. Rhoda continued in school and, of course, spent time with Yosef. Aliza worked in the hospital and grew her baby. It was one afternoon, when she was performing heart surgery that she calmly announced her water had just broken. She finished the delicate operation and then asked the young doctor assisting her to close the incision as she needed to go have a baby or two. She left the operating room and went directly to the delivery room, asking someone to call her husband and ask him to come by, if he wasn't too busy.

Jim and Yosef were both there in less than ten minutes, out of breath from running from the shop. They had not put Aliza in the delivery room yet, but she was in a waiting area and being examined by the doctor who aided in the delivery.

Jim grabbed Aliza's hand and she squeezed his hand so hard he thought she would break his fingers. She smiled and said, "I will have more sympathy for patients after this. It really hurts a lot. Husband, I may have a surprise for you!"

Jim told her he loved her as they went into the delivery room.

The delivery was probably normal, but for Jim it was traumatic. Aliza did not scream, as some did, but she moaned with the contractions. The baby was a boy, and as the nurse cleaned him up, the doctor then stated, "This one is a girl!" No one had mentioned to Jim that Aliza was carrying twins; she knew, of course! Doctors know things.

When the pain subsided, Aliza looked at Jim with a big smile and said, "By the way darling husband, we are the parents of two children! Surprise!"

Jim played along with great surprise, although he had suspected there were twins. At one point during the pregnancy Aliza's mother, Ruth, had commented, "Twins are common in our family."

Just a few hours later, Aliza was up and walking, holding Jim's arm. "It is best after surgery or childbirth for the patient to get up and walk. I have said that many, many times. From now on I will have more empathy for my patients," she said as they slowly walked down the hall to the nursery window. Their children were, of course, the best-looking babies anywhere. Jim was pleased they both had red curly locks, unusual in Israel.

She could have stayed longer but Aliza came home the day after the delivery. Jim took the Jeep, along with Rhoda and her constant companion, Yosef, to transport Aliza and the two babies the short distance from the hospital to their house. He picked her up and sat her in the seat of the rather high Jeep. She didn't protest as she normally would.

The nursery was located adjacent to the master bedroom as Aliza had directed when the house was being planned. On entering, Aliza stopped, and seeing two cribs, one with pink and the other blue, exclaimed "Jim, you knew. Having twins was supposed to be a surprise! How did you know it would be a boy and a girl?"

"My dear, I did notice when the babies were kicking there seemed to be more than two feet so I borrowed your stethoscope and listened when you were sleeping. I heard two heart beats. Besides you were huge," he said laughing, then continued, "Yosef and I made these two cribs and the changing table weeks ago, but I confess, I ordered two blue and two pink accessories for the beds as I couldn't guess the sex. So, we now have a spare for each bed."

Aliza sat in the rocking chair, which matched the other furniture in the room, and smiled at both of the men in her life, clearly happy with them.

They named the babies, Jonathan and Dinah, biblical names. Jonathan was the son of Saul the first king of Israel and friend of David, the second king. Dinah was a daughter of Jacob. His name was changed by God to Israel, the current name of the nation. They were good names, though not unusual in Israel.

It was a happy time for the city of Jenkins. The name seemed to have stuck to this rapidly growing community. The large archeological dig of the ancient ruin continued to expand to the south of the city requiring the new city to build to the north. New immigrates from all over the world came and settled, and some Jews from the southern desert areas moved into the area. The farming expanded as the soil was fertile and the Lord blessed them with regular rainfall. Life was good.

The evaluation of the writings from the jars found in the tunnel progressed very slowly. The scrolls were the most ancient written records ever found. Previously unknown information about the Manasseh tribe, the tribe assigned to this area by Joshua, was uncovered. In addition, copies of the Books of Moses were found, much older than any previously found. This was the greatest find of the century, even greater than the Dead Sea Scrolls, found in 1947.

However, being in the northern part of Israel where invasions throughout history had begun, the IDF had a strong presence. There was regular testing of the alert system which warned of a missile attack and the people went to shelters. Jim's basement was a popular shelter as they always provided snacks and they had a clean bathroom, unlike most shelters. Jim, always the prepper, maintained a supply of freeze-dried food in case of an emergency. In addition, he kept the motor home in 'ready to go' shape in case he needed to send his family south quickly.

One day the missile alarm was not a test but a real alert. The IDF had sensors to detect launches of missiles all along the front. The missiles they detected landed far away but everyone scurried to the shelters for safety. Israel retaliated by firing at the launch sites, but likely the men or boys that fired the missiles were gone. Of course, Israel was criticized for defending themselves by the UN and the world's press.

In Israel the next few years were peaceful, except for regular missile drills and the occasional real attack. None of the real attacks were effective and none near the town of Jenkins. By any measure fear subsided and normalcy ruled. The crops in the area were good and the city flourished economically, as did Jim's household. Aliza presented him with another set of twins, again a boy and a girl. Jim, now forty-eight years old, wondered how he could handle young children at his age. He felt fine now, but 'good grief', he was not a young man anymore. They named the children David and Ruth. The girl was named after Aliza's mother who passed away that year. Ruth had Aliza's good looks and red hair, but David looked very much like Jim, born with thick black hair. From the very first, David was different. It was said he was born an adult, and in many ways, it was true. He was a smart and happy baby, but always seemed mature for his age.

Rhoda married Yosef on her twentieth birthday, no surprise. They built a house on the edge of Jim's property, with Jim's financial help, and settled in. Their first child came quickly; Jim liked to say, "Nine months and fifteen minutes after the wedding!" An exaggeration, as it was actually nine months and two weeks, no hesitation on their part. Yosef made a good living for them from the new woodworking shop, also built on the property. Jim got a small cut of the profits as he was the primary investor.

All in all, everything was peaceful in Israel and in Jim's family. Not so in the rest of the western world. The US remained in a deep depression. It had been six years since the EMP attack and industry was still not up to speed. Everything had shut down after the attack and tax revenue dropped to nearly nothing. The situation was much worse than the big depression in the early 1900's. The national debt was enormous. The tax revenue wouldn't even cover the dept payment. Government social services ended, welfare payments, and even Social Security paychecks, quit coming. The military budget was severely cut, making the country less safe. The government did provide some funding for soup kitchens to keep people from starving, primarily in the big cities. The depression spread to Europe and most of the rest of the world. China suffered but was clearly the single superpower left. European countries were in a terrible condition. The millions of Muslim immigrates had overwhelmed the original inhabitants and demanded the right to rule. In several cases they were the majority population as they had many more children than the native population. The ancient dream of Muslim rule of Europe had been accomplished without a major war. The result, of course, was Theocratic rule, discrimination of Non-Muslims, and poverty. It was a mess.

In looking at the world situation, Jim observed they were in the best country at this time in history. Israel at peace and prospering; could it last?

CHAPTER 29

Wars and Rumors of War

YEARS PASSED, THE CHILDREN GREW and Jim grew older. He was now near sixty years old but blessed with good health and the strength of a much younger man. Aliza at forty-eight continued to look like she was in her thirties and was often mistaken for Jim's daughter. She found this amusing and Jim pretended it bothered him, but it didn't. Yosef and Rhoda had three children. She declared that since she had them one at a time, instead of in twos like Aliza, she somehow paid more for them, in pain at least. With four young children of his own and three grandchildren, he had an exceptionally large family, all living right next to each other. Yosef, running the woodworking shop, made high end furniture and was highly successful. He had become one of the larger employers in the city. The Lord had blessed them greatly; it was hard to believe it could be so good.

While the peace between countries held, the prosperity in Israel enjoyed was not seen in the rest of the world. Muslims, as always persecuted the Non-Muslims. Jews from all over Europe fled to Israel, and Christians to the United States. Non-Muslims remaining in Europe were badly mistreated. As always happens in Muslim controlled countries, the rulers became rich while the populace were controlled with a heavy hand. Non-Muslim women were particularly under pressure. Many were attacked on the streets and some raped and even murdered. The perpetrators claimed the women were prostitutes or asked to be attacked as they did not dress in a burka and were unaccompanied by a male relative. Women were afraid to leave their home, even during the day. A few resorted to carrying firearms, but risked strong punishment if caught, due to restrictive laws. Many of the native-born residents acknowledged they were living under occupation, the same as in war. Groups of resistance fighters known as 'RFs' sprung up to combat the occupiers. The RFs were brutal groups who would wipe out entire Arab families if the Muslim men attacked women on the streets. The cities separated into armed camps of Muslim and Non-Muslim occupants. There was no joy in Europe.

In the US the Muslim population had dwindled after the EMP attack. Persecution there was minimal, but the country never fully recovered to its previous economic and political strength. It was, however, making progress. Industry was improving and farming was increasing production making the US a major exporter of food.

Of course, 'Good' in Israel could only last so long, at least until the Lord returned. Ten years after the war the youth in the many countries which hated Israel grew to military age. Hate speech about Israel and their presence in what they considered Muslim land increased. This was nothing new but the intensity increased.

The peace treaty, negotiated by the UN, had been enforced in the past, but for some reason, it now seemed mute. Even Arie, the leader of the UN, began to speak harshly toward Israel. He was unhappy with Israel for some unspoken reason. UN troops were assigned to encircle Israel, stating it was to protect them from attack. However, the troops assigned this duty did not seem to be there to protect Israel but to prevent Israel from defending themselves or responding to an attack.

It was more than just speech; the countries surrounding Israel increased the size of their militaries, arming them with advanced weapons from Russia and China. The surrounding Islamic states which had been soundly defeated ten years earlier now had millions of young men ready to take on Israel again. Even Iran, under military leadership since the mystery attack, was supporting the hatred toward Israel.

Israel responded to the verbal attacks by building up its military and adding defenses. They were alone in the world. The US verbally defended Israel and vetoed several resolutions in the UN but did little to provide assistance due to their own problems.

Jim became a news junkie, watching the world news several hours a day. He watched alone as Aliza and the rest of his family wanted to ignore the situation; it was uncomfortable to contemplate. He became convinced Arie, was in fact, the Anti-Christ and the world was moving toward the Great Tribulation and a final great war. Most Israelis, didn't share his concerns as things continued to be good and people prospered. Jim understood their city was located very near the front lines of any future conflict, so he prepared to evacuate his family by repairing and servicing the old motor home. The motor home had been used to travel to several countries in that part of the world by his family. Occasionally Rhoda and her family used it for vacations. However, most of the time the vehicle was unused and stored in the garage. Jim replaced the tires and batteries and updated all systems to ready the unit for a speedy evacuation. His family kidded him about his ambitious plans for evacuation. One question nagged at him—where could they flee that would be safer than Israel? It did not deter him from preparing.

It was six months later when the first alert came in the form of a visit from Shalom Heymes, now a general in the IDF. He was touring the northern provinces and stopped to visit Jim. The now aging man and Jim sat in his rather spacious living room while Aliza came with more coffee, water and pastries. She interrupted often with the food and drink but was excused; after all she was a Jewish wife. Finally, she sat and joined them.

The general, after a few minutes of small talk, catching up, said, "Jim, the government is concerned. There is a massive build up in Turkey and in western Iraq. The troops are quietly coming from as far away as China and are stationed in massive camps. Just to feed all these men must be an enormous cost. We have questioned the UN, who deny the buildup, but we, of course, have people out there. Something is happening and it doesn't look good."

"Could this be some kind of exercise?" Aliza asked, hoping the implications were not as they appeared.

"It seems doubtful. There is no reason for a military exercise, especially on this scale. After all, there is a peace treaty which most Arab countries have signed. I am genuinely concerned as are senior military leaders. Your city is near the front lines if an attack comes. It would be prudent for civilians to take a vacation down south in the next few weeks, or at least plan such a trip. If something happens, we'll not have much warning." With this dark news the general shook Jim's hand and hugged Aliza and left.

The visit strengthened Jim's resolve to prepare for evacuation, much to Aliza's displeasure. In her mind she knew Jim was right, but she did not want to acknowledge the good times may be coming to an end.

Jim spent three days loading freeze dried food, water and clothing for his family in the motor home. They would be able to survive, more than survive; they would do well for several weeks, maybe a couple of months. Whatever happens should be over by then. His plan, not mentioned to his wife, was for her to drive the motor home with their four children and Yosef to drive the Jeep with his family. He would stay and fight. It was a good plan.

There was an immediate snag in Jim's plan. He presented it to Rhoda's husband, Yosef, who responded, "Father, this is not right. You should take the family south and keep them safe. I'm going to stay and fight. I am IDF and trained. Please don't be offended but you're not a young man. It would be better if you took the family to safety."

"You may be right, Yosef, but understand, I may have few years left but you have a responsibility to your family. Who knows how bad this might get? They will need you and I can contribute something to defend Israel, even if I am old," Jim replied, trying to lighten the conversation.

"Then we'll both stay; I could not live with myself if I ran from the front in time of need," Yosef responded, ending the discussion.

The two men prepared their packs with supplies for the conflict. Jim took his regular pack with the tent and sleeping bag, big enough for two if they were very friendly. In addition he added boxes of cartridges for his .338 rifle, the rifle with the expensive scope. He could hit targets well over a mile away with it. Yosef had a pack, an M-16 with a scope, and ammunition for it. In addition, they carried pistols. Jim hoped he would not have to walk far as he could barely lift the pack. In addition to the packs, they each had tactical vests with armor and pockets for clips. They would certainly look the part of warriors, even if they were carrying so much weight they could hardly walk. Jim chuckled a bit thinking about it; Yosef did not ask why but looked at him strangely.

Both men, father and proxy son, had no idea how to tell their wives about their plans. Both were fearful of the task and put it off as long as possible.

CHAPTER 30

War – The Final War?

THE ARMIES CONTINUED TO GATHER in very large numbers, north and east of Israel. The UN claimed this was an exercise and not a real attack; everyone should relax. No one believed them, especially Israel. General Haynes came by again and warned the city they should prepare to move south on a quick notice. The people accepted this warning without comment, like it was an everyday thing. Jim was amazed at the Jews acceptance of impending disaster and thought if this happened in the US the people would panic.

A month later the time came. Israel announced civilians should move south, further from the likely front. The City of Jenkins was within missile range of the enemy. If the attackers moved a little closer, they would be in range of long-distance artillery. It wouldn't be safe to stay.

Implementing Jim's plan was not going as well, as he expected. Aliza broke down crying, "Jim you must go with us! You are not in the army and we need you, I need you! You must understand you are not a young man anymore. Come with us we need you!" She said this as her four children surrounded her. All except David were crying. He rarely ever cried.

"I must go and do what I can and we'll be in God's hands," he replied taking her in his arms.

"Then I will stay. They will need me in the hospital."

"The army is evacuating everybody in the hospital except a few army medics. You need to take the children south. I have a place you can park the motor home and even hook up the utilities," Jim stated. Aliza looked into his eyes for a long time and then turned and gathered a few things for each of the children, things Jim hadn't thought of. It was a trying time.

Yosef, having a similar discussion with Rhoda, reached similar results. Lots of tears were shed.

The two women, mother and daughter, decided they would all ride in the motor home. It would be them and seven children, crowded but doable. They would tow the Jeep which could be packed with more supplies. Jim hooked up the jeep with the tow bar and instructed Rhoda on how to hook and unhook it. She listened but probably already knew all about it. The RV was loaded with the most important items as everyone more or less expected what they left would be destroyed.

With lots of hugs, kisses and tears their families began loading up. Jim's son David came to say goodbye to his father and whispered as he hugged him. "I had a dream. Everything will be allright in the end."

The motor home joined the caravan of vehicles leaving the city of Jenkins. The military reserves and quite a few men gathered and waited for transportation from the IDF. The trucks and Humvees arrived shortly, apparently prearranged. A colonel came to Jim and said, "Colonel Jenkins, you are excused. You have served you country well and are not required at this time." A clear reference to Jim's age.

"Sir, I realize I am no longer young and would not do well in hand-to-hand combat, but I see very well at a distance and have a superior rifle and scope. I will be an adequate sniper."

"As you wish. You and your son will ride in the lead Humvee and we'll locate you in the hills overlooking the eastern front. The vehicle was driven by a sergeant and already contained four other men fully outfitted with tactical gear. The sergeant, probably half Jim's age, stared at him as he and Yosef climbed into the back of the vehicle. It was loaded with duffels which were at least soft. They threw their packs in and climbed in with their rifles. There were eight vehicles in this group which carried the men from the city. They quickly sped north toward the Israeli border, passing lines of vehicles going the other way as the northern providences were evacuated. It was not far. About twenty miles from the border the southbound traffic ceased, and they were alone on the road.

It happened as they rounded a curve in the highway. A RPG shot from a line of trees came directly at their Humvee. The explosive round hit the left front tire and destroyed the front of the vehicle, turning it on its side. The seven men in the vehicle all were thrown out. The next vehicle in the line machine gunned the line of trees and cut down several men trying to run away. Jim felt a sharp pain in his left side but did not lose consciousness. He got up slowly and moved to Yosef, whose left arm was bent wrong. He also had a lot of blood on his shirt. He was cursing under his breath as he looked at Jim, very glad to see he was alive. The driver and the front passenger were dead, and the other three men shaken up but alive, one injured badly.

Men spread out to secure the area, but it seemed this was a small group who had crossed the border. A truck arrived and two medics jumped out. They insisted the survivors in the vehicle go to the field hospital. The two uninjured men indicated they were all right and could go on. Even though Jim didn't seem to have any strength in his left arm he stood with them. As they prepared to take Yosef, Jim went to him in an attempt to encourage him. Yosef grabbed Jim with his right hand and pulled him close really hurting his arm. "Father,

I promised mom I would keep you safe. For the love of God, please do not get hurt. Mom would never forgive me. I love you dad."

Jim was almost brought to tears; it was the first time Yosef had called him dad. The boy, well now a grown man, was badly hurt but from a quick look his injuries didn't seem to be fatal.

The injured were loaded and the vehicle sped off in the direction they had come from. A truck pulled up and General Haynes stepped out of the cab. He looked at Jim for a moment, and then asked, "Your Son?"

"Injured but alive. Taken to the hospital."

The general noticed Jim was not standing quite straight but said nothing. He turned to one of his men in the back of the truck and said, "Load this equipment and just stack it in the floor."

Jim's pack was picked up and put in the truck. He was glad someone else got it as he didn't think he could pick it up. It was heavy due to the extra ammunition for his rifle. The general made a slight nod with his head and a man gave Jim his seat on the end of the bench. Jim could sit with his left arm not touching anyone.

"Colonel Jenkins, you are bleeding," one of the men stated as the truck began moving. Jim didn't recognize him and, of course, he was not a colonel, but he had grown tired of correcting people. "It's just a scratch," he replied. Of course, it was not just a scratch, he had broken ribs. He knew this as he was married to a doctor and had learned something. It was painful but not serious unless he coughed up blood indicating a punctured lung.

The plan was to put small groups of men, a sniper in each group, along the high places overlooking the eastern border. At the very north end of the ridge would be a command post and the station for the general. About half the men had been dropped off when they came to ruins of a building. At one time it had been at least three stories, a factory of some kind. Now it was just parts of the floors held up by pylons. It did have a good view of the valley to the east. The truck stopped and the general directed two men to carry Jim's backpack and rifle up the remains of a staircase to the second floor of the building. The general held Jim's right arm as they went up the stairs. He had not done this with any of the other teams. The second floor, what was left of it, was bare concrete with broken blocks scattered about. The two men were directed to move several of the concrete blocks to the eastern edge of the open floor and set up a crude shooting station. The general shook Jim's hand and said, "I wish you luck Colonel Jenkins, you are a wonderful friend to Israel."

As the general and the two men went back to the truck, one of the men, a corporal stated to the general, "Sir that man is seriously injured, why are we leaving him here?"

"Corporal, Colonel Jenkins was awarded the 'Hero of Israel medal' for his service in the last war. He is now giving his life for Israel and what little we can do to help him is why we are leaving him here."

The corporal just nodded, not knowing Jim or much about the previous war, but understanding this event was meaningful to the general. The truck drove on.

In the building Jim set up the rifle on one of the concrete blocks and his spotting scope on another. He had a seat, another block. It was actually fairly comfortable. He had his own handheld radio to communicate with the rest of the army which he took from his pack and set the frequency. The men had left a jug of water, so along with it and his canteens and freeze-dried packets of food, he was good for several days.

Suddenly Jim felt he could not breath and began coughing and spitting up blood. This was not a good sign, but afterwards he felt better and could breathe easier. He prayed, "Lord the pain is bad, but give me strength to help in this cause. I know you don't need me or any of us to fight but we desire to help. If I die, please comfort my family."

Through the spotting scope, Jim could see activity in the distance, a lot of vehicles and men moving toward the border. It wouldn't be long.

He had been there for a couple of hours and was eating an apple from a tree in this yard when the radio came alive. "This is home station, check in." The sniper stations began responding, "Station 1 receives, nothing but dust to the east." The eight stations responded with similar reports. Jim didn't have a station number but knew he was between six and seven so pushed his transmit key and stated, "This is station six and one half. I receive. The enemy is eight kilometers distance with many tanks and trucks. In addition, separated to the south is a group of missile launchers and trucks. The men with them are dressed in full body isolation suits."

General Haynes in the Home Station to the north was stunned by the report. Poison gas had not been used in previous attacks. He immediately put in a secure call to his headquarters in Jerusalem requesting additional gas masks. The response he got was sobering. "General Haynes, we regret to tell you but Tel Aviv and Haifa have been attacked by nuclear weapons. We do not know the extent of the damage, but it is extensive. The weapons were apparently planted earlier as no aircraft were detected in the area."

The general paused for a moment before passing on the information, wondering if he should. He decided he would want to know. He pressed the transmit button on his radio, "Men this is General Haynes. I have had a report that Tel Aviv and Haifa have been attacked by nuclear bombs. I don't know the damage. Israel is fighting for our existence. Be brave and trust in the Lord God Almighty." No one responded.

Two hours passed and Jim experienced another painful coughing fit and spit up more blood, when a report came from one of the other stations. "There are drones coming."

It was a few minutes when Jim saw one. It was a larger version of the drones used as toys. These were about six feet in diameter and had cameras and maybe small bombs under them. Jim looked through the scope on his rifle and when the drone turned toward him, he fired. It just simply blew into many pieces, but Jim did not see it. The recoil caused a pain in his side so severe it nearly caused him to lose consciousness. A few more shots rang out from the other snipers and soon the drones were gone.

Jim prayed again, "Lord I have fired only one shot and it hurts. Please do something so I will be able to help." He then had another coughing fit and spit up more blood, this time it was black. He had no idea what black blood meant.

It seemed like just a few minutes and they were there—a huge army moving south in the valley just east of them. It reminded Jim of an anthill that had been disturbed; it seemed the whole earth was moving. The general had put the snipers in a perfect place. Jim began firing, aiming at men who seemed to be in charge, standing in tanks or riding in better looking vehicles. He had ten clips for his rifle, each with ten rounds. The clips were all emptied in very short order. Each shot brought a stab of pain in his chest and he was having more and more trouble breathing. It would be better if he stopped and coughed up some more blood, but the targets were there, so he kept shooting. Trying to load a clip with one hand didn't seem to work, so he took his box of loose cartridges and loaded a single round each time he fired.

The enemy, of course, noticed the continuous fire from the hills and the many casualties they were having. Their orders were to move south as quickly as possible, so they didn't stop but turned their guns toward the hills and fired as they went. Machine gun fire peppered the area around Jim and cannon fire from the tanks exploded all around. Apparently, they couldn't determine where the sniper fire was coming from or, perhaps, they were just bad shots. In any case he was not hit, although a shell hit the other end of his building and collapsed the area where the steps were. He was left on a long concrete beam held by two or three columns.

He was slowing down as it was difficult to take the single rounds and put them in the chamber at each shot. He stopped when he heard a quiet voice behind him say, "Let me help by loading the clips for you."

Jim turned and there was a young man with brown hair dressed in army fatigues. He looked very familiar, but Jim couldn't place him. In this dirty dusty area this young man was clean, very clean. It didn't make sense; how did he even get here with the steps gone? He realized his thinking was muddled as he couldn't get a good breath of air, so perhaps the man's presence did in some way make sense.

The man loaded all the clips, emptying the box of loose cartridges and Jim continued firing. He was almost out of ammunition when a new target appeared. It was a fighter jet approaching low over the enemy troops, firing its machine guns at the hills. Jim aimed his rifle at the craft and fired a single shot. The chance of a rifle shooting down an aircraft was very small, but the Lord intervened. The bullet hit a blade in the engine, causing an imbalance. A piece of the engine compressor broke off and pierced the cockpit, hitting the pilot, mortally wounding him. The dying man pulled the control column back and put the aircraft in a steep climb. The engine, damaged as it was, continued to put out thrust and the aircraft started into a big loop. The pilot passed out at the top of the loop and the plane went into a dive, straight down crashing into the group of missile launchers and the trucks with the poison gas. The aircraft held a full complement of bombs and missiles. It was a big explosion. In addition, some of the missiles with poison gas on the launchers exploded and others actually launched into the crowds of troops. A plumbe of gas filled the valley. Fortunately, the wind was away from the hills where the snipers were or they would have been victims. The valley was filled with the dead and dying. The new troops coming from the east walked or drove into the cloud of gas without realizing it was there. Thousands died. It was a big victory but a small percent of the invaders.

Jim, out of targets and very nearly out of ammunition moved from his stone seat to the side where he could lean against a rock, slightly more comfortable. He still couldn't get a good breath, but not firing the rifle helped with the pain. He ate a fruit bar and drank the last of his water, then coughed up another glob of black blood. Leaning back, he was almost comfortable. This position made him more vulnerable to possible enemy fire if, they were a very good shot. Somehow this was allright as he had no real plans to leave.

Praying out loud he said, "Lord if you wish to take me, I'm ready. I ask you to care for my family. Comfort them and protect them. I believe all the little ones will grow to be good Christians. Please talk to them when they wander off the path."

He stopped praying when he ran out of air and just sat there.

It was less than an hour later, maybe later than that as he had dozed off, when he heard voices. He couldn't understand their words as they were not speaking in Hebrew or English. He assumed this was the enemy who had escaped the poison gas by climbing the hill. They would not likely find him as he was twenty feet above the ground on a concrete beam with no access. His rifle had a few rounds and he had his pistol with several clips, not good odds against AK-47 rifles. In any case he seemed to be in his final place as he had no energy left.

In addition to the men below him, the invading army began moving into the valley below, heading south. They simply drove over the dead and around the damaged vehicles. The poison gas must have dissipated. It didn't take long before it looked like it had when he first fired on them. He thought, 'we accomplished nothing'.

Jim snoozed on and off. Each time he woke, he was surprised he was alive. He coughed up blood again so he could breathe a little better. He was awake when the sky changed in the east. It was now evening but in the east the sky lit like a very lovely sunrise. In fact, it was more beautiful than any sunrise he had seen. The sky was a multicolored picture, colors he could not even name. It was wonderful. He thought this must be the Lord Jesus coming for his Church, His believers. I will be taken to heaven with my family; this age is over. He was wrong.

The vast enemy below halted. They also saw a light in the east, only they saw a wall of fire, from the ground to as high as they could see, and it was coming toward them. They panicked and tried to run, but to where?

As the wall of fire moved north over the army it wiped out everyone, leaving crushed dead bodies, no survivors. But to Jim the wall was a cool comfort, a feeling of floating and no pain.

The next thing Jim knew someone was calling him. "Colonel Jenkins, we are here. You are going to the hospital."

It was General Haynes. He was with several men and they were moving Jim on to a tank, which had pulled up to the structure. Men were climbing on the tank then onto the floor to Jim's location. They put him on a stretcher and moved him to the ground and into a helicopter. He had been unaware of the approach of any vehicle. He passed out again.

"Jim, my darling, you are in the hospital. I have wired you back together and inflated your left lung. Your left arm was broken and is in a cast. We are all allright and back in Jenkins. Sleep now. You are safe." It was Aliza leaning over his clean bed. She kissed him and then left.

Later, Jim opened his eyes and there was Aliza in her doctor outfit. He reached up his hand and touched her breast. "When the man on the ship wanted to touch you, I could not be angry at him because you are the most beautiful woman alive."

She didn't brush his hand aside but smiled at him and replied, laughing, "You are talking about the Greek sailor, my heart throb."

"Yosef?" Jim asked.

"He is healing well and you should have come back when he did," she replied with a fake scowl. She took his wandering hand in both of hers and leaned over to kiss him.

Left alone, Jim dozed off again.

As she walked out of his room, Aliza met a nurse who was trying to suppress laughter. "Be careful around him, he may not know the difference between you and his wife." The nurse gave up and just laughed out loud and said, "Yes, Doctor!"

Jim, in a dream-like state due to anesthesia, prayed out loud, "Lord I don't understand. If this was the final war, I thought you would take us away."

A voice came from the side of the bed, "Men are often confused but be certain, God knows what He is doing and His plan is perfect." The voice was the same as the young man who had helped him reload his clips.

"Where are you?" Jim asked.

His eight-year-old son, David, climbed up on a chair and onto the bed and snuggled up to him.

"Where did you hear that God knows what He is doing?" Jim asked him.

"I have dreams sometimes and a man talks to me. He said you would be all right."

Jim hugged his son and thought, 'David has always been an unusual boy. What will he become?'

CHAPTER 31

After the War, the Final War?

THE WAR HAD CAUSED ENORMOUS loss of Israeli life. Tel Aviv and Haifa were both hit by tactical nuclear bombs. The cities were severely damaged but could be rebuilt. A major problem was the dead everywhere. Syria was uninhabited, there seemed to be no survivors in the country. No invader seemed to have survived and many of the Muslims living in Israel fled or died. The UN would state it was some kind of infection or virus, of course blaming Israel. The United States representatives joined the Israeli investigators and announced this was clearly an act of the Lord God Almighty. This view was supported by the many videos of the final phase of the war. Several countries had working satellites which monitored the wall of fire moving across the land, wiping out the invading armies and apparently thousands, or maybe millions, of civilians. No country had a weapon this powerful and attempts to explain the event, other than the act of the Lord God, came across as just silly. It was clear to anyone who watched the videos that a weapon of this power could wipe out all of mankind. A sobering thought.

Something happened to the people of Israel. Belief in Jesus as Savior swept the land. It seemed revivals happened on every corner and few refused to accept Him.

Jim remained in the hospital for two months while his ribs and arm healed. It was probably not necessary, but Aliza wanted to keep watch on him. Yosef recovered more quickly and got his now very successful furniture business up and running.

Jesus did not come and take them to heaven and the New Jerusalem did not come down, but on Temple Mount, peace did come. While the expected end time's predictions did not come in the way expected by Jim, many things changed.

On his discharge from the hospital, Aliza stated, "Jim, I think we should take the children and go see the progress on the temple in Jerusalem."

Jim was eager to go as he was very tired of lying around and doing nothing, although he was not physically one hundred percent or even fifty percent. His left arm was still in a cast and a sling. His breathing was labored and painful, but he did not complain. Aliza was keenly aware. She had become an expert of reading his body language.

Gathering their two sets of twins and Rhoda with her three children, the motor home was full and noisy. Jim was planning on driving, but Rhoda jumped into the driver's seat stating, "Pop let me drive, you can enjoy the kids and rest."

The drive was peaceful and short. Rhoda, an excellent driver, got them to the city gate nearest the path to the Temple Mount. "Everyone get out and I will find a parking place in the hotel lot," Rhoda said.

Since parking was almost non-existent in Jerusalem, frequent visitors paid hotels to allow them to park in their lots. Jim had a current account. In the past everyone would walk from the hotel to their destination, but Rhoda didn't think Jim was up to the task. Aliza had given Jim a wooden cane and insisted he use it. He objected, of course, but was glad to have it as they waited for Rhoda. She arrived in short order in the company of three young female IDF solders all happily chatting at the same time. None in the group were armed and neither was Jim as the Temple Mount was a no weapons location. There seemed to be no danger at all. The streets were crowded as usual but Jim noted the crowd was different than his previous visits. Fewer men were wearing beards and yarmulkes. The most noticeable thing was the lack of women with burkas' or full head scarves. Another observation was the large number of people wearing a Christian cross on a chain or cord around their neck. Christians were commonly seen in Jerusalem but the disproportion of the Christian population had exceeded that of traditional Jews.

Coming to the entrance to the Mount, the security check point had always been a little congested as backpacks were checked and with people going through the metal detector. None of this was present. There were guards but they were relaxed, chatting among themselves and with the people freely passing by. There was no security at all—a big change.

The two women and seven children walked slowly up the stairs to the wide flat temple area, slowly because Jim could not seem to get enough air in his damaged lungs. He went directly to a bench when arriving at the large open area and sat, breathing deeply to get enough air. Aliza sat by him in case the problem escalated. The children played in the open area before them, supervised by Rhoda.

The ruins of the Dome of the Rock, destroyed in the war, had been removed as had the mosque at the southern end. Construction of the outer walls of the new temple was complete but work continued on the interior walls and other buildings on the on the Mount. For such a large construction job, it was very quiet. No big machinery was operating or even present. How they were moving the large stones without equipment was a mystery.

Jim recovered quickly and was feeling much better when he noticed two young women and a teenage girl walking toward them.

"My God, what am I seeing?" he asked.

"Prepare yourself husband, things have changed," Aliza remarked as she also watched the group approaching.

The teenager ran to them and knelt before Jim. She took his hands and said, "Father, I am Blessing! Thank you for my name."

It was his daughter by his second wife, Hannah. A daughter he had never seen since Hannah died before she was born, in fact, before they knew for sure she was pregnant. The second woman was his first wife Nancy, who had died many years before. Both women looked like they were in their early twenties and quite lovely. Jim thought of them more like daughters than wives.

"It is not time yet, but we will be waiting," Nancy said with a big smile.

The two women and teenager continued walking away.

"Would you like to see?" someone beside him asked.

Jim turned and there stood young man who had helped him load his clips during the battle.

"David isn't it; you look very familiar," Jim replied.

Jim stood and the entire area of Temple Mount changed. It was much larger, extending flat as far as he could see. There was a beautiful garden of flowers and plants; many unfamiliar to him. It was the most beautiful place he had ever seen.

The pain was gone as he walked with the young man around the garden to a building. The structure was huge and had very large open doors. In the center of the building's side was a stream of water that flowed from under the wall. They didn't go into the building but continued walking around the garden.

"My son's name is David also and you look like him, but he is only a boy," Jim said, looking at the young man.

The man David smiled and said, "You will understand one day; things are different here. In your time, tomorrow follows today and that remains constant. Here time is like a scroll and can be rolled out. Time from the start to the end can be seen on the scroll and it is possible to enter the time the Lord God wishes."

"Are you David, my son?" Jim asked.

"Pop, are you awake?" David asked. His small son was on the bench beside him and was shaking him. "You called my name!"

Jim woke up and there his son sat, practically on his lap. Aliza on his other side, also waking up, smiled and said, "It is going to be beautiful isn't it?" She again had shared his dream with their grown son.

Jim looked at David and asked, "Son do you have any idea how to load bullets into a rifle clip?"

David just looked at him like he didn't understand and then shook his head no.

"Well; we'll take care of that when we get home. It will be fun," Jim said as he rubbed the boy's head.

David ran off toward the others to play.

"Your two wives are very lovely," Aliza said smiling.

"My three wives are gorgeous," Jim replied.

Still smiling she said, "I wonder when all of this will happen?"

"I don't know but God does and it will happen in His time. For now, however we are here and will do whatever he wants us to do.

The latest war was over with the attackers defeated by God Himself. There was no peace treaty or surrender as the attackers were totally destroyed. God's involvement was clear, a fact which was undeniable to any thinking person. Satellite images showing the wave of destruction moving across the country and ground images of the resulting destruction provided a clear picture. The government news agencies in Iran and a few other countries stated their defeat was a result of a new weapon, probably made by the US, and used by Israel. The claim was that the weapon was a weapon of 'Mass Destruction' and an investigation should be made by the UN. Anyone building such a weapon should be punished. The position was stupid on its face.

The war was over and God had given Israel the victory, although the damage in Israel was great. The tactical nuclear devices in the two largest cities caused much damage and loss of life. Rebuilding would take years.

The wave of destruction had continued north and destroyed all the people in its path. New borders of Israel were expanded. The West Bank and Gaza were deserted and would be occupied by Israel. Southern Lebanon and Western Syria were unoccupied. The Israeli Army proceeded north to Beirut and occupied it. It lay in rubble and deserted. This area would eventually be resettled with Jews coming from all parts of the world. They also occupied the territory east of the ruins of Damascus. Israel had more than doubled in size. They would not make the mistake again of giving up territory in exchange for a promise of peace, peace which would never come.

Jim and his family return to their home in Jenkins, happy to just recover and repair the war damage to themselves and their property.

In the next two years, Jim continued to heal. His lungs would never be the same. He couldn't jog more than a few feet and he continued to be susceptible to pneumonia, but he felt well most of the time. He and his family were happy.

CHAPTER 32

Visitor from the United States.

AN EARLY SPRING DAY FOUND Jim in the garden on a bench. This was an almost daily event for him, sitting, drinking his coffee, doing a little Bible study and enjoying life. A car drove up the now paved driveway, through the open gate and stopped in front of the house. Captain Masters, Jim's commander from the conflicts in the US, stepped out and stood looking about. The captain, a big man, well over six feet and with a strong body, looked younger than his forty-two years.

"Captain Masters, welcome to Israel," Jim proclaimed as he walked from the garden with an out-stretched hand.

"Jim Jenkins, it is you and you have not changed a bit!" the captain declared, lying, but with a smile. "I'm surprised I was able to find you so easily."

The front door of the house opened, and Aliza stepped out, smiling broadly. "Captain, it is so good to see you! We don't get many visitors from home!"

"Mrs. Jenkins, you look as beautiful as ever! It is good to see you. You have a beautiful place here," the captain remarked, truthfully on both points this time.

"Come in, have you had any breakfast?" Aliza questioned as she opened the front door wide.

"I have eaten, but the coffee your husband has does look good."

Jim took him to a sitting area, with windows facing east toward the distance ruins of Damascus. Aliza brought a tray with coffee and a stack of pastries, a Jewish thing.

"It is good to see you Captain! I am anxious to know how things are in America and how you happen to be here," Jim stated.

"Call me Mike. I am on somewhat of a vacation and because of my military connections was able to catch a flight to Tel Aviv. When I arrived, I inquired about you and found an immediate response. The man at the airport said you were probably in Jenkins. I thought I misunderstood him, but he repeated that a Colonel Jenkins had founded a city north of the Golan Heights and it was probably you. I rented a car and here I am!" the captain commented with a smile, followed by a bite of roll, then a drink of coffee.

Aliza smiled and chuckled a little, but Jim, not smiling responded.

"We were the first family to build a house on this hill and someone called the hill Jenkins. The town has grown, and I have tried to get the people to come up with a Jewish name, but no one seems willing to put in the effort. There is no good reason to name this town after me."

Mike smiled and understanding Jim's discomfort, responded, "Well accept it as an honor."

To change the subject Aliza asked, "Mike, what brings you to Israel and how long do you plan to stay?"

The captain paused a moment then replied, "I'm afraid I do not have a short answer. It has been ten years since the attack and the situation in the US continues to be awfully bad. It seems the country cannot recover, at least in a reasonable time. The electricity is working in most places part of the time, but the country wide grid is not close to coming online. The damage is far worse than we were led to believe. In addition, most of the parts needed are only made in China, not a friend to the US. Vehicles are still partially blocking roads, and few are being repaired. There is some manufacturing in the country making parts for vehicles, but it is slow. The federal debt is so great, and the tax income is practically nonexistent, so the US government for the first time ever defaulted on its debt payment. All the federal payments for Social Security, Medicare and Medicaid stopped. Money, in fact, has lost much of its value."

Mike looked down at the floor, gathering his thoughts. "The loss of life has been enormous. Many people, especially in the cities, could not get food or medicine and starved or died of treatable illnesses. Some towns formed militias to protect themselves. Unfortunately, some of them became gangs, rulings the citizens by force. It is sad indeed and even some of our previous comrades became part of the problem. There is some good news, however. Some communities have strong religious beliefs that guide how they operate. It is difficult for them as they must be on guard to keep the gangs out."

The room was quiet as the captain took another drink, still deep in thought. "My roll had become just a policeman, watching country roads. When an opportunity presented itself to leave, I took it. I never forgot your joy when you came here, and I wanted to somehow find that for myself. Selfish, I know, but I am in fact Jewish, on my mother's side of the family. We were never religious, but I realize that I need to be focusing on my spiritual well-being. I bought a bible and have been reading it and have come up with a few hundred questions."

"I am sure we can find some answers, and you will stay here until you get moved and settled in," Aliza offered with a smile.

"I don't want to impose on you," the captain replied.

"Nonsense! You are most welcome, and we are interested in all the events that have taken place in the US. Besides, having another good man in Israel is a good thing!" Jim added.

"Come, let me show you a room. It belonged to Rhoda before she moved into her own house."

Jim went with Mike to his car and retrieved his two suitcases containing everything he had brought from the US. Aliza showed Mike to the bedroom.

So it was. The Jenkins accepted a semi-permanent house guest, the captain, now usually addressed as Mike. Aliza realized she would be hearing many war stories. She also knew the comradery would be good for Jim.

Mike rose early the next morning then joined Jim in the garden where he was drinking coffee.

"I think I'll walk into town and just have a look. I'll need some additional clothes and I need to stretch my legs after the long flight," he remarked to Jim.

"Mind if I join you?" Rhoda asked as she came strolling up the driveway.

"Oh my, Rhoda! You have grown into a lovely lady!" Mike exclaimed as he gave her a hug.

"It's good to see you, Captain. May I go along and show you the town?" Rhoda repeated.

Without another word, the two of them walked away from Jim, toward the town center, a short distance beyond the hospital.

"This place is amazing; it has grown so fast! New stores are opening nearly every day or two. People are coming from all over the world, mostly Jews, but not all," Rhoda explained.

"That's amazing! I had almost forgotten I have Jewish ancestors, but suddenly I felt the desire to come here. Knowing your family, of course, has something to do with it, but it is more than that. The desire has grown with time. I am not alone. Other friends have mentioned a feeling, a pull to come here. Some were unaware of Jewish roots, until they investigated." Mike paused for several seconds, then continued. "I came to believe this feeling, or desire within me was more than just curiosity or a whim. There is an urgent need to be here. I have not been a believer in God or anything, but I now know this is something beyond myself."

Rhoda who wished she had prepared herself to witness, responded, "You will find things different here. It seems God and His angels are near. My little brother, David, has a connection and understands what will happen before the rest of us do. Even at his young age it seems he is unusual. Perhaps you will experience things that make your calling clear."

Mike paused in front of new construction of small rows of apartments and small houses. "These look very interesting; I wonder if you buy these or rent them?" he asked Rhoda, but another voice answered.

"You can rent or buy them depending on how long you plan to stay," the woman said, as she came down the sidewalk from the houses.

It was Yenta. She was dressed in a casual dress instead of her usual long work pants and wide brimmed hat, making her look nice.

"Yenta, you are not working today!" Rhoda exclaimed.

"I took off early to prepare for Sabbath and I have some shopping to do. Who is your escort today?"

"Yenta meet Captain Mike Masters, my first commander in the conflict in the United States. Captain, this is Yenta Neumann. She is the head archaeologist in the big excavation south of the house," Rhoda said as she smiled at the two of them.

"Please call me Mike. It is good to meet you," he said as he smiled and bowed slightly as he and took her hand.

Yenta smiled at the greeting and replied, "It is good to meet you, Mike. May I accompany you two into town?"

"Of course," Rhoda exclaimed, enjoying the obvious attraction her two companions had for each other.

The three walked into the town center which consisted of a dozen businesses.

"Anything you need in particular?" Yenta asked, directing the question to Mike.

"This area is cooler than I expected, so I thought a heavier jacket would be useful."

He looked at the signs on the store fronts, all written in Hebrew and all unintelligible to him. "I think I'll just look in the windows to see what they sell," he said. In his mind he was thinking, 'If I settle here, I will certainly need to learn the language.'

Rhoda was going to make a suggestion, but Yenta spoke first. "The store on the corner has a good selection of clothing, mostly work stuff but they have some dressier things."

As they walked past a grocery store, Rhoda said to them, "I need to stop in here and pick up some things for my family."

The other two others simply nodded and continued walking. Rhoda watched them for a moment and thought, 'I have never seen two people bond like this. They will be married before nightfall.' She laughed out loud as she went into the grocery store.

Yenta and Mike continued to the clothing shop hardly noticing Rhoda had left them.

Mike was looking for a jacket but stopped at the men's pants rack. The pants were made of a heavy canvas material that looked very warm.

"Those are a good choice for a working man. My team wears them to dig for artifacts. We also wear knee pads since we spend a lot of time on them," Yenta added with an unspoken assumption that he may one day need a pair, also.

The sizes were mainly in metric, but these were also in inches. Mike took a pair and put them over his arm. He then followed Yenta to the coat rack, where she had already taken two coats and held them up for his review.

"This one matches my pants." He slipped on the coat, which was heavy canvas, the same color as the pants. She had correctly guessed his size.

Jokingly she pressed on. "You are hired, you can start Monday, after the Sabbath and Sunday. We are just starting a new excavation in the old city which may uncover an extraordinarily rich person's house."

"I'll be there; it sounds like fun!" he replied with a smile on his lips and a sparkle in his eyes.

On the way to the front of the store, Yenta picked up a pair of gloves, knee pads and a hat with a very wide brim.

The lady at the front rang him up using a new cash register and gave him a price in shekels. He had no idea how much this was in dollars, but he offered her two one-hundred-dollar bills. She took the money and referred to a posted exchange table then gave him his change in shekels. Now he was really confused because not only He did not know how much he had paid for his purchase, but how much change, he received.

"I can see I have much to learn if I stay here," he said to the clerk and to Yenta.

"Yes, but it will come easily," Yenta answered.

Yenta had her purchases rung up, paid for, and then pulled a canvas bag from here shoulder bag. She stuck all the purchases for the two of them in her bag. Then she placed the hat, which she had paid for, on Mikes head, and said, "You will need this in the sun on Monday."

"I thank you mam, but you shouldn't spend your money on a stranger," he replied.

"When you see what I pay for labor, you will understand," she said, laughing. Yenta had not informed him that her laborers were volunteers.

As the two left the store, Rhoda met them with a big smile. "Well, you two seem to have had a successful trip," she said indicating the bag Mike was carrying. "Good looking hat," she added.

Rhoda had her purchases in a backpack she always took when going to town.

The three walked back and stopped in front of the row of houses where Yenta lived.

"How big are these units?" He asked Yenta.

"They are small compared to the Jenkins estate, but adequate for most Jews," Yenta answered. "Come in and I'll show you my place. The rest of these are under construction but I don't know if any finished units are available."

"I am going on, while you two house shop," Rhoda said as she smiled at them. Walking toward her parents' house, she could hardly wait to share some interesting news about their new male guest and the blossoming relationship with their friend, Yenta.

"Come in!" Yenta said as she led Mike into the complex. Her apartment was on an upper floor and consisted of a sitting room, one bedroom, a kitchen and a bathroom. It was small and had little storage space. To Mike it was a little larger than a motel room in the US. There was no storage other than a single clothes closet and kitchen cabinets. For one person or even a couple it would be adequate. Mike, however, had several large boxes in the US, ready for shipping if he made the final decision to stay.

"This is nice, but I have several boxes of stuff in the US to ship. I'm not sure all my junk would fit here."

"I understand. My work gear is stored at the dig site. The only things here are my clothes. There is a bigger unit in the next building. It's not ready, but we can see it," Yenta replied as she led him from her unit.

The next apartment was larger; it had two bedrooms a larger sitting area and kitchen, but still a single bath. "These units are normally for families with children. I know it is small compared to the houses in the US, but people here simply don't store a lot of things they seldom use." Yenta explained.

"This would actually be fine for me. I could use the smaller bedroom as a storage area. If I found a woman who would put up with me, I would hope we could both use one bedroom." He winked at her to indicate he was kidding. She smiled and laughed a little.

Mike left Yenta at her door, regretting leaving her. He did not sign up for an apartment at the facility. None were ready and he felt he needed to check out other options in the city. He returned to the Jenkins's house and the room they had provided.

Monday, early, Mike arrived at the archeology site before anyone else, dressed in his new work clothes. Three college aged students showed up a half hour later. Two girls and a boy. They were chatting about the dig site on the way, but became interested in the new, older volunteer. He was obviously an American, by his speech. His inability to speak Hebrew pegged him as a new arrival.

Yenta arrived accompanied by a dozen other young volunteers and three others in their early thirties. She greeted Mike and introduced him to each of them. He repeated each name as they were introduced; he would remember about half the names. Everyone was happy and rested after the Sabbath and anxious to start uncovering ancient secrets. Without referring to any paperwork, Yenta assigned the work for the day to each group. The teams left chatting among themselves. Happy groups.

Yenta and Mike were left alone, and she said, "Mike I want to show you the cave we found under the Jenkins property. It is quite impressive."

They walked around the site of the ancient city nearly a mile to the entrance to the cave. The site was now covered with a tent and some canvas to reduce the dust which could blow in. There was no guard or a locked fence, things Yenta had requested.

Yenta led the way down the steps and stopped when they were aligned with the writing on the side wall. She took a small flashlight from her belt and shined it on the writing.

"This writing refers to King Solomon and was probably written during his reign. Solomon was King of Israel in 970 BC, around 3000 years ago. The words are Hebrew but an ancient version. We can read parts of it, but scholars around the world are studying it to arrive at the most accurate translation possible."

Mike stood just staring at the cuneiform-like figures. The ruins of the city they had walked around were certainly impressive, but this writing was amazing. He could see the tool marks left by the person who had cut the letters in the stone. It was almost as if that person were there standing beside him.

"I cannot believe this! This is so clear, and I can almost feel the person who wrote this!" he said very quietly.

Yenta turned to him and smiled. "Welcome to the world of archology!" she said, as she reached out and touched his arm.

Walking down the steps, Yenta found the switch and turned on the lights. Lights run by a long extension cord plugged into the Jenkins's house. The tunnel lit up its entire length.

"My Lord how did they do this without any power tools?" Mike exclaimed as he stared down the long tunnel.

"I am sure it took a very long time and dedicated people!" she said, not concealing the excitement she felt at his obvious interest in something she loved and had dedicated her life to discover.

Yenta, resisting her temptation to take his hand, walked down the tunnel explaining as she went. "There where bone boxes in these notches, many of them. They will be returned after they are examined in the laboratory. We think they contain the bones of the local priests and perhaps the leaders of the tribe."

Mike followed her not saying anything, but observing with great interest.

"These notches had many jars which contained scrolls. They are the oldest, and we hope the most complete copies of the Old Testament writings ever found. If so, this is the most important discovery in our lifetimes. These writings were nine hundred years old when Jesus walked right in this area. The jars are now in the laboratory in Tel Aviv. Scholars from all over the world are reviewing them. It will take many years to review all of them."

Yenta walked on and Mike followed without replying. He could not absorb all she was saying. This was just too amazing.

Yenta stopped at a larger opening on the side of the tunnel where the body of the scribe had been found. "This was a place where a man worked, and he allowed the tunnel to be sealed with him inside. We don't know if he planned to remain permanently or if something happened and the people outside had to leave. He was working at a wooden desk or table sitting on these stones. The wood, of course, is deteriorated but it may have been covered with scrolls, oil lamps and writing pens. His body was found here," she said as she pointed behind the rocks and debris. "We will go through all of this dirt and dust with a fine screen. I expect to find more small items the man was using and perhaps something to identify him."

"I would like to help you with it," Mike said, overwhelmed with everything he was seeing.

The close feeling between the two was interrupted by a voice from the entrance to the tunnel.

"Hello, Yenta is that you?" Jim said as he stood at the bottom of the stairs with his cane. "I heard voices from the vent in my garden and was concerned someone unauthorized may be in here." He continued.

"Hello, Jim, I am just showing Mike the wonderful discovery Rhoda made!" Yenta answered.

Jim stayed just a few minutes, then excused himself and left, feeling he was interrupting special moments between the two.

CHAPTER 33

Glorious Discovery

IKE WAS QUICKLY OUTFITTED WITH a work belt containing a brush, small dustpan and a few tools from the work shed on the site. In addition, Yenta gave him a bright battery powered light. He put on the belt and carried a bucket and a framed screen used to filter the dust and retrieve any items.

In response to his smile, Yenta returned his smile and said, "I will check on you in an hour or so, do not overdo it, and drink water."

Mike walked back to the tunnel carrying his equipment, filling both hands. He thought 'This is certainly different than sitting at a check point in California waiting for someone to misbehave.' He also realized for the first time in a long time he was happy.

He went back into the tunnel to the notch were the body had been found. He turned on the battery powered light and set it on the rock which had at one time held the desk where the ancient scribe had worked. The light was very bright.

Instead of starting on the large pile of decayed wood and whatever, where the desk had disintegrated, he began on the pile of dust and dirt along the wall adjacent to the desk area. As he worked, screening the dust, he found nothing. The particles simply went through the screen into the bucket. They seemed to consist of fine sand and a powdery substance. He put his hand in the bucket and took a handful of the power and went to the light. It looked like something he had worked with before, years ago in construction. It looked like plaster which had dried out and flaked off.

"Why would anyone put plaster on a solid rock wall?" he said to himself.

He examined the wall where he had been working and noticed it was different than the rest of the tunnel. It was straight and relatively flat compared to the other walls. He used his brush on the wall and dust and sand fell off, adding to the pile at his feet. Continuing to brush, he then saw the line in the wall, it looked like a mortar line, just like on found in a block wall.

Mike knew he should send for Yenta, but he could not stop. He found a small pry bar in his tool belt and began scratching along the motor line. The mortar was dry like the plaster and dropped out quickly, exposing the top of a cut block. He went down the wall and quickly found the bottom of the block, this time without mortar. The block was made to fit closely with the block it was sitting on. There was a slight notch in the block, along it's bottom edge. He stuck his pry bar in the notch and hit it with his hand, driving the bar under the block a small distance. On the third hit, bruising his hand, the block moved. He could then push the bar further under stone and slowly move the block out. It was thinner than he expected, only about six inches thick. It came out quickly and it was heavy. It was all he could do to keep it from falling. He lowered it to the floor. The block below it was also knocked loose and he also removed it, making a hole in the wall about three feet high.

Mike paused, standing in the front of the hole in the wall, and thought, 'My God, this has not been opened in thousands of years. How could You have allowed me to find this?'

He then took the light and leaned into the hole extending his hand with the light. The reflection was blinding. Bright articles inside the chamber reflected the light. Without even thinking, he squeezed his shoulders through the opening and then crawled inside. The air was very stale but the thought of leaving never crossed his mind.

Just at that time, Yenta came down the stairs, carrying a bag with some bread, sliced meat and a flask of water.

"Mike, Mike!" she called. No answer.

She ran down the tunnel and stopped when she saw the hole in the wall and a light shining from within.

"O God, Mike don't go in there!" She shouted, which was silly, as he was obviously already in there.

She ran to the hole and looked in. Unable to control herself she jumped through the hole, not difficult due to her smaller size and joined Mike sitting on the floor.

To the side stood a large Menorah, at least five feet tall. It had three arms on each side topped with a bowl for oil. The seventh lamp was in the center. It was all gold, solid or plated, it was gorgeous. As lovely as it was, it was the box in front of Yenta and Mike which had their attention. Sitting aside from the other debris and clutter, it was about five feet long and three feet tall. On the top were two angels with their wings spread. They were facing each other. It was the 'Ark of The Covenant'. It was all silver and reflected the light.

"The original that Moses made was made of wood and plated in gold. This must be a copy. It is tradition that Solomon made several replicas to give away. Perhaps he gave one to the Queen of Sheba when she came to visit him," Yenta said quietly.

"You need to get out of here, I feel like I am about to pass out," Mike said quietly.

"You must come with me," she replied.

"I have come here, met you and seen these marvelous things. What more could I want out of life?" he said, barely audible.

Yenta realized they were in deep trouble. She lay her head on Mike's shoulder and waited for the end, barely awake and unable to stand.

Just then her hat blew off and her hair blew into her face. They were engulfed with fresh air from behind them.

A voice said, "David, wait!"

Each of them felt a small hand on their head and heard a voice, "Take deep breaths, please!"

They began recovering almost immediately.

Behind them stood a young boy. It was David, the son of Jim and Aliza. Aliza followed, scrambling through the small opening and joining them. Soon Jim and Yosef joined the group and began jarring loose more blocks from the opening. A large fan was sitting in the main tunnel and blowing air into the new room.

Aliza had a small oxygen bottle with a small hose to attach to the nose. She put it on Yenta's nose first and told her to breathe deeply. After three deep breaths, she moved it to Mike, and repeated the procedure.

"I remember how cautious you were about coming into the tunnel when we first opened it. What happed here?" Aliza, with an unpleasant look on her face, asked Yenta.

It was Mike that answered, "It was my fault. I looked in and did not even think when I saw these marvelous things. I just bolted in."

"How did you know to come help us?" Yenta asked.

Aliza answered, "It was David; he was looking at a book and just jumped up and said we need a fan to help someone in the tunnel who will run out of air. We hurried but it took us fifteen minutes to get the fan and get here. David seems to know about things before anyone else does and we have learned to pay attention."

"I don't think I was even in this room fifteen minutes before you came," Mike said, as he looked at David, who was now standing by the silver box with the angels on the top. He was running his hand along the wing of one of them. Mike continued, "He knew before we were in trouble."

Jim went to his son and knelt on one knee to be even with his face. "David, how did you know there was a problem here?"

David continued touching the angel and replied, "Sometimes I hear a little voice in my head and sometimes I dream about a man, also named David. He tells me things."

David then went further back in the room toward some other objects, not seeming to notice all the attention he was receiving from the others.

Yenta and Mike recovered quickly with the fresh air and the oxygen from the bottle. In just a few minutes their close brush with death seemed to be forgotten. They took pictures of the objects in the room, at least the ones they could get to. The small room was crowded with shiny tables and other unidentifiable objects stacked on each other. They could get to the Ark, however, no one seemed inclined to touch it as it was forbidden in the scripture for anyone except a priest from the tribe of Levi, and only then once a year. This, of course, was not the original Ark, but the concern was still there.

Jim stated, "David has touched it and did not seem to be bothered. I think we can remove the top and see if anything is inside."

"We should wait, but I can't stand it. Do you think you and Yosef could lift the lid?" Yenta said to Mike.

Without answering, Mike and Yosef stood on each end and lifted the top with the angels on it. It was very heavy, but the two were able to lift it and very gently set it on the floor.

Yenta brought a light to illuminate the inside of the box. It was almost full of gold cups and other gold and silver objects. On top of the precious objects lay a small cylinder, made of silver, with a sealed top. Maybe a scroll. The Ark was being used as a storage box for many articles used in a temple.

"I am shocked; this looks like objects from the temple, but there is no record of a second temple here or anywhere. There may be an answer in this cylinder," she stated as she removed the cylinder from the box. "Please replace the top and we will not disturb the Ark further until more experts come."

The two men, with great effort, carefully replace the top of the Ark.

"If these objects were placed here shortly after Solomon's day, they are in remarkable condition. Surely the tables and cabinets are made of wood and covered with gold and silver. The wood should have deteriorated long ago," Yenta said quietly, then continued. "I believe, without a doubt this will be the most valuable find in modern Israeli archaeology."

Yenta went to Mike and took his hand and said, "Mike on your first day on the job you have made an amazing discovery! What will you do tomorrow?" She then raised up and kissed him on his cheek.

"We need to all leave before someone inadvertently damages something," Yenta said as she led all present from the tunnel to the outside where her cell reception worked. She made three quick phone calls, careful not to reveal the details of the find, but emphasized the value.

"We will have visitors soon. The military is sending a detachment of solders to provide a full-time guard to protect the tunnel and I believe the Prime Minister and several of the government's officials are on the way. This is going to be a busy day!" she announced to everyone.

All in the tunnel had exited and were standing outside when the first helicopter arrived. It was small and carried four men, military police. They immediately set up a guard station at the entrance to the tunnel along with the rather baffling orders to allow no-one to enter, apparently including the ones who had just left the tunnel. The men were polite and apologized but explained their rather confusing orders. In any case, the tunnel was now protected.

Everyone who had viewed the discovery retreated to the Jenkins' house for a break and to discuss the find. Food and drinks were, of course, placed on a table in the main room. Most were sampled.

Yenta opened the discussion, "This is an unexpected discovery. We know the tunnel was opened when Solomon was king, as documented by the engraving on the wall at the entrance. We do not know how long it was in use and when it was last sealed. The Ark of The Covenant is not the one made by Moses, as that original one was made of wood with gold plating. So, this Ark is a copy. The question is, why are these things here? It appears the Ark and the gold tables are articles from a temple. But the temple is in Jerusalem and there is no record of one here or anywhere in the Northern Kingdom."

Jim spoke up, "I am certainly no expert, but is it possible a group of devout people in the Northern Kingdom, made a replica of the temple with its furnishing, and carried on the worship normally done in Jerusalem?"

"That is an explanation, although we have not uncovered any evidence of a temple in this city." Yenta paused then continued, "Perhaps the scroll we discovered in the Ark or one of the many in the tunnel will give some evidence of the purpose of these articles. In any case, this is a wonderful find."

Their discussion was interrupted when a helicopter flew low over the house. At the same time, vehicles drove up the drive and stopped in front of the house. One of the vehicles was a light-colored limousine and was led and followed by Humvee's, each equipped with machine guns on the top. Men exited the Humvees and took up stations as guards or escorts as Prime Minister Salon got out of the limousine, followed by General Steinhoff.

"Oh, my God, I have nothing ready to serve!" Aliza almost shouted as she ran to the kitchen, with Rhoda following. It seemed that not having something to set in front of guests, even if unexpected, is an unpardonable sin for a Jewish woman.

Jim went to the door and greeted the two men, the most powerful in Israel.

"Mr. Prime Minister, General Steinhoff, welcome, come in," Jim said, probably not a proper greeting to these high officials.

The two men came in and met the others already in the main room of the house. Yenta had met the prime minister, but not General Steinhoff. Mike, of course, had met neither.

"Mr. Prime Minister and General, this is Mike Masters from the US. He was my commander in the militia in the conflict. Mike, meet Prime Minister Salon and General Steinhoff."

The men shook hands, and the prime minister said, "Welcome to Israel, Mike, and we are known as Joshua and Benjamin to our friends. I understand we have you to thank for this grand discovery, and on your first day on the job. Yenta, it seems like this man is a good addition to your team."

Yenta smiled and replied, "Yes sir, I expect great things from Mike."

Aliza entered the room with a tray containing a coffee pot and a pitcher of an iced drink. She was followed by Rhoda with a tray containing glasses and cups.

"Gentlemen, coffee and tea is available, and cakes are in the oven and will be ready soon," she stated.

The PM greeted Aliza, "Aliza, you are as lovely as ever and you do not need to fuss over us. Before your cakes are ready, perhaps we could see this new treasure."

Yenta, indicating Mike should walk with her, led the group to the tunnel. Several armed soldiers walked just behind, watching all about.

As they stood in front of the Ark, the PM said quietly, "This is a surprise, is it not? I was not aware of anything like this ever being in this area so far north of Jerusalem."

"Yes, we are all surprised, and are speculating on what it could mean. We found a scroll within the Ark itself which should have some answers when it is read in a controlled environment," Yenta replied.

The PM looked at Yenta and asked, "What do you recommend we do with this treasure?"

"These items should be placed in a controlled environment to be studied and displayed where they can be seen. This is something our nation and people will be proud of. This proves our heritage in this land. No one can doubt our history here," she answered, not quite controlling her excitement.

"Since our northern border has been extended, it has been suggested we have another center for scientific study and display. I think the City of Jenkins would be a grand location for such a facility," the Prime Minister stated with a flourish of his hand.

Yenta could not contain her excitement as she jumped a little and even squealed. "I think that is a wonderful idea. There is much to be found here in this city and there are many places north of here which need to be investigated."

The prime minister walked across the yard and stood looking at the ruins of the ancient city slowly being uncovered. "This city may have been more important than anyone envisioned," he said. "You may need more people to help dig it out. In addition, I would like you to recommend a location for a laboratory and a display center," he continued, looking at Yenta.

As they walked back to the Jenkins' house, General Steinhoff said to the Prime Minister, "Sir, we have control of two levels of Mr. Jenkins garage, which are now underutilized. The artifacts could be stored there and out of the tunnel."

"Yenta, what do you think about moving them to the guarded location here?" the PM asked her.

"It would be good to get them out of the cave where we can look at each object more closely. We will need to be careful in moving anything as they may be structurally unsound," she replied.

"Keep me advised as to your recommendations. I consider this an especially important project."

General Steinhoff did not consider Jim's offer of his garage, but simply requested the basement under the garage be cleaned out. This area was and always had been under some control of the military.

Moving the articles out of the tunnel was an experience. The tunnel was either made for the tables or the tables for the tunnel. Men had to lift the tables to the top and carefully maneuver them to avoid damage. The Ark was emptied of the small articles and was very easily carried out.

Hoping to do the move in secret was not possible. It appeared as though everyone in the city had gathered to watch the objects being moved. Even covering everything with a sheet did not conceal the identity of the items.

The pastor/rabbi of the Church/Synagogue in Jenkins joined Jim as he watched from his side yard.

"I thought these holy objects were only to be moved by members of the tribe of Levi," Jim stated to the preacher.

"That is true, or it was in the forty years before returning to the Holy Land. When the Temple existed in Jerusalem the Holy Objects were not moved. Only some rabbis were allowed to see them, especially the Ark. These objects are not from the Temple, as far as we know. However, these men are all believing Jews and upstanding citizens of the Synagogue, and while we do not know for sure if they are from the tribe of Levi, they are the best we have for this job. I have asked God to forgive our lack of knowledge, to bless our efforts, and thanked Him for giving us this gift," The Pastor/Rabbi stated.

When all the objects were safely in the basement below Jim's garage the people dispersed. The army did not. They assigned a company of IDF soldiers to provide guards for the priceless ancient objects. No one was allowed inside the basement without the approval of General Steinhoff and the head of the Archeological Foundation. Members of this foundation were allowed access, and in time all of them came. Yenta and Mike spent twenty hours a day there, studying and documenting what they found. While the original Ark and the tables, commissioned by Moses, were wood, covered with gold as described in the Old Testament, these items were all metal. The Ark was solid silver and the tables were some type of metal with gold plating. This was an unknown type of construction for the time, but explained the lack of deterioration of the objects.

Jim and his family were allowed entry to inspect the objects. No one seemed to be more interested than young David, who walked around each object and crawled under some of them. He even discovered names written under the tables which had not been noticed by the archaeologists.

Every few days a group of experts from all over the world arrived to view the find. Jim's property seemed to always have several cars and a bus or two to transport the crowd. In addition, news crews came and set up on his property. Everyone was well behaved and polite, so there were no problems.

CHAPTER 34

THE CITY OF JENKINS

A COMMITTEE MADE UP OF NOTABLE Israeli archeologists met in Jenkins in the basement of Jim's garage, where the artifacts continued to be secured. Jim was not invited but Yenta was and had a strong voice. She wanted a larger display building than most of the others had envisioned. Her argument was simple: there were many sites which needed to be dug out in the captured territory north of Jenkins. They were also finding many Christian artifacts from many sites, so the building should have a wing dedicated to Christianity. The discussion went on and on resulting in a building plan larger than even Yenta had envisioned.

The head of the committee was Rabbi Stedman. After the meeting he approached Jim.

"Mr. Jenkins we would like your permission to locate a design team in the basement under your garage."

Jim thought it strange they would ask him as the military had more control of the basement of the garage than he did.

"I certainly don't object but the military might, although they have not used it recently. However, I suggest you consider the basement of my house. It has the advantage of a restroom and easy access to my kitchen, which my wife seems to always have something prepared to eat."

The two men went into the basement which was nearly empty except for cots which were broken down and stacked. Constructed by Jim and Yosef to be used by the locals in the case of an attack, they had only been used once.

"This is much better, better lighting, more electrical outlets and a bathroom," the Rabbi stated laughing.

The next day a large van arrived with desks and large drafting tables along with a dozen chairs. Shortly after, the workers arrived mostly young architects, engineers and two secretaries. With the people came computer equipment. Yenta had a desk, away from the rest. She seemed to be a supervisor, although no one had a title. By the second day the basement took on the air of a professional office while sketches began appearing on the walls of the floor plan and the building as viewed from the outside. Even the initial draft of the structure showed an impressive and beautiful building.

A week later, in mid-morning, Aliza and Mike walked down the stairs with a large tray of baked goods and a large pitcher of fruit juice. Aliza was horrified to see David, her nine-year-old son, drawing on one of the computer-generated pictures on the wall with a crayon. All the workers were standing around him intently watching him. She was about to yell at her son but Yenta, who was standing right beside David saw her and held up her hand. Aliza walked up to the group to see what was going on and hear what was being said by David.

"It would be pretty if the roof had a peak and windows here." He then drew a Star of David with a large cross on top. "These could look like gold and be lighted at night. If it faces east, they could catch the morning sun and look nice," David said as he lay the crayon down.

Aliza had not noticed Rabbi Stedman, but he was standing right next to David watching his sketches intently. "David have you seen a building like this before?" The Rabbi spoke to the boy like he was an equal, a much older person.

"No, but I have a friend who told me about one. He saw your sketch and suggested this modification. He saw a building in Poland like this and it was attractive." David replied.

The Rabbi then looked at his crew and stated, "I like this idea; come up with new sketches to show it!"

The young designers nodded in agreement and seemed pleased with the suggestion, even if it came from a child.

Aliza went to David and placed her hands on his shoulders and said to the Rabbi, "I hope my son has not been a bother. I will try harder to keep him from coming down here."

"Please don't. He is a joy, and this suggestion is just what this building needed. I was unhappy with the look we were coming up with, it looked like an apartment building, not a building for something beautiful and meaningful," the Rabbi responded, smiled, then continued, "Yenta told me about David sounding the alarm when she was in trouble. He is a special lad and if he wants to help us, I will welcome it."

Aliza, taking David by the hand prayed as she went up the stairs 'Lord what have you given me to raise? I am in need of Your help to not do something wrong. Please guide me and Jim to help make David what you want him to be.'

Two days later Aliza was in the kitchen and there was a knock on the door to the basement. Aliza opened it and Rabbi Stedman stood there at the top of the stairs.

"It is not necessary to knock, you are welcome at any time," she said as the rabbi entered. He took the coffee and the seat at the table, smiling broadly.

"Mr. and Mrs. Jenkins, I have some information which I am sure will interest you. I contacted a leader of our Synagogue in Warsaw, Poland, and sent a picture of your son's drawing of the new building. I will read you his answer."

"Rabbi Stedman, it is good to hear from you. I did not need to do any research on the building you sent. It is almost identical of a rather famous Synagogue near here. At the time it was built there was a rather small number of Jews and a small group of non-Catholic Christians. These two groups pooled their resources and built a Synagogue/Church. I believe a first in all of Europe. I have included a picture of the building and as you can see is nearly identical to the drawing you sent me. The surprising thing is this building was destroyed in 1941 by the Germans and never rebuilt. I am very interested on how you came up with this design."

Jim and Aliza were silent. The rabbi continued, "As you can see in this very old photograph, the building is identical to the sketch David made and the locations of the Jewish Star and the Christian Cross is identical. Even the location of the windows is the same. The question is how did a nine-year-old know about a building destroyed so many years ago?"

Jim answered very slowly, "Rabbi, there is something with our son, David. At one time when we were on Temple Mount I dozed off as I was recovering from wounds I received during the war. I dreamed of a young man showing me around a new and wonderful expanded Temple Mount. This young man was also named David and I believe he is my son, David, as an adult. I think he may be in heaven but comes to visit. He did explain to me that in heaven, time is like a scroll laid out and he can enter our existence in the past or maybe the future. This David visits my son and tells him things."

Rabbi Stedman was silent for a very long time. Then he stood and said, "You and your family are Christians, yes?"

"Yes," Jim replied.

"I welcome your son to participate in our planning downstairs any time he is inclined to come. I will not discuss this information with anyone, but after a time I would like to discuss, with you, what it would take for me to be a Christian."

With that comment, Rabbi Stedman went back down the stairs to the basement.

After a moment, Aliza turned to Jim and said, "God does work in mysterious ways."

"Yes, and we need to do our best to follow His leading!" Jim replied.

A site was selected for the new Archaeological Office and Display building just to the west of the ancient city being excavated. The location was on a hill overlooking the old city. The site was in clear view from Jim's garden where he often took his morning coffee.

There seemed to be a rush on the construction as the land was being excavated before the details of the building were completed on the plans. The digging stopped when building stones were uncovered. For some reason, a structure had been overlooked by the ground-penetrating-radar. A more detailed search with the radar discovered the foundations of a large building. It seems the ancient builders had also thought a building overlooking the city was a good plan. For the following year Yenta put her entire crew, including Mike, on uncovering the site and identifying the building as a smaller version of the first Temple in Jerusalem.

This Temple, or a copy of the actual Temple, raised many questions. Did Solomon have this built as a second worship site? Or was this built by the divided Northern Kingdom as a worship site for the more devout Jews to discourage them from going to Jerusalem? The second idea was more likely as the scripture is clear about Jerusalem as the site God chose as the Temple location. Perhaps the scrolls from the tunnel would answer the questions when they were finally translated.

The delay in the construction of the new Archaeological building lasted about a month then it was decided to modify the plans, making the ancient temple a display on the first floor of the building. It would mean making the new building larger, but the excavation could continue and be interesting for visitors.

CHAPTER 35

THE UNITED STATES

JIM AWOKE AS USUAL BEFORE the sun rose with the sky beginning to lighten by the dawn. He did not disturb Aliza as he got up and went outside with his coffee and Bible. It was a beautiful early spring morning and still cool. Unusual for Jim, he was disturbed. He had dreamed about the US and his visit in the small town, named Hermosa, in Colorado, were he met the widow of the pastor, named Alice and the policeman, Teddy. Jim could not remember the details of the dream, but felt he needed to check on these people, but how to do it?

Taking his old, but usually faithful, laptop computer he did a search on the name of the church and the town.

It came back immediately with a nice web site, showing the church, nicely rebuilt and with a pastor's name and picture, a man Jim had never met. Apparently, things had recovered somewhat in the United States. Not surprising as it had been over ten years.

He opened a message window and typed the church e-mail address and the message addressed to the pastor of the church:

Pastor Morris

Pastor, we have never met, but my name is Jim Jenkins. About ten years ago I stopped by your church while passing through Hermosa. I was driving my motor home and parked on the back of your lot on a Saturday afternoon. I met a police officer named Teddy. I have forgotten his last name. On Sunday I also met the widow of the previous pastor who had been recently killed. The church had a nice service on Sunday morning and a lunch afterward.

I doubt if anyone remembers me, but last night I had a dream that I should contact your church; I do not know why.

Since that time I have come to Israel and married. I have four children and a lovely Jewish wife. At the present time there is peace here. We live in a city, unfortunately named Jenkins. There are many better Jewish names, but we were the first here and the name seems to have stuck. This is the location of an ancient city with an unknown name and is being excavated by a team of professional and volunteer archaeologists. They have made a rather amazing find in a cave. It is a copy of the Arc of the Covenant, several gold tables and a large Menorah. It appears there was a smaller replica of the Temple here at some time in the past.

Perhaps this message could be given to Teddy and Alice if they are still around. When I was there, it was suggested that I was an angel because Alice's daughters had prayed for someone to bring some sweet bread. I made some muffins for breakfast that Sunday morning and shared them with the girls and the young girls considered me an answer to their prayer. While I am not an angel, there may have been one there that day. While I was driving down the road, a young man stood in the road and waved me into the parking lot, and I stopped there for the night. More recently, in one of the battles here, I saw him again. I was wounded and he helped me. This young man may, in fact, be an angel, and I have met him several times in dreams, dreams that seem to be very real.

Thanks for your time. If you can locate Teddy and Alice, I would be happy to hear from them.

Jim Jenkins

He sent the message not knowing if the web service even worked in that rural Colorado town.

Jim received no answer that day but sometime during the night there was a reply. The next day when he got up and turned on his computer there was message from the policeman, Teddy, in Colorado.

Jim Jenkins, Israel, City of Jenkins,

Jim, it is so good to hear from you. We have wondered many times how you are doing and where you are. I assure you no one in our church has forgotten you and your muffins. We have an annual supper here at the church and the ladies bring their muffins, each in the hope of duplicating your recipe. For several years Alice made a few from the boxes you left to remind the judges of how good yours were. By the way, Alice finally agreed to marry me about a year after your visit and she blessed me with two sons. You can imagine how well cared for they are by Alice and her three daughters. These daughters are now young women and quite lovely.

As the sheriff I formed a militia to protect the town to hopefully prevent another attack like the one that killed our pastor and destroyed the church. We had lookouts that warned us of a group of thugs coming to ravage the town again so we set up an ambush. God was gracious and we wiped them out. Surprisingly, they were carrying a truck load of weapons, so we are now a well-armed group and able to protect ourselves. There have been no other attacks as we seem to have a reputation for being able to defend ourselves.

The church has been completely rebuilt and a second larger sanctuary built next to it as the church has grown in membership. Many people are coming as refugees from towns throughout the areas which not have recovered. We screen the newcomers as well as we can to keep out any who would cause trouble later on.

The city has rebuilt an old mill and we now grind wheat into flour and sell it statewide. In addition, we have a new factory which builds electronics for vehicles to repair the damage from the EMP attack. So, we have many vehicles running and send the electronics all over the country.

As you can tell, we are proud of our city and hope you will someday visit us again. You will be received as a dignitary as you are remembered. You may not be an angel but certainly were sent by one.

I would warn you that while our city is quite safe, many parts of the country are not. There seems to be cities or towns which are religious and peaceful, and others are like the old west where there is no law at all.

Perhaps someday things will get back to normal for everyone, or maybe it never will.

I understand Israel is preparing to send missionaries to many countries in the world. If some are sent here, we will happily receive them and help in their ministry in any way we are able. We would also be excited to welcome you or any members of your family should you choose to come this way.

God Bless you and yours,
Teddy and Alice Ashman and our five

Jim made several paper copies of the letter which contained information about conditions in the US. He hadn't heard about Israel sending missionaries to the world. He would discuss this with the local Rabbi/Preacher a little later in the morning.

As his usual routine, Jim took a copy of the e-mail, his Bible, a muffin and his third cup of coffee and went to the outside table in the garden. He had just sat down when a voice from behind him stated, "Good morning Jim, I hope I am not disturbing your study." It was Rabbi Stedman the Rabbi/Pastor of the local Synagogue/Church.

"Good morning, Pastor. Have a seat and I will get a cup of coffee for you. I think you will find this letter from the United States interesting," Jim replied, as he got up and went for another cup for the pastor. He returned with additional muffins, a cup and the pot of coffee.

Pastor Stedman looked up from the copy of the e-mail with a smile and a rather astonished look on his face. "You received this, this morning?"

"It was sent sometime overnight, and I just read it a few minutes ago," Jim replied.

"This is the Lord's doing. I just returned from Jerusalem, late last night where I attended a meeting with the Evangelistic Society. The main topic was plans for mission outreach to countries all over the world, including the United States. A meeting your friend in Colorado could not have known about except by the intervention of the Lord God!" the pastor stated, then paused as he ate some muffin and took a drink of coffee. He continued, "I think this is directing us to send a team to Colorado as the Lord has work for us there."

"I would like to go," stated a small voice from the doorway. There stood little nine-year-old David.

"David, you are too young for such a trip, there will be many opportunities later," Jim said to the boy.

Rabbi Stedman leaned over to Jim and whispered, "Jim it is your decision, of course, but David's age is not a problem; many young people will probably want to go."

David came to the table, carrying a juice and took a muffin and started eating it. Jim thought David had overheard the Rabbi's whispers but did not comment on it.

"We will need to discuss this with your mother," Jim stated to David, who just smiled.

"Discuss what?" Aliza said from the door, holding an empty cup. "I see you have taken the coffee pot from the kitchen," she said with a mocking voice.

"The church is discussing sending missionaries to the United States as there are so many problems there, and David has indicated an interest in going," Jim said her.

Aliza did not speak but looked at each of the people at the table, one at a time, ending by staring at David.

From the door, Rhoda chimed in, "I will go, and David and I can look out for each other. That is if you and Jim will watch my kids."

Rhoda then filled Aliza and her cups and took the empty coffee pot back and put on the second of several pots of the day.

After a long silence at the table, Rabbi Stedman finally spoke, "We are concerned that the ones we send should speak the language of the country and I think David can speak English, can he not?"

David answered in English, "Mom and Dad taught me."

"David speaks better English than I speak Hebrew. He would do fine as far as the language goes," Jim replied to the group.

The discussion ended with the statement from David, "I think I should go."

Without a clear decision, the Rabbi left with the promise that Jim would get back to him soon. Jim then left his coffee and went into the garden where he was alone and got on his knees.

> Lord, I need your guidance on this. I believe a trip is
> what You want Israel to do, but should I send David,
> and should I go with them?

Jim waited for an answer, but nothing happened. He got up and turned to see Aliza getting to her feet. She had been praying right behind him.

"David should go, and we should support all of them with our prayers from here," she said without any doubt in her voice.

Jim knew this was not her choice to send her child away so he felt this must be from God. She had received an answer for his prayer. The difficult decision was made for them. He sent a message to Rabbi Stedman on his phone telling him of their prayer and the answer they had received. He then went to tell David who was not surprised.

CHAPTER 36

MISSIONARY TRIP TO THE UNITED STATES

THE PLANNING WAS ACCOMPLISHED QUICKLY for such a significant trip. There would be 120 Christians going of which David would be the youngest by several years. A private flight, using an Israeli Airlines passenger aircraft would be used. It would stop in several US cities and leave teams of missionaries to meet with local Christian Churches to use as a base for their mission work. David and Rhoda, along with four others, would depart the aircraft in Denver and then travel to the church in Hermosa were Jim had met Sheriff Teddy Ashman and his wife, Alice.

With all the planning, one thing seemed to be left out. When would the trip be over and when would the teams return to Israel? The leaders, including Rabbi Stedman, could not agree on a fixed date, but finally stated the end would be decided by the Lord and His guidance accepted. Jim was told about the decision and hoped the trip would be less than a year while Aliza hoped it would be no more than a month. David was excited to go and even pleased that Rhoda would be there to watch over him. He talked almost non-stop about the trip, something unusual for him.

They would all go to the airport in Tel Aviv. With both families and seven children the motorhome was the necessary vehicle. With the 120 passengers there was a huge crowd. Rabbis and pastors, most who Jim did not know, had a victory service to send off the missionaries. David and Rhoda hugged and kissed everyone good-bye. Everyone was excited to see them off, but all knew they would miss each other during their separation. The well-wishers seeing the missionaries off waited until the aircraft took off and was out of sight before leaving.

Aliza went to Jim and as he hugged her, she said, "I knew this day would come but not this soon. I will miss David so much." Their three remaining children came, along with Yosef and his three who joined in a group hug. Jim wondered if it was wise for Rhoda to leave them, but he was glad she was with David. He didn't understand why the Lord did not allow him to go, but the direction seemed clear.

The Israeli aircraft flew through the night and everyone was too excited to sleep. It was a party all night with singing in Hebrew and then English. The groups assigned to various cities got together and discussed their plans for ministry. By the time they landed in New York all were exhausted. Of the one hundred twenty, fifty got off. They would break into smaller groups and travel to cities up and down the east coast. The aircraft's next stops would be Nashville, Kansas City, Dallas, then Denver where Rhoda, David and twelve others got off. Rhoda and David would team with four others and go to the town of Hermosa for their ministry. The aircraft would not fly to California as the US Government would not allow it due to safety reasons. There were still significant areas where rebels and gangs were still in control of parts of several cities.

In the waiting area of the airport stood a young girl with a sign which read:

David Jenkins and party.

Behind the girl with the sign stood a tall, good-looking policeman. Both were sporting big smiles. The policeman stepped up to greet David first and extended his hand to shake David's small hand. "David, I am Teddy Ashman. I met your father several years ago."

David introduced Rhoda and the other four, acting more mature than he felt. Teddy then introduced the girl he was with as his daughter, Wanda Ashman. Wanda was fourteen, four years older than David, but seemed to accept him as an equal.

Teddy helped everyone with their luggage, a lot of it, and loaded the luggage and the new arrivals into the church bus from the church in Hermosa. As the trip progressed all from Israel fell asleep except Rhoda who brought Teddy and Wanda up to date about Jim and his family. While she made it sound as good as possible it was a sad story with Jim's wife dying in Israel, his return to the U.S. for several years before meeting his current wife, then moving back to Israel. She relayed how Jim was injured in the war but had mostly recovered.

"Rhoda, may I ask you if your dad is some sort of an angel? We all thought he might be when he came by. He was so clearly an answer to our prayers just the night before," Wanda ventured.

"No, Dad, not my real father of course, but Dad is not an angel. However, our family seems to have contact with heavenly spirits, more than others. Dad had a young man help him in the war when he was gravely injured, a man that was not physically there. Dad was also in the firey wave that God sent to destroy the invading army. To Dad it was just a cool breeze. The one of us that seems to have the closest contact with angels is David. He seems to know things that he has no way of knowing. When David says he thinks something is happening we all believe him and take whatever action he suggests." After Rhoda spoke everyone was quiet for a lengthy period of time and everyone glanced at David, who now seemed to be waking up. Obviously hearing this discussion, David responded.

"I don't know what's going to happen, but my "friend" tells me things. His name is also David, and he may be an angel or something like one. I think he helped my dad once during the war," David said. David's "friend" wasn't further discussed.

The plan was for the six Israelis, with Ted as the guide and protector, to go to a small town south of Hermosa and witness to the people there. The town, named Deadman, had suffered greatly and had been attacked at least once by the invaders from the south. Only about fifty people were left in the town, and they were in great need. The missionaries would take the old school bus with a trailer loaded with provisions for the winter. Hermosa was supplied by the train which ran through the town. Additional supplies were left for the smaller towns near them, towns the train did not pass through.

After a night's rest, the group got underway. The bus was driven by Ted, who was armed, apparently the only one in the group. In addition to the six Israelis were four adults from Hermosa, and at the last moment, Wanda decided to go. She sat near David who seemed deep in thought, not unusual for him. Rhoda, uneasy at not being armed, talked with the adults in the group and told them about Israel, as they rode along.

David turned to Wanda and asked, "What do the people in the town think we are going to do, and what kind of a name is Deadman for a town?"

Wanda smiled at him and answered, "The people are mostly ranchers. They raise cattle and some sheep. There is a mine but it's been shut down for years. The story is the prospectors who found the mine also found a dead man nearby, so they named the town after this unknown man. The story may not be true, but it is the west, so it could be."

The two young people chatted the entire trip, clearly enjoying each other's company. Rhoda watched them with pleasure as David tended to be a loner, and to see him interacting with this girl was very encouraging.

Currently, in Israel, it was early in the morning and Jim and Aliza had been asleep. Together they both sat up in bed, fully awake.

"David and Rhoda!", they said at the same time. "We need to pray!" Jim said. He was out of bed and on his knees while Aliza called the Rabbi/Preacher Stedman on the phone. "Our missionaries are in trouble; we need everyone to pray!" she said, and then hung up the phone without waiting for an answer.

The Rabbi, immediately called two church members in the prayer chain; each of them called two others. In just a few minutes the entire church was notified and were praying for the missionaries for whatever problem they were having.

Ted drove the bus down the main street in Deadman and suddenly stopped when a line of armed men walked across the street in front of them. Ted cursed himself for driving into a trap and thought to back up and get out, but another group of men were behind them. The men looked mean and tough. Some were dressed in all black and looked like the Arab Terrorists he had seen many years before.

"Everybody out the back door!" Ted yelled, louder than he intended.

"What is happening?" Wanda said to David. "Something wonderful," he replied with a smile.

Immediately the terrorists behind the bus saw a group of soldiers coming from the rear toward them. They were being led by a Humvee with a machine gun mounted on the top. The terrorists began screaming loudly and shooting toward the soldiers behind them. Needing reinforcements and in fear of the soldiers, the group ran past the bus toward the main group of terrorists in the front of the bus, ignoring the bus and its passengers.

The leader of the terrorists was a large man, well over six feet, with a face permanently in a scowl. He looked mean and vicious. He was with the group in front of the bus, a group of men now seemingly confused. The leader pulled his AK47 up to fire but did not notice the sling caught on a hand grenade on his belt. It pulled the pin. The explosion blew the man apart and spread shrapnel and body matter among the group. Men went down all about him.

One of them, a young man with no gun, named Ata, was wounded in the arm and one leg; he went down. He also had a nasty wound on his forehead which was bleeding badly. Ata was sixteen and had been born in Tucson, Arizona. His family had legally come to the United States from Iraq years before. Because of his ancestry, Ata had been recruited by this group of terrorists when they went through Tucson. He had not wanted to join them, but they threatened his family. He aided in stealing food but did not kill or rape anyone as the others did. Most of the men running by the bus were unharmed by the explosion and they continued running past their downed comrades and out of the town.

Ata lay on the ground as the arriving soldiers surrounded him. They did not shoot him or any of the wounded terrorists. A female soldier came to him and went down on one knee and said, "Ata, you will be fine, I will patch your wounds. The Lord has called you for His service."

Ata was scared and confused; how could this woman know his name? He saw she was attractive with long red hair. She opened the bag she carried and cut his clothes to expose the wounds. She expertly cleaned the wounds and bandaged them. The woman then ran her hand through his hair, smiled, then walked away.

Ata, with effort, sat up and leaned against the wall of a building. The soldiers and the Humvee were gone, maybe following the few remaining terrorists. Even the woman who had just treated him was nowhere to be seen. As he looked around confused, the missionaries from the bus approached him. They were led by Teddy, a tall man with a pistol, the only weapon visible. The bus driver looked at him and seeing he was unarmed went to check on the other men in the street. It seemed all the terrorists who had not fled were dead.

Noticing how frightened and alone he looked, Rhoda and David felt compelled to make a connection with this young man.

Approaching Ata, Rhoda spoke. "My name is Rhoda, and this is my brother David. What is your name?"

"I am Ata," he replied in a shaky frightened voice.

"You were injured in the explosion; how did you manage to bandage yourself so quickly?" she asked.

"One of the soldiers, a woman helped me," Ata said, now very confused. After all, they were not far away and could have seen the woman.

"What soldiers?" It was the tall man, the only armed man in this group.

"The group of soldiers that just came through here, they ran off the bandits I was with. You had to see the big Humvee with the machine gun on top!" Ata insisted, more confused than he had ever been.

David knelt beside the wounded boy and looked at his bandages, then asked, "What did the woman who treated you look like?"

"She had long red hair and was pretty."

David and Rhoda looked at each other for a moment, then Rhoda opened the pouch tied to her waist, removed a wallet and took out a picture. "Is this the woman?" she asked, showing the picture to Ata.

"That's her, but she was dressed in army clothes!"

Rhoda showed the picture to the people who had come in the bus, now all gathered around the wounded boy. "This is our mother; she is a doctor, and she is at home in Israel!" she said with a big smile.

David, turning toward his fellow passengers, said, "The Lord has sent deliverers, our people in Israel, to protect us."

The group was silent with this news and Rhoda's ringing cell phone sounded very loud.

Rhoda answered the phone and before she could say anything, Jim's voice yelled, "Rhoda, are you and David all right?"

Rhoda, smiling broadly and laughing, put her phone on speaker so all could hear.

"We are fine, Dad! We all want to thank you for saving us!"

Jim replied, "Your mother and I were wakened in the night and felt the need to pray for all of you. The entire church has been praying; tell us what happened!"

Rhoda began the story. "We arrived on schedule in Hermosa and met your friends, Teddy and Alice Ashman. They have two boys of their own, in addition to the three girls, which you met. Teddy accompanied us to our missionary site several hours away. Things suddenly went badly, and we were blocked in the street by two groups of terrorists, one in front and another behind our bus, many were heavily armed. We were all frightened, except, of course, David. After everything was over, we found a wounded boy, one of the bad guys. His name is Ata and I think he will be able to tell the story better than I."

Rhoda handed the phone to Ata and indicated he should tell what had happened.

Ata's hand shook a little, but he spoke clearly. "Sir, my name is Ata, and I was born in Tucson. My parents came from Iraq. The men came through our community and took the boys who looked like me. They needed us to carry the supplies. They did not give us guns. We were going through small towns and taking anything of value and any food. There were not many people in this town, and they are locked up in a barn a block over." He nodded in the direction to the barn. Teddy and two men went in the indicated direction to check.

Ata continued. "We saw the bus coming and Evilall, the leader, divided the group so some would be in the front of the bus and the rest would be behind. I was in the group in front. We wanted the bus because our truck broke down. The bus stopped when they saw us, and we were going to take them and lock them up with the others and take the bus. Our men behind the bus started running toward us and screaming. Behind them I saw a group of soldiers with a Humvee coming down the road. We had not seen these soldiers before. Evilall took his rifle to shoot at the soldiers but he suddenly exploded. He always kept hand grenades on his belt, and they seem to have all exploded. All the men around him were killed and I was wounded in the arm, leg and my head. I was bleeding badly when the soldiers came to us. A woman soldier with red hair came to me and treated my wounds. The woman here showed me a picture of the woman who treated me and said she was far away. I don't understand but I am all bandaged up now. The soldiers went after the other men in our group, and I didn't see them anymore."

Aliza, in Israel, spoke into the phone. "Ata, this is David's mother. My name is Aliza, and I am a doctor. The person who treated you may have looked like me, but I am far away in Israel. The soldiers and the doctor were angels. We were praying here for our people in danger and the Lord God answered our prayers by sending angels. He chose to have them look like us, who were praying. You and your men saw them and acted by running away. I don't know why God chose to not reveal the angels who came to your rescue."

Jim then spoke into the phone. "Ata, this is Jim, David's father. The Lord God has given you a great gift. He has shown you a great miracle. I believe God has a plan for you and you need to seek Him to find out what that is."

The people from the town, who had been locked in a barn came into the street. There were about sixty men, women and children. None had been injured when they had been dragged from the street and locked up. Most of the town's people were farmers and ranchers. The plan to raid the homes for food was disrupted when the terrorists saw the bus coming.

The mayor of the small town was a woman named April. She stood on a step and said in a loud voice, "We have been saved by these visitors. I suggest we place tables in the street and the women go home and fix lunch for everyone and let us hear what these missionaries have to say. They have come from Israel to tell us something important."

The luncheon came together quickly. Tables and chairs were gathered from businesses and nearby homes. They were set up in the middle of the street and women began bringing food from their homes. Within an hour the tables were all covered with sandwiches, salads and drinks. Someone provided stacks of paper plates and plastic forks. The guests were provided seating at a table while most people stood to eat. An older man led a prayer of thanks for the meal and the safety provided by the guests.

As everyone was finishing their meal, the mayor stood and stated, "Everyone, something wonderful happened today. Something I do not understand. We have guests from Israel who have come to update us on world events. They are with Teddy Ashman from Hermosa, who many of you know. I will ask him to introduce his guests."

Teddy, always an imposing figure, stood and introduced the guests from Israel. He briefly mentioned Jim's earlier visit and the impact on their church. He then asked Rhoda to come and tell them about what was happening in Israel.

She stood, and speaking as loudly as she could, said, "My friends, God is moving in miraculous ways in Israel. I will tell you more later, but we came on this missionary journey to spread the good news of Jesus. As we were here this morning, my parents, Jim and his wife Aliza were both awaken at the same time, with a feeling they needed to pray for our safety. They called the pastor of our church, and he called the leaders of the prayer ministry group, who in turn each called two or three people in the prayer chain. In just a few minutes the entire church was praying for us, even though they did not know what danger we were in. As we came into your town, the road was blocked by men from the terror group which had taken your town."

Rhoda paused, then looking at Ata, smiled and said, "I think my new friend Ata, previously a captive of the terrorists, should continue this story as he saw more than I."

Ata, with a clean shirt on, stood up and looked unsure but spoke loudly and clearly. "My name is Ata. I was born in Tucson; my parents are from Iraq. I was taken from them by the group which came to your town today. This group has done this many times before. They did not kill everyone but took everything they could take. This time they locked you in a barn and planned to rob your homes. Their plan changed when they saw the bus. The truck we had been using was broken and barely running and they wanted the bus. Evilall, our leader, divided the group so some would be in front and some behind the bus so it could not run away. The bus stopped. The group behind the bus saw the soldiers first and started running past the bus toward us. Behind them were soldiers and a Humvee with a machine gun on the top. Evilall was going to shoot at them, but he just exploded. He always carried several hand grenades and maybe they exploded. A lot of the men were killed, and I was wounded. All the rest ran away. A woman soldier with red hair came and treated me and bandaged my wounds. She was nice and somehow knew my name. The soldiers left and the people on the bus came up. I told Rhoda about the woman and she showed me a picture of her and said it was her mother in Israel. The people on the bus did not see any of the soldiers, I don't know why because they came right by them. Rhoda's mother called her and said that she was not the soldier, but the soldiers were angels that looked like the people in Israel who were praying for them. I think Rhoda's mother is right. The soldiers must be angels, or everyone would have seen them. The woman who bandaged me said the Lord has called me for His service. I must study and find out about the Lord and do whatever He wants me to do."

Ata went and sat by David and Rhoda. The people were quiet for a time, not understanding what had happened in their town.

The afternoon was spent cleaning up the town. The bodies were loaded on a farm trailer and hauled out of town. A tractor with a front loader dug a trench and the dead were thrown in and covered up without any service. The town lived up to its name of Deadman. The guns were gathered and put in the mayor's office.

Teddy and the missionaries were put in two houses for the night, separated by gender. The accommodations were not plush, but everyone was happy to have a place to rest. David and Ata sat on the porch to talk and were joined by Rhoda and Wanda. After a bit Teddy also came and sat nearby.

Ata said, "I feel like I need to know more about how the soldiers rescued your group. It seems your people in Israel caused angels to come. I don't understand how that could be."

Rhoda answered, "Ata, we will teach you about Jesus and His plan for salvation. We will give you a Bible which we believe is God's word to us. You have a family in Tucson, and they may want you to come back."

"No, I don't need to go back. They consider me an adult and want me to be on my own. But you will go back to Israel someday," Ata said, looking at Rhoda.

"My father and I live in Hermosa, not far from here. We will take you there where there is a good church," Wanda added.

It was decided, Ata would stay with the missionaries as they moved from town to town, spreading the gospel and strengthening churches. In the next two months they moved across southern Colorado and northern New Mexico. During this time Ata read the Bible the New Testament four times and most of the Old Testament. He had an amazing memory and could quote scripture better than most of the others in the group. He was baptized in a watering tank for cattle a week after they left Deadman. Everyone believed God had a mission for this young man.

After the two months were over, the missionaries were excited about going home. Teddy, Wanda, and now Ata, were anxious to see Alice and the other siblings. The Israelis were also looking forward to seeing home. This was the longest most of them had been away. The trip had been a tremendous success, as the number of new converts was in the hundreds and existing Christians had taken on a new desire to evangelize. Ata had quickly become an asset and dynamic speaker in giving his testimony. He would have a good future in missionary work in the United States.

The last day before leaving, they were all staying in an old but nice motel, a gift of the local church. About two o'clock in the morning, David was awakened with a start. He set up and heard a voice say, 'Leave the building, NOW!'

He jumped out of bed, slipped on his shoes and went for the door, yelling at the other men in the room. He ran outside, still in his night clothes and banged on the doors where the women were sleeping. "We need to get out of the building! Now!" he shouted.

Amid fearful cries and chaos, stumbling and questioning, the motel was evacuated. Even those not with their group followed. Rhoda encouraged the ladies who wanted to rest, but everyone assembled in the parking lot. Most had grabbed some clothes, which they put on. Others wrapped themselves in a blanket or had just whatever they slept in.

The group stood for a couple of minutes and some of those, not in their group were grumbling and starting back to their rooms when the slight tremor began. It was only a few seconds later when overhead power lines and the trees began to sway. The quake was not severe but ended with a shock powerful enough to bring down the old motel.

CHAPTER 37

ANOTHER DISASTER

THE EARTHQUAKE IN COLORADO WAS relatively minor even though there was damage, mostly to older structures. The severity of the shaking increased to the west.

A man, Doyle Johnson, was rich by anybody's standard, living in a multimillion-dollar house north of San Francisco and working downtown. He made six million last year on investments and foreclosures, much of it coming as benefits from all the rioting and violence. He worked in a building in the heart of San Francisco which was guarded by twenty full-time guards. With a wife and two girlfriends, he suspected they knew about each other but with the money he supplied them, they didn't care. By his standards, he was a great success.

This morning Doyle was driving south on highway 101 from his home twenty miles north. He was in his brand-new luxury Lexus and was feeling great; he had the world by the tail. Doyle started onto the Golden Gate bridge and was just passing the northern tower when he saw more than felt the shaking. The huge cables which held the bridge swayed back and forth. He had never seen them move before. Doyle, not being stupid, knew in an earthquake a bridge is not the place to be. He thought about speeding up and getting off the bridge to the south but looking at the big tower at the southern end of the bridge, saw it moving. He could not believe it. The tower actually moved to the west. In a panic he spun the car around to go back north, going the wrong way on the south bound lanes. The traffic was lighter than usual but still there were a lot of vehicles. He made some progress and was back at the northern tower when more people tried to turn around causing accidents in the middle of the highway, completely blocking it. He jumped out of his car and started running through the wreckage and ignoring the cries for help from people trapped. There was a loud bang, a noise louder than he had ever heard before. It was so loud the shock of it nearly knocked him down. The big cable to his right fell, crushing several people and cars. He was shaking so badly he could hardly stand. He kept going, even pushing others fleeing the chaos out of his way.

Doyle finally reached the solid pavement, which was also shaking, but he felt safer. He turned to look back and saw the city of San Francisco moving to the west. The bridge was gone, and parts of the city was moving into the sea. A woman behind him said, "O my God, all those people!" Doyle's only thoughts had been about the buildings and not the inhabitants. For the first time, he felt remorse for the people, but more for his wealth, which was all in the city. In a matter of minutes, he lost his investments, his job and his savings. He had a large mortgage on his house, which he had no way of paying. He felt sorry for himself, not the city's inhabitants.

San Francisco was gone, but the city was only the northern most part of the earthquake's destruction. The split went south following the fault line some thirty miles from the coast. All the cities along the coast south of San Francisco into Mexico were gone, including Los Angeles and San Diego. In Mexico, the peninsula of Baja California became a small island; just the southern end survived. The southern part of the western coast of the United States was gone, and with-it millions of people, and a huge amount of the wealth of the country.

The disaster was not over. With the collapse of the land mass into the ocean, a tsunami was triggered which went west. Hawaii had some warning, and many people ran for the hills. There was not sufficient warning for everyone to escape, and the loss of life grew by millions more. The cities along the coasts were wiped out. The islands of Hawaii were desolated. The waves continued and hit Japan and the countries along the coasts from Russia south. The damage and loss of life was impossible to measure. The earth with its economy and way of life would take centuries to recover. Some countries would never recover.

The Middle East and China were not affected much by these disasters. China had damage along its east coast but not its industrial centers. The Middle Eastern countries, including Israel, were in a quiet zone for this earthquake.

In Colorado, the team of missionaries were unaware of the magnitude of the damage. Teddy counted heads to insure everyone was safe. "We need to get back to Hermosa and see that everyone there is all right!" he said, obviously worried about his family. He then turned to David and asked, "Any word from your friend about Hermosa?" Teddy, as well as the others in the group, had accepted that David had an insight into what would happen in the future. David shook his head and replied, "No, I am sorry."

While the group was getting into the bus, Teddy located the motel manager who was with them in the parking lot to tell him they were all right and leaving. The rooms had been paid for by the local church. As they drove out of town, Teddy had one of the men call the pastor of the church so he would not worry about them.

It was dawn when they reached the church in Hermosa and Alice was waiting with two of her daughters and both of her young sons. She hugged Wanda and then gripped Teddy for a long time, sobbing with relief and joy.

Wanda introduced Ata to her mother and the church preacher, Pastor Morris, who had just arrived. "This is Ata. He has been with us for several weeks and is a great asset to our ministry."

"Welcome to our town, Ata!" Alice said to him as she gave him a hug.

Pastor Morris shook his hand and said, "Young man, I look forward to hearing your testimony. I have been told it is quite impressive."

The next day was Sunday, and the missionaries were asked to come to the front, and those who chose spoke to the congregation. The pastor encouraged Ata to give his testimony, which he did. After the service, the church prepared a luncheon, a part of the welcoming of the missionaries. Serving lunch was a regular occurrence for this church.

After eating a small amount, David left the crowd and sat alone outside, trying to understand what had happened. Ata, walked up to him and asked, "May I join you?"

"Of course, I am just trying to understand what has happened to this country. It seems California has had a major disaster. We were sent to spread the gospel here and now God has chosen to do this."

Wanda came and quietly sat by Ata. Conversation seemed unnecessary.

After a few moments Ata addressed David "You have a friend, an angel or someone, who tells you things. Has He told you anything?"

"No, he has not, but His message in the Scriptures is that God is in control of events. Events we may not understand," David said.

"David, when you talk to your friend, if you could, ask Him to help me know what God wants me to do here. I would appreciate it," Ata stated quietly.

Before David could answer, a voice behind them said, "Ata you are chosen by God Himself to a service He will choose. You can talk to Him and He will answer you. If He sends me to you, I will come and help you along the way." Then the voice added, "The Lord has a plan for the United States. If they turn back to Him, He will use this country to be a great witness for Him."

The three young people turned and there stood the David previously known to only young David. They all saw him, and then he was gone.

In great awe the three just stared for a moment then Wanda said, "Thank You, Lord for allowing me to see your angel." The two boys added, "Amen."

The three young people shared what had just happened with Rhoda and Teddy. Repeating the encounter numerous times, with questions from Rhoda and Pastor Morris they all rejoiced for this heavenly visitation and knew it was a conformation that God was in control.

The church sent the missionaries on their way with thankfulness and promises to keep in touch. As Teddy drove the bus he reflected on the events of the recent days. It was a happy trip to the airport.

The news of the destruction in California was slow in being broadcast as the major news stations in the area were now gone. The entire area was in chaos with fires and panic. A young woman newscaster from Oakland stood on the shoreline of what once was the east side of San Francisco Bay, now the shoreline of the Pacific Ocean. She stood, weeping as she spoke, with the camera sweeping the open sea with floating debris. She tried to express the feelings of loss, loss of life and wealth, from the destruction so great that it was indescribable. She ended her broadcast with the statement, "Lord God, how could you have allowed this to happen?"

After the weeping newscaster went off the air, the station reverted to their home station in Washington DC. Another newsman, a well-known figure in the news business, came on the air and stated, "This prayer asks a good question. We have connected with Pastor Billy Samuels of Dallas, TX, for a comment." The camera switched to his location.

Pastor Billy Samuels came on the air. He was dressed in casual clothing and stood outside a large church. "The question about why God allows bad things to happen is often asked when disasters occur. Sometimes there is no answer, but that is not the case for the United States. For many years, the country has forgotten the Lord God, our Creator and Savior. We have stopped worshiping, and our churches are mostly empty. We as a nation have accepted and even glorified actions that are against the Lord's teaching. We abort many thousands of children each year and we accept and even celebrate ungodly, homosexual lifestyles. We have expelled Him from our government, our schools and our personal lives. How can we expect God will continue to bless us?"

The news broadcast cut the pastor off and returned to the station and a now frustrated newscaster. "Thank you, pastor, for your thoughts, but we know there is no answer for why these things happen," she said.

At the airport the missionary group watched the TV and after the broadcast Teddy stated, "At least some people understand! We need to turn back to God, and He will help us through this."

The same aircraft which had brought them from Israel arrived to take them home. A large number of people deplaned and came into the terminal. They explained that they were missionaries, assigned in Israel with the task of going into California, which was now open to them. Two couples of the homeward bound group decided to stay and join the new group. Rhoda looked at David questioningly and he replied, "We will come back again." They got on the aircraft to return to Israel.

When the aircraft reached altitude, a woman stood at the front and commented, "I know many of you had wonderful experiences. Does anyone want to share?"

Many did so beginning at the front of the aircraft. People stood and talked about their mission experiences. Everyone had been accepted by the people where they were witnessing, and none had been concerned about their safety.

When her group's turn came, Rhoda stood and spoke about the men who attacked their group and the rescue by soldiers, believed to be angels. She explained how they did not see the angels, but the terrorists did. She told about the young man, Ata, who was wounded and later joined their group. "Please remember this man, as I believe he will be a powerful influence for God's kingdom in the future." She concluded her report with the comment, "We all saw another angel, named David. He appeared to us and spoke to Ata and told him the Lord had a duty for him to accomplish. This angel has appeared to my brother several times and given him warnings and information about what would happen. Every time the information has been true. We are living in a time when God is working miracles to spread the Christian message to the world. Be strong, for God is with us!"

The aircraft was quiet for a moment then someone began clapping then another shouted "Glory to God." The weary travelers broke out in a Hebrew song, a song praising God and His great power. It was a wonderful expression of their adoration, love and thankfulness to a wonderful Savior and friend.

CHAPTER 38

IS THIS THE END OF TIME?

Jim and Aliza met the aircraft with the church bus, the same as they did after the first trip the missionaries had taken. It was a joyous meeting, even more so than the first time. With the disaster in California and the attack on the missionaries by the bandits, it had brought fear and worry to the parents and relatives of the missionaries, but all had returned safely and happy. The trip back to the city of Jenkins was noisy and exciting with the young people telling their experiences, sometimes all at the same time. Jim watched his wife as she enjoyed her children, laughing with them and listening to the stories. He could not remember her being so happy.

The next day was Saturday, Sabbath for the Jews. Almost everyone in the city attended the services as returning missionaries had been asked to report on their trip to the United States. The service began as usual, then the Rabbi introduced the returning missionaries and asked if they would like to report on the trip, one at a time—an attempt to have some degree of control of the service.

The young people were, in fact, very controlled at first, allowing one person to speak, telling what was most important to him or her. Several of the youngsters told of the attack of the terrorists and the saving of their lives by the Jews praying in Israel. They told of the identification of Aliza by the young man, Ata, who identified her by the picture Rhoda produced.

The meeting went on well into the afternoon, past the normal lunch time. Finally, some of the women went into the church kitchen and prepared some sandwiches and drink. When announced that food was available the service broke up with many people going into the kitchen, continuing their conversations, while some went home. Jim and his family were still at the church when one of the leaders came in and announced to everyone that something was happening in the US at Yellowstone Park. Jim had been experiencing a strange feeling of dread for the last few hours. He suddenly rose and loudly announced, "I am going home and tune in the US news on TV. I have a bad feeling!"

Aliza and the children went with Jim, hurrying home as quickly as he could, limping as always.

Jim's house had connections to several satellite TV services, one which was a United States system that allowed him to view the national network systems directly. He tuned on the popular conservative network, the one he often watched to keep up with what was going on in his home country.

A familiar newscaster was broadcasting and just reporting. "For an update on the events occurring in the Yellowstone National Park, we join our reporter Josh Hawkins on site."

A younger man appeared on the screen who was outside in front of the resort. Jim recognized it as the one near the Old Faithful Geyser. The man looked disturbed as he spoke. "As you are aware, there has been unusual activity in the park for several days. In the time we have been here the ground shaking has been nearly continuous. In addition, there is a constant sound, like a roar or a growl surrounding us. The Old Faithful Geyser has been continuously discharging, and it has changed from water to mostly steam. Visitors and employees have been asked to leave the park and we will be leaving after this broadcast. Our station has installed cameras fixed in several areas of the park, two are here, one points at the geyser and the other at the lodge. These will continue to broadcast after we leave. I believe it is very dangerous here; the ground is shaking and feels unstable—gel-like."

The screen went blank for a moment then the newscaster returned and said, "We have an interruption of the broadcast from our team, but the stationary cameras are still working. This is a view of the Old Faithful Geyser from the fixed camera."

The scene switched to the camera and the geyser came into view. It was spraying steam and then fire. The camera began shaking and then seemed to topple over. The TV scene shifted to the second camera in the area showing the lodge which was fully engulfed in flames. The newscaster stated in a shaky voice, "My God, I hope our people are ok!"

Another reporter came on the air and said, "We seem to be having technical difficulties with the reporters in the park. We will switch to Mark Hadley on a ranch west of the park."

The image switched to the reporter, who was obviously not ready. He picked up the microphone and stated, "We are at Masson Ranch, 10 miles west of the park, with Mr. Masson who has reported some unusual events with the wildlife."

The camera switched to Mr. Masson, a mid-fifties man, dressed in bib-overalls. "I have never seen anything like this. A large herd of buffalo came first, knocking down our fences, and then came deer and bears. They were all running west. I guess they are coming from Yellowstone!" he said, nearly yelling.

The camera went back to the reporter who started to comment about the animals when his eyes got very big and said, "Good God, look at that!!"

The camera swung around to point east to a scene of a huge column of smoke and fire going straight into the air. Another voice, probably the cameraman said, "Let's get the hell out of here!!"

There was a tremendous sound of an explosion, and the screen went blank.

The scene on the TV went back to the station, to the speechless and confused newswoman who just stood there with a terrified look on her face. Nothing happened for several seconds, then a commercial came on.

After the commercial the screen went blank for several seconds, then without any introduction a man appeared. He was dressed in casual attire without a tie. He was standing in a cluttered office filled with books and charts. He began speaking as if everyone should know who he was. "We have been studying the super volcano in Yellowstone Park for many years and it seems it has now erupted. This is a major problem for the United States as the plume from a very large volcano will be massive and will travel for great distances. Depending on the length of time it erupts it could blanket the northern states all the way to the east coast with a layer of ash, in which nothing will grow and there will be no foliage for animals to eat. Unless this stops in just a few days, this is a major disaster." He spoke showing no emotion, but at this point he stopped and said sadly, "I am sorry to report this. It is very bad news; God must be very unhappy with us." The man then lowered his head and said no more.

The screen then switched back to the station and a man at a desk spoke. "If you are just tuning in, a volcano at Yellowstone has erupted and it seems to be a major explosive eruption. What we know now is the plume has reached at least forty thousand feet and is several miles wide. The eruption started with an explosion that caused damage for miles around. We have no reports of casualties but there are probably many. We have been told the President will address the nation in a few minutes. I am sorry this has happened to our great country." With that statement the man lowered his head into his hands and appeared to cry.

The picture remained on the reporter while a voice announced, "We are switching to a station in Buffalo, Wyoming, approximately one hundred ninety miles east of the park."

An unclear image came on the TV looking over a city and, on the horizon, a black column reached the top of the picture. It looked very wide. The only sound was voices speaking in the background. "Zoom in a little so they can see what a mess thts is." The picture got larger, showing the massive up-flow in the column and particles falling outside of it. "What is this crap in the air? When I breathe it, it burns my lungs and it is starting to get dark." Another voice answered, "I don't know but this pollution will kill us if we breathe it very long. We need a mask to filter the air. I think we have to get out of here!"

The sound stopped for several seconds then a voice said, "We are now switching to the President."

The picture went to the Oval Office, where the President was sitting behind the desk. He had on a suit coat and a tie, except the tie was pulled down and his collar open. "My friends, we have had another disaster in our country. The super volcano which created the Yellowstone National Park has erupted, the first time in thousands of years. I am told this will cause a lot of fallout across the northern part of the country and it may cause a darkness over the entire globe. It may not, but this could be a worldwide catastrophe. I have been praying a lot lately about our country. First, we had the electrical problems, caused by an enemy, then a major disaster in California which caused an enormous loss of life. Now this volcano which will affect our entire country, particularly the cities in the north and possibly as far south as Phoenix, AZ. My friends, something is not right. I believe this is the Lord trying to show us the errors of our ways. I am making a commitment to the Lord God and promise to do as He wants. I have been told there are missionaries from Israel who have been requested by God to witness to the entire world. I ask these missionaries to come here and witness to all our people as the Lord directs. If they come, I ask everyone to welcome them. In closing, I ask everyone to pray for our country."

The TV switched back to the newsroom where a reporter continued to talk about the volcano, a subject he clearly knew little about.

Jim left the picture on but muted the sound. He looked around the room at his entire family who had been watching TV. "I think the call is clear, we are all called to be missionaries. I think I should go to the United States."

The room was silent for a moment then Aliza and David spoke at the same time.

"We should all go, and quickly!!"

Jim and Aliza's other three children stood with David indicating their willingness to go, all were smiling.

"I and my family will also go," Yosef, Rhoda's husband, said quietly.

"We will pray about this, Yosef. But without a presence here I think the city would suffer. Pray about this and I will support the decision you reach," Jim stated quietly.

The meeting of the family slowly broke up and Jim went alone to the garden, his favorite place of prayer. He prayed for guidance and asked that it be clear regarding his family. He was conflicted about the children going, even though they were older teenagers.

His phone rang and while he was unhappy with the interruption, he answered it.

"Jim, this is General Steinhoff. A large cargo plane has arrived from the US. It will be here three days unloading, with plans to return nearly empty. I know you are sending missionaries to the states on a regular basis, and I suddenly thought to notify you of this aircraft. It could easily take your motor home and several passengers. I know this sounds strange, but I suddenly felt I needed to call you."

Jim stood with the phone to his ear, with a big smile. "General, I was just praying for guidance about taking my family to the US. It had not occurred to me to take the motorhome, but you have spoken to me for the Lord. I will prepare the vehicle and be at the airport before your flight time. I have never had such a clear answer to a prayer. I thank you."

"I have never spoken for the Lord, Jim, but I am grateful that God saw fit to use me. He is speaking very plainly now, isn't He?"

When the call ended Jim put his phone in his pocket and stood. Behind him stood Aliza with a big smile. She had overheard the conversation. "Three days and we leave!" she sighed, still smiling.

Jim called the garage who serviced his vehicles with instructions to replace the tires and to service everything on the vehicle, in preparation for a long trip.

It was late the next day when Jim brought the RV back to the house with new tires. His family began packing for an extended trip. The family needed clothes for any weather condition as the length of stay was undefined. They begin loading the next morning. The family of six, two adults and four teenagers required a lot of clothing, most of which had to be stored in the bins under the motorhome. Jim also took several boxes of the freeze-dried emergency food, uncertain about conditions in the United States.

In addition to Jim's family were fifteen others from the church, going as missionaries. They would ride in the church bus to the airport. In this group were brothers Harold and Ralph Taylor, a pastor and a doctor, a great addition for the mission. Rhoda and her family came to see them off. She was sad, as she really wanted to go, but understood Yosef's decision to stay. In addition, many members of the church arrived to send them off, promising to support them with prayers.

Jim led the group driving the motorhome and towing his Jeep. The bus followed. At the airport Jim was surprised to see General Steinhoff at the gate to the military side of the airport waving them through. The general got into a military Jeep and led them to the runway were a large C-5 cargo plane was parked. The Jeep stopped and the general stepped out with a big smile. As he approached the motorhome he called to Jim, "Jim, it is good to see you on this special Memorial Day!"

Jim shook the general's hand and replied, "General, it is so good and surprising to see you. I must have missed something. What memorial is this day?"

The general smiled, a larger smile than Jim had ever seen. "I wanted to wait and tell you in person. I have seen an angel of the Lord!"

Jim was stunned. He placed his hand on the general's shoulder and said, "Tell us, my friend."

Still smiling he said, "Just before I called you and before I even knew about this plane, I was sitting in my office looking over some papers. When I glanced up, sitting across the desk from me was a beautiful woman. She had flawless skin. Without introducing herself, she said, "General, an aircraft is arriving from the United States. It is to carry missionaries and Jim Jenkins's motorhome back to be used by the Lord God. The airplane is arriving now."

"I looked out the window and saw this aircraft on final approach to land. When I turned back to the woman, she was gone." The general paused, so excited he could hardly speak, then continued. "I knew my young aid could not have missed a beautiful woman walking into my office, so I called him in. He said no one had come into my office. This woman had to be an angel. I feel so blessed. That is when I called you."

Jim had never seen this man so happy and excited. "My friend, you truly have been blessed. The Lord is doing something great in the world and we are all fortunate to be present to witness it."

With that statement, Jim reached out and hugged the general, something he would never have done before this moment. The general was so emotional, he hugged Jim back.

The general stepped back and said, "Let us load up your vehicle so you can be on your way to see what the Lord has planned for you!"

The general signaled four men, Israeli soldiers, who quickly disconnected the Jeep and drove the motorhome into the aircraft, followed by the jeep. An American airman directed the placement of the vehicles. In addition to Jim's vehicles was a small bus, already tied down.

The general shook Jim's hand and each of the childrens' hands and for the first time ever, hugged Aliza. Then, still with a big smile, said, "Go with God my friends!" He then turned and walked away.

Jim went to his wife and said, "He has truly seen an angel of the Lord!"

"And he is changed forever!" she confirmed.

The airman who had directed the loading came to Jim and said, "Mr. Jenkins, I am Captain Evans. If your crew will board the aircraft, we will get underway."

Jim, his family and the missionaries with him boarded the aircraft, taking seats along the side. In the front of the cargo bay were several rows of seats, all filled with passengers. This was a full flight.

As always in a cargo plane the sound during takeoff was deafening. A few had ear plugs or earmuffs, the rest put their hands over their ears. At cruising altitude the noise was still loud, but more tolerable.

The airman, Captain Evans, came by and indicated to Jim that he and his family could ride in the motorhome which would be a little quieter. Jim's family and the Taylor brothers went into the motorhome, accompanied by Captain Evans. The unit was crowded, but quieter.

Speaking to everyone, Captain Evans stated, "I know you are aware of the volcano in the US. You may not be aware of how bad it is. The fire and gases close to the eruption have been bad, but the main problem is the gas and ash from the eruption. The wind from the west has carried the ash across the northern part of the country. The ash has covered much of the land all the way to the east coast and in some places it is thick. People and animals have died from the gas, which is fatal to breath. The crops in the area are destroyed, maybe for years. This has crippled the United States. We will be landing at a military base near Oklahoma City which is still clear. I hope your message to us, the citizens of the US, will encourage everyone as most do not understand why God has done this. I am glad you have come to help us."

Without waiting for a reply, the captain left the motorhome.

It was quiet for a moment then Pastor Harold Taylor remarked, "My God, I had no idea the gas was poisonous. The cloud has drifted across the most populated cites of the country! The loss of life must be enormous."

As the word of the conditions in the US spread, the mood in the aircraft became more somber. It was a terrible report that poisonous gas had spread across the northern part of the country. While Jim was not an expert on volcanoes, he had never heard of toxic gases spreading very far from the eruption.

Long before reaching the coast of the US the aircraft encountered a haze which intensified as they continued. The pilot veered a little south and found cleaner air. As they continued, haze to the north intensified as a black heavy cloud.

The pilot came back on the intercom and stated, "As you can see, the air to the north is polluted. It is spreading across the world as it moves and will likely affect the climate over the entire earth."

He said no more but the attitude in the aircraft became very somber as everyone looked at the black cloud.

They landed at the airbase near Oklahoma City and unloaded everything. Jim loaded several passengers in the motorhome and instead of towing the Jeep, allowed six to ride and a young man to drive it. They had arranged for a bus to carry the rest of the missionaries.

Jim made a stop at a camper supply store where he had called ahead and ordered ten sets of filters for the engine and cabin of the motorhome and Jeep. When he arrived, he was told the limit had been set at two as the demand was high and the supply very limited. The manager of the store explained they had established the policy to help as many people as they could. He then explained how the filters could be covered with a porous cloth which could be removed and shaken out to extend the life of the filters. This seemed good to Jim, and he thanked the man for his help.

The bus took most of the missionaries and dropped them off at their prearranged sites from Oklahoma City north to Kansas and Nebraska and Iowa, the furthest north they could go due to safety. Jim took his family and twelve others west. The six in the Jeep dropped off in Amarillo where a local church would provide rooms and transportation. Jim, with the Jeep now in tow continued toward Phoenix, their assigned city.

As they drove west on Highway 40, Jim noticed the lack of traffic. "I have driven this road many times and except for right after the EMP attack have I seen so few cars," he remarked.

"And look at all the cars broken down along the road," Aliza replied, then continued. "It seems the country is in a lot of trouble."

They entered Arizona at a corner of the Navajo Reservation and noticed the small towns seemed deserted. Jim's oldest daughter stated the obvious. "This looks spooky. What is going on?"

Not knowing what to say, her parents did not reply.

Reaching Holbrook and an open truck stop, Jim pulled in to refuel. People inside the station just looked out the window at them. The pump accepted Jim's credit card and he filled the tank, which would take him to Phoenix.

As they traveled on toward Flagstaff conditions seemed to improve. Most of the highway was clear of abandoned cars, and the traffic increased. The small communities had people moving about as normal.

At a shopping center on the outskirts of Flagstaff, Jim pulled into the nearly empty parking lot and parked.

From the back of the bus, someone said, "What is Mexican food, and can only Mexicans eat it?"

Jim replied laughing, "Everything on the menu is good, only it might be better to stay with the less spicy selections. Some food here will be a little hot if you are not used to it!"

All twelve of them went into the restaurant and chose tables, which they quickly pulled together. The only waitress came and welcomed them to the establishment. She was a middle-aged woman, and chatty. She handed them menus and said, "Welcome to Arizona! My name is Jane, where are you all from?"

She was looking at Jim with a large smile, so he answered her. "We are from Israel and are on a missionary trip to your country."

Her smile faded to a serious look and replied, "Let me get my husband, well, boyfriend. We are both very interested in what is happening to our country."

A man, several years older than Jane came out of the kitchen with a look that indicated he was not happy to be interrupted. Without introducing himself he stated, "If you are missionaries can you tell me what God is doing destroying our country. California fell into the ocean and the Yellowstone Volcano is destroying everything else. After all we are a Christian Nation, everyone says so! Why is God doing this!" As he spoke his volume increased until everyone in the restaurant was paying attention.

"Perhaps we can examine the situation. First to introduce myself, my name is Jim Jenkins and I now live in Israel, but I was born in the US and lived much of my life here in Arizona. These others are my family and friends, coming in the hopes we can encourage people here to come closer to God."

Jim paused as more people came into the restaurant and stood around listening.

Jim asked, "Tomorrow is Sunday. Is the church at the end of the street open?"

Someone in the back of the room spoke up. "It is open but almost no one goes."

"Well perhaps there will be room for us," Jim stated to the surprise of his group. They had not planned to spend the night in this town.

Jim continued, looking at the cook and waitress, "Perhaps you, your wife and two daughters could come with us."

The statement brought an immediate reaction from the waitress, Jane. She shook like she had been electrocuted and all the color drained from her face. She would have fallen except a woman next to her grabbed and held her. A man near them retrieved a chair from the next table and they helped her sit down next to the cook.

The cook whose name was Dick said, "We are not actually married, no one gets married anymore."

Jane started talking before Dick was finished and said with tears flowing down her face, "My babies were girls! I never knew. They told me it was too early to know."

She paused, now crying uncontrollably, then said "I had two abortions. I killed my daughters!"

Dick, also very disturbed replied, "It was just the wrong time to have children. We were just trying to get the restaurant going and it wasn't illegal. No one knew." He then sat back in his chair and looked like he had been struck.

No one said anything for a full minute then Dick looked up and said in a loud voice, "We are the reason God has done this to the country; we have completely turned away from Him. None of us has been to that church for years and we have sinned so greatly, can God ever forgive us?"

"We are all fortunate that the Lord God is a forgiving God. He will forgive us if we confess our sins and change our ways," Jim said quietly.

"This restaurant will be closed tomorrow; we are going to church," Dick stated.

Dick seemed to recover, and he selected two young men from the crowd to help him and went into the kitchen to prepare food. Jane, however, remained seated and quietly asked Aliza, "Is there some way I can find out if my daughters are all right?"

Smiling, Aliza replied. "Include them in your prayers and perhaps God will answer you with some assurance about them."

David, sitting beside his mother, added, "Your girls would be happy if you would give them names and pray using their names."

Jane smiled for the first time in a long time and replied, "I thank your family for helping us and showing us the way back. I will pray for your mission."

She then hugged Aliza and David and returned to help the women who were taking orders from the now full restaurant.

The food was good, although many things on the menu were not available.

Jim caught Jane's attention and asked, "Jane, we need a bill, and we can clear these tables."

She smiled and replied, "The meal is on the house, you have given us much more than money."

"Thank you we will see you in church tomorrow," Jim responded. He then left three one-hundred-dollar bills by the cash register when she wasn't looking. Aliza smiled at him in agreement.

She then commented, "I guess we are spending the night here somewhere."

"It seems like God wants us here for another day," Jim confirmed. Everyone seemed to agree as many nodded their heads.

Jim, Aliza and their four children would sleep in the motorhome. The other six would need rooms. Jim was looking for a motel or hotel when a man came running up to the vehicle. He went to the window by the driver's seat, which Jim opened.

"Hello, Mr. Jenkins, my name is Pastor Saul. I am pastor of the church just down the block, The Fourth Baptist Church. We have some rooms set aside for the homeless and travelers to use. It is not luxurious, but they are clean and free. A member of our church was at the restaurant and told of your witness. We would be happy to provide housing for you."

The statement was directed to Jim, but Aliza answered, "That would be wonderful. We are grateful! Come around to the other side of the RV and I will let you in."

The pastor, a little over thirty, was welcomed by the group as he got in and was directed to the right seat in the front, across from Jim. "We are two blocks down this road and have a place with hookups for your motorhome. At one time a visiting pastor came and spent some time with us and paid for the hookups for his motor home. It has not been used for some time, but I believe everything works," he said with a smile.

In the parking lot of the large church was an area with a large tree. The area around the tree was separated from the parking lot by a curb and within the small area was a sewer pipe, a water valve, and an electrical box on a post, everything needed for a long stay in an RV.

"You can leave your Jeep hooked up and just pull through. The parsonage is on the other side of the parking lot," the pastor said with his continuous smile.

Jim parked the motorhome, aligning the bin where the electrical and water connections were located with the facilities in the ground. Jonathan, Jim's oldest son, jumped out and hooked up the utilities. The electrical connection required an adapter which posed no problem, as Jim carried various ones in a box. Everything worked.

The pastor led the entire group into the church to see the rooms set up for overnight guests. As they walked, Pastor Saul said to Jonathan, "Jonathan, we share a biblical name."

David, from nearby asked, "Your name is Saul, like the first king of Israel?"

"Yes, and your name is David, the second king of Israel. We both obviously come from religious families," the pastor replied.

They entered the church through a side door and went down a flight of stairs to the basement. There, down a long hallway with doors on both sides, he opened the first door on the right to a large room with eight beds in two rows.

"This room is for the boys. There is a bathroom with a shower right next door. The girls' room is just past the guard station, which we man most of the time," the pastor stated, smiling.

"We have two boys who will need beds. My family can stay in the motorhome," Jim said casually.

"I will stay with Ben and Mossel, just to keep them company," Jonathan said.

Jim nodded in agreement. Jonathan at twenty-one, an adult, did not need permission and the motor home would be crowded with all six of his family.

The group continued down the hall to the guard station. An older man sitting behind the desk rose when the pastor came by. This station was located at the main entrance to the basement and was the hub of the security system for the church.

The pastor explained the station. "During the conflict with the invasion years ago we strengthened the security of the church. Several families spent a good deal of time here. This station monitors all the doors in the building and can lock them from here. Of course, the doors will open if someone needs to exit the church. We keep a security person here on weekends and continuously if we have guests. Mr. Simons here is part of our security team."

Mr. Simons smiled and shook each hand saying, "Call me Doug. I will be here spending the night with you."

Doug did not appear to be armed.

The pastor showed the group the room for the girls, which was identical to the room for the boys. Jim thought it humorous the guard station was between the rooms.

Pastor Saul turned to Jim with a serious look on his face. "Jim, I hesitate to bring this up to you, but I think I should. We have a girl in the town, about the age of your girls. She is an orphan and Jewish. Her entire family was killed in the invasion several years ago. She isn't happy here; her only desire seems to be to return to Israel. She isn't doing well here, and I fear for her health and future."

Aliza, standing beside Jim, answered the question directed at Jim. "Pastor does this girl have a passport and does she know any of her family background?

The pastor showed obvious signs of relief at the interest of his guests and responded. "I have talked with the girl, and she seems to know some of her ancestry. She doesn't have any relative in this country and our letters to Israel have been unanswered."

"I would like to meet her!" Aliza replied, with an excited look on her face.

The pastor replied with a big smile, "I am very happy you are willing; she is in my office waiting for us."

He led Jim and Aliza toward his office. Jonathan went with them, unusual for him as he rarely joined them on matters of this nature. As they opened the door, a woman who had been seated stood. She was middle aged, and with a serious expression said, "I am Mrs. Johns and am from the Welfare Agency, and this is Hanna Salon. She apparently is from Israel but has no identification and there has been no response from the Israeli Embassy. She speaks very poor English, and I believe she is mentally disabled."

Hanna, perhaps around eighteen, but looked younger, had not stood but looked up and said, "hello." English clearly was not her first language.

Aliza moved toward the girl but was surprised when Jonathan stepped up first. He leaned over and said in Hebrew, "Hello Hanna, I am Jonathan, and I am from Israel. I am very happy to meet you."

In an instant the very plain looking girl changed from dowdy to quite pretty when she smiled a very broad smile and replied in Hebrew. "Hello Jonathan, will you take me home; I have been here so long." While speaking, she took Jonathan's hand and held it.

Aliza then took charge and said in Hebrew, "Hanna, my name is Aliza Jenkins, this is my husband, Jim and my son Jonathan. We are from Israel and are on a missionary trip to this country. If we can make the arrangements with the Welfare Agency, you are certainly welcome to join our family. We plan to return to Israel in a month or maybe a little longer."

Hanna smiled and had tears of joy on her face as she hugged Aliza. She then reached and took Jonathan's hand again.

Jim looked at Mrs. Johns and asked, "What would we need to do to take Hanna with us?"

Mrs. Johns looked embarrassed and slowly explained, "I didn't think she could really speak very much. She just didn't understand us! Since she is over eighteen, she is free to go. I will update our paperwork in the office." She then looked at Hanna and said, "Hanna, I am sorry you have been treated so badly; I wish you well."

With that statement, she started to leave but, paused and said to Jim, "She had nothing but the clothes she is wearing."

Pastor Saul spoke for the first time. "Well Jim, I think that went very well. It seems you may have a new daughter."

Aliza then added, "I think this girl needs some food."

Hanna was very thin, looking like a starving third world refugee.

"I think we can help in that area. In addition, I will contact someone from home to get papers for her. She surely has some family left there," Jim added.

Hanna held Jonathan's hand until she was introduced to his sisters, Dinah and Ruth. She joined them and all three began talking at the same time, and seemed to understand everything, a talent a man does not possess. Hanna would fit in this family very well.

The three girls talked for several minutes and then Dinah came to Jim and said, "Dad she has nothing, and our clothes are too big for her, she is so thin. We need to go shopping."

The girls, still all talking at the same time, prepared to go, taking the Jeep. Again, surprising everyone, Jonathan volunteered to drive them. Jim handed over some US money with the request to return any remaining funds, which got a giggle from all of them.

Following directions to a ladies clothing store the three girls went shopping. At their request Jonathan did not go in but wandered about in other stores while they shopped.

Entering the store a clerk greeted them, "Welcome, how can I help you?" She looked at the two sisters and then her smile faded a bit as she stared at Hanna.

Dinah explained, "We need everything for Hanna, she has been abandoned due to the war. We are all from Israel and are here as missionaries."

She then changed to Hebrew so Hanna could make selections. It was quickly obvious that Hanna was most interested in saving money and was only looking for cheap items. The two sisters began covering the price tags and helped her pick nicer things. When finished she had several dresses, shorts, and shirts for day-to-day use. She also got underwear, and all the other things girls need. They discarded the clothes she was wearing as they were worn and the wrong size.

When they came out, Jonathan smiled and said, "My word you look quite lovely." Hanna returned his smile.

While in the store Dinah and Ruth witnessed to the clerks and encouraged them to come to the church next Sunday. They responded favorably.

The made another stop at a drug store to purchase things girls need, again Jonathan stayed outside.

It was a happy group which returned to the RV in the church parking lot.

All the children decided to sleep in the church mission rooms, leaving Jim and Aliza alone in the RV, the first time since leaving Israel. All enjoyed the night's rest.

The next day, being Saturday, was Sabbath for the Jews. Aliza as usual prepared for the Jewish service. She set up the table with the menorah and the drinks usually served with this service. The five youngers arrived at the proper time, and they all came in and quietly sat down.

Aliza recited the prayer she learned as a child from her mother, who had learned it from her mother. As usual she spoke in Hebrew, which all understood. The part about "Next year in Jerusalem" was more meaningful this year.

After the prayer, Hanna was smiling with tears on her cheeks. Aliza noticed and asked, "Hanna, are you alright?"

"Oh, yes. I remember my grandmother doing the same things in Israel. My mother did not carry on the tradition, but I remember my grandmother."

Just then a male voice from outside spoke, "I apologize for over-hearing your service. I am Rabbi Stevens from the synagogue here."

"Come in and join us for breakfast," Jim replied.

"I would be very pleased to have breakfast with Jews recently from the Holy Land!" he replied as he stepped in the door Jim had opened. "I heard about your family and your missionary efforts here and wanted to meet you."

After introductions all around, Jim stated, "Rabbi, I hope you understand that we are Jews but have accepted Jesus as our Savior and are considered Messianic Jews."

"Yes, I assumed so since you are in a Christian church parking lot. I have many Christian friends, including the pastor of this church. While I don't agree with everything about Christianity, I find it intriguing and worth considering." He paused briefly, then continued, "However my purpose in coming is to invite you to speak to my people about the situation in Israel. We are considering a permanent move."

"We will be most happy to come and meet with your people!" Jim replied.

The family accompanied the rabbi to the synagogue for the meeting which would start in thirty minutes. Jim's family included his wife and four children and Hanna. It was not clear whether Hanna was his daughter's friend or Jonathan's lady friend.

As they approached the building, the Rabbi pointed out the chips in the stones, across the front of the building. "As you can see, we have some 'Jerusalem pox' here which we accrued during the recent conflicts. Fortunately, no one was injured in the gunfire."

As they entered the building, the Rabbi said, "We have some yarmulkes for the men but they are not required."

"Yes, we want to show respect, every way we can," Jim replied as he and his sons put on the caps. Aliza and the girls covered their hair with scarves.

The synagogue looked very much like Jonathan's church. There were pews where men, women and children were sitting together, unlike the more orthodox seating which separates men and women. While most of the people had head coverings, many did not. It seemed this was a less conservative Jewish congregation.

Jim, his family and most of the other Israelis took seats on the front row, the only ones available for their group. Rabbi Stevens went to the front of the synagogue and addressed all present.

"As you all know, this is a meeting to discuss moving our congregation to Israel. I have invited the Jenkins family to tell us about the conditions in Israel. They are here on a missionary trip to witness about the Messiah. They are Messianic Jews. The head of the family is Jim Jenkins. He has agreed to speak with us about moving."

Not having anything prepared, Jim said a silent prayer as he stood. "Lord, give me your words to say to these your people."

"My contact with Israel began years ago, just after the EMP attack on our country. I was part of a group of volunteers fighting the invaders. During the conflict, I met and married, a Jewish woman. While our group was moving to California to continue the struggle we met with a group of people, mostly Jewish, who were finalizing plans to go to Israel to help in the war there. My wife and several others with us felt called to go. I, of course, agreed to go. We flew to Israel in a large cargo aircraft and took my motor home, the one we still have. While fighting in the final battle of the conflict for the Golan Heights, my wife died in the hospital where she was working. Her cause of death was never determined as there were so many casualties. I returned with the rest of the group we had come with, and I settled in a cabin in Colorado. I was pretty much a wreck. A few years later I met and married the lovely Aliza, another Jewish woman, and a doctor. When we met, her church members were planning a move to Israel, much like you are now. This time we went with nearly the entire town on a ship. It was a wonderful trip. When we arrived, we were encouraged to settle just east of Mount Hermon, in the northern part of Israel, on the border with Syria. This was land taken in the previous conflict. We settled there and built a home. Aliza worked in a nearby hospital, and we were blessed with two sets of twins, each a boy and a girl. They are here with us. As you undoubtedly know there was another conflict very recently. The Lord intervened and saved Israel. I was a witness to this miracle, and the Lord awarded me with this gimp leg and a limp so I would never forget. At this time the Lord impressed on us and many Israelis that we should share with the world the message of God and His Son. We are convinced we are in the final days. Our purpose of this trip is to spread the news of the Jewish Jesus, son of God who came and gave His life for salvation for all. I pray you will consider this message, particularly in this time of turmoil in the world. In any case we, will all face eternity eventually and our message 'Jesus is the answer.' As Jews you should return to Israel, it is God's plan, and you will be welcomed. If He delays returning, we hope to return to our home when our missionary journey here is over. When you return, you will be welcomed and there will be a place for you. I am sure it will be a joyous return."

Jim paused and noted the reference to Jesus seemed to be acceptable to the audience. He continued, "I would like to introduce my wife, Aliza. She has been confused as my daughter by several present here, but she is my wife."

Aliza stood and touched Jim's hand as he sat down. She smiled at him and the audience.

"Hello, I was born in Colorado as Hadassah Aliza Fitzgerald to a rather conservative Jewish couple. Our family are Messianic Jews and have been for several generations, and I accepted Jesus as my Savior at an early age. I have been asked to tell you how Jim and I met. It will be difficult for you to believe, but it is true. I am a doctor and after a day in surgery was very tired. I went to bed early in my house in Homestead, Colorado. Suddenly I was wide awake, sitting on a rock and looking at a lovely sunset from the top of a mountain. Off to my left in the distance, I could see a large lake. The mountains and sky were just beautiful. A man walked up, just a few feet away and was looking at the sunset. He did not notice me. I spoke to him, and he turned to me, and I noticed he was quite good looking. Just then, very suddenly the sky turned dark, and the wind picked up. I turned and my little blue tent just blew away with all my things. I was left with nothing but the clothes I was wearing. We ran to his tent as the storm grew furious. He had a small circular tent, maybe eight feet in diameter. We could sit up but not stand. It was small. The very cold storm continued for days. I felt comfortable with Jim. We were there for a long time, many days. Jim had a pack with food and water, which never ran out. It was a wonderful time for me, the first time I had ever felt like I was exactly where I should be. Then I woke up in my bed in my house. It had been a dream, but it seemed so very real. I went for several days thinking I was dreaming and wanting to go back to the real world in the tent."

"The next Sunday, I was to teach a class in Hebrew in preparation for our move. The Rabbi announced a man was coming who had recently returned from Israel and would speak to us. Jim walked up to the front of our church. I stood and would have jumped in his arms except I was in the middle of the row. He stopped and looked at me for a long time, it had been real, he knew me just as I knew him. I don't remember what he said about Israel but after the service, he came to me. My parents did not understand how a man I just met could be considered my husband in my mind."

"After a few days we left for Israel in the ship, again taking the motor home. It was a good trip, and the seas were kind. We were married the day we arrived in Israel. We were encouraged to settle in an area north of the Sea of Galilee and purchased a lot on a hill north of the community and built a house. A new town built up around us and some people named it Jenkins, a name my husband dislikes. We now have four children and a happy life. In the last big war, my husband again volunteered and was severely injured. Twenty-four pins and staples, along with several pieces of metal are a permanent part of his body. I prayed long and hard for the Lord to preserve his life. Praise God for answered prayer. The Lord has been very kind to our family, and we pray we will be of some service to the Lord Jesus."

Aliza paused and with a big smile concluded, "While I was pregnant with our first twins, Jim and I went to the top of Mount Hermon. It was exactly the same as in our dream. We found a piece of my blue tent where I had set it up. We again put Jim's tent exactly where he had placed it when the Lord put us there. He drove the stakes with the same rock he had previously used. We were really there by the Lord's love."

Still smiling, she sat down.

Rabbi Stevens paused for just a moment then stood and said to the audience. "I am touched by this message of God's miracle in this family's life, and I welcome them to our synagogue." He paused and considered commenting on the reference to Jesus, but thought, 'This was not the time for controversy.' He continued. "We have our usual snacks available and invite our guests to stay and provide answers to our many questions."

The room for the lunch or snack time was a large open room. Along one wall were tables covered with food for snacks or a substantial meal. If there was a shortage of food in the country, it was not evident here. As they entered Aliza whispered to Jim, "They have the tables set up for three separate groups." Jim looked around and just nodded.

As they went through the line, the purpose of the three groups became evident. The men went to one set of tables and the women to another. The third group was for young adults, like Jim and Aliza's children. Aliza whispered to Jim, "Well husband, it seems I am not welcome to eat with you, this day!" She took her plate and drink and went to join the women and Jim went to the men's table.

Jim took a seat at the men's table with his plate of food. The men had begun to eat before he arrived so apparently grace before a meal was not the norm. One of the men asked Jim a question. "Mr. Jenkins, were you involved in the war several years ago when the Syrians were defeated?"

Jim, surprised at the question, replied. "Call me, Jim, please. I was involved. I was injured at the start of the conflict when the Jeep I was in was hit by a rocket. My left arm and ribs were broken, and my older daughter's husband was more seriously injured. My wife was angry with me later when she learned that in spite of my injuries I went on to the front. I was stationed in an old frame of a building alone as my partner was taken to a hospital. The enemy came and it reminded me of ants, swarming from an anthill. They were so thick they just covered the ground. All along the ridge we fired, and they returned fire with machine guns, rockets, and mortars. We took out a lot of men but there were just too many. When I ran out of ammunition, I had to stop. My wounds were agonizing, and I really thought my time had come. I just sat there waiting to die when I saw the front coming from the south. It looked like a wall of fire, hundreds of feet tall. I had never seen anything like it. The opposition saw it also and began to run back north, the way they had come. It was total confusion with tanks and trucks running over people. The wall of fire came quickly and went through their ranks. There were no survivors, but the trucks and tanks were unharmed. When the wall got to me, I was surprised it felt cool and refreshing, like God had touched me. I guess I passed out because the next thing I knew, my wife was treating me in the hospital. After several surgeries I became as good as I am now."

Jim was silent for a moment as he remembered the relief of being treated by Aliza in the hospital next to their home.

The men in the group were quiet, giving Jim a time to reflect. A middle-aged man, a man with military looks asked, "Jim, does Israel have a weapon that produces a wall of fire? I have never heard of such a thing."

Jim smiled and replied, "No sir, that was the hand of The Lord God Almighty. He destroyed the entire invading army. He cleaned the West Bank and the land to Beirut, the northern boundary of the Promised Land. It involved millions of people, but not all died. It seemed God judged each of them and spared others."

Jim paused, then added, "Go to Israel. There is much land available, and you will be welcomed by the people and by God Himself." Jim then continued, "Be aware, God is active in the world, especially America and Israel. The US is being disciplined by the natural disasters and Israel has been given peace for a time. I pray all of us will be receptive to God and His message, for I believe the end times are upon us and Christ Jesus may return at any time."

At adjacent tables, Aliza met with about fifteen women. One of the ladies about Aliza's age asked, "What is it like living there and what are the houses like?"

Another asked, "How big are the houses and do they live in apartments or single-family homes?"

The questions came in rapid succession and Aliza answered them as honestly as she could. She discussed in some detail about the need to learn the Hebrew language, emphasizing the need to join the Israeli people as an integral single people. When some looked concerned about the language, she added, "Learning Hebrew is very important but there are classes for language and many people speak English, so the time of adjustment is not difficult." With that comment the women relaxed somewhat.

Meanwhile at the young people's table, Jonathan and his twin, Dinah, seemed to be the oldest. The ages ranged from ten to twenty. Jonathan spoke up first and told the young people about the sports in Israel and about the active schools. He also discussed the lovely landscape and the ability to take hikes in the mountains. He then explained most of the people in their town met in the same building for worship, the Jews on Saturday, and the Christians on Sunday and most attended both services. The implication being there is no difference between the two groups.

When Jonathan paused, David spoke up and further explained, "The Lord God is moving in a great way across the world and particularly in Israel. There have been several wars where invaders came to Israel and were defeated by God Himself. Our father saw the wall of fire which destroyed them and cleared the land north of the country for additional settlers. At this time there is peace but understand God is at work and will change everything. The structure on Temple Mount in Jerusalem was destroyed in the war and a new Temple is being constructed, using the best information on Solomon's Temple. When completed the plan is to reintroduce the Jewish sacrifices as done in the Old Testament time. How the

Christians there will respond to this has not been discussed as far as I know. We should all be aware that prophecy of Christ's return will be fulfilled, and He will take the Christians to heaven. While no one knows when this will happen, everything is in place now. I understand that many Jews do not believe that Jesus Christ who came long ago is the Messiah, but I ask you to review the scriptures and decide for yourself. This is important."

At the women's table, Aliza noticed something a bit strange among the group of women. There were two separate conversations going on at their table. One group was talking about preparing meals and taking care of the group that day. The other group was discussing the need for some of the local women to travel with the missionaries to their next destination. She then glanced at the table with the young people where there were obviously two groups there also. One group, including David and her two daughters and more than half the other young people, were discussing the upcoming missionary tasks. The second group seemed to be congregated around Jonathan and the new girl, Hanna Salon, discussing the differences between living conditions in the US and Israel.

In the men's group, Jim also noted there were two topics being discussed. In one group, includig himself, was the pastor or Rabbi, and about half of the men. They were discussing the missionary tasks and the religious importance of getting God's message to all the people. The other half of the men seem to be discussing the mechanics of getting the services like water and fuel approved. In addition, they were planning the mechanics of really moving to Israel.

After the meetings, Jim and Aliza got together to discuss what they had perceived during lunch.

Aliza spoke first. "Jim, most of the women's group were eager to work with the missionary effort but some seemed more interested in working on survival issues and improve the situation here for the long term. Does this seem strange to you?"

Jim stated, "It is confusing. Part of the men seemed to be focused on the need for urgent missionary work while others on survival here and a future move to Israel. The young people also seem to have two discussions going on. I don't know what this means, for both are important but we are here to be missionaries."

Their discussion was interrupted by the lights going out in the synagogue. Even in the middle of the morning the light coming through the windows was dim, due to the pollution in the air. The Rabbi spoke up and announced, "Don't be alarmed, the power is on a rolling system. We have power for about three hours a day. Unfortunately, we have been shorted today."

The Rabbi came to Jim and his group with a very serious expression on his face. "Jim, the power situation here is not good and is getting worse. We have many solar panels and windmills that do not work, as the air is so polluted. The few power plants that still work on natural gas must be shared with many, many people. We were promised four hours a day, but it is getting less all the time. The plan is to reopen some old gas fired plants, but it takes lot of time and effort and money to get them up and running. I don't know how much longer we can stay here."

The Rabbi paused for a moment then continued. "The people who have come from the north, closer to the volcano, have brought disturbing news. The pollution from the volcano contains small bits of what seems to be glass. When breathed it causes damage to the lungs, and many of these people who came are very ill. They reported the land near the volcano is full of those who have already died with no-one to bury them. We will soon all be wearing masks to try to protect our lungs. The sooner we leave the better. It is becoming obvious to me that the prophecy in the book of Revelation is at hand."

The Rabbi's reference to a book in the Christian New Testament surprised Jim. "You have read the Christian Bible?" he asked.

Smiling, he replied, "Yes, many of us have and we believe that it is true. I have not made any announcement to the people in my synagogue as I feel all of them need guidance. It has become a burden for me. If I become a Christian, what will the rest of my flock do?"

"Each person must make his own decision about accepting Jesus as their Savior." Jim replied.

The Rabbi lowered his head for several moments and then spoke without raising it. "Jim, will you address and introduce Jesus to my flock in tomorrow's service, the Sabbath service?"

"Rabbi, I am not a preacher, but I will speak to your people and pray for Jesus to reveal Himself," Jim replied.

CHAPTER 39

THE FINAL SYNOGOGUE SERVICE

THE SERVICE THE NEXT MORNING, commenced as usual with singing and a prayer by the Rabbi. He then introduced Jim as a Christian from Israel to discuss the current situation in the US and the situation in Israel.

Jim, dressed in a suit and tie, like most men in the congregation, stood before the assembly. He did not go to the elevated podium reserved for the Rabbi.

"My friends and fellow Israelites, I bear greetings from Israel. While I am not a Jew, I am married to a lovely Jewish lady and have been welcomed to Israel. The Lord God defended His Country in the latest war with a mighty hand and drove out many who opposed us. I witnessed this purifying wall of fire. Israel was greatly increased in size by this war, so if you choose to go you will be welcomed and it is God's plan that you go. As you know I and my family are Christians who believe that the Jew, Jesus Christ, is the son of God and is the Savior of the world for all who believe in Him and put their trust in Him. In our church in Israel, we have a Saturday service for the Jewish congregation and a Sunday service for the Christians. Many, including my family, attend both services. But be assured we believe in Christ as our Savior. I know this may upset some of you in this congregation, but I ask for your tolerance. I ask the Lord God to give you a sign, a sign from Him that you should be open to the truth of God's word in the Holy Scriptures."

The last statement shocked everyone, including Jim, who had not planned on saying such a thing. Aliza and David who had accompanied Jim were also shocked as was the Rabbi.

There was an eerie silence as a few looked around at fellow worshipers.

Within seconds there was a tremor, a rather weak earthquake, not unusual for this area in recent times. Collective gasps were heard, then a loud crash in the front of the synagogue. The wall with the ornate figures in the front of the room just fell away. There was not a lot of smoke or dust, it just fell away, exposing the congregation to the outside.

Outside it was very cloudy and dreary as usual, but then a ray of sunlight broke through. It illuminated the steeple on Pastor Saul's church which was on the next block.

No one in the synagogue panicked or spoke a word. Everyone quietly stood and gazed at the cross on the steeple.

Rabbi Stevens, now standing beside Jim, lowered himself to his knees and said in a low voice, which somehow carried throughout the building, "My Lord and my God, I thank you for this clear sign and this message that Jesus is your Son and our Savior. I am sorry for all my many shortcomings and ask for Your forgiveness. I pledge I will do all I can for the remainder of my time on this earth to tell this story of Your wonderful revelation. I pray for my people here that they will accept this sign and tell everyone of your message that Jesus is Lord of all."

David, standing beside his mother said, "We should all go to Pastor Saul's church."

David approached his dad, and took his arm, and led him down the aisle toward the front door. Aliza followed them, while the congregants followed her toward the exit.

Rabbi Stevens remained at the front of the room watching in amazement. Not everyone left. A group of several families remained seated. The Rabbi went to them and said, "You have seen this wonderful sign, a clear sign from the Lord God. You surely cannot deny this."

One of the men, an older patriarch, replied, "Rabbi, I have seen the sign and felt the earthquake, but I cannot accept that everything I have been taught for my entire life is wrong. I just cannot accept it."

"I understand, I will pray for you all every day that God's will be done," the Rabbi said quietly, as he followed the larger part of his congregation out of the building.

Pastor Saul noted the presence of Jim and his family with the Jews. He smiled broadly while he opened the door to the sanctuary of the church. As the Jews filed in, the pastor enlisted a man standing nearby, "Deacon Jones, please contact the staff and ask them to come in, including the organist and the choir. We are seeing a wonderful miracle."

The pastor stood at the front of the church, still dressed in his yard working clothes, as the Jews took seats near the front of the church. Jim and his family sat behind the group and watched.

Pastor Saul, without anything in his hand and with no preparation for this service, spoke about the Old Testament prophecies concerning the coming of Jesus. He then spoke of the teachings of Jesus in the New Testament.

As Pastor Saul spoke something happened, something Jim had never experienced. A feeling came over the room—a feeling that God, or something or someone was moving among the people. Most of Jim's family felt it, but David saw it. He saw several angels, near the ceiling sprinkling something over the crowd and images of angels moving among the people, touching each worshiper. David was the only one of his family to see this.

"Jesus asks you to come forward and accept Him," said Pastor Saul, to conclude his message.

The crowd stood as one, went to the front and kneeled around the pastor. David could see the angels surrounding them all. After a time of prayer the new converts gave testimony to the pastor and those summoned to come. During the entire time Jim and Aliza stayed in their pew and prayed. It was an experience no one present had had before. Baptisms were scheduled for the next day, which was Sunday, after the morning service.

David noticed one of the young women in the group of Jews, was watching the angels moving among and above them. After the meetings with the church officials had been completed, David went to the woman who seemed to be able to see the angels. He said to her, "Hello, I am David, son of Jim Jenkins. I think you could see things others could not."

She smiled and responded, "My name is Sarah and yes, I could see many angels. Could you see them?"

"Yes, I could. I don't think anyone else could see them as you were the only one looking up," David replied.

"I didn't say anything to my friends because they have teased me before when I see something they cannot see. Has this happened to you?" Sarah stated as she moved a step closer to David.

"My family accepts what I see, others not so much," he replied.

David's parents, Jim and Aliza Jenkins walked up, and David introduced them to Sarah and then added, "I have invited Sarah to come with us when we move to our next missionary site."

Aliza looked surprised but replied, "Sarah you are certainly welcome to come with us, but we will need to discuss it with your family."

Sarah, now smiling broadly stated, "There will be no objection. My parents died soon after I was born and having no close relatives, I have been passed from family to family my entire life. I am sure everyone will be glad to be rid of me."

So it was, and a new member of the family was added. It was clear that David and Sarah were meant to be with each other. They were alike in so many ways and from that day forward were inseparable.

The Jenkins family remained in west Flagstaff for three months, ministering daily to the community. The attendance at Pastor Saul's church increased so much they went to two services on Sunday. In addition, missionaries from the church went to other churches in and around Flagstaff. The results were truly amazing, attendance at all the churches increased greatly and many Jews accepted Christ as Savior.

Jim went to Pastor Saul, along with Rabbi Stevens and stated, "Pastor, we feel it is time for us to move on to a new mission field."

"I understand. It is impossible for me to express my gratitude and thanks for what you and your family have done here. We were close to losing our lives. but now are alive. I know the Lord will bless your ministry wherever He leads you." With this affirmation, Pastor Saul hugged Jim and Rabbi Stevens.

As Jim and Rabbi Stevens were walking away discussing travel plans, David, standing on the sidewalk waiting for them, spoke. "Dad, I think Sarah and I should get married."

Jim and the Rabbi stopped and looking at David, paused for a second. Then Jim said to his son, "David, you have only known her for three months and what does Sarah think of this?" In addition to the question, Jim was thinking, 'What will his mother say about this?"

"I haven't mentioned it to anyone, but I would like to be with Sarah if we are called home."

"Have you been told something? Jim replied seriously and quietly.

"No, it is just a feeling that the time here is short," David said quietly.

Jim replied, "David you and Sarah are two very special people and I see no reason why you should not be married. However, it would be good to discuss it with Sarah and your mother. I expect they will both agree and will be very happy, as I am."

David took Sarah and went to see Aliza. Jim stayed in the back to watch his wife's reaction. David had obviously asked Sarah to marry him as she had a smile that covered her entire face. She also seemed to glow; she was so happy.

Before David could say anything to his mother, she came to Sarah and hugged her and kissed her on the cheek and said, "Sarah, you are intelligent, like-minded and beautiful and will make a wonderful addition to our family!"

Jim's entire family joined them in a big group hug, with laughter and joyous voices.

That afternoon, Aliza took Sarah to a bridal shop, and they purchased a wedding gown. It would take the shop a day to make the modifications to fit her. Jim bought David a new suit to wear, off the rack, as David's normal desire to save money decided.

The wedding service followed the Sunday worship service in Pastor Saul's church. Many of the church members remained, as did all the new Christians from the Jewish church. In addition, many of the Jews who had not been saved arrived in time for the service, the first time they had been in the Christian church.

The wedding was beautiful. The church choir stayed and sang several songs. Sarah's white gown added to her beauty, a sharp contrast to her looks when Jim and Aliza first met her. David, handsome in his new suit, never took his eyes off his bride.

Since Sarah's father was gone, Rabbi Stevens walked her down the aisle. Pastor Saul conducted the service.

After the service, all were invited to the church's social room which seated many people at tables. The room was packed, and the plentiful food was provided by the congregation. Pastor Saul came to Jim and said, "Our church has not been this full for many years. I want to express my appreciation for your missionaries making this possible."

"It is not us; it is the Lord's work," Jim replied.

One of the members of the church owned the local motel and a wedding gift gave David and Sarah a week's stay—very generous.

After a joyous day, David took his bride to the motel room.

The next morning, Aliza got up as usual and made coffee and started breakfast in the motorhome. She saw Sarah coming down the street from the motel just a block away. Aliza opened the door so she could step in.

"Good morning, Sarah, how are you today?" she asked.

"I am good. I think married life agrees with me! David will be along; he is still sleeping," she replied laughing.

Aliza handed her a cup of coffee and Sarah then stood in front of the long mirror viewing her reflection from the side. She patted her abdomen and said, "I hope to see some swelling soon."

"Sometimes it takes a while," Aliza commented.

"We will just have to keep trying," Sarah replied laughing.

Then Sarah leaned over and kissed Aliza on the forehead and said, "Have a great day, Grandma," as she ran out the door to look for David.

Aliza's eyes got big as she looked at Jim and then smiled at the thought of becoming a grandmother.

Jim, overhearing the conversation, almost burst out laughing, but controlled himself. He came in and sat by his wife, kissed her on the cheek and whispered, "Good morning, Grandma."

Sarah's idea of being with child was confirmed when her monthly cycle stopped. Something like this would normally be a secret but Sarah did not seem to understand what a secret was. She told everyone that she was with child, and it was a boy, a comment most thought was funny. How could she know this early what sex her child was?

While Sarah continued to check herself for swelling, Jim, the Rabbi, and the local preacher began to discuss moving the missionaries to another location. The work there had been very successful as

Pastor Saul's church was now packed, even with two Sunday services and they were reaching out to other churches in the Flagstaff area. It was a very enjoyable location to serve and to live, but they were missionaries and other places were calling.

Jim called a meeting and in attendance were Pastor Saul, Rabbi Stevens, and several of the Jews from the synagogue, including some who had not accepted Christ.

Jim opened the meeting by saying, "My friends, we have come as missionaries to this area and the Lord has done marvelous things here. I feel it is time to move on and witness somewhere else. The Phoenix area seems the logical place; it is just south of here. Phoenix is a very large area and has several million people in the greater area. I don't know about accommodations in the area."

"I can help you there," Pastor Saul stated. He continued, "There are several churches in the Phoenix area that I am closely acquainted with. Some have accommodations for your motorhome and have room to house people. They are in the condition you found us in, with low attendance and nearly empty churches. I believe you will be successful in the Phoenix area as you have certainly been in our area. I will make contacts with several churches."

Jim was relieved at the statement as their missionary group had grown much larger. They had added most of the local Jews, both those converted to Christianity and those who had not. They all had decided to travel with Jim and his group, and accompany them when they, hopefully, returned to Israel.

The caravan of vehicles assembled on the church parking lot. It consisted of Jim's motor home, a church bus and eight cars. A rancher arrived in a pickup truck with several jugs of gasoline in the back, a blessing as gasoline was difficult to obtain. After a service consisting of singing, prayers, and speeches, all requesting God's blessing and help, they got underway.

Jim drove the motorhome, with Aliza in the passenger seat. The vehicle was full of Jim's family and many guests, and those who did not have cars. The Jeep followed with Jim's son Jonathan driving. His friend Hanna, always very near, sat in the right seat and three passengers crowded in the rear seat. The cars followed and the bus brought up the rear. It was a rather interesting looking convoy.

Pastor Saul, acting as the guide, directed Jim to a beautiful church with a very large parking lot. As they drove in, several men came out of the building to guide them. One of the men directed Jim to an area near where several busses were parked and to a location with a sewer hookup and available water. There was an electrical hookup, although electricity was available only four hours every other day. Even with limitations it was a great place for the motor home.

The church also had a three-story building for classrooms which were now mostly unused as church attendance was very low. A few of the classrooms were used as living quarters for people without options. The entire third floor was unoccupied, so the new visitors moved in. There were several bathrooms along the hall, but the nearest showers were in the nearby gymnasium which also included clothes washers and dryers. Their sleeping beds consisted of inflatable mattresses, all donated by church members.

Others in the group which accompanied Jim preferred to stay in the nearby hotel, including David and his wife in one room and Jonathan in a separate room. Where Jonathan's girlfriend Hanna stayed was not discussed. Jim, his wife and two daughters stayed in the motorhome. Everyone was very pleased with the arrangements.

The next morning everyone gathered in the dining area of the church for breakfast of hot oatmeal and several choices of cereal. A simple but tasty meal. Jim was happy with coffee. The group included Jim's family and the fifteen others from Israel who had accompanied him on his trip, the fifty or so Jews from the synagogue in Flagstaff, some converted to Christianity and some not. In addition, some twenty people from the Flagstaff church had joined the missionary group. All in all, there were over a hundred people in their group, a significant burden on this church.

The pastor of the Phoenix church was a man named Mark Remington, but everyone calls him Pastor Mark. He was a very serious, God-fearing man with a great love for God and his church.

As the breakfast was finishing up, Pastor Mark called the gathering to order to discuss the plans for the missionary effort. After introducing himself to the group he called Rabbi Stevens to address the crowd.

Rabbi Stevens stood before the rather large group and stated. "My friends, my name is Rabbi Stevens, and this is the fourth day of my life as a believer in Jesus Christ. I, like all my Jewish friends here, wish to return to Israel, however my current mission is to witness to the saving power of Jesus Christ. I believe there are about twenty synagogues in the Phoenix metropolitan area. We have enough Jews, both those who have accepted Christ and those who have not, to contact each of these groups. We will have three important messages to give to these Jews. The first and most important is the message of Jesus Christ as the Savior of all. The second is to verify their safety in this difficult time. The third is to notify them of our expected trip back to Israel and determine their interest in going with us."

The Rabbi paused a moment to let the rather strange message to sink in, then continued. "As we go to these Jewish groups, our group will include the Jews present here, both believers in Christ and non-believers as this point. In addition, we will take any non-Jews who are called to go with us. My friends, I believe the end times are upon us and our most famous Jewish ancestor, Jesus Christ, son of God, will soon come back for those who believe in Him to take us to Heaven. Our mission is to give every Jew we can reach the opportunity to take this trip, the most important trip of a lifetime."

The organization of the missionaries went very quickly. Teams from three to six were assembled and they consisted of Jews, both those who had accepted Christ and those who had not. In addition, some non-Jew Christians agreed to go. Rabbi Stevens contacted each synagogue and offered the services of the missionaries.

Surprisingly, all the Rabbis at the synagogues welcomed the missionaries, even when they understood the message would include a presentation of Jesus Christ and, most hopefully, a plan to go to Israel. With the air quality in the US being so bad it made going to Israel look very attractive.

CHAPTER 40

TUCSON

J
IM AND HIS FAMILY WERE welcomed as missionaries to a synagogue in Tucson, south of Phoenix. The members there were willing to accept the Christian Jews and their message, mainly because of the plan to go to Israel. They moved the motorhome to the synagogue parking lot where there were full hookups, a seemingly common accessory with the churches and synagogues in the south. While the water seemed to be reliable the electricity was off much of the time. Jim, his wife and daughters lived in the motorhome while David and his wife took a room in a nearby motel provided by the Jewish owner. Jonathan also took a room in the same motel. His girlfriend Dinah also stayed there, perhaps in a separate room from Jonathan.

The air in Tucson was some better than in Phoenix but everyone wore a mask in the hopes it would help.

Early the next morning at an abandoned store with an old picnic table in the front, there was an old car parked nearby and a man sitting at the table. There were others in the vehicle. He was dejected as his car had quit running the night before just as he got it off the road. His wife quietly got out of the car, trying not to wake their two young girls. She said to her husband, "We need to find some food for the girls. Any idea what is wrong with the car?"

"No, I hope it will start after it cools off. I am doubtful though," he replied.

"Maybe God will help us." she replied.

"I don't even know if there is a God, but I doubt if he cares about us even if He exists. It would be nice, however, if He could provide a cup of coffee about now."

From the car window the voice of his daughter, eight-year-old Julie, called out, "Daddy an angel is coming!"

The two looked and there was a beautiful woman with a long house coat. She had long red hair and seemed to be floating rather than walking. In one hand she had a stack of paper cups and a coffee pot in the other. She looked completely out of place in this desolate location.

The woman came to the table and said, "Hello, my name is Aliza and I saw you from our motorhome and you look like you need a cup of coffee."

"Hello, my name is Sam, and this is my wife, Jane and my daughters Julie and Becky. We seem to be broken down."

Sam smiled but Jane sat, wide-eyed, as if seeing a vision.

Little Julie stood near Aliza and looking up said, "Are you an angel sent by God?"

Aliza stooped down to address the girl, eye to eye and replied, "No dear I am not an angel, but I believe we are sent by God to this area."

Aliza then stood and poured coffee into three of the cups and set one in front of each of the two adults.

Sam sat and just stared at the coffee in front of him.

Finally, Jane, still wide-eyed, spoke. "I cannot believe this; Sam just said that he did not really believe in God but if He did exist, he would like for Him to bring a cup of coffee. Then you, looking like a goddess, came with coffee."

Before Aliza could respond, Jim walked up behind her and said, "Yes, my wife is lovely, but she took all the coffee and left the oven on!"

Jim, laughing, set hot rolls in a basket on the table and a jar of cold orange juice beside it, along with additional paper cups. They poured orange juice into cups for the two girls who attacked the hot rolls aggressively, obviously very hungry.

Sam quickly drank the cup of coffee and Jim gave him a refill.

"Isn't that a synagogue where you are camping?" Sam asked.

"Yes, it is. While I am not a Jew, my wife and children are. We live in Israel and are here on a mission trip. There will be a meeting this evening at the synagogue for Jews and non-Jews. We will be discussing what is happening in Israel and in Yellowstone, and we'll present the message of Jesus as our Savior. You are certainly invited to come!" Jim stated.

Jane looked very serious as she spoke, "My mother and grandmother were Jews, but they married non-Jews, just as I did. No one in my family has been practicing any religion. We never went to church or synagogue at any time in my life."

Aliza then smiled and said, "We are Jews but have accepted Christ as our Savior and now are considered Christian, or some say Messianic Jews. Many Jews are accepting this message and in Israel there are many Messianic believers. There is an interest in immigrating to Israel by many Jews in this country where the air is much cleaner."

Sam paused, deep in thought, then looked at his wife and said, "Jane, I have not considered moving out of the country, but it could be an answer to our problems."

Jane, looking at Jim, asked, "Would they let us move to Israel?"

"If you could show your Jewish ancestry, they would welcome you and your family with open arms. There are many jobs in the northern part of the country which are just now being settled," Jim replied.

While he was still talking, Jonathan and his ever-present girlfriend, Hanna, walked up. "Dad, someone took the coffee pot," he stated, laughing.

Jim made introductions all around and then asked Jonathan, "Would you look at Sam's car? It just stopped running."

"Sure, I will get my tools from the motorhome," Jonathan replied.

"Jonathan is good with cars; maybe the problem is minor," Jim stated to Sam and then continued. "The meeting is starting in synagogue soon; would you like to come? We will be talking about belief in Jesus Christ and planning a migration to Israel sometime in the future."

Sam smiled and Jane answered for them, "We would be delighted to come!"

The group walked the short distance back to the motorhome for a quick breakfast and more coffee and juice before heading to the synagogue for the morning meetings.

In the meantime, Jonathan, driving Jim's Jeep with a tow strap and with Hanna steering Sam's car, towed it to a spot just behind the motorhome. He opened the hood and began checking the electrical controls, continuing while the service in the synagogue began.

The service in the synagogue commenced with the usual prayers recited by the local Rabbi Morris. He introduced the guests. "My fellow Jews, we welcome guests from Israel, the Jenkins family. They have come to tell us about how it is in Israel and a possible migration there. They are Messianic Jews and will tell you a bit about the Jew, Jesus, a center of their belief."

With that rather interesting introduction, Jim stood and spoke to the congregation, smiling. "Fellow Jews, my family and I have come to America to tell you about the events in Israel. The Lord is moving there in an amazing way. The country is rejoicing about the victory over its enemies, a victory that has expanded the borders of the country to the size of the rule of King Solomon. It was not our victory but the Lord's. I was a witness to the great wall of fire that destroyed an entire invading army. The wall of fire passed over me and I felt, not flames but a comforting coolness. It was like the Lord

Jesus came to me to aid me. And I ask for that same Jesus to come to us now today."

Then it happened. It started with a gentle breeze coming from the ceiling and a low sound like a hum. Then there was singing, most voices singing in Hebrew. Jim looked at the crowd and all were singing in a language most did not know. They were singing, "Come Lord Jesus the Son of God, the Savior of the world." No one there knew it, but it was the same song the Jews sang when Jesus' rode into Jerusalem on a donkey a few days before He was crucified.

No one saw the angels, but all felt their presence. David's wife, Ruth, took his hand and placed it on her extended belly. He could feel the baby within her moving around to the beat of the music. The entire crowd was looking up and holding their hands up, at the energy coming from above. Even for Jim, the pain which had been with him since the war, left him and he felt completely whole.

Rabbi Morris, stood and with his hands raised said, "This is what has been missing from our lives, this is what worshiping God and His Son is like!"

Most, but not all, of the people in the room were joyful. Some did not seem to sense anything other than being irritated that the Sabbath service was being disrupted. They felt displeasure that their normal quiet service had turned into a spiritual riot.

In the back of the room, stood the pastor of a local Baptist church, known as Pastor Jim, who was a Jew and cousin of Rabbi Morris. They were close friends. He occasionally attended the Jewish service as a visitor, just to enjoy the service. He went to the front and hugged Rabbi Morris, both with tears in their eyes. "Rabbi, are you now ready to be baptized as a believer in Jesus Christ as your Savior."

The Rabbi with a huge smile replied, "Yes and I think most of these will want to be baptized also!" With this comment he indicated with his hand all the people in the synagogue.

The Sabbath service ran long as the revelry just would not stop. The group moved outside of the synagogue and continued discussing the service. All those who had experienced the visitation were joyful, while those who had not, left unhappily.

Jonathan and Dinah drove up in Sam's car. He got out with a big smile and started explaining how he replaced a computer part. He was surprised when no one seemed to care, even Sam and his family.

David explained, "Jonathan, this was an amazing service. I believe God's spirit came and the people responded. I think most all of them will want to be baptized as Messianic Jews."

Jonathan thought, 'I am sorry I missed this service.' But a voice in his head said, 'They are probably exaggerating what happened.'

The voice was wrong. The results of the service changed everything. Baptisms were carried out in a public swimming pool. Pastor Jim baptized the two Rabbis first, then the three of them continued to baptize the rest of the new believers, a total of one hundred seven. The choir of Pastor Jim's church provided music. It was an amazing service.

The results of the synagogue service changed everything in Tucson. The new Messianic Jews went to all the other synagogues in the area and told of their conversions and described how the Holy Spirit had come upon their service. In most cases the event was repeated in the other synagogues. In just two days most of the Jews in Tucson were saved and became Messianic Jews.

The new Christians spread the Word, and a great revival spread across the city. As the numbers of new believers grew, both Jews and non-Jews, sent word to friends and relatives in other cities and to other countries. Word came back from many of the contacts that similar events had happened in their cities, also. The Holy Spirit was moving across the United States and the world in a powerful way and the results amazed everyone. The new Messianic Jews also went to Christian Churches as missionaries and preached salvation to churches that had grown cold in their beliefs. The revival spread across the United States. Churches which had been nearly empty in previous years were now overflowing. It was a great revival.

Jim and Aliza had planned for the mission trip to the US to last about six months. But after the six months, with the amazing power of God's moving, they decided to stay longer. In a regular phone conversation with their daughter Rhoda, she stated, "Dad, wonderful things are happening here. Everyone in Israel, seems to have found the Lord. Miracles are happening every day. Jews are going as missionaries to almost every country in the world. What do you think? Could this be a sign of the end times?"

"Well Rhoda, it could be, but the time of the end is not for us to know. I think a revival is predicted just before the return of Christ and this may be it, or it could be a periodic revival because of the disasters in the US. I don't know, but we should be prepared to meet Christ," Jim replied.

Rhoda paused then added, "Dad, I would like to be with you and Mom, I just feel like something is going to happen."

"We will be together soon," Jim remarked as the call ended.

CHAPTER 41

THE END AND BEGINNING

AN ADDITIONAL TWO MONTHS PASSED, and a planned revival was scheduled. A football stadium was reserved, and the meetings widely publicized throughout the entire state.

Much of the organization of the revival was carried out by Jim's son Jonathan. He seemed to have a talent for organizing and in general getting things done. He was a great help. But Jim was bothered a bit by Jonathan's lack of interest in the actual salvation message. In fact, he rarely attended the meetings as he was busy with other things and his constant companion, Hanna. Jim included all his family in his prayers but prayed especially for Jonathan. He was in prayer just before the big revival meeting and again asked for assurance about Jonathan's salvation. Jim rarely got an immediate response to his prayers but this day, an answer came. It was not verbal, but a message came clearly to his mind, "Jonathan has an important duty, and he will fulfill it!" Jim understood the clear message and pondered what it meant.

The day of the revival arrived and people from miles around came. Many were from other states, especially refugees from northern states where the air was still polluted. The stadium was packed, and even on the field people were standing around the platform for the speaker. People had become receptive for a message that gave them hope for something better.

The people present represented distinct groups. The largest were people of varied backgrounds who claimed to be Christian as they had attended a Christian Church at some time in their life. The second group was of Jewish ancestry, and most were interested in learning about a planned trip to Israel with cleaner air. A third group, smaller in number but noisier, consisted of protesters. They consisted of gay persons, dressed in rainbow colors along with devil worshipers, who wore horns on their heads. These people concealed themselves as they entered and pasted the police guards.

The local pastor, Pastor Jim, opened the service with a prayer asking for God's guidance for the country and for salvation for those in attendance. The choir and audience sang The National Anthem followed by the famous hymn, How Great Thou Art. Many people joined in the singing.

Pastor Jim preached an evangelistic sermon telling the people they can receive salvation by confessing their sins, receiving Jesus into their lives and asking Him to help them turn their lives around. He indicated they could do that in their seats and then attend a church and have a discussion with the pastor.

While he was preaching the protestors became active. Revelers drifted onto the field in large numbers. Gay people came out in their rainbow clothing waving gay pride flags. Men, dressed as women and real women with scanty clothing began dancing and wildly jumping, acting foolishly, just to get attention and disrupt the service. Initially they were ignored but as they grew louder that was not possible. Pastor Jim stopped preaching and then David stood and walked to the microphone, raised his hands above his head and shouted, "Lord God, we ask your intervention to stop this disruption!!"

In the open stadium, the sky suddenly became dark with rolling black clouds. There was loud rumbling thunder and the ground shook with a slight earthquake. With great fear the protestors became quiet and stood looking up. In the clouds a face appeared, the face of a man with a golden crown and a staff in his hand. Only the protesters saw this man, who pointed the staff at them. There was a loud bang, more like a gun than thunder. The protesters all lost strength in their legs and collapsed. The stadium was very quiet as the clouds rolled above them. Then a second figure appeared, only visible to the people who had been saved by Christ. This figure was a man with a loving face, it was Christ Himself, as the people who saw him knew it was Christ. He stretched out his hands and said, "MY CHILDREN COME UNTO ME!"

Most of the people in the stadium saw none of the figures in the clouds but they saw what happened next. The true Christians in the stadium were changed to standing figures dressed in floor length white robes. Then with their hands raised they were all lifted into the air and disappeared into the clouds. There was a glorious sound as large numbers of rising voices sang "Hallelujah!" Everyone remaining in the stadium was dumbfounded, silent and frozen in their seats.

On the row where Jim's family had been sitting, only Jonathan and Hanna were left, the rest had risen. Jonathan walked to the microphone and spoke into it. "My friends, we have witnessed a great miracle. The Lord God has taken His children and left us unbelievers. This event was predicted in the Bible. We who are left are not saved, but we can correct that now." Jonathan then raised his hands and said, "Join me in saying, Lord God, I ask you to forgive my many sins and take me into your family. I will reform my ways and serve you to the best of my ability. If you have really meant what you have said God will accept you into his family!"

Someone in the audience shouted, "Will God take us to heaven now?"

"No, my friends, I do not believe God will take us now, this magnificent event we witnessed is a one-time event. We who are left have a duty to witness to the rest of the people in the world before the final end time. We all have a crucial duty to serve the Lord and witness to as many people as we can so God will save them also," Jonathan stated.

Jonathan looked at the crowd and estimated that no more than twenty percent of the people had been taken. In some cases, one of a married couple were taken and the mate left. Some children were taken and some not. Those who were left would have great difficulties, as time would show.

CHAPTER 42

What to do??

WHILE MANY PEOPLE IN THE stadium came forward, asking for help most of the crowd simply went crazy. People were missing; people they came with and lived with were gone! Some were pastors, many of whom understood what had happened, and were confused as why they were not taken. They did, however, assist those asking for help in finding salvation and led many in prayer.

Hanna came to Jonathan, still on the platform and asked, "What are we to do?"

"The first thing we must do is get married. God does not approve of our lifestyle."

Her only response was "Yes."

It was not a dream wedding. The pastors they knew had gone to heaven. They were married by a Justice of The Peace in a city office. It took about twenty minutes, one hundred fifty dollars, and resulted in a wedding certificate.

The city as well as the entire nation was in turmoil. Many people were gone, some communities were nearly vacant, while others were unaffected by the Lord taking the saved people to heaven. In some churches many of the members were taken and in other churches they were almost unaffected. The news media personalities were full of comments about the event and discussed what happened, with all kinds of theories, none of which were 'God has taken His children home.' UFO invasions was a popular theme.

It took less than a day for things to fall apart. Communities where thieves thought Christians had lived were looted. It was not just sneak in and steal small items, they brought trucks and loaded furniture and emptied the houses. In many cases the people had not been taken but were just not home. Some police personnel were taken, and so they were shorthanded and could not respond to all the calls. In some areas the homeowners shot looters and the looters shot back. The dead covered the streets in some communities. It was a huge mess.

In some countries, particularly Muslim countries, a few people were taken. The governments of these countries quickly suppressed the news, not allowing any mention of witness testimony. In Israel the opposite was true. The government praised the event, reporting the taking of Christians as proof of God's existence. They avoided the obvious fact that the resurrection of Christians had been foretold by the Bible.

Jonathan spent his time reasoning and witnessing to people in Pastor Mark's church. Pastor Mark and many members were resurrected along with most of the leadership of the church. The remaining members, knowing they had missed a great opportunity, welcomed Jonathan and his message.

Three days after the resurrection, Jonathan received a visitor at the church. The man was dressed obviously as a Catholic Priest indicated by his attire. He came to Jonathan and stated, "Hello, I am Father Murray of the Catholic Diocese here. Tell me about the event in the stadium, why some people were taken and some left."

Jonathan paused a moment then replied, "The Lord took those who had accepted Christ as their Savior, as predicted in the New Testament. Those who had not, He left. We who are left and have now accepted Christ as our Savior are tasked to witness to everyone in hope they will accept Jesus Christ as their Savior."

Father Murray paused for a long time, looking at Jonathan, a much younger man than he. He then responded, speaking slowly, "I have been a priest since I was very young and studied the catechisms very diligently. I have followed all the teachings of the church and have never been with a woman in a physical way." He paused then continued, "In the Diocese I lead, about seven hundred people, only two families are missing, and I assume taken by the Lord. The rest of us were left."

The man sat with his head down while Jonathan thoughtfully responded. "I knew a woman at work one time. I tried witnessing to her, but she finally told me her church would save her. Is it possible your faith is in your church and not the Lord? I was raised by a strong Christian family, and my father saw several miracles. But when the resurrection came, I was left. I must conclude my faith was not in the Lord but in doing things here, right things I believe, but not faith in God. An error I have corrected. We were both left but now have a job to do. We are to make every effort to tell others about God's saving grace so when the time is finally over, we will all be taken to heaven to be with God."

"I just don't understand, I spent my entire life helping fellow Catholics feel better about themselves. I listened to confessions and gave instructions on how to improve their lives. I prayed to God every morning. To the best of my ability, I did nothing wrong," Father Murray stated, now with tears on his cheeks. Perhaps all those confessions should have been made to God, not me!"

Jonathan replied, "A few days ago a family's car broke down nearby. My father took them into the church and led them to Christ. I on the other hand took the car and repaired it. It runs fine and is sitting outside now. I did nothing wrong by working on the car, but my father worked on something more important, the salvation of a family. This has been true my entire life. I work on physical things while my father's view has always been on higher things, things about eternity. I now understand the things I have been concerned with are temporary and I need to concentrate on things about God and salvation, things infinity more important. Perhaps you would like to join me in this effort."

Father Murray went to his knees and with his head bowed, asked the Lord to forgive him for his sins and his erroneous lifestyle. He felt the Holy Spirit come upon him and rose smiling and happy. "I should have done that, years ago," he commented.

Catholic Father Murray was baptized by a Jewish Rabbi in a pool previously owned by a Baptist deacon, now in heaven. The service was attended by Catholics, Jews and several Christan church members. What a glorious day. As he came out of the water, with a loud shout said, "I have met the Lord Jesus, and he has saved me from my many short comings and sins!"

Jonathan was invited to the Catholic Church the next Sunday for the service at 9:00 in the morning. He sat at the front while Father Murray was on the raised platform. When it was time for him to speak, he rose and went to the podium. There was nothing usual about his presentation that day. He raised his hands and bowed his head and prayed. "Holy Father and Jesus Christ, we worship you today. I pray you will give me your words today. Everyone here wants to be Your child and servant. Guide us I pray."

This must have been an unusual prayer as there was some murmuring in the crowd, which Jonathan noted.

Father Murray continued. "As you may have heard, this week at the meeting organized by the Israeli Church, there was an event, a onetime event by God. I was there, as were many of you. I believe the saved in the crowd saw the Lord Jesus in the clouds and He requested them to come to Him. I did not see the Lord. I did see the people, the saved people, raise their hands and as they rose into the air they were clothed in bright white robes. It was absolutely breath taking."

He paused again, seeking God's help with a bowed head. He continued, "I am certain this was the Rapture of Christians, as promised in the Bible. It was clear to me what had happened, but I was confused because I was not taken. I was not a child of God. This means that if I died before this time I would not have gone to be with Jesus, a devastating revelation. I have spent my life preaching and teaching the gospel of Christ, and yet somehow, I missed the most important point. The point is Christ will save those who confess their sins and accept Him as their Savior and Lord. It is not the church who saves, it is Christ Himself. I was misled in my training, and I misled many of you. It is not the church who saves but it is Christ Jesus as the Bible clearly teaches. I am so sorry that I did not accept this truth before the Rapture. I am happy however that I now have the opportunity to tell everyone the true path to salvation and provide assurance of Christ's acceptance for each of us when He calls us home. I ask you all to pray with me the prayer our Savior gave us as the path to salvation."

Father Murray stepped to the side and got on his knees and prayed, "Lord God, we ask you for forgiveness for our many sins and short comings and ask for You to come into our lives and guide us and save our souls. We are sorry to have missed your Rapture, but we now ask that you use us to advance your kingdom on earth and give us strength and guidance to follow Your will for each of us."

The Spirit of the Lord came upon the church, a church which rarely showed any emotion, in the form of a feeling of goodness and power, a feeling of the presence of God Himself. Not all, but many of the people came to the front of the church and they went to their knees and raised their hands above their heads. It was a clear acceptance of the belief in Christ as their Savior. A great moving moment.

After this amazing Sunday, the newly saved Catholics went to the churches all over Tucson and spread the Word that belief in Jesus as the Savior was the only way to salvation. There was an interesting addition to the message, that the word of God came from the Jews, just as predicted in the Bible in the book of Revelation. The word these new Christians spread was well received by each church and the numbers of saved greatly increased. Several pastors and other leaders of local churches joined with Jonathan and formed an informal alliance to plan for the next phases of the missionary efforts. Their goal was simply to spread the word of God to everyone everywhere.

This also was happening in Israel; thousands were taken into heaven. With the reduced population there was room for many more people. Jews from all over the world were coming home in great numbers and the expanded lands were being filled with new arrivals. The desire to be saved and then spread the word of Christianity was a national desire. New churches were built, and teams of missionaries were trained and sent to every country in the world. It was a truly great religious revival across the entire world.

While the good news of a growing salvation in the United States was being broadcast, not all reports were good. Gangs were forming, and they roamed around causing havoc. Food supplies were running short as the economy was collapsing. Crime was on the rise with unrest everywhere. Many conflicts ended in brutality and killing. Communities divided into two camps, Christians, now missionaries, and violent gangs. This was something never seen in the US, not even in the days of the wild west.

The United States was collapsing. Crops would not grow because of air pollution. Electrical power was unreliable because the country depended on wind and solar, both required clean air and wind to keep the power on, neither of which were available in the current situation. The government was in distress as the tax base shrank because, so few were working. The very high debt the nation owed caused inflation to soar. Since the debt could not be paid the value of the dollar on the world market plummeted. It was difficult for the country to buy food, because food shortage had become a worldwide problem. Some countries had food but no fuel for transportation. International trade was hampered by transportation and money problems. In addition, all countries seemed to have a problem with crime as some people saw opportunities to take from others. It seemed the entire world was entering another dark age.

The evangelism work Johnathan and his team continued for several months with good results. The Lord was with them. Jonathan's wife, Hanna, was three months with a child and now showing a bump. The team was pleased with the great numbers of new Christians and with the new child within Hanna. On Sunday morning a large church was selected to hold the service. The denomination of the church had become irrelevant as all churches were welcoming new Christians and anyone else who was interested. Father Murray and Jonathan stood outside the church greeting congregants as they arrived.

The peaceful and solemn event was interrupted by a large group approaching, coming down the middle of the street. Dancing and shouting they were led by men dressed as women and a few women, barely dressed at all. They looked foolish but the men following them did not. They were dressed in military garb, carried rifles, and wore vests with clips of ammunition. They were not singing but looked very angry. Behind these two groups was another who was shouting threats against the church and Christians. It was difficult for Joathan to estimate the number of people but clearly over two hundred in the crowd.

The people waiting to enter the church rushed inside, leaving Jonathan and Father Murray to face the crowd. Jonathan did not understand what these people were angry about, but he stepped forward to question them. At that time from around the corner of the church came three men, each dressed in heavy canvas clothing. Each of the men was extremely tall and heavily built. No words were spoken but the three men lined up between the marchers and Jonathan, creating a security barrier between them.

At the sight of the three large men the gay people at the front of the crowd faded behind the armed men. One of the church haters, a big ugly man, came forward and shouted, "We have come to burn this building. There is no room for God here anymore. Get out of here and you won't be hurt." He followed his statement with curses and profanity, then raised his rifle and pointed it at one of the large men in front of Jonathan.

The seven-foot man protecting Jonathan raised his empty hand toward the ugly man and a stream of fire came from the hand and consumed the man pointing the gun. He burned with a flame for a moment then fell. All that was left of him was a small pile of ash with a rifle lying by it.

Everyone was silent after this event. Most of the crowd quickly dispersed as a Jeep with a heavy machine gun mounted on it came roaring up to the front of the crowd. A man was standing behind the gun ready to fire.

Another one of the defenders pointed a small cylinder-like object at the Jeep and fired something at it. The Jeep erupted into a huge ball of fire and seemed to melt into a puddle on the pavement. Some of those from the crowd who had lingered were burned by the heat and ran screaming from the church. There was a moment of silence then the entire crowd turned and ran. In a short time, order had been restored!

The three large men turned and walked around the corner of the church. No one followed them.

A young girl came out of the church and said to Jonathan, "Who were those giants?"

"I believe those were angels sent by God to save us," Jonathan replied.

"I thought angels sat on clouds and played harps."

"Angels are powerful beings who follow God's command. They can do anything God wants to do."

The girl looked mature for her age as she replied, "I think they certainly saved our bacon."

Jonathan, not sure what the term, 'saved our bacon' meant, smiled, and replied, "We need to start the service," as he entered the church.

The service was up-lifting, in no small measure, due to the visitation of God's angels. It seemed someone in the crowd had a video recorder so the entire event was on the evening news. By evening the national and international news had picked up the amazing story, how a mob attack on a Christian Church had been stopped by three giant men with surprising ability. No one seemed to know who they were. Of course, there were a few commentators who questioned the death of some of the mob and whether this was a violation of the law. All in all, it was an amazing day. The most important, but unreported, occurrence that day was that nearly all the people in the church that evening accepted Christ as their Savior.

That evening in the motorhome Jonathan and Hanna were finally alone. "I have been thinking about going back to Israel. We have been here longer than our original plan. I know we are doing the Lord's work and are having success but now there are several leaders who can carry on without us. I know we must do what the Lord wants us to do. What do you think?" Jonathan asked his pregnant wife.

Hanna smiled and laid her head on his shoulder and replied, "Well husband, I would love to go back home; it has been so long since I was there. We must do what the Lord wants us to do. He has blessed us so much.

As usual, since their salvation that evening, Hanna and Jonathan got on their knees and prayed. This evening, they made a specific request for guidance on whether they should return to Israel or remain in the United States. They were just finishing their prayer when someone knocked on the motorhome door. It was Rabbi Stevens.

The Rabbi entered and apologetically stated, "I am sorry to come so late, but it is important. We just received a message that a ship is leaving from Houston to Israel in ten days. There have been communications about missionaries' travel arrangements. The ship just brought a large group from Israel. Some will come here, and some will go to Central and South America. The ship will return and take any Jews wishing to go to Israel. Apparently, those in charge were concerned about the air quality and decided not to send aircraft. I think a lot of our people will want to go and I know you have considered going home."

Jonathan and Hanna both smiled, and Hanna replied, "Rabbi, we were just praying for guidance on returning and as we finished you knocked on our door. I believe you are the answer to our prayer and maybe my baby will be born in Israel."

CHAPTER 43

HOME, THEN FINAL HOME

THE PREPARATIONS FOR MOVING TO Israel were chaotic. People who thought perhaps they had Jewish ancestors tried to document them so they could meet the requirements for immigration to Israel. Everyone wanted to go, even those not Jewish because there was peace and clean air. However, the requirements for immigration were clear and enforced. Non-Jews could go if married to a Jew, otherwise there had to be some proof of Jewish ancestry. Many Jewish women received proposals of marriage in the hope of joining the group to move out of the country.

Jews who had decided to migrate were given four days to be ready to leave, which was too soon for most, but they all made the best arrangements they could. Those who owned houses listed them with realtors. Houses were listed as fully furnished. Owners knew they would take a great loss if the houses sold at all. Sales proceeds would be deposited in a bank account in the seller's name. There were few buyers, but a few of the houses sold and the rest were signed over to a broker. A few people had a moving company pack some of their things, including some furniture which would be shipped to Israel.

Rabbi Stevens and most of his congregation were planning to go. Also, Jews from other cities came and joined the now large group of travelers.

Pastor Saul came to Johathan's RV in the campground and spoke to him. "Jonathan, my friend, I will be sorry to see you go, but I understand, and I think it is God's plan for the Jews to return to Israel. You may not know it, but I and my family, are Jewish and there are many Jews in my church. I would love to go with you, but I have a duty here."

"Pastor, I know this is difficult for you but if the Lord is leading you to stay then that is His will and He will be with you," Jonathan replied and then continued.

"We have this motorhome, and I don't know if we can take it on the ship. We brought it here in an aircraft in a special arrangement with the government. I wonder if you could make use of it in your ministry."

The pastor smiled and put his hand on Jonathan's shoulder and replied, "Jonathan the Lord already has a use for this motorhome. My church has several Jews who have no transportation and desire to go home to Israel. I had hoped they could ride with you to the ship."

Jonathan smiled and replied, "Pastor, all who can crowd in are welcome. A good second driver would be most welcome as we do not have much time before the ship leaves."

It soon became obvious that Pastor Saul had been planning the trip for some time. The people he had selected and counseled were all Jewish Christians and were anxious to go to Israel. The group included eight older people who no longer drove, and a family of six consisting of a man, his wife and four children. The man was a truck driver and the pastor thought he could assist Jonathan in driving the motorhome. It was decided by someone that the motorhome would tow a sizeable trailer instead of their Jeep. The jeep would provide extra seating. The Jeep would accommodate five adults and would tow a trailer. The trailers would transport smaller items. No one would be taking furniture due to a lack of space. Several families had contracted a company which took possessions in shipping containers on freighters to Israel.

They prepared to leave on the morning of the fourth day. Each vehicle had at least two drivers as they planned to drive straight through to the ship. The distance ahead was about twelve hundred miles, a two-or three-day normal drive time. The decision was made that the motorhome would lead the convey as it would be a recognizable vehicle.

Jonathan encouraged everyone in the vehicle to go to the restroom in the gas station before they left as the holding tank in the motorhome was not large. The people on board did not seem insulted but thought it was funny. A few women were still in line at the bathroom when Pastor Saul came to the door of the motorhome. "May I come in?" he asked.

Instead of answering him Jonathan jumped out and gave him a hug. "I was afraid I would not see you before we left," he exclaimed.

The pastor laughed and replied, "Well Jonathan, it turns out there has been a change in plans."

Then Jonathan noticed the pastor's family was with him, his wife and two daughters, along with four suitcases. "It looks like you are going on a trip to somewhere!" he said with excitement.

"Yes indeed, we are going to Israel. My assistant pastor took over my duties and we are going along with almost all the Jews in our church. It seems to be God's will, and my family certainly wanted to go," Pastor Saul remarked with a big smile and then continued. "However, we gave our car to a family who needed a car in better shape than the one they had. As a result, we now need a ride to the ship. Do you have room?"

Jonathan laughed and stated, "We will make room for you and your family!" He opened one of the storage compartments under the vehicle and after rearranging some items was able to put two of the suitcases inside. The other two would go inside a storage compartment under a seat. Pastor Saul took a seat beside Jonathan requiring Hanna to move to another seat.

The caravan finally got underway two hours late. As planned, Jonathan led the convoy of about ten cars and trucks, several pulling trailers. He stayed in the right lane and drove the speed limit, no speeding. After several hours, Pastor Saul got a call on his cell phone from someone in the line behind them. After the call he said to Jonathan, "There is a rest area just ahead and the call requested a bathroom stop; also, it is time to change drivers."

Jonathan just smiled and nodded. He was ready to stop and use the bathroom in the motorhome. It had been in almost continual use since they left.

Pulling into the rest area, Jonathan parked next to the sewer dump station. It didn't take long to hook up the drain line for the sewer and wastewater tanks. He drained them and left the valves open as some people from the cars were lining up at the RV door to use the bathroom. It seemed the restrooms in the rest area now had long lines waiting to use them. There was a freshwater hose to fill camper tanks. Like his father, he did not trust this amenity, but after tasting the water decided to fill the tank in the RV as his passengers were using a lot of water.

Pastor Saul took over the driving while Jonathan took a nap in a rear seat alongside his wife. The trip went very well. All the vehicles stayed together, and they made good time. They stopped every four hours, or as close to it as they could, always trying for a rest area or a large truck stop. At each stop they changed drivers, so they kept moving, arriving at the shipyard by afternoon the second day.

At the main gate they were met by Houston Police officers who directed them to a second gate. Surprisingly this gate was manned by unarmed Israeli soldiers in uniform. They quickly checked each person's ID to verify Jewish ancestry or citizenship. Everyone in their group was accepted and they drove to the ship, only it was not one ship but two. The closest ship was a very nice, large passenger liner. The second ship was a freighter and not particularly attractive. Jonathan was directed to the freighter where he was met by several Israeli soldiers. An officer came to the motorhome window and in very broken English asked, "Is this the motorhome owned by Jim Jenkins?"

"Yes, it is, I am his son, Jonathan," Jonathan replied in Hebrew.

The officer smiled and in Hebrew stated, "Thank you, we were requested to watch for this vehicle and will take it aboard this ship. All your passengers will ride in the passenger liner. Park in that area and take what you need for the trip and leave the vehicle unlocked and the keys in it. All your people will be driven to the passenger ship."

Jonathan parked the RV where directed. The passengers took their belongings and waited for the ride to the passenger ship. It was a little more difficult for Jonathan and Hanna as their things were stored all over the camper. They quickly packed two suitcases and a sizeable plastic box with everything they thought they might need on the cruise. In fifteen minutes, they joined the others waiting outside the vehicle. When the RV had emptied, a man from the ship moved the RV onto a frame attached to a crane on deck. The RV was picked up and set on the deck alongside some storage containers.

Soon an open vehicle pulled up. It was a flat frame with rows of seats. They loaded their luggage and drove the short distance to the passenger ship. Their IDs were checked again, and they boarded. The couples were assigned cabins and the singles were assigned to large cabins with rows of beds. The ship was very close to capacity as people from all over the US had arrived for the trip to Israel. Some, like Jonathan were Israeli missionaries heading home. Many others had Jewish ancestors or were married to a Jew and were fleeing the US due to the poor conditions here—a first for the US.

The ship left the dock and to the crew it was strange there was no one on shore waving goodbye. The friends of the passengers were on board. Although Jonathan was unaware of it, this ship leaving for Israel had become a regular event occurring every month—each one packed with Jews leaving the country. In addition, Jews were flying home to Israel and shipping their belongings by commercial freight delivery. This trip was part of a large exodus from the US.

The seas were calm and the trip smooth, with much activity on board. Many of the Jews on board were missionaries and they were aggressive to convert those who were not. There was a line at one of the swimming pools for baptism, for both the passengers and crew. Every evening several services were held at various locations throughout the ship to sing joyous songs and preach the gospel. It was a great trip.

As they entered the Mediterranean Sea, they met a fleet of US ships heading out, returning to America. For several months the US had been withdrawing its forces from around the world, another indication of the reduced influence of the US on the world. The traffic in the Mediterranean was heavy; the economy in this part of the world seemed to be doing well.

As they approached Israel, the passengers gathered on deck in anticipation of seeing their new homeland for the first time. A loud shout sounded when it was sighted. At that point two Israeli war ships escorted them toward the harbor, with their cargo ship close astern. Jonathan also noticed there were Israeli warplanes regularly flying overhead along the coast. It seemed the military was on some kind of alert.

The ship docked to the shouting of a large group waiting to welcome them, unlike their departure. There was a great deal of shouting and waving from both sides, however, there was no-one to greet Jonathan and Hanna, or Pastor Saul. They were not surprised. Within a matter of a few hours the group was headed north to the city of Jenkins. It seemed there were several empty houses there as the population in the city had been greatly reduced when the Rapture had occurred. Jonathan again noticed the presence of the military in significant numbers; something was going on. They were making good time until the traffic was stopped to let a convey of military trucks pass, also headed north. Several of the trucks were carrying tanks and others had cargo in military trucks. Others were transporting troops. A powerful army was moving north.

As it was getting dark they arrived at the city of Jenkins. Jonathan felt a sense of peace as they came into the city. Not much had changed. The church on the hill was lit and beautiful. When they arrived at his house things looked very different. The military was everywhere. Trucks were parked in the driveway of the separate garage and armed soldiers were standing guard. Jonathan pulled the motorhome into the driveway at the house and stopped. A soldier came over with his rifle at the ready. He asked, "Are you a Jenkins family member?"

"I am Jim Jenkins oldest son. My name is Jonathan," Jonathan replied.

An officer came over and the armed soldier stepped back. The officer stated, "I am Major Levin. The house is unoccupied. Perhaps we could go in and talk."

The officer and everyone in the RV entered the house, the one Jim Jenkins had built. Jonathan had a key, but the door was not locked. They went into the main area and removed the covers from the furniture, covers Jonathan's mother Aliza had placed there before leaving. Major Levin, with an armed soldier standing behind him, sat on one of the chairs. Some of the new arrivals sat and others stood as the informal meeting got underway.

The Major began "Mr. Jenkins you may not be aware of the situation here as the news has been suppressed. The enemies of Israel have raised a massive army all around us. Our entire country is now on full alert, and the army, including the reserves, are on full duty. As you know, this property is partially controlled by the military and the facility over your garage is being reactivated. We will move the vehicles out of the driveways so it will not be obvious the military is here. We will use the upper and basement floors of the separate building, just as we did before. We will try to maintain a low profile, but in case of attack, you should consider leaving or at least stay in the basement. We don't know when or if an attack will happen in this area, but we are preparing and will be ready."

Jonathan replied, "I understand. We will move in for now and will prepare to do what is necessary. A sizeable group from the US arrived with us and several wish to settle in this area. I understand some of the houses are empty because of the Christians being taken to Heaven."

The Major looked startled at the comment about Christians being taken and replied, "I know about reports of some people missing, but I don't know anything about it."

Jonathan smiled and answered, "I was present when my family was taken. My parents, two sisters and a brother were taken. I was with them and saw them turn into spirits and taken to Heaven in a time of glory. I was left because of my unbelief. I hope to discuss this event in the church service next Sunday. I hope you and your troops will attend."

The officer and the two men with him looked startled and then the Major replied, "I heard of such reports but dismissed them. I and my family will plan to attend the service. It seems the church has not been having services for some time; it will be good for it to open again."

The Major and his men left the house and Jonathan turned to Pastor Saul who was standing by the front door. "Pastor it is late, and everyone is tired. There is room for everyone to stay the night. There are four bedrooms so there should be room. The house has been unused for several months so there will be dust; try to overlook it."

Jonathan went to his old bedroom and gathered up some clothes and moved them into his parents' room, now his. Pastor Saul and his wife took a second bedroom and the three women stayed in the other two. Everyone was happy with the arrangements.

The guests with Jonathan and Hanna stayed almost two months. The ladies helped Hanna clean the house and prepare food. Their company was a pleasure and not a burden. It took some time for the new immigrants to buy homes in the city. Ownership of many of the houses was not clear. Legal ownership of homes previously held by those raptured had to be established. Slowed by the process, home buying could be delayed for years in some cases.

The city council finally decided and allowed houses with no clear heirs to be sold by paying off existing debts and taxes. It was a good deal for the newcomers. Pastor Saul, with his wife and two children, bought a three-bedroom house next to the church, now closed, as most of the members were taken. The three single ladies, who had come in the motorhome purchased a three-bedroom house nearby.

Most who had come from the Southwestern part of Arizona also purchased homes or moved into apartment buildings. Everyone found a place to rest and reflect, not knowing what the Lord had in store for the future. The city of Jenkins went from a city of empty homes to a thriving community again.

CHAPTER 44

A time of peace?

AS TIME PASSED, THE ISRAELI Army remained on full alert and continued to increase in size as many new arrivals joined their forces. The enemies around them talked very aggressively but did not attack. It was deduced that they were continuously increasing in strength and still planning an eventual attack in the future.

Amidst all this international pressure, the city of Jenkins seemed to thrive. Jonathan restarted the woodworking shop and hired several employees to make furniture. Pastor Saul was called to be the pastor of the local church and conducted a service in English as he learned Hebrew. A second service was conducted in the Hebrew language by an Israeli native. The city flourished and everyone seemed happy.

In perfect timing, Hanna gave birth to a son, which they named Jim, for his grandfather. A little more than a month after giving birth, she seemed to be pregnant again. After nine months and the birth of twin girls, another month passed, and she was somehow pregnant again. It was soon determined to again be twins. This would soon produce five children for the young couple, which in this town was not that unusual. In the church services it was usual for many of the young women to be carrying an unborn child along with babies in strollers. It seemed the Lord was repopulating the country after the Rapture.

Jonathan questioned Hanna about the large family they were having and his concern for her. She replied, "Husband, do not be concerned; I love carrying a baby. It makes me feel complete, and I love caring for babies. Everything is just wonderful for me," as she gave Jonathan a big kiss.

The visitor arrived on a Saturday morning, unannounced. Jonathan was surprised as he usually heard a car arriving, but this time he first heard the man ringing the doorbell. He was a nice-looking man, a little older than Jonathan and dressed in a suit with tie.

The man introduced himself. "Hello, Jonathan, my name is Billy Austin, and I have just come from the US. I was informed that you were interested in what was happening there."

Jonathan was surprised by the statement as he had not told anyone about his interest in the US but had prayed for the missionaries and asked for safety of the country. He had sent letters and made phone calls to people he knew there but had not gone out of his way to search for information. He noticed this man was a little unusual in several ways. He was spotless, even without dust on his shoes and his eyes, looked a bit strange, almost as though he could see through you. Another thing Jonathan noticed was there was no car in front of the house. If he had walked from town along a dusty road, he would have dust on his shoes.

"Come in. Would you like a cup of coffee?" Jonathan asked, as he opened the door fully and stepped aside.

He led his guest to the office and invited him to sit across from his desk. Before any discussion, Hanna came in with a tray containing two cups of coffee and a pot, two plates with some hot pastries, which she set on the desk. After the introductions she smiled and left the room, leaving the door ajar.

The guest took a sip of coffee then sat down. Smiling, he began explaining the purpose for his visit. "I have just come from the

United States where I traveled about and observed the situation there." He spoke in Hebrew which was good for Jonathan and very good for Hanna, who listened near the door. Billy continued, "It would be wonderful if your wife could join us. She might be interested in the situation there."

The door opened and Hanna, with a cup of coffee, stepped in and took a chair next to her husband, facing Billy. She remarked, "Thank you, but I can only stay a few minutes. The children will be waking up shortly."

Billy, continued to smile and said, "As you know, the Lord God, Bless His name, has power over everything. He has created mankind and given him power to make decisions about his life. Based on these decisions, the Lord allows them to influence others, to have faith in Him and accept Him as Lord God. Those who accept the Lord God, will be accepted into His kingdom forever. For this reward He requires people to acknowledge Him as Lord God and worship Him. As you know, people and nations sometimes follow the Lord's direction to worship Him and then fall away. This means the Lord will punish those people and those nations so they will turn back to Him. The Lord God, in His wisdom, created and chose the nation of Israel to inform the world about His plan for mankind. This nation followed the direction of God sometimes in its history but often did not. In their time of apostasy, God punished them and removed them from their land. In God's time He sent his Son to bring the message of salvation to the world and selected Israel to be the bearer of this message. The nation of Israel rejected this message. There were and are many exceptions who did become witnesses for Christ's saving message which they spread around the world. Shortly after the Lord Christ returned to heaven, God removed the nation of Israel from the land, the Holy Land, for hundreds of years and dispersed them across many nations. He recently returned them to the land for their future mission."

Billy paused, took a sip of his coffee then continued. "The Lord also chose America to be His messengers, and they claimed they were, in their founding. Over time many lost that message and became hostile to the gospel. Because of this America has been punished. This seems to be the way of mankind; he will do right for a while then turn away and God will punish. Throughout history nations have risen and then fallen, never to rise again, at least not to their previous power."

With the short pause, Hanna asked, "Sir, we have been taught there will be a seven-year tribulation after the Rapture of the saints, which happened three years ago. Could you explain these events more fully?"

Billy smiled and replied, "Some believe the seven-year tribulation occurs immediately after the Rapture. There may be a short delay to allow the new believers time to spread the Gospel to the world. The exact date is known only to the Lord God, bless His name. The time is short."

He paused again, then continued. "The time is short. Israel has been assigned the task to bring the message to the world to promote the salvation of many. The time is short. You are encouraged to accept this task and spread the message of Christ's saving power. The time is short."

With that statement, Billy Austin stood and turned toward the door. He opened the door and turned back to the couple and added, "Jonathan and Hanna, both of your parents send their greetings and look forward to seeing you again."

Jonathan and his wife were so shocked they did not respond. Billy walked down the steps and down the dirt path toward town. Jonathan noticed he did not leave footprints in the sand.

As they watched him leave, Jonathan said, "I believe we have been visited by an angel."

"Yes," she responded, then continued, "Do you think we are now in the seven-year tribulation period now?"

"I don't know for sure, but the signs are all about us. The armies of our enemies are on our borders and ready to attack. It seems we should be very ready."

The next Sunday in the church service, Jonathan asked the pastor for a moment to make an announcement. He stood and told of his visit and repeated the message as best he could. The congregation listened intently. He concluded his message with the comment, "We who witnessed the Rapture saw a great thing; we who did not believe were left behind. We now believe and have work to do to spread the message that God is real and will forgive us and take us later. Perhaps we will experience pain and suffering but will be taken to heaven later when the Lord dictates if we are faithful until the end. I am sorry to have missed the first Rapture of believers because of my unbelief, but He has given us a job, an important job to tell the unbelieving world about the Lord God and His Son. In addition, I believe God is going to do amazing things in Israel and we should always be prepared to move up to Jerusalem."

It turned out the church had been making a video recording of the message and Jonathan's talk was added to the end. This video was, as usual, played on the local TV station. It was later broadcast on the Israeli national TV station. After a few days the broadcast was replayed in the United States on one of the few national TV stations still in operation.

The broadcast gave encouragement to Christians around the world.

CHAPTER 45

NEW WORLD

THE COUNTRIES IN THE WORLD, including the United States, seemed to all have problems managing their countries. To help with the situation, countries made agreements with each other to manage many of their problems. Most already had agreements about travel and trade, but the new agreements included much more, like shared leadership, finances and immigration. Europe, already closely joined, became almost like a single country. As a European country they elected a leader for the entire union. The man's name was Gaddie, which seemed strange as he was born in the city of Rome and now lived in Poland where he was a lawyer and a businessman. He was well liked by everyone in the entire union and stated he wanted peace in the world. His wish seemed to come to pass as the world was completely at peace. For months there had been no conflict, and nations seemed to be friendly and got along well worldwide. The nations of the world all seemed to listen and follow the leadership of the man Gaddie. To many he became the leader of the entire world.

However, as the months and years passed the situation in the world seemed to grow more serious. The buildup of troops around Israel seemed to grow even though there was no violence of any kind. The troops were from Muslim countries and Russia. The troops were encamped in permanent housing but seemed to be rotated at a two-month interval. This put a burden on Israel as they were required to be on full alert continuously. Even though tensions were high the country was at peace. Jonathan and his family lived happily in their home with their children in the city of Jenkins. The local church prospered, and teams of missionaries were sent around the world.

Young Jim was just taking his first steps when the international situation grew more critical. It was noticed the enemies around the country seemed to be increasing in numbers. The two-month duty time seemed to have been extended to a permanent posting and as new troops arrived the number of soldiers around Israel grew to a great number. In addition, the US was still recovering, and their aid to Israel was limited. Israel seemed to be alone. They were not alone, of course, for The Lord God was with them.

Even more troubling was the fact that Gaddie had moved to Jerusalem and seemed to take charge of the economy. He stayed on the Temple Mount in a temporary structure and started holding meetings about how the nations of the world should behave and function. While discussing peace and no violence, he was directing each country on what they should be doing. One of his primary objectives was the buildup of foreign forces around Israel, something he had been encouraging for some time. There was much discussion in the media everywhere about Gaddie and he was continually referred to as the king of the world.

Israel monitored the buildup and considered attacking the encampments before the invasion could take place. However, this seemed futile as the massive number of enemy encampments were more than Israel could attack. In fact, it seemed to the Israeli military that the defense of the country against this massive horde was impossible.

On the world stage, things were changing. Mr. Gaddie, the president of the European Union became more powerful and popular around the world. One of his goals was to take all the weapons away from the populace. It was rumored he had been killed by an assassin and then after three days, rose again, a copy of Christ. As a result, of this and other things, it was rumored that Gaddie was God. Because of these things, the Muslim countries, along with Russia and China joined with the European's and took Gaddie as their leader. The new leader's headquarters was in Jerusalem and also in Rome at the Vatican, and the Pope seemed to be his assistant. It was rumored that it was the leaders desire to have Jerusalem as his worldwide throne.

During this time the US seemed to stay out of world events. The tensions in Israel, however, grew with these changes in the world situation.

Jonathan and his family walked to church on Sunday morning as usual. The parents tried to conceal their concern about the tensions in Israel from their children by being joyful with them. The youngsters went to their classes and the adults to the morning service. It was an unusual service as the pastor led the people to pray and ask God for forgiveness and help with the situation in the country.

The pastor then introduced an officer of the military. The man was a general of the IDF and came to the front of the church with two armed soldiers. The general did not smile as he stood to speak.

"My friends and fellow Christians, I have come with some disturbing news. On our borders a large army has been gathering for some time, and we now have indications of an impending attack. This is a very large force, and we encourage the citizens north of the Sea of Galilee move temporary south for your safety. We don't have an exact time but strongly suggest a move in the next few days. We intend to stop any land invasion, but the artillery attack will likely be deadly.

With that statement the general thanked them and walked out of the church. No one moved for several moments then they all rose and began talking in groups. Pastor Saul came to Jonathan and said, "We need to organize a caravan to go south, maybe several. I don't know where we should go but I am sure the government is planning something. I hope you will help me with this."

Jonathan agreed and started checking out the old motorhome. He checked the tires, oil and filled the water tank and topped off the fuel. He then began loading the vehicle with mostly food and extra water containers. Hanna loaded clothing and lots of baby things to care for her five very young children. Jonathan then put in many of his father's firearms and ammunition. The motorhome rather quickly began to fill up. He then took an enclosed trailer, used for delivering furniture from his shop and filled it with survival items from his house. He loaded tents and blankets and many clothes to help people survive. The trailer was only half full when he finished. He thought the rest could be used by others as they moved. Hopefully this move would be temporary but something told him it would not be so.

Two of the three women who had come with them from the US rode with them. They had been a help to Hanna with her five children and keeping up the house. In exchange Jonathan had paid them rather generously, money well spent.

As they proceeded south toward Jerusalem the traffic grew very heavy. It seemed all of the northern parts of the country were evacuating.

Approaching Jerusalem, the impossible and unexplainable happened. The clear air suddenly became cloudy and foggy. It was not normal. They went from clear vision to almost no vision at all. Jonathan steered the vehicle to the right and slowed to a stop, or he thought he stopped, but everything continued to move as if the vehicle was floating.

The motorhome Jonathan drove stopped when it came to a group of people standing in front of it. One of the men was immediately recognized by Jonathan as his brother David, who had been raptured along with the rest of his family and the Christians at the time.

David opened the door to the motorhome and stepped inside. He seemed to be a younger version of himself. His hair was darker, very neat and he had a nice smile on his face. He continued smiling and said, "Greetings, Christians, you are now in the New Jerusalem. The mist will soon clear, and it will look to you like the old Jerusalem with new housing, where you will live for now and be protected by the Lord, bless His name."

David paused for a moment then with a serious look on his face continued. "I have been sent to tell you what will happen from now on. We are now in the time of the Tribulation, as described in the Book of Revelation of the Bible. You will continue to live your lives and have more children. God, bless His name, will protect you and your family. One day Christ will return, and we will all be at home with Him, bless His name. While here you will be tasked with witnessing to the world to save all that will be saved. The world will from now until the end will be in turmoil with much pain, but with some happiness which your message will bring. Our father and the others of your family will be near to help and watch over you. At some point in the future, we will welcome you and your family into the New Jerusalem and presence with the Lord Himself, bless His holy name." With that statement David smiled and nodded to his brother and left the motorhome.

Those in the motorhome were quiet for a full minute, then Hanna said, "That was David, Jonathan's brother who was raptured with the rest of the family."

After another pause, Jonathan said, "Yes, it was my brother who was taken. He came back to tell us what is happening. I think we are in the TRIBULATION as described in the book of Revelation in the Bible. This is a seven-year time period—the first half is peaceful, and the second half is total violence. I believe we are now in the second half and worldwide violence. The Lord will protect us here, but we still need to witness to people everywhere."

The cloudy air cleared and the place where they were was not familiar to anyone. There was row after row of apartments on many levels, the outsides looked like the stone of old Jerusalem, but looked newly installed. It was clear, these were their new homes, protected by the Lord God Himself. Jonathan and his family left the motor-home and walked down the sidewalk. A door opened as they passed it. They were surprised as no one was around. They stepped inside and were shocked to find their furniture there from their home in the north. It could not be clearer; this was their new home for some indefinite time. Hanna laughed and ran around the rooms, almost dancing.

Jonathan and his family went for walk around the neighborhood. There seemed to be walkways but no cars or streets. In addition, there were people, people they knew and were friends with. Several of their friends joined them as they walked and discussed what they were seeing. They came to a quite lovely park and found benches to sit on. The adults took seats, and the children ran and played, everyone was very happy.

As they relaxed a young man walked up to them and greeted them saying, "Fellow believers, as you can see you are in the safe place provided by the Lord God, bless his name. As predicted in the Bible, you are in a safe place within Jerusalem which will be protected for the remainder of the time. Members of your group will be selected to go to the world to spread the message of salvation to help those who will be saved. The Lord, bless His name will be with you.

So it was. Both men and women, somehow knew when they were called and arranged to go to somewhere on the earth as missionaries.

The missionary effort resulted in thousands of people being saved all over the world. However, due to the gangs and rioters, many missionaries were murdered. Most considered it a price worth bearing.

There was a Christian Church in the neighborhood which they attended almost every day. The first time they went into the building it seemed the attendees occupied most of the building, but each successive time more people came, and the building grew larger. While this seemed impossible, they were not surprised.

Their home seemed to be in a bubble, hidden from the world, but outside the world continued to decay. Gaddie was referred to as "King of the World" in every publication. He seemed to direct the countries on what they should do, and they all responded without question. He wanted and got peace everywhere in the world except Israel where all nations seemed to have troops around the country, threatening it. The exception was the United States which no longer had troops and wasn't involved in worldly affairs any more.

The city of Jerusalem was divided into two groups; the unbelievers lived in the ancient city with old buildings and narrow rough streets, while the Christian believers lived in a pure clean heavenly section. The two realities existed within each other, but the people only saw the sections depending on whether they had accepted Christ as Savior. The unbelievers were very confused as they were told about the glorious existence of the believers and quickly sought to become one. Very quickly the majority of the people in the city became Christians.

The actual look of the city seemed to change and seemed to glow and looked marvelous. Seeing the glory over Israel the enemy armies did not understand what was happening and ordered an attack. They fired their weapons toward Israel, but they fell among the camps of the men from countries which had come to attack Israel. The Lord caused a massive confusion among the great armies, and they attacked each other and eventually were all destroyed.

CHAPTER 46

NEW JERUSALEM
THOUSAND YEAR REIGN

ALL AROUND THE NATION OF Israel lay destruction and death. Then the Lord waved his hand, and the land was cleared and clean. The mountains were also moved, and an entirely new landscape was created. In this landscape was a new glorious city, a giant city was instantly created.

It was a massive change that affected the entire world. The news everywhere covered the change in Israel. Pictures of the new city appeared everywhere but none from inside the city. In addition, the city seemed to grow everyday as more and more people, new Christians, arrived.

The next day a visitor arrived at Jonathan's apartment. The man was a younger version of David, Jonathan's brother, who had been raptured.

Smiling, David said, "Greetings, brother and family. I welcome you all into the thousand-year final time period. From now on, visits between our groups will be common. You who are physically alive will live, have families and at some point, die and then join us. After this thousand-year period, will be the end of human life, as you have known it. During this time, you will have an important job to tell the rest of the world about the way of salvation by accepting Christ as Savior. This is a most important job, and you will be helped by those of us who have already gone ahead to Glory. We will be with you more closely and more openly than in the past. This is a most important job as the word of God must reach every living person in the world. For this time, Satan and his angels are locked up, and will not interfere with your efforts. But he will be released later at the end of time."

A new and completely different time period has started and will last for one thousand years. It will be generally a time of turmoil in most places. There will be angry people who will not accept the word of God and refused to listen to the Gospel. These people are doomed! There will be missionaries in most places, and some will die in the service, however, a great number will accept Christ as their Savior.

So, the thousand-year period explained in Revelations started and continued. With Satan and Gaddie carried away and locked up, many people accepted the message of Christ and most, but not all, were saved.

As time went on Jonathan and his family lived and, in their time, died and moved to the eternal side, joining their family.

And when the thousand-year time ended, and judgment had taken place, all unbelievers were sent to Hell and believers in Christ joined him in the permanent Kingdom which would last forever. Just as THE LORD GOD promised.

The End of the present age.

Discover more titles by Rondel W. Osborn:

Voyages of Evening Light   Final Voyages of Evening Light